MANAK-NA'S STORY, 75,000 BC

BOOK TWO OF WINDS OF CHANGE, A PREHISTORIC FICTION SERIES ON THE PEOPLING OF THE AMERICAS

BONNYE MATTHEWS

Since 1978

PO Box 221974 Anchorage, Alaska 99522-1974
books@publicationconsultants.com—www.publicationconsultants.com

ISBN 978-1-59433-373-6
eISBN 978-1-59433-374-3
Library of Congress Catalog Card Number: 2013908395

Cover photo of Neanderthal by Okologix.
Cover background photo by Vitaliy Krasovskiy

Manufactured in the United States of America.

Other Book in the Winds of Change Series:
Ki'ti's Story, 75,000 BC, Book One

Manak-na's Story, 75,000 BC

BOOK TWO OF WINDS OF CHANGE,

A PREHISTORIC FICTION SERIES

ON THE PEOPLING OF THE AMERICAS

BONNYE MATTHEWS

Dedication

For Skip,
also known as Lorene Signi Lyster—Tibbetts—Meggitt—Henderson,
a true friend, wonderful artist, and excellent editor. To use the terms of the
People in the first two books in this series, Skip has gone to Wisdom,
and it rips my belly.

Acknowledgements

Without the assistance of several people, this book would not be. These people are, first, my brother, Randy Matthews, and then Skip (Lorene) Henderson, Sally Sutherland, Barry Wise, Patricia Gilmore, Robert Arthur, and Pat Meiwes. Each contributed far in excess of what could be expected or hoped for on the basis of family or friendship or love of reading. I also thank my publisher, Evan Swensen, who had the courage to take on this project.

Pre-Clovis Archaeological Sites
in the Americas

Old Crow (Yukon Territory)

25,000—40,000 years ago

Possible flaked or cut large mammal bones

Bluefish Caves (Yukon Territory)

12,000—28,000 years ago

Mammoth bone core and flakes, microblades

Mud Lake (Wisconsin)

15,000—16,500 years ago

Lanceolate point, blade like flakes, charred basket

Manis (Washington State)

14,000 years ago

Antler point in mastodon rib

Hebior (Wisconsin)

15,000—16,500 years ago

Stone tools, butchered mammoth bones

Wilson Butte Cave (Idaho)

17,500—18,000 years ago

Modified bones and flakes

La Sena (Nebraska)

17,000—22,000 years ago

Flaked mammoth bones

McMinnville (Oregon)

46,000 years ago

Broken mammoth bones; bison tibia chopper

Meadowcroft Rockshelter (Pennsylvania)

13,500—17,500 years ago

Lanceolate point, charred basketry, flakes

Paisley Cave (Oregon)

14,300 years ago

Human coprolites

Saltville (Virginia)

15,000—16,000 years ago

Stone, fractured & polished bone

Fort Rock Cave (Oregon)

15,500 years ago

Stemmed points

Cactus Hill (Virginia)

17,000—19,000 years ago

Lanceolate points, blades, blade cores

False Cougar Cave (Montana)

17,500 years ago

Stone artifacts and human hair

Topper (South Carolina)

15,000—16,000 years ago

Stone tools

Dutton (Colorado)

14,000—17,000 years ago

Flaked and polished mammal bones

Sloth Hole (Florida)

14,400 years ago

Stone tools, cut mastodon tusks

Jensen (Nebraska)

22,000 years ago

Flaked-mammoth bones

Toca da Esperanza (Brazil)

204,000—295,000 years ago

Carbonate, breccia

Little Salt Spring (Florida)

14,000 years ago

Shaped wooden stake in extinct
tortoise shell

Shaffert (Nebraska)

17,000—22,000

Flaked mammoth bone

Sitio do Meio (Brazil)

8,800—18,600 years ago

Artifacts

Burnham (Oklahoma)

22,000—40,000 years ago

Flaked tools, extinct fauna

Caldeirado de Rodriguez (Brazil)

9,480—17,000 years ago

Artifacts

Lovewell (Kansas)

22,000 years ago

Modified mammoth bones

Pedra Furada (Brazil)

6,150—50,000 years ago

Painted fragments, quartz tools, hearths

Pendejo Cave (New Mexico)

14,000—55,000+ years ago

Pleistocene fossils, bone, hair

Alice Boër (Brazil)

14,200 years ago

Artifacts

Valsequillo (Mexico)

200,000—245,000 years ago

Skull fragment, artifacts, art

Pikimachay (Peru)

14,700—22,200 years ago

Collagen, sloth bones

Buttermilk Creek (Texas)

13,090—24,420 years ago

Tools: bifaces, core, flakes, blades, gravers,
lanceolate forms

Monte Verde (Chile)

10,860—42,100+ years ago

Wood, charcoal, peat ball, unburned wood

Pubenza (Columbia)

15,050—17,790 years ago

Calcareous seed, humic clay

Taima-Taima (Venezuela)

12,980—15,000 years ago

Mastodon butchering, twig mastication

Tequendama (Columbia)

28,690 years ago

Charcoal, waterfall

Introduction

Manak-na's Story, 75,000 BC is the second novel in the Winds of Change series that focuses on prehistoric peopling of the Americas. This novel mainly takes place in what is today Asia and Mexico.

The novel series deals with two issues:

(1) Clovis-First vs. Pre-Clovis Views

Clovis-First View: Clovis-First is an opinion that no humans were in the Americas until the Holocene (11,700 years ago to present). Proponents of that view are C. Vance Haynes, Aleš Hrdlička, Paul Martin, and Tim Flannery. The Clovis-First View recognizes no Pre-Clovis sites in the Americas. Along with the Clovis-First View is the idea that intelligence along with body shape evolved.

Pre-Clovis View: Pre-Clovis is an opinion that humans were in the Americas in the Pleistocene (2.6 million to 11,700 years ago), and may have been present here as far back as hundreds of thousands of years ago. The Pre-Clovis proponents are: Thomas Dillehay, James Adovasio, Christopher Hardaker, and Michael Cremo. They point to some 400 Pre-Clovis sites in the Americas. This view conceives that humans have always had the same level of intelligence; they just applied it to different sets of circumstances and built on different bases.

(2) The Intellectual Level and Life Styles of Neanderthals

Neanderthals have been viewed as hunched over, dark-skinned brutes, without the function of spoken language. We know today that Neanderthals had fair skin, and some had red hair, and blue eyes; could speak as well as we can; were intellectually bright (catching dolphins, something which can't be done from shore), killed mega fauna with spears, and survived temperatures that would be a challenge to our best outdoors men and women; buried their dead with red ochre and/or flowers; and cared for their disabled. It might be noted that many people today carry residual Neanderthal DNA.

The series explores the Pre-Clovis View and speculates on the mores and lifestyles of a People who could endure for hundreds of thousands of years without killing off others or their own kind. *Manak-na's Story, 75,000 BC* portrays mingling of Neanderthals, *Homo erectus*, Cro-Magnons, and Denisovans.

Manak-na's Story, 75,000 BC focuses on the life of Manak-na, who has dreamed of an exploratory adventure since childhood. He participates in a boat trip from Asia to Mexico, where people have already been living for a significant period of time, while his People head toward the Lake Baikal region, having been forced to move by an increase in earthquake activity and reduced game where they lived. The plan is that Manak-na will return to resume his life among the People. Manak-na's adventure is not as free as he expected, because he unintentionally invites his young nephew to join him. Read to see whether Manak-na can keep the commitment of a single adventure as he promised his wife, or whether he has become, as a result of his travels, an adventurer.

Manak-na's Story, 75,000 BC contains a bibliography.

For more information see: http://booksbybonnye.com

Manak-na's Story, 75,000 BC: Book Two of Winds of Change, a Prehistoric Fiction Series on the Peopling of the Americas

NANICHAK-NA

Hahami-na + Blanagah
- Patah
- Mota
- Siff

Grypchon-na + Likichi

Manak-na + Domur
- Tuma
- Mhank

Late Addition Mol:
- Gumokut + Fiinee
- Lolmeg + Maylue

Minagle + Sum-na
- Meeluf
- Song
- Halmi
- Shukmu
- Luga
- Mona
- Sofa

from the Place

Where the Sun Rises:
- Tikarumusa
- Ahna

Ki'ti + Untuk
- Yomuk
- Elemaea

from the west
- Kipotuilak

Frakja-na
- Tin
- Lakut
- Shud

Mootmu-na + Amey

Kai-na + Mitrak
- Ketra

Ekuktu-na + Wemumal
- Ekoy
- Rish
- Smig

Lamul-na + Meeka
- Hupu
- Yoah
- Koi

Olintak + Slamika-na
- Keemu

Lamk-na + Liho
- Bun
- Mingugno
- Kal
- Seenha

Ermol-na + Flayk

Ermi-na + Shymukuk
- Trokug
- Gratu

Arkan-na + Ey

Alu + Guy-na
- Minal
- Fife
- Lag
- La
- Van
- Solu

Lai-na + Inst
- Walu
- Humko
- Smosh
- Mouku
- Tita
- Maig
- Lakop
- Din
- Phelen
- Olmot

Tongip-na + Aryna
- Cam
- Elet
- Tiki
- Meta
- Truto
- Mefu
- Luko
- Kuma

Boatbuilders:
- Pah
- Komus
- Rokuk
- Mogil
- Fengren
- Gurst
- Mirk
- Ralm
- Piman
- Skuku
- Mokul

13

Chapter 1

Nanichak-na struggled with anxiety. His white hair blew about in the breeze as he rubbed his upper arms. He was a seasoned hunter governed by a logical, common sense approach to life. This trek was the source of his frustration. Ki'ti was leading. Nanichak-na knew she was thirty-one but at his age of seventy-six, he continued to see her as a young girl. Until now, seasoned hunters had led treks. Specifically, *he* led treks. Not Wise Ones. In the past Wise Ones were placed towards the rear of the line for protection. This was unprecedented! It felt all wrong. In his lifetime he'd seen the simple life of the People complicated by the Winds of Change—something that happened when Wisdom exhaled. Even the Minguat and Mol were now People. *Didn't matter what you looked like anymore,* he thought thoroughly irritated, *Now everyone was People! And, they didn't even smell like People!* Nanichak-na spat. He thought that if the huge man-like apes wanted to, they could probably become People, too. Things used to be so simple! Life was getting too complex. He yearned for the past, but he also had a bit of curiosity about how things would come to be in the future.

The line came to a halt. Again. Nanichak-na stepped out of his place in line to confer with the Wise One. Where once he had been convinced that they must move from the long tree home in the valley, now he had serious misgivings about the Wise One's leading the refugees to a place unknown. He admitted that earthquakes had been increasing and game animals were harder to find, but it was a good place. *Who knew what the new destination would be like?* he wondered, agitated. Ki'ti's brother, Manak-na, and Untuk, her husband, walked beside her, but they were there to protect her, not to lead.

When Nanichak-na reached the front of the line, he could see the reason the line had halted. The ancient path they had been following had disappeared in a landslide. He edged closer to the Wise One, who appeared to be gazing out into the air above a lush, summer-green lowland.

"Wise One?" he said quietly.

Ki'ti turned and looked at the old hunter who had pierced her spiritual moment. "Yes?"

"What happened here?" he asked.

"Come, sit with me on that point," she offered.

He shrugged off his backpack. Nanichak-na wasn't really enthusiastic about sitting but followed Ki'ti to the promontory where the two sat alone overlooking the immense lowland. He tried to maintain composure but remained slightly impatient, and he was acutely aware that she knew it. Her hair blew in loose tendrils around her face but did little to hide her piercing blue eyes from which he could never hide his thoughts.

Ki'ti allowed some time to pass before she spoke to him. She smiled to herself. Since childhood she had been fascinated with the hunter's wiry, long white eyebrows that stuck out at the sides. They still did. His tunic was new. Likichi, Ki'ti's original mother, made it for him when his last one had fallen apart. Getting him into the new garment tried the patience of Likichi to the extreme. He wanted to keep the old one and she wanted to be sure that he did not. Finally she succeeded, but the battle was hard fought. The new tunic was made like his last one with a strap over the left shoulder. Down the side of his tunic were a series of new holes he'd made with a medium awl and widened by cutting the leather with a sharp blade. The holes represented people whose deaths brought holes to his life. He had never spoken to anyone about what they represented, but from time to time he could be seen fingering one or another of the holes. Each hole represented a specific person whose life had gone back to Wisdom. He wanted to keep the old tunic because that is where he first made the holes. No one understood with certainty because he did not discuss the holes, but several people had accurately guessed the meaning.

Finally, Ki'ti said, "This was foretold. You know that, Great Hunter." She also wore a tunic that was new. Made of a deerskin that was cut into a rectangle, there was a transverse slit for her head to go through. The sides were pierced with an awl and laced together with thin leather strips. It was very soft.

For a moment his heart melted. Her use of the epithet, Great Hunter, originally used by her sister, was for him alone only when the two of them were by themselves. It was, he had realized, her way of showing her real respect for his leadership and for him.

"You're telling me that you've seen Kimseaka and you know where to guide us without the path?"

"Great Hunter, can you not see the light yonder?" She pointed to a spot below. His hunter's eyesight, remaining acute at his age, could see no light below. She really didn't know whether he or anyone else could see the light or only she could.

"I see only the light that leaps to the sky from that stream," he admitted.

Ki'ti rose from sitting to kneeling and rested her weight on her heels. She noticed that Untuk had caught their daughter, Elemaea, to prevent her from interrupting the meeting. He would remind her again to leave her mother uninterrupted when she was talking. He was glad he'd made the intercept. So was Ki'ti. His daughter liked to act and then think, he mused. She was yet very young.

"Great Hunter, be still, rest your thoughts and concerns for a brief time." With her attention no longer divided, Ki'ti lowered her head and shut her eyes.

Suddenly Nanichak-na felt surrounded and looked around himself, the hair on the back of his neck standing on end, showing his increased anxiety. This sensory awareness resembled how he felt when he *knew* a predator watched him, only it was significantly more intense. *Were there many?* He wondered. He scanned their surroundings.

"Wise One, please, this is not my world," he quietly implored her, hoping that she would remove that presence he could not see. "I agree, Wise One, Wisdom *is* with you."

"You really don't see, do you Great Hunter?" She put her hand on his forearm.

"I see nothing. I *feel* the presence of something unseen now. It awes me more than facing," he showed ten fingers twice, "enemy warriors—alone. I'd rather face the warriors. I'd know what to expect."

Ki'ti looked into his eyes. Their worlds and ways of knowing were so different.

"You are in the presence of Kimseaka, and you are aware. Most of the time on this trek, none of you are aware that Kimseaka, our great messenger from Wisdom, has been among us. We will not be forsaken by Wisdom."

Nanichak-na relaxed when he realized that he didn't need to get his hunter tools for defense against an enemy, certainly not one he couldn't see. Nanichak-na's awareness of Kimseaka's presence slowly left, but it had been overpowering to the old hunter and he was having difficulty reestablishing his equilibrium. At present, he had no sense of where they would go without the ancient path they had followed.

Ki'ti smoothed out the dirt at her knees. With a stick she drew the low-land below. She showed the mountains they'd crossed and placed a tiny stone to mark the promontory where they sat. She showed a continuation through the mountains to a place where a tree grew horizontally from the rocks below. Beside it was a great boulder jutting out, but they would have to go carefully around it to find again the ancient path that would take them to the lowland. The huge boulder hid the path.

Nanichak-na looked into the eyes of the Wise One. "You have never set foot upon this land." He put his flattened palm on the dirt where she had drawn. "Yet you have seen this tree and the boulder?"

"Great Hunter, you remember the cave of the animals where images were drawn?"

He nodded.

"Wisdom makes images in my mind web so I can see just a little ahead. Not far enough that I would become puffed up thinking I could do without Wisdom, as if I were somehow able to see this on my own, but just far enough to assure the safety and right direction of the People. Great Hunter, walk with me. When we reach the tree and boulder, you'll see. I ask you to stand at the boulder to make sure that all pass around it safely. It's a steep place with little foothold." She stood, ending the meeting.

Nanichak-na rose. At seventy-six he was in remarkable condition physi-cally and mentally. He had nodded to Ki'ti showing his willingness to walk with her and to assist at the boulder. He didn't understand her spirit ways, but he'd be interested to see whether the tree and boulder existed. As an afterthought, he struck his left palm with his right fist, and Ki'ti did the same. They exchanged bittersweet smiles. That once important gesture was falling into disuse by the People. Soon the palm strike would no longer affirm agree-ment or add emphasis to their speech.

The People reassembled this time with Nanichak-na beside Ki'ti at the fore-front and Untuk and Manak-na next in line. They walked for quite some time along the edge of the cliff. Nanichak-na continued to wonder whether Ki'ti really knew what she was doing. A pine tree growing horizontally from the side of the cliff came into view. Beside it was a huge boulder. Nanichak-na looked at the little Wise One only to find her eyes already on his face. She knew he doubted. Her ways of knowing were so different from his. This and the obvious boulder she'd described restored his faith in Wisdom. For the first time, he also grasped the truth that Wisdom was leading *through* Wise Ones. Wamumur and Emaea, former Wise Ones, had both tried to explain it to him. He hadn't understood how leadership could be from Wisdom *through* someone. Wise Ones, he reasoned now, were serving *for* Wisdom. He wasn't following Ki'ti but rather he was following Wisdom who communicated through Ki'ti what to do. It came as a profound understanding to the old hunter. He had always thought that Wise Ones initiated strange things, not that they were following directions directly from Wisdom. To him there was no denying that following the lead of Wisdom was superior to following the lead of a hunter or Wise One. He bowed his head deeply to Wisdom and touched the two holes in his garment that represented Wamumur and Emaea, previous Wise Ones. They had tried to explain what he now understood. He wondered why, not for the first time, it took getting old, really old, for him to understand some things. He wondered whether the mind web changed with age.

Nanichak-na positioned himself at the edge of the boulder. He motioned for Untuk to come down with Elemaea. Then he motioned for Ki'ti to descend. One by one he called those who waited above. In the midst of helping the People around the boulder, the dogs also needed assistance when they dragged poles with skins laden with heavy items or carried heavy back-pack loads. Manak-na came with the responsible girls to help unload and reload their burdens. Finally, all had made safe passage back to the path made by the ancient Mol, and they progressed down to the lowland where they would stop for the night.

Nanichak-na returned to the end of the line. He no longer had concerns that the leadership should be in the hands of a hunter. No hunter on this trek had been to the big lake. No hunter knew the land. With Wisdom in the lead showing their Wise One where to go for safety, his concerns could rest. He'd seen how Wisdom had shown Ki'ti the path. He knew now that he could use his hunter skills to look for predators, enemies, and food, or to assure that they were not being followed, and leave the leading solely to Wisdom. Even if it did look like Ki'ti was leading. He admitted to himself that a hunter probably would have missed the connection to the path, as hard as that was to admit. Then, he realized he was feeling hunter's pride again. He lowered his head to Wisdom in shame. Wisdom had chosen Ki'ti. He'd had all the facts for years. It just now made sense. He wondered whether he'd ever grow up in things that pertained to Wisdom. In that respect he knew tiny Ki'ti was a giant.

Manak-na was alive with the new experience. He thrived on exploring, and their group had been sedentary for so long. Certainly, he and others had explored around their cave and the tree home to a radius of about a twenty-day hunter walk, but they covered basically the same ground each time. Instead of exploring, they were alert for changes that would show the presence of humans that might pose threats to the People or wildlife that might provide food. This trek was new and exciting. You never knew what would unfold. He felt that he was seeing better than he normally did—his awareness heightened in strange places. His energy seemed limitless. Midway down the mountain he noticed a tree with oddly unique flowers. The petals, their shapes discernible though past their prime, hung as upside down white ovals with a great brown center in the rounded part of the petals. If you were to hang a fish by the mouth, a fish with a very large eye, that's how it would look, he thought. He showed the tree to Untuk.

"Spirit tree," was Untuk's response in the Mol language. Then he translated. The Mol had lived in this north land from the beginning of days. They knew the plants and animals. Only recently had they become sedentary, so none of these current Mol trekkers had ever been this far north on the path, but the plants were still familiar to them.

Almost at the lowland, Amey slipped and slid down the path. Rocks gouged her legs and her ankle was twisted, but not severely sprained. It took a while for her to rise. The major concern was stopping the bleeding. She could walk with a limp. Likichi brought leather strips and the honey bladder. She smeared honey on the significant wounds and wrapped them with leather strips. When they reached their camp, she would clean and wrap them again. She was concerned that the honey was running low. Returning to her place in line, Likichi smiled at children she passed. She approved their behavior on this trek. They had been remarkably well behaved. Minagle and Sum-na's ten-year-old daughter, Luga, and Meta, Aryna and Tongip-na's daughter of the same age, had been given the responsibility for the dogs. They had done commendable jobs. Both Ki'ti and Minagle had watched the young girls handle the dogs and remembered a time when that job had been theirs on a different trek.

The People reached the lowland and found a grove of oak trees on a little knoll about 200 hunter strides from the path, and they chose that as their campsite for the night. Hunters quickly scoured the immediate area for poisonous snakes and harmful spiders, while others went to the river bank to examine tracks that would tell them of animals in the area. The area appeared safe. The young girls showed the dogs to an area downwind, where they told the dogs to stay. They brought water and sticks of dried meat and fish for the dogs. They removed burdens from the dogs and set the animals free. The dogs would walk a short distance from their assigned place, but they wouldn't stray.

The season of colorful leaves was coming fast and the nights were chilly. Soon, Ki'ti thought, they would have to find a place to shelter during the season of cold days. She liked the lowland, which seemed a good place to avoid winds in the cold times. She would, however, unquestioningly defer to what she was shown by Kimseaka. Hunters left to hunt as soon as they established camp. Small groups went off in four directions. It was not long before two were back, each with a deer. The deer weren't large, but the two animals would feed the group that night. Later, the other two groups would return with three more deer.

At the men's council, which took place this day before instead of after the evening meal, it was decided to camp a few days. Hopefully, by then, Amey would be walking better. They would replenish meat supplies, gather available plants, and rest before continuing on. It also gave Manak-na and Kai-na time to explore this new area. Before they could set forth on their expedition, the camp had to be established. It took time to set up the temporary lodging for so many people. The two hunters decided to go out the next morning early to explore the area.

The number of the People was ninety-two, just over twice the number that left the caves in the ash for their northern cave twenty-five years earlier. There were, in addition, four Mol who had decided to join them at the last moment, when the People said their last farewells at the Mol cave before crossing the river to go north on the path the ancient Mol ancestors had made.

After the evening meal, Tongip-na and Ermi-na walked back up the pathway to survey the evening sky. They were checking to see whether any hearth fires were visible in the vast lowland. Both had great vision and if a column of smoke rose, they'd see it. Only one point in the vast lowland showed smoke, and that was their camp. The hardwood trees still dense with leaves diffused theirs. Nevertheless, hunters knew how to spot smoke diffused or not. They walked a little higher on the path—even then, no smoke was observed rising anywhere else. Wordlessly, each looked at the face of the other. Where were the people? Their unspoken thoughts had more volume than if they'd been spoken. Still they waited. Perhaps a few hunters had come to the lowland. But even in the dark, no smoke other than theirs was visible in the sunless sky as far as they could see. They returned to camp.

The People traveled as lightly as possible, so there were few skins or poles for lodges. Consequently, many lean-to shelters facing small fires in rock surrounds covered the knoll. The lean-tos were covered with branches, wood, and grasses, whatever it took from what was available to keep the area dry and provide a little warmth. Some were simply a slanted horizontal plane and others were enclosed at the edges. A few shelters were floored with pine boughs brought to cushion the sleeping places and provide insulation from the cold ground. Manak-na and Untuk provided those for their families and then gathered some for two sets of the elders: Grypchon-na and Likichi and Ermol-na and Flayk. Other younger men provided for the other elders. Not only were pine boughs pleasant for comfort but also the fragrance was balm-like. Some lean-tos were floored with grasses, and some very young men used no flooring whatever, sleeping only on skins. This was so very different from how they had lived all together in a single huge cave or single structure made of bent trees.

Ki'ti sat on skins over pine branches. She needed rest. She unbraided and slowly combed through her long, light brown hair streaked with lighter lines from the sun. She noticed a few gray hairs among the brown. Her fine hair easily worked its way loose from braids, no matter how tightly she braided the strands. It annoyed her when even a light wind would blow hair in her face. She remembered having her hair cut short when they shared the cave with Minguat, because head lice were rampant. It was during the ashfall when she was very young. She considered having it cut again to keep it from her eyes. Ki'ti parted her hair down the center and braided it, tying the ends with narrow strips of leather that did not match.

She surveyed the camp. It was good. She looked down and there, with a question on his face, was a pup from one of the last litters. He was the smallest. He could hardly carry any burden. She smiled at him and he climbed into the sling her tunic made as she sat with crossed legs. No dog had claimed the place of her last dog. She had really missed having a dog. *Was she,* Ki'ti wondered, *gaining a new dog?* She didn't have to wait long. She looked down and again two brownish eyes looked into her blue ones. She put her hand on the pup's head. Tiriku, she mused, very tiny wolf. Ti, a word used infrequently, meant a single grain of sand. Riku was the word for wolf. Again a dog had chosen to be with her. Silently she thanked Wisdom. She stroked Tiriku. He looked just like her first dog, Ahriku, who came to her in her childhood in the same manner as had this dog. Tiriku, however, was far smaller than Ahriku had been when he came at about the same age. No People had the same close relationship with an animal that Ki'ti had, though a few had wondered when Ki'ti would have another. Now they would know.

Wisdom was beginning to suck color from the lowland behind the mountains. Song, Minagle's oldest daughter and second child of Minagle's first husband, Ghanya, stood outside the oaken canopy and gazed at the stars above. In the chill she hugged herself with her hands on her shoulders. Suddenly she felt large hands cover her smaller ones.

"Such a big sky, is it not?" Humko asked, breathing the natural scent of her.

"It is so," she replied.

His arms surrounded her and they star gazed together, speaking little the sweet words they had for each other while the sides of their faces touched. Humko became rigid and whispered urgently, "Don't move!"

Song fully opened her dreamy eyes to discover she was looking at the face of a huge hooded serpent. She froze. Without Humko, she might have fled and been struck by the snake. His strong hands steadied her.

"Keep your eyes shut," he cautioned her, not knowing whether the cobra was a spitter, and then he whistled the HELP—SNAKE signal and hunters came running as light-footed as possible. Two hunters turned and ran to pick up snake sticks.

From years of experience with snakes, the hunters got between Song and the cobra. They distracted it from Song and carefully moved it away with the snake sticks. Rather than have to wonder about the location of the snake if they freed it, they chose to kill it. They cut off the cobra's head. Hunters buried the head far from the dogs, covering it with a heavy rock. They took severed pieces of the snake's body to ring the camp to warn other snakes to keep out.

At the first hint of light in the sky, Manak-na and Kai-na left to explore. They headed in a northwest direction following the path, which quickly was lost to sight. They tried to guess its location among the areas that were free of trees, but that covered too much space. They established their own landmarks and began serious exploration. They planned to sweep the area in expanding arcs to find the path, while taking the time to savor the differences in this environment. They were wise hunters, but they also had a bit of youthful exuberance in the freedom of exploration, a joy of discovery inherent to both of them. It gave lightness to their steps, clarity of vision, and an openness to see things not in their previously learned experience.

When Wisdom returned color to the land, young hunters teased Humko mercilessly about using Song for a shield against the cobra and waiting for others to kill it. They'd seen him standing behind her. They knew their words were false, but they made sport of Humko, and they laughed at the young man who blushed and didn't know how to respond. Ki'ti overheard and immediately gathered a large number of hunters by name. Even those not called were interested. She had the attention of all who were within earshot of her call, while the uncalled listened trying to appear busy with something else. A change in routine excited their curiosity.

Ki'ti was agitated. She asked the young hunters which of them had dispatched the cobra. All hung their heads. She asked again, "Who killed the cobra?"

Bun, who had been teasing Humko replied, "It was my uncle, Ekuktu-na."

"And why wasn't it you?" she asked looking at Bun. "Or you?" she asked, looking at Cam and Mhank and Patah.

Cam looked at her and said quietly, "I am afraid of snakes. I don't know why I fear them, even the non-poisonous ones, but I do."

Ki'ti looked out over the group of hunters. She stood as straight and tall as she could. "It is not good for hunters to tease one another—to pretend somehow that one is better than another. Our way has always been one of humility, one of seeking the good for all, not one. Remember the lesson Sum-na brought with him when he left the ruined Minguat sea-coast camp to become People? The Minguat hunters postured and talked of their prowess, but the bigger the talkers the quicker they fell to weapons of the coastal Minguat. They died at the hands of Minguat, not People, not Mol. Minguat fought Minguat. Think of the wasted lives such fighting brought. Pride undid them. And it starts with little seeds of teasing where one erroneously feels elevated at the undoing of another. That leads to the posturing and bragging about one's own ability or potential over another. Remember the essence of Sum-na's story. It avails one nothing to compare himself with another person. Instead, it takes People a great distance from truth. That makes them vulnerable."

She paused and looked at the ground. She was greatly conflicted. Their way was not direct teaching, but she could not stop herself. She looked up and continued. "You think you're smart; you think you're strong; you think you'd be victorious in battle? Let me make this clear. Each of us came from the dirt of the ground, handmade by Wisdom. Do not forget that your lives are governed by Wisdom, not by your imagined thoughts. None of us stands or walks upon this land except by the unmerited favor of Wisdom. You think your efforts make you strong? Remember Kai-na's accident. He was one of the stronger young men then. He lived and lives in Wisdom's hand. All his exercise and hard work practicing did not prevent the accident when his leg was broken. For much time he was unable to walk. He had to depend on others. Then Wisdom gave him back his leg. He's strong enough now to explore with Manak-na. They went out before Wisdom restored color to the land. Now, you must remember each of us is vulnerable." She looked each one in the eye slowly before continuing. "We reside in the hand of Wisdom. When we get puffed up, we leave the hand of Wisdom and then are very, very vulnerable. Like the Minguat who lived without Wisdom."

"We may work hard to learn to use slingshots and spears, but we have no success without Wisdom. Wisdom makes us and governs us not because we deserve it, but rather because Wisdom chooses to favor us. Wisdom can change our circumstances in the blink of an eye. Remember the story of Maknu-na and Rimlad? They lived, but what of their People? Their People seriously offended Wisdom and in an instant they were all gone. And that doesn't mean that Kai-na did something Wisdom didn't like. Sometimes Wisdom chooses to let misfortune befall one who has done nothing wrong at all to discover how others will respond. You could say that Wisdom tests us individually and as we treat others."

She looked at Nanichak-na. "Yesterday, I talked with Nanichak-na. When he felt the presence of Kimseaka, a spirit messenger from Wisdom, he told me he'd rather deal with," she showed two full hands of fingers twice, "enemy warriors alone than the presence of one from the world of the spirit of Wisdom. Is he a timid hunter?" she asked.

All said, "No!" There were a few palm strikes. Everyone knew Nanichak-na was one of their best and bravest hunters, even at his age.

"Nanichak-na knows that fear of Wisdom is the beginning of right reasoning and understanding. Nanichak-na has felt the presence of one sent by Wisdom. Have you?"

She waited while they responded negatively.

"Just because you haven't felt the world of the spirit of Wisdom, does that mean that world doesn't exist?"

They gave negative responses. Ki'ti's agitation had not subsided. Instead it made her focus sharper and she could not contain the flood of knowledge she felt these young people should know.

Then she said, "That word *Wisdom* is used by us as another name for the One Who Made Us: the uncommon, unusable, separate name we speak not often and with great care. We do that so pride won't grow in us from having been made by the hands of Wisdom, unlike all else that was made by Wisdom's speaking it into being. Like it or not, Wisdom made us and Wisdom rules us. Because we follow Wisdom, we have lived since the beginning of days—and will continue. If we lose Wisdom, we die as surely as did the Others by the sea."

The hunters were spellbound. Never had they heard so much at one time from their Wise One when she told the stories in the season of cold days. Their mind webs were capturing every word. This time, they didn't have to figure it out from the stories. The Wise One was making it plain. Many now understood Wisdom far better than they ever had. They understood better their own places in relation to Wisdom. Many found answers to questions they'd had but didn't know how to ask. The former Minguat and Mol gained much understanding, understanding that they hadn't realized they were missing.

Ki'ti continued with force. "Teasing will cease among the People. Think before you act. Remember, though, that all among us, from the oldest to the youngest, male and female, original People, former Minguat, former Mol— all of us now People—are, in the eyes of Wisdom, nothing special on our own account, just Wisdom's creations. Wisdom thinks no more of one of us than another. Do not think I am special because I represent Wisdom. I am simply used by Wisdom. Some of you may remember well how hard that was to achieve." She sighed remembering.

There were some gentle laughs from the older People, some of whom had gathered to listen on the fringes of the meeting to this new teaching. Grypchon-na and Mootmu-na both struck their left hands with their right fists, making a sound. Nanichak-na raised his large eyebrows listening to the sound of the palm strikes. The Winds of Change left so many differences. He felt old. None were older than he. *Being the oldest is a lonesome place,* he mused.

Ki'ti continued. "All of us are equal. None better, none worse. If you cease to believe that truth, you believe a lie *you* have created. Never forget we are equal in Wisdom's eyes and in our own. We must remember to keep it so. Finally, would you want to be teased?"

The assembled People indicated they didn't want to be teased.

"Then," she continued, "Don't tease anyone else. If you don't want it done to you, then don't do it to anyone else. Consider. Last night Humko held Song very still in the face of the snake so that she would not move and get struck. His bravery filled both of them. It was extraordinary quick thinking! Could you have thought that well? He reminded her to close her eyes in case the snake spit. Would you have remembered? Or would you have run in fear, leaving your special one to fend for herself?" She paused. "That is all I have to say," she said following her words with a palm strike.

For a few moments the assembly froze. The Wise One had spent time teaching directly, something different from the teaching through stories or through demonstration where the younger were to observe and figure out the lesson. Like the path that had disappeared in a landslide, they had moved off Wisdom's path. The Wise One yanked them back by teaching directly. Teasing would cease for the present. Very slowly the group broke apart to get back to the day's activity. Glances and nods were exchanged among Nanichak-na, Mootmu-na, Ermol-na, Grypchon-na, and Ki'ti. The men's council that night would hold a surprise.

Yomuk ran to the hunters to share his discovery, but waited patiently and marked well the words his mother was speaking. When the group broke up he found Grypchon-na and Mootmu-na talking together.

As soon as they recognized him, Yomuk said, "I have found bees. I know our honey bladder is nearly empty. I looked carefully for bees. I found some and located their hive."

The older men were astonished. Yomuk at age ten was young to be demonstrating such responsibility and foresight. They agreed to gather supplies and to harvest the honey and wax with the boy.

On the way, Grypchon-na asked, "How did you find the hive, Young Hunter of Bees?"

Yomuk smiled. He was not a real hunter yet, but he was thrilled at the epithet, Young Hunter of Bees. His eyes sparkled in a beaming face. His squared jaw gave him a visage of strength. His hair neatly combed and held back with a leather band from his forehead to the back of his head was black with a blue shine and it was trimmed to the shoulders. His tunic was new and just covered his knees. It was held at his right shoulder. "I have watched bees," he said. "They fly from their flowers straight to the hive. They don't curve their flights. So I watched bees when they left those yellow flowers over there. I saw them head straight for that deadfall log and the upright next to it. It's over that hill. The honey is in the upright log near the top."

Grypchon-na wore an old tunic fastened over his left shoulder. He had long white hair pulled back atop his head, braided, and folded, held in place with a wide strip of leather. He was fifty-one, slightly stiff as some older people were. His hairline was receding. He preferred short hair, but said he felt stronger when it was long. He carried a torch, an ember, and a small antler to pry open the hive. He also carried a bladder to hold the honey and a piece of stiff leather that was bent down the center. Mootmu-na was sixty-three. He wore the same style tunic and had long hair that fell free and was kept from his face with a headband Amey had made and colored red. She said she could spot him in a crowd with the red headband. Her eyesight was better up close. Mootmu-na carried hunter tools that would be required to defend them, if the need arose. He didn't anticipate a need. There had been no sighting of strangers or large animals. Yomuk carried a snake stick and his spear along with an additional bladder. All were barefoot.

The men hiked over the hill following Yomuk. It was a sunny day and the warmth was welcome. Yomuk was savoring his first time as a leader of any kind other than of his sister, knowing as soon as he reached the site that role would end.

"It's just as you described it, Young Hunter of Bees," Grypchon-na stated. There was the deadfall log with the upright next to it. "Are you able to remain calm enough so the bees don't become enraged?" Grypchon-na asked skeptically and continued, "Even if you are stung?"

"Yes, I do not fear a sting," he replied more from bravery than certainty. He immediately realized with those words he was committed and would have to remain brave.

"Then take this ember," Grypchon-na said, "And get the torch lit."

Yomuk made a nest of dried grass in a scooped out area and gently introduced the ember. The grass caught and he added a few twigs. Then, he took the torch and held it over the little fire. He twisted the torch very slowly until it caught thoroughly. He gave it to Mootmu-na. Then, he carefully put out the little fire he'd started.

Mootmu-na held the torch so smoke would blow to the upright log while Grypchon-na pried off a large section of tree bark that was covering the honey, gently laying it aside. Then he pried off a woody section and laid that piece aside, exposing the honey. Grypchon-na took the stiff leather gently placing it directly under the honeycomb. He directed the dripping delicacy and bits of comb into the bladders.

The bees did not ignore the invasion. Agitated, many took flight to defend the hive. Mootmu-na got a sting on his shoulder and on his leg. Yomuk got a sting on his back and two on his arm. Grypchon-na was stung on his face twice and had shoulder and back stings and one on his chest. Grypchon-na was grateful. He knew that following bee stings, his arthritic pain improved temporarily.

Yomuk's reaction was not gratitude. He tried to remain brave as he watched the hunters appear unaffected by the stings. It was painful to him to have one of the stings but several tried his bravery. He wanted to cry, but forced himself to concentrate on the honey gathering and think of nothing else. Occasionally he'd wipe under one eye or the other as if he were doing anything but removing evidence of a tear. The men politely pretended not to notice, exchanging grins between them.

When they finished gathering the honey, Mootmu-na extinguished the torch by covering it with dirt. Then, he shook the dirt from it when the fire was out because the torch was reusable. Grypchon-na carefully replaced the woody piece and the bark he'd laid aside when opening the hive. He checked to be sure that the hive would be protected against rain. One area was exposed, so he looked around and found a suitable piece of bark to cover it. The piece of bark needed to be held in place, so Mootmu-na handed him a strip of leather to tie the protective piece to the log. Yomuk checked again to be sure the fire starter area was cinders with no smoldering embers. Then the men checked the stings on themselves and each other to be sure the bees' stingers were removed from their skin.

The hive was a big one so both bladders were full. They returned to camp and left the honeycomb-filled bladders with the women. The women would separate the honey and wax and save both. The three went directly for a welcome bath in the river. Yomuk walked as tall as his body would stretch. He was already as tall as Grypchon-na and Mootmu-na. His father, a Mol, was very tall. Yomuk knew he had taken a significant step toward becoming a hunter. He smiled. It wouldn't be easy, he concluded, but it would be worth it someday to be called hunter. He delighted in the idea. Surely, the stings weren't so bad after all, he decided.

At the camp Elemaea was visiting with her aunt, Minagle, and playing with her same-age cousin, Mona, when her brother walked by on his way to the river. Elemaea saw the bumps on his skin and on the men. She ceased playing and ran to Minagle.

"Auntie, what are the bumps on my brother and the men? Are they sick?" she asked breathlessly.

Minagle was startled with Elemaea's impulsiveness. The child reminded her of her own sister, Ki'ti, when she was very young. She reached for Elemaea's hands. She slowed her own response in an attempt to slow Elemaea.

"The men and your brother have been gathering honey. Bees aren't happy about having their hives invaded, so they fought back by stinging the men," Minagle told her.

"I got stung by a bee once," Elemaea said. "It hurt terribly. You put mud on it."

"I remember that, Elemaea. Yomuk and the men will be fine."

Elemaea smiled and returned to play with Mona.

Minagle looked at the children. She remembered her girlhood. She looked so different from People then. She was thin while the People were stocky. Her hair was thick and black while the People had fine hair ranging in color from red to brown. Some had hair that spiraled. Her eyes were brown while most of the People had blue eyes. She looked like the Minguat, those her People used to call Others. She had grown up with many insecurities, because she looked so different from the People. Both sets of her children had Minguat fathers, and though they all were People now, she and her family looked Minguat. Elemaea, her sister's daughter, was part People and part Mol. She was, unlike her brother, tiny. She was thin compared to People but shorter than normal for real People. Neither she nor her brother had the protrusion on the back of the head that characterized the People. Minagle mused that standards of beauty had changed. *Today—with the mixing—all children were strikingly beautiful despite or, perhaps, because of their many differences,* she thought. Minagle approved.

Somehow Wamumur had put the differences in appearance in their rightful place long ago when he proclaimed that all who remained with them were People, Minagle remembered. There were no longer Mol or Minguat—all were People. Somehow, all differences were seen as People differences. There was a new flexibility in what one saw as beautiful after that. Had she grown up at this current time, she felt, she would not have had the insecurities it took so long for her to overcome. Two Minguat left after Wamumur's proclamation because they didn't want to be People. Minagle shivered when she remembered both those who left had died when they ran into a bear at night. But all the rest were pleased to stay and most had already considered themselves People. She knew that the older People were concerned with the problems the original People had with childbirth. For most couples, the mixing seemed to make childbirth easier, although it hadn't helped her sister, Ki'ti, Minagle realized. Ki'ti had been pregnant frequently, but had only managed two live births.

With the warmth of the sun on her skin, Minagle stretched. It filled her with joy to realize how happy she was. She thought of her brother and Kai-na exploring somewhere. Manak-na loved to explore from the time he was very young. He'd taken her with him from the time he was seven and she was four. She rubbed her arms. She considered that she might be the stronger today for his leading her to new places when they were children. He had definitely taught her to examine her surroundings with care, to read the sky and the position of the sun, to tread quietly, and to listen acutely. Girls, of course, were taught these things, but not with the same intensity. Manak-na taught her, as if her life depended on it. He told her someday it might. It hadn't saved her when Reemast had abused her. It hadn't happened when she married Ghanya, who, she thought, was wonderful and so sensitive, but who turned against the People, thinking somehow that he was superior to them as Minguat, and ended up killed by a bear. But in the long run she'd found Sumna, and life was better than at any other time in her life, including when she was young and exploring with Manak-na. She wondered where Manak-na and Kai-na were.

The two men traveled swiftly. They had been unable to locate the path, but they had already made wide, sweeping searches across the area where they assumed the path should be. The sun was almost overhead when they stopped along a creek. They ate some of the dried meat sticks they carried and drank from the creek instead of from the water bladders they carried. Fresh bubbling water was always better. With his few burdens laid on the ground, each man carefully studied the area.

"Look at that spider!" Kai-na said. "I think it's called a wolf spider."

Manak-na looked at the spider and smiled. "I think you're right. Don't let it bite you," he laughed. Both were aware of its potent bite. "There's a lot of game here," he continued. "Out here I noticed numbers of antelope and deer. It would be good to harvest for winter, if we were going to stay. I also think those hills are worth exploring for shelter. Agree?"

"Agree!" Kai-na said enthusiastically, gathering his burdens from the ground.

Manak-na, too, gathered his burdens. They crossed the creek, headed into a treed area, and walked toward the hills, despite the fact that this was a distinct deviation from their planned extended arcs to seek the continuation of the path. The sky was clear and the cool air was perfect for their quickened pace. They reached the hills and could see that, in fact, there were some caves in the hill. Some were at ground level; some were mid-way up the hill. They crossed a swift creek. Very carefully they examined the area. It appeared that no people were around or had been for a very long time. Few traces of animals were visible on the hill side of the creek, though they could see many when they looked back across the creek. Scarcity of animal life was a curiosity to the men. Regardless of the apparent lack of life in the area, the men approached the area stealthily with extreme caution. Both used every sense available to them.

Kai-na pointed to the cave that appeared larger than the rest. It was at ground level and appeared to slope downward. Kai-na pointed to himself and then the cave, signaling that he'd enter the cave first. Manak-na, concealed in the brush, raised his spear as an unseen protection against anyone who might harm Kai-na. The effort was not required, for there was no one in the area.

Kai-na whistled the signal that the cave was unoccupied. He followed that with the whistle that meant no scent of living things. Manak-na checked again all around him outside the cave, lowered his spear, and joined Kai-na in the cave. The men were no less surprised by this cave than they had been when they saw the caves with the images of animals on the wall long ago.

This cave gave them the impression they had shrunk. The cave was huge by any standard. A few tools lay about. At least Manak-na concluded that they were tools. But they were much larger than tools they used with similar shapes. Tools looked like the ones made by the Mol. Fire pits were larger than any they'd ever seen.

"Mol giants?" Manak-na muttered the question, holding what looked like a spear tip, a spear tip at least four times larger than his own. A spear tip crafted of opaque flint that was beautiful, a little like the ones the Minguat used years ago to kill the man with the green bag. The man with the green bag was a Mol they'd found near the caves they just vacated. When they found him he had been dead a very long time. Manak-na's mind web was evaluating what he was seeing, but it kept stopping without answers—unless giants had inhabited this cave. That was just too incredible. He returned the spear tip to the place he'd found it.

Kai-na went outside. He wanted to explore the cave higher up the hill. He found what seemed to be hand and foot grips on the hill face, but they were too far apart vertically and horizontally. Kai-na had begun to dig out additional grips for hands and feet when Manak-na came out. Manak-na noticed a crack in the rock face off to the right where another raised cave could be seen.

"Kai-na," he said, pointing, "Do you think that one might be easier to explore?"

Kai-na looked at the other raised cave. He laid down the tool he'd been using and went to the cracked wall. He wedged himself into the crack and moved himself upward with his legs and feet first, and then he used his back and arms. When he reached the level of the cave he could see large hand grips, but he had to strain hard to reach them safely.

In a matter of moments after Kai-na entered the cave. Manak-na could hear Kai-na's voice tinged with anxiety, "Oh! Oh! What's this? Wisdom—protect us!" It alarmed Manak-na.

"Kai-na, are you well?" he apprehensively called to his friend. Manak-na didn't take his eyes off the cave entrance.

Moments later Kai-na staggered to the cave entrance with a skull he was holding. The sight of Kai-na with the skull, framed by the gray walls of the cave entrance was a sight for which Manak-na was totally unprepared. It took a moment for his mind web to comprehend what he was seeing. The skull had long red hair and some skin attached. What was truly awesome was the size of it. Kai-na held the lower jaw in place. The skull and jaw were equal in height to the distance from Kai's waist to the top of his head. Kai-na turned and placed the skull back where he had found it. He returned to the cave entrance, looking somewhat pale to Manak-na. With great care, but as quickly as possible, Kai-na returned to the ground.

Manak-na asked, "Are there more of them up there?" He wasn't certain he wanted to know the answer.

"It's filled with them," Kai-na acknowledged quietly.

Manak-na looked at the ground, seemingly conflicted. "I don't want to do this Kai-na, but I think we must cut short our adventure to go back. I think the Mol should see this—maybe Ki'ti."

"You're right, of course. My first instinct is to flee this place, but it's probably due only to the size of the dead. Do you think there are live ones nearby?" Kai-na adjusted the shoulder strap on his tunic. His eyes narrowed as he looked off into the distance. He ran his hands over his arm muscles distractedly.

"There has been no sight of fire at night. My mind web persuades me this is something from long ago. Long, long, long ago. I don't think any living giants are here. At least not in large numbers. Think what it would take to feed those giants! Think of the number of animals we saw over there earlier. Nobody's been eating them." They walked to the creek where Kai-na automatically washed his hands and arms.

"Straight from the mind web of a good hunter, my friend," Kai-na replied. "Let's go." Kai-na and Manak-na gathered their burdens and retraced their route from earlier in the day.

As Wisdom began to suck color from the land, back at the camp, Tongip-na and Ermi-na climbed again the path to the huge boulder. They looked for camp fires. They could spot their own, but nothing else.

"We should be able to see Manak-na and Kai-na's fire. They'd have one by now," Ermi-na said in a voice touched with concern.

"I agree, Ermi-na, but look over there in the distance between those two clusters of trees. The two spots there seem to be moving. Could that be the explorers returning already?"

Ermi-na finally found the two moving spots. "That was fine vision, Tongip-na. Fine vision! Let's get down there to hear why they returned."

Both moved quickly down the hill.

At the camp the evening meal was almost ready when Tongip-na and Ermi-na arrived from one direction and Manak-na and Kai-na from another. People rushed to Manak-na and Kai-na to hear why they returned until the booming voice of Likichi rang out that the evening meal was ready, and Manak-na and Kai-na could share their adventure at the council after eating. The adventurers laid down their burdens, washed the dust from their hands and faces, and happily went to eat whatever it was that smelled so good. Manak-na took a moment to smile at Domur from a distance and Ki'ti a little closer. Kai-na greeted Mitrak with a hug.

After the evening meal, the men's council began. Ki'ti nodded initially to Nanichak-na.

Nanichak-na stood. He said quietly, "Humko, please come here."

Obediently Humko rose. He stood before the old man wondering what help Nanichak-na would need.

Nanichak-na put his hands on Humko's shoulders. "No longer will your name be Humko. From now on your name is Humko-na."

Humko had not anticipated the honor. His face turned bright red in confusion and he lowered it as far as possible. When Nanichak-na released the hold on his shoulders, Humko-na returned to his seat still dumbfounded. He guessed it had something to do with the snake episode but was unsure. He just didn't expect anything like this.

Neither did the young People who had teased Humko earlier in the day. They learned another lesson that night, after having learned several earlier from Ki'ti.

Nanichak-na nodded to Ki'ti indicating he was finished. Ki'ti nodded to Manak-na.

Manak-na began. He told of their plan to travel in expanding arcs to look for the path. He told of their inability to find it. He told of their distraction and subsequent visit to the hill where they found caves. He asked Kai-na to stand in front of him. He put one hand at Kai-na's waist and one on the top of Kai-na's head.

"Kai-na," he asked, "What does this measure?"

"It measures the size of a giant skull and jaw we found. The giant had red hair," Kai-na replied.

Silence covered the camp with a great heaviness. Only the very young failed to realize that meant giants were real, and that they were two to three times larger than adult People. Manak-na and Kai-na returned to their places.

Manak-na continued, "We considered that the People who used to be Mol should come to this place. We also considered that Ki'ti should also see it." Manak-na nodded to Ki'ti.

Tongip-na made eye contact with Ki'ti. She nodded to him.

Tongip-na looked at Kai-na and then Manak-na. He asked, "Do you think the skull belonged to one of my relatives from long, long, long ago? Maybe one of the path builders?"

Tongip-na nodded to Kai-na, who replied, "The skull was only one of many. We hardly explored the area before turning around to have you come to see this for yourselves." Kai-na nodded to Tongip-na.

Beyond the circle of the men's council, Yomuk was listening. He was ready to go, his interest so intense. *What a grand adventure!* he thought.

Tongip-na nodded to Ki'ti.

"What is your thought about this?" Ki'ti asked, nodding back to Tongip-na.

"I definitely want to see this. I'd think most formerly Mol would like to go, too. The bodies could be Mol giants. We've only heard about giants, never seen one. Ki'ti, if you joined with us could you possibly gain information for us from what you see there?"

Ki'ti shrugged.

Manak-na almost moaned. He knew Tongip-na was probably right, but Manak-na knew it could be dangerous for Ki'ti to get involved in another time. They would have to guard her. Manak-na looked up—right into the eyes of Untuk. They both acknowledged that they'd have to be on guard. Ki'ti saw the exchange. How she missed Wamumur and Emaea. Her heart ached. Thanks to Wamumur she knew with confidence how to protect herself from those in other times—even from giants.

Tongip-na nodded to Ki'ti, who said, "Those Mol who wish to go to this place with Tongip-na, Manak-na, and Kai-na, be ready when Wisdom has returned color to the land. I will go. The rest of you will remain at this camp until we return."

The council ended and Yomuk was on his feet making his way to Untuk.

"Father," he said, "I must go tomorrow."

Untuk had not planned for that. He expected Yomuk to help look after Elemaea.

"Father," he continued, "I am half Mol. Those could be my people." Yomuk's sincerity was palpable.

Untuk thought briefly. "You may go," he said. Untuk wondered how Ki'ti would feel about his decision.

It was dark and with travel for some the next day, the group dispersed and sleep came quickly. Gripchon-na and Ermol-na stood guard for the first part of the night until the tail on the large snare in the sky pointed eastward. Then Mootmu-na and Arkan-na would take over until Wisdom restored light to the land. Gripchon-na watched as the big snare rotated around the star in the north that never moved. The device that gave them direction and their watch periods at night, a true gift from Wisdom, never ceased to awe Gripchon-na. He lowered his head and thanked Wisdom for the big and little snares in the night sky. The night was huge with bright stars everywhere with a quarter moon rising. It was breathtakingly beautiful.

Wisdom restored color to the land. Arkan-na took two medium sized rocks and hit them together three times. It wakened all the People. There was much hurrying and fixing of food to take and to eat before the travel. A few dogs were used and the men carried backpacks. Yomuk got his backpack and Ki'ti noticed. She went to her son and asked what he was doing.

"Mother, I am going. I asked Father. He agreed. I am part Mol. These giants are my ancestors, and I am old enough not to be a burden on this travel." Ki'ti was shocked at his presentation. He was a son to approve.

"I want to go too!" Elemaea shouted from Minagle's arms wiggling to free herself.

"You may be mature for your age, but you are not old enough. Keep your facts straight, Yomuk. Very well. Fill your backpack with dried meat. We do not know how long this will take." Ki'ti walked over to Minagle and looked sternly at Elemaea. "You shouted out, and that was not good. How can anyone approve you when you constantly act impulsively? You are no longer a little child. Stop acting like one. I have told you that you will remain here. That is the end of it. Behave yourself well or when I return you will have regrets. Do you understand?"

Yomuk had lowered his head in respect and hurried to fill his backpack as full as he could. His backpack was not as large as the men's backpacks, so he went to his uncle Frakja-na and asked whether he might use his backpack for dried meat for the trip. Frakja-na was a little surprised that Yomuk would be taking the trip, but he handed him the backpack with a smile. Yomuk transferred the meat and went to add more until the backpack was completely filled. Frakja-na watched the young man leave to make the meat transfer and to place bedrolls on the backpack. He chuckled as he mused; *He's got the same desire to explore that his uncle Manak-na has.*

All the travelers had grouped together. Above the quiet chatter, Manak-na asked, "Who has not eaten yet?"

In his haste Yomuk realized he'd forgotten, so he said, "I have not eaten yet."

Cam, Tongip-na and Aryna's oldest son, said, "Nor I."

Ki'ti said in a small voice, "Nor I." She wondered how she could have forgotten that rule of travel. She hurried to take the bowl Likichi handed her. She stood to eat, something she almost never did. The cooked grains were warm, and the food filled her with a feeling that the day would be profitable for the People.

Finally, those who needed to eat were filled and all the travelers gathered. Manak-na took inventory of the travelers. There were former Mol: Tongip-na and Untuk, Gumokut and his wife Flinee, Lolmeg and his wife Maylue. There were half Mol: Tongip-na and Aryna's older children, two boys, Cam and Elet, and Tiki, the girl. And, of course, Yomuk. Then, there were Kai-na, Ki'ti, and himself none of whom had Mol ancestry. There were thirteen People. Since Cam was sixteen and Elet was fifteen, Manak-na considered there were seven hunters. That did not count Yomuk who was practiced but not tried in hunting or Untuk whose primary job was to guard Ki'ti. Manak-na was satisfied that they had enough hunters for protection. He noticed that the dogs were ready and that Ki'ti was handling the dogs with help from Tiki. Tiriku, Ki'ti's personal dog, was also burdened with a small pack. Manak-na lined up the travelers the way he wanted them to walk. He and Kai-na would lead; Ki'ti and Untuk would be next, followed by Cam and Elet; next Tiki and the dogs were placed centrally to keep things moving; then Tongip-na and Yomuk; following them were Flinee and Maylue; and at the end were Gumokut and Lolmeg, because both had great ability to keep track of what was before and behind them.

Manak-na whistled Start and the line began to move. It was soon that they found the pace that all could keep. It was quicker than when they had travelled with the entire group. They crossed the flat land easily, surprised by the wildlife they saw. By high sun, they had reached the creek.

The creek was deep in some places. The dogs had to be carried across with their burdens. Ki'ti picked up Tiriku, crying out as she lost her footing on a slippery rock, landing with a splash in the swiftly moving current. She and the dog were instantly carried away at a rapid rate. With her backpack she had difficulty righting herself. She held fiercely to Tiriku. In a blink of an eye Untuk was out of his backpack and sprinting down the creek bank trying to get ahead of her. Everyone else looked in horror at their Wise One being swept away. Manak-na ran down the opposite creek bank ready to help if he could. He could not keep pace with Untuk. Untuk entered the water where it was fairly deep and the creek was just coming up on a section of the rapids, swimming as fast as he could. Ki'ti was bouncing around rocks. Finally in a great burst of speed Untuk grabbed her backpack and got his footing. He pulled Ki'ti still gripping a terrified Tiriku through the water over to the shore opposite where she had entered. Ki'ti was tired and cold but not injured except from some bruising around her shoulders. She still held onto Tiriku and his backpack. For a moment Ki'ti did not want to turn loose of Tiriku, but she did put him down on the ground where he shook and shook to get the water off his fur. He looked at Ki'ti with eyes that seemed bigger than normal. Untuk removed Tiriku's lopsided backpack and Tiriku shook more water from his fur. Ki'ti was a bit confused, as she walked with Untuk and Manak-na back to the others whose relief was obvious on their faces. On the way Tiriku kept butting his nose into the back of Ki'ti's leg. It was a way he had of asking for her attention. Ki'ti hardly noticed. When they reached the group, she appeared to have regained her composure. Manak-na was greatly relieved. When she had entered the rapids, Manak-na had not been at all certain that Untuk could save her. From that moment, hunters accompanied the rest of the People who were crossing the creek.

Before exploring the caves or any other activity, Untuk got a fire going and took Ki'ti's new tunic and put it on a stake near the fire to dry. He covered her with soft leather that was made for sleeping. She sat near the fire to warm up, for she was shivering. The dogs were shown to their places and their burdens were removed. Tiriku would not leave Ki'ti's side. Flinee and Maylue started food for the evening meal. They put some small new meat pieces into a pot of greens and the odor made everyone very hungry. Yomuk asked Tiki if she'd like to help him find firewood in case they needed it later. She eagerly agreed to help. No one was permitted to enter any cave until they were told they could. Their anticipation was hard to control. Working helped.

When Ki'ti stopped shivering, she got up and felt her tunic, finding it still soaked. She asked Untuk if he'd cut a slit through the leather he'd wrapped around her. He agreed and she put her head through the opening. She took two small pieces of leather from her backpack. They were wet but useable. She emptied her backpack so the contents and the backpack could dry. She placed the contents on tree roots to keep the dirt from turning to mud on the things she carried in the backpack. She asked Untuk to cut two tiny holes on either side of the leather so she could tie the sides together. Finally, with the sides tied, she was ready to see what the giants had to tell. Her braids were still wet and when they touched her skin it chilled her. She ignored it.

Meanwhile Untuk had removed his leather, which he wore threaded front and back through a leather strap tied around his waist. It kept him clean when he sat. He replaced it with a dry one that went from between his legs up through the leather strap and hung over in both front and back. It was standard dress for formerly Mol men until cold weather came. It was simply called leather. Untuk much preferred it to the tunic which the People wore.

Ki'ti ate and decided to walk over toward the caves. She didn't need permission. She walked into the largest cave that was at ground level. She noticed the huge tools that were lying on the ground. An overwhelming sense of sadness came to rest on her like the moisture in a thick swamp fog. As she went further into the cave, the sadness became more oppressive. She could see where the fire pits were. She could see the air vent at the top of the cave toward the back. Despite the sadness, she realized this huge cave had once been good for living. She wondered what they had to do to keep it warm. Their fire pits were definitely larger than the ones they made. Ki'ti looked back into the light and saw Manak-na who had just walked up to her. He wore a questioning look.

"Brother, where are the giants' caves?"

Manak-na was startled. Not often did she call him Brother. He wondered why, but he pointed toward the caves that were elevated.

Ki'ti carefully assessed the caves and their entrances. Although she was good at traveling, there seemed no way for her to reach the caves.

Manak-na interrupted her thinking, "We decided we could get you up there by making a loop in a rope for you to sit on and pulling you up from below. It's not going to work for you to climb. While sitting on the rope, you can walk up with your feet so that you aren't dragged up the side."

Ki'ti thought about that for a moment. "Who will pull me up?" she asked.

"Since Tongip-na has the strongest arms, we thought he was the best choice. He also can climb up there easier since he's so tall."

"Let's get started," she said.

Manak-na quietly went to find Tongip-na. He picked up his backpack and pulled out the rope he had put aside for this purpose. All gathered around the fire. Manak-na explained that they were going to take Ki'ti up into the giants' cave so that she could see what happened. Then the Mol could go to see their ancestors. All would stay back by the fire and maintain quiet while Ki'ti went into the cave. She might need quiet. The People nodded. They wanted Ki'ti to be safe and would be very quiet to avoid distractions for her. They did move around a bit to find a good place from which to watch the activity unobstructed.

The People watched as Tongip-na climbed up to the cave using the hand grips. He had difficulty reaching one of them so he decided to swing to the side and up to grab it. Kai-na hadn't made hand grips all the way up. With the swing technique, Tongip-na was tall enough to manage the hand grips instead of wedging himself against the wall. He had the rope slung over his head and under his left arm. When he got to the top he started to pull off the rope but his curiosity got to him first. He began to look at the bodies of the giants.

"Wisdom protect us!" he cried out before he thought to say anything.

Everyone below, including Ki'ti, was instantly alert. Manak-na remembered Kai-na's similar shout when he saw the giants for the first time.

When Tongip-na had composed himself, he began to lower the rope to Ki'ti. She sat on the circle of rope and waited for Tongip-na to pull her up. Tongip-na was looking to Manak-na for a signal. Manak-na nodded and Tongip-na began to pull the rope that would bring Ki'ti to the cave. He was surprised at how light she was. Manak-na showed her how to use her feet to keep from sliding along the cave wall. She did well.

Tongip-na pulled her up to the last part of the edge and with a swing brought her inside. When her eyes adjusted, she felt overcome again with great sadness. Tongip-na coiled the rope and set it aside. Ki'ti walked among the bodies she could see. She looked at Tongip-na and asked for a torch. She had difficulty seeing the further back she went. Tongip-na went to the cave entrance and asked Manak-na for a torch. Manak-na got one and Untuk, who had watched the climb Tongip-na took, offered to take it up. Manak-na gave him a sling to put over his head and under his arm so he could carry the un-lit torch on his back. He gave him a small ember in its carrying case.

Untuk climbed up the same hand grips that Tongip-na had used. He was a bit taller so the swing wasn't necessary. He arrived in the cave prepared to be amazed. He could quickly see why Tongip-na had shouted out. He had never seen a giant. *These giants,* he thought, *must be as big as Gar!*

With the torch, Ki'ti walked among the bodies. She noticed that many giants had six toes on their feet. Some had six fingers on their hands. She thought of Keemu, Olintak and Slamika-na's son, with six toes. When she saw skin still attached, she studied it. On one corpse she noticed the skin was covered with awful looking sores. She continued to search and found more and more of these skin lesions everywhere. Then she became restive. She could feel the pull to another time. She prayed that Wisdom would protect her and remain close to her. She let the pull take her. Toward the back of the cave she could see a body moving. She noticed that where there had been no skin, skin was reappearing. She went toward the body. It leaned on an elbow seeming to look at her, and she heard words that she could not understand. She looked at Tongip-na and Untuk. Their faces were stricken with grief.

"Did you hear the words and understand the language?" she asked them.

"Yes." Tongip-na replied, dumbfounded that he'd heard words from a dead man. He realized this must be common to the Wise One. He wondered how he'd heard it. The mouth of the corpse hadn't moved. He continued. "The dead man spoke the same language as the Mol. He was the last. He said all had gotten sick from sores that drooled and hurt badly. They sickened and died. He was the last. He wanted someone to know. The sores had taken his family."

"Did you see him as he was before he died or as a corpse?" she asked.

Tongip-na answered, "As a corpse, of course. What do you mean?"

She said, "Say these words three times in the language of the Mol, 'We know your story. We will not forget. Now you can sleep.'"

Tongip-na was confused, so Untuk said loud and slow in the Mol language, "**We know your story.** We will not forget. Now, you can sleep. We know your story. **We will not forget.** Now, you can sleep. We know your story. We will not forget. **Now, you can sleep.**" Untuk's emphasis changed each time he said the words. He tried to be convincing, and he spoke with great feeling.

Ki'ti watched as the man let himself lie back and change from a very sick man to the corpse he was in her time. Ki'ti was greatly alarmed. She asked to be lowered back to the ground and for the men to join her. Ki'ti tossed the torch to Lolmeg and he put it out before she was lowered to the ground. All gathered at the fire pit.

Ki'ti began to speak. "I know you want to see the giants. I will not stop you, for it is your heritage. What I will say is this, 'Go to satisfy your curiosity—do it quickly and return. Look at the bodies you can see from the entrance. Do not walk among them. Do not touch them. Then you must go to the creek and bathe every part of yourself carefully. Do not touch your mouth or your nose until you are totally clean. Clean under your nails and your hair. You must shake out your tunics or leathers very well and brush water against them for cleansing—not to get them wet. Be sure a hunter is there to keep you from drifting off in the current.' Do you understand?"

Everyone nodded.

"The giants died from a terrible disease which made sores all over their bodies. It must have been very painful. I don't want anyone here to develop that sickness. You must clean yourself, if you go up there."

Flinee leaned toward Maylue. "Are you going up there?"

Maylue thought a moment and replied, "No. It isn't worth it to me."

"Me either," Flinee said.

Manak-na said, "Whoever wants to go up come over here."

Yomuk rose and went to his uncle. Gumokut and Lolmeg went to the gathering place followed by Cam, Elet, and Tiki.

Manak-na asked Kai-na to oversee the viewing. Untuk touched Ki'ti's shoulder. "Come to the creek with me. You must get clean. You, too, Tongip-na." They followed him quietly, bathed thoroughly, and returned to sit by the fire, while Manak-na went to help oversee the viewing. The three by the fire were speechless. What could they say after what they had seen and experienced?

Ki'ti sat on a log by the fire with Tiriku at her side. She was troubled. This place was a potential danger to anyone who might pass it and have curiosity to enter. She felt that there should be some means of warning people, but she could not imagine how.

Maylue came over and sat beside her and asked, "Ki'ti, this has been quite a day for you. Are you cold?"

Ki'ti hadn't considered how she felt. She was a little chilly. "Yes, I am, Maylue."

Maylue went to her own backpack and pulled out a leather piece to which fur was attached. It was a blanket she normally would have put under Lolmeg and herself for sleeping. Maylue put it around Ki'ti with the fur touching Ki'ti's skin. Maylue, being formerly Mol, was much taller than Ki'ti and the blanket covered Ki'ti well. Ki'ti smiled at Maylue. Ki'ti's placing her hand on Maylue's arm and looking into her eyes expressed her gratitude for Maylue's kindness. Ki'ti was extremely tired. She pulled the covering around herself and held it tightly. Tiriku came to her and sat by her feet.

Untuk sat beside her on the log. He put his arm around her and she leaned her head on his chest. For some reason that she failed to understand, she wanted desperately to cry but held off tears and sat there dry eyed.

"What it is Ki'ti?" Untuk asked.

She looked deeply into his eyes. She was quiet and then said, "Yesterday, I got so angry and impatient that I taught directly. That is not the way of the People!" She did a feeble palm strike. "I wanted to be certain that everyone got the message clearly and I was so angered, I just let my words fly. I even used the word Others instead of Minguat. Then, today, by a careless step, I was swept away by the creek waters. I thought I would die. Just now, I saw the giants and learned their sad story. I also learned that giants are real, not just a story. It ripped my belly with pain to realize what happened to the giants. And, now, I know we must find a way to warn People to stay away from here, but I cannot think how. I am just so very tired and cold."

Untuk realized that her composure outside did not match the feelings that were roiling inside, and he ached for her. She took everything deeply to her belly when she experienced things that others did not even know existed. But he'd have her no other way. He lifted her to a standing position and pulled the covering so that it covered her completely. Then he sat on the ground and pulled her to his lap. He wrapped her as he'd wrapped little children when they were cold. Untuk took a moment to unbraid Ki'ti's hair, so it would dry quicker. He noticed Tiriku standing there looking at him. He picked up the little dog, dry now, and put him inside the cover with Ki'ti. *That'll also help to warm her,* he thought. Tiriku looked at him as if he were smiling. Untuk watched him curl up to rest against Ki'ti's belly. Untuk could feel Ki'ti relax into sleep. Untuk was not cold. He was filled with thoughts from the creek rescue to the sounds of the man who seemed to talk from the dead. The man spoke but Untuk was unsure whether he heard the words with his ears or his mind web. He realized he experienced a tiny piece of what Ki'ti's life was all about in hearing those words from the dead man. What it must be like to live in the world in which Ki'ti lived. He considered the difficulty when young—how hard it must have been to know what was real and what was of another time. He'd prefer the one he lived in. Of that he was certain. The short experience gave him even greater respect for the little woman who was his wife. He looked at her sleeping face. He wondered, *Do we ever really know another?*

Gumokut, Lolmeg, Cam, Elet, and Yomuk had all been up to the cave and seen the giants. Tiki just wasn't able to reach the hand grips. She was afraid of the crack in the wall and using her back and feet to get up there. Tongip-na agreed to climb back up and pull her up by the rope. Finally, the feat had been accomplished and all went to the creek to clean themselves of anything that could cause them to become sick. Rarely had there ever been such silence in a group of the People. Tongip-na washed Manak-na's rope and hung it over bushes to dry.

Flinee, Maylue, and Tiki began to start the night meal. Soon Wisdom would be sucking the color from the land and they needed to set up camp and eat to fill their bellies. Untuk was still seated with Ki'ti on his lap. Manak-na stopped by.

"Don't get up, Untuk. Ki'ti needs rest and she will get it with your holding her."

Untuk looked at Manak-na with concern. "She is deeply troubled about something Manak-na."

"I should think she'd be troubled by more than one thing right now," Manak-na replied.

"Yes. One thing stands out, though. She is convinced we need to establish something that warns others to avoid this place. I've thought and thought and cannot come up with anything. Ki'ti is certain that whatever sickened the giants could sicken others who might go into the caves. That's why she wanted everyone to bathe thoroughly."

"After we eat we will have a men's council. We will discuss ways to warn others. Please, Untuk, just stay where you are and let her sleep."

"You have my word," Untuk said with a smile. How grateful he was that Manak-na wanted what was best for Ki'ti.

Men brought firewood into the camp for the night and scouted around the area. Yomuk, Elet, and Tiki found dandelion greens with roots and some lake greens that would make a good addition to the evening meal. They brought them back to the group after stopping at the creek to wash the dirt off. The People did not know whether to set up camp in the large cave or outside, so they decided to wait until Ki'ti was awakened for the evening meal before they began the routine appropriate for the cave or for outside. They did gather evergreen boughs of fragrant spruce, and some sticks for lean-tos just in case. But they did not sweep the cave for spiders and other unwanted living things or check again the surrounding area thoroughly for snakes or where lean-tos might best be built.

Ki'ti finally roused just before she was to be called. She had warmed up and wondered how long she'd been sleeping.

"Just a while," Untuk reassured her. "The People want to know whether to prepare camp inside the cave or outside," he said, since it was nearing the time Wisdom would suck the color from the land.

"Outside would be best. I do not know what lies in the cave except great sadness," she responded. "Whatever caused the sores could be inside."

Hunters began to put the lean-tos together with supplies they'd gathered while Ki'ti slept.

Ki'ti smelled the food about to be served and was ravenously hungry. As the evening meal was served, Ki'ti began to worry about a way to mark the place as something to avoid.

"What's bothering you?" Untuk asked.

"The sign to avoid this place," she told him.

"We have that as an item to discuss at the men's council tonight."

Ki'ti handed Maylue's cover to Untuk and asked him to return it to her. She went to the place she'd emptied her backpack earlier so it and the contents could dry. She picked up her comb to detangle and braid her hair. Then, she joined the group for the evening meal.

Ki'ti relaxed. She realized that she didn't need to solve the problem of a sign. There were many good mind webs in this little group. She ate in peace.

When the food was cleared, and the men's council began, Manak-na caught Ki'ti's eye and she nodded to him.

Manak-na stood. "I ask Untuk to come here," he said.

Untuk went to Manak-na, unsure what he'd be asked to do.

Manak-na smiled at Ki'ti. He put his hands on Untuk's shoulders. "From this day forth, your name is Untuk-na." Untuk-na turned to face Ki'ti with a question, noticed she was surprised, and then immediately lowered his head as low as he could get it. He had thought he'd never be given the title of a superior hunter because it was his job to guard Ki'ti. Today, however, he'd put his life in jeopardy to save hers. He realized why he had been given the name, and he was humbled. He returned quietly to his seat.

Manak-na looked at Ki'ti. She nodded again.

"Ki'ti had made it clear that this place is one that requires a warning to others to stay away. We need to come to some agreement on a way to make it appear that bad spirits or something terrible is here and to avoid it for their safety. Think for a bit and speak when you have an idea."

Kai-na said, "We had the caches on the way from the ashfall cave to our last cave, what about a cache? The creek is full of rocks."

Tongip-na said, "If you put up a cache, others may take it apart to see what's inside."

"What if you took some of these long flat rocks and made them serve as arms and then put a rock on top that looked like a head with an upside down smile carved in the rock?" Lolmeg offered.

Everyone visualized it.

Kai-na looked at Manak-na who nodded to him. Kai-na said, "I like that idea but think that we should make a number of them to block off the caves in an arc. Each could have its arms almost touch the other's. That would make it clear that people should stay away."

All approved the idea. Gumokut was a great rock carver, so that function belonged to him. The youngsters could gather rocks and the older People, who knew how to build a cache so it would stand, would build. They'd build one first and if that was approved, the rest would be built that way.

Wisdom had sucked all the color from the land and the stars were twinkling as the men's council ended. The People were well ready for sleep. Manak-na and Kai-na would take first watch and Gumokut and Lolmeg would take the second.

Just before falling asleep in the lean-to, Untuk-na asked Ki'ti, "What did you see of the corpse that spoke?"

She murmured, "I saw him fully fleshed with painful, weeping sores. He stank. Tears flowed from his red eyes. I've never seen anything so gruesome. I hope never to see anyone so sick."

Untuk-na put his arm around her. In their lean-to they snuggled together gratefully after an incredibly stressful day. They were soothed by the scent from spruce branches under the sleeping skins. Ki'ti savored the scent of Untuk-na's skin, nuzzling his chest. How she enjoyed the feeling of safety he gave her! He gently kissed her cheek, awakening his desire that no way could he fulfill this night. Ki'ti slept.

When Wisdom returned color to the land, the People were up, ate quickly, and the young people went to the creek to gather rocks. They brought the rocks to a place Manak-na had specified for them to pile them for the construction. A hunter stood by to guard those who waded into the creek for rocks. They did not want anyone else to be swept away by the current. Gumokut was busy making the upside down smiles on the faces of the dome shaped rocks. When they found one with a dome shape and a flattened bottom, they took it to Gumokut, because it was the ideal shape for making the cache barrier heads. The older men began to construct the base of the single cache that would eventually appear to be a stone guard with arms outstretched and a head with a frowning mouth.

By the time for the middle-of-the-day meal, everyone was surprised to realize they'd been at work so long. They had thoroughly enjoyed what they were doing. The first warning cache had been finished, and it clearly communicated a warning. They all agreed that the construction was effective, so the second and third were being constructed on either side of the one that had been built. Ki'ti was delighted. Tiriku stayed right at her heels, occasionally poking her heels with his nose.

It took two days to complete the warning arc, but all agreed that if they came upon it, they'd stay away. It looked a little like a group of men holding their arms out to prevent entry. The upside down smiles were frightening along with the mean spirited eyes that Gumokut had carved. The People slept outside under the stars again and the next day traveled back to the camp.

When the group arrived back at camp at high sun, they noticed that everything was astir and the fires were out. Dogs were being loaded with packs or drags. Manak-na saw Nanichak-na and asked what caused the commotion.

Nanichak-na was obviously concerned. "Minagle took Elemaea and Sofa for a long walk. From an overlook at the top of this mountain, they saw a group of Minguat who were practicing fighting. There were no women. We are convinced that it is time to leave this place."

The People called an immediate men's council. They decided they must leave as soon as they could pack. The People were heading north. The Minguat were located to the southeast in a small valley. They hurried to pack and to start moving. Ki'ti began to lead them but instead of following the path, she went just to the east of it. Tongip-na and Lolmeg were concerned to be leaving the path. They tried to argue with Ki'ti, whose calm assurance that she was going where they needed to go, irritated the men. She told them how to find the path that Manak-na and Kai-na had not been able to locate. They had great confidence in the path built by the Mol. The two men would find and follow it to meet up with the People later. Only Tongip-na and Lolmeg continued on the path. As the group left, Tongip-na and Lolmeg carefully swept the camp area to clear it of evidence of their campsite. At the end of the group of trekkers, Nanichak-na, Hahami-na, Mootmu-na, and Ermol-na used branches to try to obliterate their tracks.

The People trekked as quickly and quietly as they possibly could. They did not stop for the evening meal until they had rounded a conical mountain and found a rock overhang that was suitable for a concealed camp. It was dark. That night they had no fire and ate only uncooked jerky for their evening meal. Normally Tongip-na and Ermi-na watched the night sky for fires. Since Tongip-na was gone on the path, Lamul-na volunteered to accompany Ermi-na to climb the mountain to search for fires. In the dark they climbed with difficulty, but from the top there was no evidence of fire anywhere. Since Tongip-na and Lolmeg had taken only dried meat with them, the men did not expect to see evidence of fire in the direction of due north from their last campsite. They waited a long time. Again, there was no evidence of fires anywhere.

The People ate and quickly slept. The watch called them just before Wisdom returned color to the land. They rose, packed, took some aurochs jerky, and began trekking while they ate. They moved again as rapidly as possible. Amey's foot was much better, but she walked with it wrapped and supported by strips of soft leather. When little ones tired, they were carried. For five days they continued on, trying to put as much distance between themselves and the Minguat warriors as possible.

Luko, Tongip-na and Aryna's, six-year-old son, was tired, hot, and irritated with the hurried trek. He dropped to the ground and began to shriek. Amey went to him as quickly as she could. She pinched his nose and held his jaws and lips tight together. He finally stopped struggling. When he opened his eyes, she told him that it would be better that he die than for the People to have to fight warriors who were training to fight. She told him his behavior was disapproved. She told him to behave in the manner of the People or suffer what he had just experienced—though he might die in the process. Fear straightened Luko's behavior.

They only ate cold trek meals to avoid the risk of being observed. As they left their overnight stops, they carefully concealed evidence of their passing. Finally they saw what appeared to be the path. Ki'ti assured them that they were back on the path. She had been following the light provided by Kimseaka, which no one else seemed able to see. Off to the side was a small cave. The People climbed the slope to the cave and waited while hunters inspected it. Nanichak-na whistled the all clear sound and the People gathered their things and entered the cave, where women set to sweeping it immediately. Wisdom had not yet sucked the color from the land.

Manak-na heard the dogs shifting and growling low in their throats. He went to the entrance to the cave and warned the dogs to be silent. In the distance he could barely see two dots moving toward them. He could not determine whether the dots were Tongip-na and Lolmeg or whether the People were being followed by the Minguat. He called to Ermi-na to see if he could determine who was moving in their direction. He cautioned the People in the cave to be silent and for hunters to be prepared if the need arose.

Ermi-na strained to see clearly whether the two were Tongip-na and Lolmeg.

"I cannot tell yet. They are both dragging something. If it's branches, then it's probably our two. But it could be some Minguat going in the same direction we are. I'll stay here until I can tell who they are."

Manak-na went inside and pulled his spear out and placed it near the entrance to the cave. He returned to Ermi-na. "Anything yet?" he asked.

"I think they're ours. They are wearing those leather strips, not tunics. Will you ask Minagle whether the Minguat she saw wore tunics?"

Manak-na found Minagle in the cave and asked her.

"They wore tunics, Manak-na. They had cut the bottoms of the tunics into little strips so when they moved the strips moved actively. They had planks that were about as wide as a person. They'd hold the planks up to defend themselves."

Manak-na thanked her and returned to Ermi-na. He shared the information from Minagle. Both men watched as the dots clearly became people.

Ermi-na turned to Manak-na and smiled. "They are Tongip-na and Lolmeg!"

"You are certain?"

"Yes," Ermi-na said emphatically with a palm strike.

Manak-na got his spear and used it as a walking stick to meet the travelers.

Tongip-na and Lolmeg, spears at the ready, were greatly relieved to find that the stranger approaching was Manak-na.

Tongip's first words to Manak-na were, "I'll never doubt Ki'ti again!"

"What happened?" Manak-na asked.

"We reached a pass where the path would obviously have gone through the mountains over there," he pointed to the west. "There had been a huge rock slide and the pass was impenetrable. We had to retrace our way to follow you. Even though we knew your general direction, finding your trail was very difficult. It gave us an appreciation of how well you can conceal a trail and for Ki'ti's knowledge without experience. How does Ki'ti know these things?"

"Wisdom tells her."

Tongip-na looked at Manak-na with his head slightly tilted. "You mean all that Wisdom talk is real?"

It was Manak-na's turn to be surprised. "Of course, it's real!"

"Well, I'm a believer now!" Tongip-na stated flatly.

"Me, too," Lolmeg added.

"Did you see any evidence of the Minguat?" Manak-na asked.

Lolmeg replied. "No. We watched carefully during our trek and at night. There was nothing to indicate we were followed. Rain clouds are gathering to the west. We may get rain tonight, and if we do, any evidence we may have overlooked will definitely be removed."

Still dragging the branches to conceal their trail, they went to the cave where preparation for the evening meal was well underway—this time with fire.

The People slept that night with a sense of relief. It did rain heavily early in the evening and then dried out. The next seven days were spent trekking. They slowed at Ki'ti's bidding when they reached what appeared to be another path that went east-west, while theirs went north-south.

Ki'ti studied the path and then looked to the west. She scanned the hillside carefully.

"See there, on the hillside behind that grouping of evergreen trees there is a cave where we will spend the season of cold days. There will be enough game animals to keep us fed and prepared for the next trek. There is water in the cave at three levels, so bathing and using water for cooking and drinking is convenient. The water comes from afar high in the mountains where there is much white rain. It flows here and through the cave. There are plenty of downed trees for firewood. There are other caves nearby."

Tongip-na was in hearing distance. He wondered, but tended to believe her this time, though he knew she'd never been to this place. He could see no cave because of the trees.

The group changed direction and headed straight toward the little grouping of pines on the hillside across from them. Sure enough, there was a large cave there with an overhang at the entrance where the dogs would stay. There was an excellent, if small, smoke hole above the main part of the cave. It appeared to all that this would be a great place to spend the season of cold days. They were just into the season of colorful leaves, and that gave them time to gather and smoke game animals for keeping. They could find what vegetation they ate and store it. The place seemed ideal.

That evening the People ate and thanked Wisdom for guiding them to the place by showing Ki'ti the way. They asked Wisdom to remain with them for protection. They had not seen anything since they left the camp that appeared to have been made by humans except the path that the giant Mol made long, long, long ago. Maybe with the help of something called dragons? They bedded down ready for a new time in their lives while they stayed in the cave at the crossing of the paths.

Chapter 2

The first full day in the cave by the crossed paths brought excitement. The new home cave was well protected from view below by the pines. The People, however, were able to see through them a great distance to know if strangers approached from the lowlands. The best viewpoint was from the new home cave entrance. It could not have been better planned. There was good flat land just outside the cave, and off to the north side there was a large pond that had water to a depth equal to the distance from waist level to the pond bottom when measured on a man of the original People. The pond would do well to preserve some of the meat. To the north, downhill from the pond, and sheltered by bushes, the People established their privy and one for the dogs.

The primary requirement of the People was to hunt game for their immediate needs and to dry an ample supply of it for the future season of cold days. They would also need dried meat to sustain them on long hunts and for dependable food on the resumption of the trek to the big lake. Secondarily, they would process skins and all parts of the animals. Some People needed boots and clothing for the season of cold days. Others needed bedding, hand and head covering, and many other things, such as food and water containers. The new home cave promised more than they could have desired to meet their needs for shelter. There was game to the north of them and in a valley to the southwest. They had found at least one other cave in the area.

Hunters gathered near the entrance of the new home cave as soon as Wisdom returned color to the land. They would need to use only their spears for hunting, because the special dropoff over which they had run animals in their former land was no longer available. The group of People was large enough that the men's council had to choose those who would be assigned to hunt. They used broomstraws for the three basic age groups: those who drew the longest straws were chosen to hunt; those who drew the shortest ones remained behind. Among the older hunters selected for the first hunt were Hahami-na, Mootmu-na, Ermol-na, and Arkan-na. Those of fewer years included Kai-na, Guy-na, and Sum-na. Younger hunters were Patah, Mhank, Meeluf, Ekoy, and Humko-na. The untried, who would be tested, were Yomuk and Shukmu. There was much excitement as the hunters feasted on the morning meal. They had seen many deer, so they expected to kill many. They had seen little else for larger meat supply. Hunting gear had been set up by the entryway and the hunters had divided up so that some would go to the north and some to the southwest.

Ki'ti stood and Untuk-na said in a voice that carried through the entire cave, "Ki'ti will speak."

A great hush fell in the cave. Everyone strained to see Ki'ti.

"Today is the first hunt. We ask Wisdom to supply healthy animals to give their lives willingly that we may survive. First, I ask of Wisdom that all our hunters return as well as they are right now, without injury or loss of life. Second, I ask of all those who remain here that they prepare for the game that will be brought here this day, so that each animal is used to the fullest and there will be no waste. It honors the animal when we use all it provides. We, too, need all that each animal supplies so generously."

As the hunters rose to file out, Ki'ti met each one at the entryway and put her hands on the shoulders of each with the words, "Go with Wisdom." She looked directly into the eyes of each hunter when she said it. It was never a perfunctory comment. She meant it from the bottom of her belly for each one of them. The hunters left in groups: those going north left first, followed by those who would go to the valley in the southwest. Among the hunters there was great excitement mixed with an understandable amount of fear of both the unknown and the known. They tried to conceal it, but the People were not filled with guile and their efforts were transparent. The poignant scent of hunters leaving for a hunt filled the cave. Dogs jostled each other in an attempt to get comfortable under the overhang of the cave near the entrance. They knew a hunt was about to begin. They also were aware that they could not go with the hunters.

Elemaea watched her mother carefully. She knew her mother was important and had recently become fascinated with what she did. She was rarely told why things were done as they were—she was expected to reason out what she saw. Her parents had explained often to her that reasoning would grow her mind web in the proper way. It was the way of the People. Ki'ti had spoken sharply to her before leaving for the cave of the giants. She had barely talked to her since her return and during the trek to this new cave where the paths crossed. She had done everything she was supposed to do to please her mother. She asked Minagle why her mother hadn't noticed her improvement. Minagle told her that People shouldn't expect approval for doing what was rightly expected. That was what they were supposed to do. Praise came from doing something well beyond what was right and expected. Doing things such as letting behavior run wild was an offense against the People and Wisdom. It would bring disfavor and prevent approval. Elemaea was silenced. She would spend much of the day thinking on these things. Her parents had told her these things, but now she heard it from her aunt. She wondered whether all the People disapproved her and just weren't saying anything about it. Elemaea felt wretched for the first time in her life.

Manak-na had been eager to go on the hunt but had not been chosen at the men's council. He and Nanichak-na decided to make a trial exploration of the area for additional caves for the processing of meat. They had spotted a cave not too far away. If there was one, there might also be others. They left just after the hunters.

"You have become a real leader, Manak-na," Nanichak-na said as they climbed the incline to the cave they'd seen nearby. "It must feel empty to you that you did not attend the first hunt."

"It does, Uncle. I really wanted to go." The older man shared Manak-na's disappointment.

Nanichak-na studied him for a moment. "Manak-na, you have been given great gifts. You still have important things to do in your life. What happens is designed by Wisdom. You still need to learn patience. Patience may save your life sometime. Remember the restlessness I felt when this trek began? My pride told me I should lead. We have to keep in our mind webs that others need to learn to lead. We must stand back for the good of the People."

Manak-na lowered his head. He knew Nanichak-na was telling him something vital about gifts and patience, but he was unsure of what the man spoke. He understood that others needed to learn to lead. He put in the forefront of his mind web to think on gifts and patience as time permitted this day. He loved the old man. Nanichak-na was as special to him as Emaea and Wamumur had been to Ki'ti. He learned from the old hunter words from Wisdom. He had to understand and make them part of himself.

They reached the cave and looked around. It was a good cave with a flat floor, but it had no water. Nanichak-na had spotted one lower down the slope and they slid sideways on their feet down the dirt and gravel slope to reach it.

Manak-na was there first and called to Nanichak-na that he could hear water in this cave. As they entered they were well pleased with the level floor and the running water. There was more room in this cave, they both agreed, than any meat preparation cave they'd ever seen. It was accessible from the flat lowland by a rocky slope. Three more pines grew in the lowland by the entrance to the slope. They chose this cave for their working the meat and skins.

Manak-na stood at the entrance to the cave to study the rocky slope. He turned to Nanichak-na and said, "This reminds me of the cave area we left. Remember how some plants grew near the cave almost too conveniently, so we thought they were purposely set to grow there?"

"Yes, I remember," Nanichak-na replied while stroking his beard. He thought a moment and continued, "You're thinking that someone purposely set the evergreens to mark or conceal our new home cave and the slope to the meat preparation cave?"

"I do think that. I don't remember seeing any other evergreens on this hill. Can you recall whether there are any?"

"I cannot pull up any others from my mind web, so I'd trust my answer only if I went back down to the lowland and looked up. It didn't seem particularly remarkable to me when we first noticed the evergreens. If I saw any other ones after making a check from down there again, I think I'd want to know whether they marked anything—and, if so—what? That can wait for another day." He smiled a slow smile. He had to put first things first.

Having completed their task, the men returned to the home cave to gather some materials that would be needed in the preparation of meat.

At age nine and fully enthusiastic about the new home cave and the hunt, Truto, Tongip-na and Aryna's fifth child, came running to meet them.

When the adults recognized Truto, he said breathlessly, "Already two are returning with a deer!" He pointed to the north where two men could be seen with an animal suspended from its legs on a pole between them.

Nanichak-na smiled at the youngster. "Then, we could use your help to take things to the meat cave. Will you find some other young people to help? We need poles taken over there." Nanichak-na pointed to the specific cave.

Truto nodded and sprinted off to find others to help.

Without a word, labor was divided among the People. In this case, Manak-na walked briskly towards the men with the fresh kill. He knew they could save some distance by going directly to the meat preparation cave up the rock slope. He'd show them the way. Nanichak-na went to the home cave to gather supplies to transport to the meat preparation cave.

When he saw Sum-na, Nanichak-na said, "We are going to need new poles quickly. Already meat arrives and we will need to prepare much of it for drying. We have few poles."

Sum-na nodded toward the old man, noted the cave that Nanichak-na pointed out, and quickly gathered others to look for young trees that were big enough to provide the proper poles. They'd have to cut them, limb them, and remove the bark as fast as possible. Then, they'd have to transport them to the meat preparation cave. All of the available men except for Lai-na and Grypchon-na, who were left to guard, went with Sum-na to gather suitable poles. The young men also joined the effort, if they were not already involved with helping Nanichak-na carry supplies to the cave.

The women were delighted when they realized they'd have a feast for the evening meal. They'd be starting roasts soon and the young girls were looking for plants to fill baskets they carried. It would be a great way to begin life in the cave during this season of colorful leaves and for the season of cold days which would follow.

Soon another pair of hunters was spotted carrying another animal on a pole each shouldered—this time it was a boar. Likichi gathered a number of butchering tools and tools for skin preparation and sent them to the meat preparation cave.

Minagle began busily straightening the cave. With so many gone, sweeping and refolding sleeping skins and washing out eating bowls, was so much easier. She knew that the women and she would be involved in the skin preparation and drying meat or home cave work. They'd alternate. Nobody ever indicated who would go to the meat preparation cave and who would remain to keep the home cave on a certain day. People simply did what was needed with no seeming direction. If there appeared to be enough People to maintain the home cave, everyone else left for the meat preparation cave. Usually Likichi remained at the home cave since she had the task of cave administration as had Totamu before her. She also took care of injuries and sickness with herbs she and Ki'ti knew.

Out in the valley to the southwest Arkan-na, Guy-na, Meeluf, Ekoy, and Yomuk had spotted a great aurochs. It was on sloping grassland upwind of a forested area nearby, and the men hoped to secure it through surprise when they burst from the forest with spears at the ready. Heavy thrusting would be required. They crept silently, still downwind of the magnificent animal. At a signal from Arkan-na, the hunters burst from the forest with great yells. The aurochs was confused and didn't know whether to charge or run. It gave the hunters just time enough to thrust their spears into the places where the animal was most vulnerable. It turned and fell with its head almost directed downhill.

Yomuk was shocked at the first kill they made. His spear still dangled from the chest of the great beast. He had never been on a real hunt and, when he saw the eyes of the aurochs change from life to death, it hit his belly like a tough punch. Seeing Yomuk's reaction, Arkan-na walked over to the boy, which caused Yomuk to look at him not the aurochs. Other men began to pull the beast to align it head downward, tail up on the hill. When its body was too heavy they found stones and used a stout tree trunk from the forest to place over the stone for leverage to move the body. They would not use their spears for leverage for fear of cracking or breaking one.

"This is your first kill?" Arkan-na asked quietly.

"Yes," Yomuk responded. He wondered whether he would keep his morning meal in his belly.

"This fine aurochs gave its life that we could live, Yomuk. It did so willingly. Did you see it run or show fear? It has happened this way since the beginning of life. It is Wisdom's plan. The animals we secure give themselves to us. Wisdom gave us the animals to eat. They keep us healthy and filled with energy. Do not be sad for the aurochs. The aurochs has honor for giving its life for us. That is the way of things."

"Thank you, Arkan-na. That will help me sort out in my mind web what I have just seen. Does it get any easier to see as you mature?"

Arkan-na thought. "Death comes to all, Yomuk. It is never easy to see whether it be People or animals. Just remember death is just a door to another life. We go to Wisdom and a new life when we die. What I can tell you is that after a while you will come to accept that the life of the People depends on the kill. The animals know that, and they cooperate. It is understood since the beginning of time. So, yes, it gets easier when you fully grasp what is happening. Use your mind web and your belly to understand that this is part of the huge life-to-death-to-life cycle that Wisdom made for us. Always remember that when you kill for food, you also kill for everything the animal offers, such as its hide, the hooves, the bones, and so on. You would dishonor the animal and anger Wisdom if you fail to use all it provided. Come now, you must be blooded."

Yomuk looked at Arkan-na confused.

Arkan-na said, "Your spear entered a lung. You will have blood placed on your forehead because you were part of the kill and it's your first. You will wear it on your forehead until Wisdom begins to suck color from the land. Then you will wash it off. It is the way of the People. It is not something you discuss. Just do as I have said." Being careful not to foster pride, he would not tell Yomuk that almost never was a youngster blooded with aurochs blood. Usually, it was deer. Yomuk was very strong and precise in his thrust for someone his age. Arkan-na approved in silence.

Yomuk followed Arkan-na to the side of the aurochs. He tried hard to push down the pride he felt in his good spear thrust. His dark, shining hair was loosed from his headband and blew in the breeze. His leather piece had slid down somewhat. The leather strip that circled his waist and held the wider strip of leather had stretched. Appearance had not entered his mind web. His total focus was to absorb everything about the hunt and ignore all else.

Arkan-na noticed Yomuk's loose clothing. He grasped the narrow leather strip at Yomuk's hip and said with a smile, "You might want to tighten this before you are unclothed."

Yomuk blushed and stopped to tighten his leather strip and pull up his wide leather covering. He thanked Arkan-na. Yomuk felt for his headband. He had lost it. His eyes scanned the scene and he saw it just uphill. He retrieved it and pulled it over his head to keep the hair out of his eyes.

Guy-na said, "We almost have the beast headed downhill. I will run to let hunters know to stop their hunt, so they can come here to help. I will also notify women at the home cave that we have an aurochs." He knew that he was likely the quickest runner, except for Yomuk, but Yomuk was too young for the responsibility and the boy needed to learn butchering. Hunters nodded at his words. He left at a run.

Arkan-na pulled Yomuk's spear from the animal. He removed Yomuk's headband and wiped the spear point across the young man's forehead. Then, he returned the spear and headband to Yomuk. The youngster put it back on despite the fresh blood on his forehead. He would clean the headband later. Arkan-na removed the remaining spears from the aurochs. The other hunters had already had a first kill, so the only one blooded was Yomuk. Arkan-na pulled a sharp blade from his backpack. He cut the arteries and blood flowed downhill from the animal.

He looked at Yomuk. "We have to get the blood out so it doesn't spoil the meat." Yomuk nodded. His father had explained the procedure, but his father was not a hunter. He paid more attention to hunters than to his father on hunting matters. He wanted to be a hunter like his uncle, Manak-na.

Meeluf, Ekoy, and Yomuk had already turned the animal onto its back, after many attempts and having to move the head of the aurochs. It lay a bit off perpendicular to the downhill slope. The animal bled out as well as could be hoped for on the slant where it lay. The two men at the hindquarters began to pull the legs forward to lift the back end, if they could. They were unable to lift it. Normally, they hung deer and smaller animals from trees to bleed them. Hunters took the legs of the aurochs and moved them as if the animal moved. By holding the legs up and moving them, the blood drained from the legs so it could exit the body of the aurochs. Arkan-na told them he would open the gut and that the intestines would roll out. He warned Yomuk without calling him by name that the interior of the beast would likely not smell very pleasant. He wanted them to hold the beast in its current position and then to catch the neck of the gut at the top of the first stomach. Ekoy volunteered to clasp it. Yomuk watched carefully. He didn't know what the first stomach on an aurochs looked like or where it was placed. He watched everything carefully. Off and on pride filled him with warmth when he thought of his spear thrust delivering a killing strike.

"You'll need to keep it so nothing leaks out," Arkan-na said.

"I understand," Ekoy replied.

Arkan-na began to slice into the beast. Yomuk thought he'd been nauseated before, but this odor was far worse. He gagged.

Arkan-na said sternly, "I warned you, Yomuk. You cannot get sick now. You have to hold the beast."

Yomuk wanted to cry but quickly reasoned that was not an appropriate response. He tried not breathing, but that wouldn't work. Finally, he continued to breathe and make himself well aware that vomiting was not an option. It was difficult! He remembered the bee stings. *This is another part of what it means to be a man?* he pondered.

Arkan-na had cut the beast from under the neck to and around the rectum where he held the contents from leaking. Ekoy had done a great job of holding the stomach. Meanwhile the intestines had rolled outside of the animal and looked like a giant gray snake to Yomuk. He was fascinated and completely repulsed. His belly still threatened to heave.

Arkan-na told the young men they had to move the intestines away from the body of the aurochs. They used tree trunks that they'd already used as levers, while others held the ends of the gut tight to prevent leakage. For heavier parts of the animal they gained leverage by using more than one trunk of a tree from the forest, still safeguarding their spears from usage that could damage them. They would have to clean out the intestines, so they would become useful as containers that wouldn't leak, but that required very careful cleaning first. They had to be cleaned away from the aurochs so they wouldn't contaminate it with the awful contents. All four of them moved the intestines from the aurochs, cut the intestines into a man's arm length, and carried them away to a nearby creek to wash them thoroughly.

Arkan-na began the skin separation process. He had the younger men turn the body of the aurochs when he needed to reach something he could not otherwise reach. Yomuk participated here rather than cleaning intestines. Occasionally, the turning required use of levers with rocks underneath to make the aurochs roll as desired. Ekoy had found a stick to use that was stronger than his spear, which he chose to protect at all costs. Arkan-na wanted to assure that they got as whole a skin as possible, so moving the beast was required. Women made wonderful things of a skin and this was a very large one of excellent quality.

By the time the skin had been removed, Ekoy looked up and noticed that hunters and women were approaching. Once they arrived, the work went faster. Women gathered hands full of damp grass and wiped down the hindquarters which had been cut off first. It took two men to carry one hindquarter to the meat preparation cave. They could have used a third man. A roast was sent to the home cave. The skin was rolled and carried by Kai-na and Ermi-na to an old skin where it was securely wrapped. The hauling skin had two strips of leather attached. The men pulled the fresh wrapped skin bundle across grass to transport it to the meat preparation cave for processing. Slamika-na and Manak-na carried the second hindquarter to the pond where they submerged it at the pond's far end. To keep it underwater, they piled rocks on top of it. The intestines had been cut into arm length strips and washed in the creek. The bladder and stomachs were separated and cleaned. Then, they were taken to the meat preparation cave for final work. Little by little the body was butchered and when Wisdom began to suck the color from the land, they had finished and those involved in the day's butchering were enjoying a celebratory bath at the meat preparation cave. Yomuk had washed the blood from his forehead and carefully cleaned his headband.

Poles had been brought from the home cave and from the trees the men had felled earlier in the day. The meat preparation cave was clearly ready for use. Skin stretchers needed to be assembled, but the major work was finished.

The hunters who would be working late in the meat preparation cave went to eat so they could return to process and guard the meat into the night. They brought oil lamps so they could see in the dark cave.

While they were eating, Manak-na passed by Yomuk, putting his hand on the boy's shoulder. Yomuk looked up at his uncle. Without a word, Manak-na made it clear that he heartily approved his nephew. Yomuk lowered his head. He was so grateful that he'd been able to keep his food in his belly during the butchering. His uncle's approval meant everything to him. He knew his father could not be a hunter, and he wanted hunter approval—most of all from Manak-na.

Back at the new home cave, Ki'ti walked outside with a small basket on her arm, and, seemingly without thought, began to follow a deer trail that went uphill from the flat land. Tiriku trotted at her heels. Ki'ti examined the vegetation for herbs they might want for food seasoning or healing. She was feeling worrisomely agitated. Ever since she had taught directly at the camp, she had been unsure of herself. It concerned her greatly. She did not want to go outside the boundaries that Wamumur and Emaea had set for Wise Ones. She wanted to be a creditable Wise One, and she felt extraordinary failure. Untuk-na had tried to reason her out of it, but it didn't help. She was harder on herself than anyone else ever could be.

Untuk-na saw her leave the cave and followed at a respectful distance. He knew she was thinking about many things, and he had no desire to interrupt. He was, however, charged to keep her safe.

Ki'ti saw several medicinal herbs and placed them in the basket, her hands functioning automatically, while her thoughts were more theoretical. She thought of Yomuk, so young and yet so tall. He wanted to be a great hunter and seemed to worship his uncle Manak-na. She felt that sometimes he was disrespectful of his own father, who could not hunt. Untuk-na had been a great hunter before they joined. He had saved her life when the creek water swept her away. But, Ki'ti thought, what mattered to Yomuk was hunting, the bigger the beast the better. He had a pride problem like she had long ago. She wondered whether it was as large a problem. And then there was Elemaea. The child was impulsive just as she'd been. She was getting a little old to be doing impulsive things, she felt, until she realized how old she'd been when she disobeyed and left for the cave of the man with the green bag. She worried about the lack of a new Wise One. Who would it be? Would there be time to teach that person all a Wise One needed to know? Her mind raced. She also knew that the Mol who joined them just as they were leaving were not adapting well to the group. They had different customs. They had a chief who issued orders. Each person was not expected to think and to reason for himself or herself. The Mol had been in one place for so long that they didn't understand the need for a group on trek to act as a tight unit, tied by understanding the group as well as themselves.

Ki'ti looked up and noticed some more pine trees. They formed rows where trees were just offset from each other so as to provide a barrier to sight. The straight lines fascinated her. Obviously, a person had set them to grow in lines. She continued walking very quietly, trailed by Tiriku, who was leaping and jumping over obstacles. Her senses were acute, but nothing gave her any indication that life existed here. Untuk-na moved up to her quickly.

He put his arm on her shoulder. "Wait," he cautioned. "Let me go into the cave first."

She looked at him, jarred from her thoughts. "Of course," she agreed. Tiriku continued behind her making more effort the steeper the path became. When Ki'ti stopped, he sat. She looked down at her dog with a smile.

Untuk-na wasn't long in his cave examination.

"Come, Ki'ti, this is most unusual," he called.

Ki'ti followed the trail upwards, crossing behind the trees to the cave. It was small with a high ceiling. In the cave there was a large slab that was made when the walls were chipped away. On the slab were a number of items laid out in straight lines: a piece of green rock, highly polished, and shaped like a snake or dragon—she was unsure which; a piece of quartz with flecks of gold embedded; a purple shell with holes at the edge, which she assumed correctly was the item that caused the friction in the Maknu-na and Rimlad story; a leg bone that was longer than she was tall, could not be encircled by her hands or Untuk-na's, and felt like rock rather than bone; a piece of rock that had been split that sparkled with fire when she licked her finger and ran it over the flat surface; a very large conch shell that tasted of salt and made a sound when placed by the ear; a bone flute that played beautiful sounds; a curved horn-like thing that looked like an elephant's tusk, but this one was almost as tall as she, and it curved almost back into itself; a wooden carved woman who was fatter than anyone Ki'ti'd ever seen and had huge breasts and feet so small proportionately that they'd never hold her up; a pile of claws from various animals and birds; a flat long stone that had scratches in it; a stone that had what looked like dark plants as part of the stone, causing her to wonder whether plants grew inside stones.

Ki'ti looked at Untuk-na speechless. Both had examined the items. Both realized this was something special but had no idea what they were viewing. Finally Ki'ti asked, "Will you look out the windows and tell me what you see?"

Untuk-na picked up a rock and set it before the window so he could stand on it to see outside. He did the same with each of the three windows. It felt odd to him to have to use a rock to gain height to look out of a window. He realized in an instant how life must be for Ki'ti with her lack of height. Before he experienced it himself, he had no idea. "Each window frames a hilltop," he said quietly.

"What would be the purpose of that?" she asked.

"I don't know unless this area used to be home to many people and they communicated by setting fires atop the hills to send messages. I suppose it could have been used to have some sense of when a seasonal change would occur if the sun, moon, or a star topped the hill on a certain day. It could have many uses, but, really, I have no idea."

"There's no feeling of people in here," Ki'ti remarked. "I do think it important to leave these items as we found them. They obviously were placed as they were for a purpose."

"My Dear Ki'ti, whoever placed these things did so a very long time ago. Look at the accumulation of dust in here. This place has been untouched for lifetimes. Probably nobody on the earth knows this place exists!"

"It may exist in stories," Ki'ti rejoined. "Look at the purple shell with the holes. That is what the People at the time of Maknu-na and Rimlad were fighting over."

"Now that you mention it, I agree totally. What wonderful dippers they'd be! Why, do you think, someone would leave these things lying here like this?"

"It seems that they are special things to someone. I'm thinking that they may have known Wisdom. Maybe they felt that they should offer something special to Wisdom. Could this be a place where they put offerings or sacrifices to Wisdom?"

"Ki'ti, that's your world, not mine. I think we should talk about this at the men's council tonight and suggest that people leave things here as we found them. If they were given to Wisdom, it would be terrible to take them or break one. We surely have no right to them."

"More direct teaching?"

"Well, how else would you get them to leave things as they are?"

Ki'ti smiled and chuckled lightly. She smiled her special smile for him.

Ki'ti sat on the edge of the stone slab. Tiriku came to sit beside her, his tongue hanging from his mouth. He looked back and forth from Ki'ti to Untuk-na resting with his ears back and eyes protruded. Untuk-na noticed him and almost laughed aloud, but cut the laughter away when he noticed Ki'ti was deep in thought. Their ways were changing, she mused, and there seemed nothing she could do to slow the rate of change. She would have to address the issue directly and definitely that night. Another direct teaching experience! It made her terribly uneasy, as if she were breaking some long established rule. Determined, she rose and reached for Untuk-na's hand. As they began to exit the cave they saw Nanichak-na coming up the path.

"What are you two doing here?" he asked resting his hand on the wall of the entryway.

"Ha," Untuk-na laughed, "We could ask you the same thing."

"Manak-na and I were talking about how the pines on this hill seem to have been put where they are intentionally. These outside this cave are placed in lines! All seem to mark something. Is this cave interesting?"

Ki'ti smiled. "Come in and look for yourself." Tiriku had stood up eagerly when Ki'ti did. He sat back down with a look of resignation.

Nanichak-na entered and drew in a breath that made a sound. "I suppose it is interesting!" he said, "I suppose it is." He carefully examined the items on the stone slab.

"It almost seems that they are laid there as a gift to Wisdom," Ki'ti said. "I feel that the People should be warned not to take anything from here or put the items in places different from where they are. There is something too special about all this. It's almost disturbing."

Nanichak-na looked more carefully at the items. "Look at this! It's the Maknu-na and Rimlad story?"

"I think you're right," Ki'ti said.

"You'll speak of this at the men's council?" Nanichak-na asked.

"Yes," Ki'ti replied. "I admit I feel strange speaking out directly to the People."

"Ah, Ki'ti, hunters do it all the time. There is a time when it's critical—as it was the other day at the camp when Humko-na was being teased. It's done to get attention focused closely so that the hearer doesn't lose the message or get it confused. When you speak out directly, the message is clear to all. There is no way to find little cracks like you used to find to avoid doing what was expected. If you did it all the time, People wouldn't hear you, but when you do it seldom, it gets attention effectively."

Ki'ti laughed at the memory. "Nanichak-na, Great Hunter, thank you from the bottom of my belly. I had been worrying and causing myself endless frustration about speaking out. I didn't realize that there are times when it is appropriate."

Untuk-na felt a great sense of relief. He was certain what Ki'ti had done was necessary and appropriate, but he had been Mol and wondered whether he was missing something when he tried to calm her about it. He knew that Nanichak-na had just handed her the means of relaxing finally. He was grateful.

"Let's go down," Untuk-na suggested, "It should be time for the evening meal."

Nanichak-na shook his head as he went down the hill. "That is an amazing group of things!" he said with a voice tinged with awe. "There is another place on the hill that has pines. I'm eager to know what those evergreens mark."

"I would like to see it. Will you wait until after the morning meal to go?" Ki'ti asked.

"Of course, I will." His eyes twinkled but the others who were behind him could not see them.

The evening meal was one of their best. They had roasted meat from the deer and wonderful greens from the hillside mixed with some root vegetables and a few blueberries. The chatter was light and optimistic in the cave until Van, Mhank and La's three-year-old son, tried to take his brother Solu's food bowl. Trying to force him to give it up, Van bit his younger brother. Mhank was swift to strike his son's mouth to reprove his action. Van whimpered at the stinging from the strike and the words, but he would not try to take his brother's bowl again.

The Mol who joined them for the trek to the big lake seemed to be enjoying the group instead of planning to leave. The men's council was filled with numbers of issues and Ki'ti addressed the need to leave untroubled the items in the cave above them. She pointed out that there was a purple dipper as described in the Maknu-na and Rimlad story, but that it would be best to look with one's eyes, not hands. She suggested that these things might be sacrifices to Wisdom, and that no one should rearrange or take anything from that cave. She let it be known that it troubled her to think what might happen to anyone who tried to take or rearrange what belonged to Wisdom. At that, everyone in the cave old enough to understand what she was talking about wanted to visit the cave, but they were warned not to trifle with Wisdom and what might be Wisdom's things. They listened carefully to the warning. Not all believed those things were Wisdom's, but they would not argue with the Wise One.

The People bedded down and when Wisdom restored color to the land, all were up and ate their morning meal and went hunting or to the meat preparation cave. Nanichak-na found Ki'ti and Untuk-na and the three of them began to walk up towards the cave shadowed by tiny Tiriku. The next set of pine trees was higher on the hill and just above the one that screened the cave where the special things were laid out.

At the cave, where the special items were, they found Manak-na. He exclaimed, "This is astounding. What a collection!"

"It is!" Nanichak-na agreed. "What did you think of that leg bone?"

"It's huge!" Manak-na exclaimed, eyes wide. "It might be interesting to hunt whatever that came from. Maybe it's a dragon leg. It's a lot bigger than the leg bones of the giants!"

"I'm too old for that!" Nanichak-na laughed. "We're going to the next set of evergreens. Want to come with us?"

"Of course," Manak-na said.

The four continued up the steep pathway. There was another cave. It was at the top of the hill, but it was hidden from below with pines. The pines did not block the somewhat strange view from there. The cave was dome shaped with a very tall ceiling that had been hammered out. The debris had been taken outside and shaped into a wall that curved outward from the cave entrance. It was carefully roofed in stone blocks that circled in decreasing layers. There was a hole in the center at the top. The far wall was smoothed and on it were spirals and circles. In the center was a round stone pillar with a diameter the length of Nanichak-na's arm. Drilled into the very center was a hole beside which lay a peg about as long as Nanichak-na's hand. He picked it up and found it fit into the hole in the center. Around the center hole were 12 other holes. If pegs fit in those holes, there were none to be found. The peg for the center hole wouldn't fit. It was too large. The circling holes seemed to be perfect distance one from another. They had never seen anything like this. Morning sunshine was coming from the doorway and it definitely lit the peg, but that meant nothing to them. Untuk-na moved a rock to enable him to see from the windows. He was surprised that the view was of the sky. The People were convinced that the cave had purposes to do with the sun, moon, and stars—purposes they did not understand.

When they turned to leave, Manak-na said, "Wait. Look at this." He pointed to the big and little snares, the zigzag, the three stars, and other night sky sets of stars. "I think the people who did this knew a lot more about the night sky than we do."

Untuk-na was amazed. The items laid out and now this display of night sky knowledge overwhelmed him. "These are all part of my giant ancestors' things, are they not?" He asked in the style of formal language the Mol used at certain times, wondering whether they would see as he did.

Nanichak-na looked directly at Untuk-na. "Untuk-na, I have thought the same. Why else would the ceilings be so high? The windows, too? And this location is right on the path your giant ancestors made. But why here?"

"Because it's a place where the paths cross," Ki'ti spoke quietly. Untuk-na noticed that her eyes were widely dilated. "The giants made both paths. The path that crosses the one we follow goes to the sea that way, she pointed out from the door, and the one going the other way goes to tall mountains. Very tall mountains! This place has not been used for many, many, many lifetimes. The giants watched the stars from here and they told them of things that would happen and when. They learned to understand the night sky here. They learned to understand the sea at the end of the path that way. They learned how to make boats go where they wanted them to go and they learned of new lands." Again she pointed out the door. "They learned of great mountains that way." She pointed to the west, away from the sea. "And the way we go," she pointed north, "they learned of the big lake and cold. On the path where we came from" she pointed south, "they learned of very warm lands and a very large land beyond the waters where many strange animals lived."

Untuk-na and Manak-na had both been fixed on Ki'ti. Tiriku had moved to the doorway but focused on Ki'ti with a very soft whine. Ki'ti had changed her features slightly and was in one of her spirit places. She was given information there which was not available to people who couldn't go wherever she went at those times. Both men were greatly concerned. Each heard what she had to say and were fascinated with the information, didn't question it, but held it apart until they were sure she had returned to the present time and place safely. Nanichak-na had been re-examining the walls.

Ki'ti seemed to begin to relax and looked at her brother and husband. "I'm fine. You wanted to know, didn't you?" she asked.

"You're sure you're back to us?" Untuk-na asked.

"Yes," she smiled.

"So this was where they learned about the sky at night?" Manak-na asked.

"Yes."

"I would really like to see the boats and learn to use them to go to new lands," Manak-na said with enthusiasm.

"You're a hunter," Nanichak-na said flatly.

"Even people who go on boats have to eat," Manak-na said, not really seriously thinking of taking the path across from the hillside.

The four went back down the hill. Each had responsibilities that required attention. There was always much work to keep the group healthy in all ways.

Elemaea, Mona, and Sofa were with Minagle at the end of the pond nearest the cave. Minagle was bathing Sofa and cleaning her hair. Elemaea and Mona had bathed and were warming in the sun. Both were excellent swimmers. It was chilly, but the pond was protected against the wind. The girls straddled a short log in the water and Elemaea spoke quietly and asked, "Mona, do the People disapprove me?"

Mona thought for a while. She wanted to respond kindly and truthfully. "Sometimes, Elemaea, People think you act before you think. That is what very little children do. It reflects badly on you and worse, it reflects badly on your mother. People know you have a good nature in your belly and would not choose to hurt People, but you are not careful of how other People feel. You need to learn to keep your mouth closed until you open it and speak as a girl growing up among the People. Sometimes, Elemaea, you interrupt People young and old. It's as if you think you're more important than they are. That's what the interruption says. You know better, but you just don't act on what you know. I think you need to slow down. It looks to me that you are doing some of that."

"Thank you, Mona. You're smart for someone my age. I have been trying to be what my mother wants me to be, but it's hard."

"You're seeing it oddly. If you love your mother, it isn't hard. I could do what you do, but it would hurt my mother so badly that I'd never be able to do it. It just means you have to think about someone other than yourself first. That, Elemaea, is what love is."

"But, but, I love my mother."

"Elemaea, you don't love her enough not to interrupt her. You don't love her enough not to do things she's told you not to do."

"I see. Do you hate me?"

"Hate you? I love you! Elemaea, you're my friend. I want to see you happy. You'll never be happy until you control yourself and start to fit into the People where you're supposed to fit."

"Where am I supposed to fit?" The idea of fitting in was one totally foreign to Elemaea. She went through her mind web and could find no reference to fitting in anywhere.

"That I don't know. You can't find that out until you control yourself and start to look for your place. Then you'll find out what you're good at doing and you'll get better and better at it. You'll see how it contributes to the People. I'm learning to make garments. I love to do it. That's where I'll fit in. I'm going to the meat preparation cave later to see how I can contribute with the skins. For you, I don't know. Each person has to find their own fit."

"Can I go with you?"

"Only if you will listen carefully and do exactly what they tell you to do. The work can be tedious and you'll want to go to play, but if you stay and work hard, you start to fit in, and it becomes a very good experience. But I don't know whether you're ready. I am."

Elemaea felt her world changing before her eyes. Mona was going to work with the women. She didn't want to work skins. It stank. She would not go with Mona. At the same time, she yearned with every fiber in her being to fit in somewhere. One thing she recognized. Everyone was telling her the same thing.

The People thrived at the new home cave. Available meat was healthy and soon their supply had just about reached the limit of their need, even at the most excessive. The weather was turning colder and new clothing had been prepared for that time. The season of cold days had arrived. When Wisdom restored color to the land, large flakes of white rain began to fall from clouds overhead. To the east, they could see the sun. The white rain was beautiful to watch. The big, flat flakes fell slowly, drifting silently in the windless air, straight down to the ground. Quickly the ground began to turn white. Likichi smiled contentedly. She knew they were well prepared for the season of cold days. Ki'ti stood in the entryway enjoying the scene and chuckling at Tiriku who pranced among the flakes, trying to catch them in his mouth. Ki'ti noticed that some flakes on the ground shone in the sun like tiny suns while others appeared in rainbow colors. White rain could be quite beautiful, she thought.

Manak-na talked to Domur, his wife, about his desire to take the path to the sea. She thought at first that he was not serious, but when she discovered that he was, she was distraught. She did not want to go to the sea. She definitely did not want to get on a boat to travel to strange lands. She also knew that Manak-na had resisted his adventurous spirit for a very long time.

But how, she wondered, could he do this to her? She knew and assumed he realized that he'd have to leave her to go to sea. She agonized over how it was possible that he could leave her for an adventure. She could not understand. She could never do that to him. She was terribly torn and hurt, although she was convinced that his desire did not have anything to do with his love for her. She was certain he loved her, but to think to be without him ripped her belly apart. She could not comprehend this need of his. It conflicted with all that she was. But she knew that the call of distant places always drew Manak-na. She would have to encourage him and hope with all that was in her that he would return safely, if he chose to go to the sea. Manak-na had not mentioned anything about a sea adventure for a few days. She felt it would be a false hope to anticipate that he had forgotten.

Ki'ti sat on furs in a quiet part of the cave and reviewed in her mind web the stories that she told every winter. Elemaea walked over to her and said nothing. She crawled next to Ki'ti and sat still on her right side. Tiriku occupied the left side. Ki'ti noticed the child and observed the change in behavior. She put her arm around Elemaea and pulled her closer. She stroked the spiraling hair. Elemaea was a pretty little girl.

"I have noticed a change in your behavior, Elemaea," Ki'ti said. "I approve."

Elemaea squeezed Ki'ti's hand. She smiled up at her mother. "I love you, Mother."

"I love you, Elemaea."

"Mother, how can I fit into the People? Mona is working skins and learning to make garments. Siff has been cooking. Tin has been learning about herbs along with Meta. I need a way to fit in, but I don't know how."

"What interests you?"

"I'm very good with the slingshot."

"Listen carefully, my daughter. I asked what interests you, not what you're good at." Ki'ti was speaking lightly, not strongly directly.

"I could say nothing interests me or that everything interests me."

"Well, sort it out. If there were something that if you could never do again, you'd feel your belly ripping apart—what would that be?"

"I don't know."

"Little Girl," Ki'ti said, using a term that was no longer used for herself, but caused her to smile wistfully as she used it, "Spend the next few days looking for that thing that is important to you. Each time you do anything, consider it might be the last time you do it. Think how that would make you feel."

After thinking on that for some time, Elemaea said, "Mother, suppose that nothing is that important to me."

Ki'ti looked at her daughter. Perhaps there was nothing that had captured the interest of her daughter. Perhaps that was the reason for her impetuous nature? Ki'ti would think on it. She replied, "Until you are certain that there is nothing that is that important to you, keep looking for two days. If you have not found something at that time, I'll set up some things for you to do to see where your interest lies. If you see someone doing something you haven't tried, ask them to show you how to do it. Then try it. Don't stop right away if you aren't good at it. Nobody is perfect at first. It takes much practice. Ask yourself questions. How does doing it make you feel? Do your hands feel that this is something they were made for? Ask questions like that." Ki'ti had no specific plan available. She would have to spend some time in thought about a plan, but she would wait one day. Instead of racing off, Elemaea sat quietly, resting her small body against her mother's. From a distance Likichi noticed and smiled.

Manak-na had gone outside and climbed to the top cave. He stood there in his furs and looked out from the door at the path that Ki'ti had said went to the sea where they built boats for travel to strange lands. It tugged his mind web and his belly. Domur also tugged his mind web and belly. Could he really have an adventure without her? Could he be happy with adventure alone? If he had one adventure would it require another in the way that eating the morning meal made him have an appetite all day long? He realized he was asking himself whether one adventure would suffice for a lifetime. He realized, too, that he didn't know the answer. He accused himself of having selfish thoughts, of putting himself first in a culture where that was inappropriate. He finally realized that he had some real fear down inside of setting out alone on such an adventure. His entire life had been spent as part of a cohesive group. None of his thoughts or reflections or realizations squelched his desire for a sea adventure. He looked at the walls around him. He was fascinated to consider what others must know that he did not know. How much information there must be to learn from cultures different from his? Sometimes it overwhelmed him. It was not the first time he had entertained such thoughts. It would not be the last. He gathered himself together and left the top cave to bring wood and bones for the home cave fire. He did, after all, have work to do.

In the home cave Humko-na and Song went to Likichi. She stopped sorting her dried herbs and looked at them questioningly, holding onto a polished bent stick that was her cane.

"We think it's time to join, Likichi," Humko-na said with a smile. "We have stopped for a while and the time seems good."

"Wonderful!" Song's grandmother replied with a grin. "We've been wondering how long it would take! Have you set up the pronouncement with the Wise One?" She placed Song's hand in Humko-na's hand and put her free hand around theirs.

"Not yet, Izumo," Song said with a lilt in her voice. "We wanted to share with you first."

"Well, now you have. You'd better go to see the Wise One." Likichi put her free hand on her hip and stood slightly bent from stiffness as she watched the two young people go to find Ki'ti. "That will be a good joining," she said aloud but not so anyone could hear. Humko-na was twenty and Song was nineteen. Both had waited very late in life to join. Then her mind drifted to Smosh at age nineteen and Bun at eighteen. Neither of them had settled down with a wife. Then there was Smig at age twenty-five! His twin had joined with Tuma long, long ago. They had a child of 3 years! Likichi shook her head. She returned to her herb sorting with a smile.

Before she could attend to that task, Tita headed toward her with Din. Tita looked concerned.

"What is it, Tita?" Likichi asked.

Fighting tears, Tita said, "He is very hot, Izumo, and I am afraid."

Likichi looked at her and very quietly she said, "Never say that aloud in front of children, Tita. It can frighten them and make things worse. You must show that you are certain all will be well. Sometimes words are a type of medicine."

"I'm sorry, Izumo," she said again using the term that meant grandmother or revered elder woman. "Now that I think on it, I understand."

Likichi had been gently touching the head and chest of Din. He was hot, but not to the severe level where she'd need to pack wet cloths all over him. She went to her bag and handed Tita a few pieces of willow bark. She tore off a smaller piece. "Have him chew on this," she said. "He should spit it out, not swallow it. His body heat should return to normal. It may rise again, so use more willow bark if that happens. If he becomes hotter than this or starts to shiver violently, call me. Even if it's the middle of the night."

"Thank you, Izumo." Tuma said.

Likichi's mind web drifted back in time to the cave in the ashfall when Tita wasn't expected to live. She was two years old and looked half her age. Her mother's milk had dried up on the trek to avoid the volcano. Her mother was Minguat. People saw to it that Tita was fed. Real People saved her life. Likichi resumed sorting herbs.

Gladly, with a sigh Ki'ti agreed to do the pronouncement of joining Humko-na and Song that night at the men's council. They would have a short dancing ceremony and the two would depart for the cave above the meat preparation cave. Even now the two young people were preparing it for their first night. At the same time, the home cave was abuzz with the final aspects of the evening meal which all would enjoy together this night. After the dancing, they would have at least one story. She wondered whether there might be a special story that should be told this night.

Against the wall deeper in the cave, Tita felt the forehead of the now sleeping Din. The willow bark had cooled him down and he seemed comfortable in sleep. Ey, Tita's mother, stopped by to see how the young one was doing and showed a real sense of relief. It was troubling when adults were sick with body heat, but when it happened to children it seemed to carry an additional concern. Ey didn't know why in general, but she knew that she had almost lost Tita once so everything specific about her daughter was special to Ey.

After the evening meal and cleanup chores had been completed, after Ki'ti pronounced Humko-na and Song joined, after the dancing and the departure of the newly joined, Ki'ti prepared to tell the story for the night. This would be a short story. All gathered around the main fire in anticipation, shadows dancing on the walls from People settling for the story and from the bright hearth fire. Little sparks floated up towards the ceiling, mostly going dark before they reached the great height.

Ki'ti began, "There was a wonderful place we called the land where the giants played. When we named it that, we didn't know that there had been giants in that land. When we said giants, we did not mean the real giants who really lived there. We didn't know giants really existed except in stories. The land where the giants played was filled with strange huge rocks. They rested on rock on the ground. We thought very huge People must have stacked blocks atop other blocks to make the structures we saw."

"One day a small rock on the ground said to one of the beautiful rocks that appeared to have been carved to look like an elephant, 'People come to look at you, and they marvel at your shape. Those People never see me. They walk all over me. It's painful to see all the mindfulness you get—while I just get walked on.'"

"The rock that looked like an elephant thought for a while and then said, 'You had a chance. You stood above me for as long as time. Rain and that flooding river ran past us and the land shook and you were impatient. Your body became stiff and unbending with anger. Finally, with all the rain and flooding river water and freezing and thawing, you broke in half and then in half again. You fell from your place to the ground where you were ground down faster. That is why People walk on you today and don't see you, while they look favorably at me.'"

"Then, here is another story," she continued without pausing. Tiriku slept soundly beside her left leg. "When we lived in the place we just left, the hunters found a wonderful dropoff. They planned to use the dropoff to run animals over it for a safer way to hunt. Kai-na agreed to stand at the edge of the dropoff to call to the animals so the animals would run towards him. Below where he stood, there was a ledge he would drop to when the animal got too close.

"The first time they tried it, Kai-na was injured by the rhinoceros as it ran over the dropoff. Its hind leg broke Kai-na's leg. People worried that the dropoff wasn't safe. It was Kai-na who explained that it wasn't the dropoff. Instead the ledge needed to be dug out so there was more room on the ledge for hunter safety. Certainly there was danger, but expanding the place the hunter could hide could decrease the risk of injury. While Kai-na's leg healed, hunters dug out the ledge and the dropoff became a wonderful safer way to hunt the animals that traveled past that grassland every season of new leaves and colorful leaves."

"Now, I want to do something different. Look at my face if you know what the story about the rocks was about."

Ki'ti watched.

Ten-year-old Luga, Minagle and Sum-na's child, immediately looked at Ki'ti.

"Luga," Ki'ti said, "What was that story about?"

"It told of a lack of patience that turned into anger and what happened because of it."

"You are right, Luga."

"Now, all of you," Ki'ti addressed them all. "In the second story Kai-na got injured and couldn't walk for a long time. Was he like the rock on the ground?"

Mingugno, Lamk-na and Liho's sixteen-year-old son, was looking right into Ki'ti's eyes. She was delighted. Mingugno was one of the quiet ones. Nobody really knew him.

"Mingugno," Ki'ti asked, "Was Kai-na like the rock on the ground?"

"No, Wise One. Kai-na was trying to help the People and was taking a great risk himself to do that. He was brave, not impatient and angry like the rock. He was not injured because of flaws in his character or carelessness but rather because the feat he was trying to accomplish was new and untried."

Ki'ti was overwhelmed that this quiet one was so very much on target.

"I approve!" Ki'ti said. "You have reasoned well."

Everyone was surprised when Humko-na returned to the story group. On first night, once the pair left, they didn't return. His eyes stared into Ki'ti's and Ki'ti said, "Humko-na, what is it?"

"On our way to our cave, Song spotted something dark in the solid white rain below. It is large, and it does not move," he said.

"We will check to see what it is, Humko-na. Thank you for informing us. Please, return to your cave now."

No sooner were the words spoken than Humko-na was gone.

Manak-na, Kai-na, Arkan-na, and Bun were on their feet at the cave entryway immediately. They dressed warmly, took spears and some leather skins, and left. They could make out a dark spot below near the path that led to the sea. With the falling white rain, in a short time the darkness below would have been covered and it would not have been clear that something out of place lay there.

Bun slid down the trail faster than the men. He was much younger at eighteen and was eager to know what the dark spot was. When he reached the level ground he began to run only to discover that his legs sank to his knees in the white rain. Instead of racing to the dark spot, he found that he had to drag one leg at a time from the white rain and step forward in short increments, making a very narrow pathway for the men who followed. That was not what he had planned, but it permitted him to provide a service to the older men, so he felt that he was doing what he was supposed to do rather than what he chose. That he had a helpful role pleased him.

When he reached the dark spot, he could see that it was a man. The man was a Mol, but a stranger. He had a bag which he carried with him. He had some spears.

Manak-na approached next and checked the man's neck. "He's alive," he said. "Bun please return to the cave as fast as you can. We could use two men, formerly Mol, to come with a stretcher. Warn the women to prepare for a man who is drifting away to death from cold."

"I will go as fast as possible. Do you want me to return?"

Kai-na looked up. "Not necessary, Bun. You have done very well."

Bun climbed up to the new home cave as quickly as possible to deliver the message. The women and men responded, preparing for the newcomer immediately. Tongip-na and Gumokut carried a stretcher down and were amazed at the narrow walk that Bun had cut to reach the dark spot. It was surprisingly straight. They laid the stretcher beside the man and all of the men together rolled the man onto it. Then they used some leather strips to hold the man to the stretcher, and the two men began to carry it towards the hillside and then to the home cave. Meanwhile, women made a sleeping place for the man and filled numbers of bladders with water and dumped hot stones in them to heat the water.

Likichi showed the men where to put the stretcher and they untied the man and rolled him onto furry skins that had been provided. So that the man would not fear when he awakened, they placed his spears on the wall near where he lay. He was terribly cold, but his hands and feet were protected and his face and head had been covered as well. His nose was not frozen. They hoped he would not lose parts of himself from freezing.

His clothing design wasn't lost on Likichi. She had seen the design years ago worn by the man with the green bag. This man had a tunic, pants, jacket, boots, a head covering, and hand coverings. He also had a huge skin that was very soft over all of the garments he wore. His tools were similar to the ones they had. He carried a bag they had not looked into. Likichi noticed that his heart rate was slow, and he did not breathe deeply. She removed his jacket with help from the Mol who'd brought the stretcher.

Tongip-na said, "He looks like the Mol who live beyond where we lived, far beyond in the high mountains. I have never seen him. Have you seen him, Gumokut?"

Gumokut shook his head indicating a negative.

Women brought furry coverings to Likichi who placed them atop the stranger. The cave, which normally resonated with quiet conversation at this hour, was virtually silent. Everyone was fascinated with the stranger. The stranger remained asleep. Likichi had tried to awaken him to no avail. She had some women take the heated water in the bladders and place the bags beside the man from his underarms to his hips. Three layers of his coverings were pushed aside and more bags were placed on the two coverings that remained on his belly and chest. Then the three covers had been laid back over the man.

Likichi had moved her sleeping skin and covers to the ground perpendicular to the head of the man. If he moved or awakened, she wanted to know. Tongip-na moved his sleeping skin and covers next to the man, so if interpretation became necessary, he'd be available without someone having to seek him out. Otherwise, all was normal in the cave.

As time passed, because the man did not awaken, the People began to go to sleep. Through the night as the man slept, Likichi and Tongip-na kept the warm containers of water placed against the man's sides and atop him to keep him warm. Both rarely slept much, as they took their responsibility for the man very seriously.

It was not until after Wisdom had restored color to the land and after the People had enjoyed their morning meal that the man showed some signs of stirring. He didn't wake up completely—just twisted a little and moaned quietly.

Finally about the time the sun was directly overhead, if it could have been seen through the cloudy sky, the man opened his eyes and instantly began to show signs of great fear.

"You are safe here," Tongip-na said to him in the language of the Mol.

"You are Mol?" the man asked incredulous.

"Yes."

"How did I come to be here?" the stranger asked.

Tongip-na explained that someone had seen a dark spot below and they had brought him up to the cave hoping to see him live. When Tongip-na noticed the man trying to move, he explained about the bags of hot water to warm him. The stranger made it clear he'd never heard of anything like that and he appreciated the help. Tongip-na began to remove the bags from around the man. Girls came to pick them up and asked if more were needed. Tongip-na replied that he didn't think more were needed at this time.

Likichi had gone to get some meat broth for the man. She returned, but he made it clear that first he needed to find the privy. Tongip-na tried to help him to his feet but he was too unsteady. At Likichi's direction, Meta brought the container that men used when they could not go to the privy. The man was horrified to have to make water in the cave, but if that's what it took, it was better than bursting his bladder. When he finished, Meta took the container to the entryway and placed it there for emptying at the privy below. Whoever went next would take it.

Likichi handed a bowl to the man and he drank the broth from it, smiling at her because it wasn't only broth—it was seasoned and had tiny particles of food in it, so it was delicious. He drank all of it.

"Ask him if he wants more," Likichi asked Tongip-na.

Tongip-na asked him.

"Please," the man said with a smile to Likichi.

Likichi started to rise, but Tongip-na put his hand on her shoulder and offered to get the broth. He knew Likichi had difficulty getting up and down.

The man enjoyed a second bowl of broth and then he lay down and pulled the covers over himself.

"I'm sorry," he said to Tongip-na and Likichi, "I am just in serious need of sleep."

For three days the man ate broth and slept. At the end of that time Humko-na and Song had returned to the home cave and the man was sitting up. He would share his story at the men's council that night. Otherwise he wanted to know what the few Mol were doing with the People. The story fascinated him. They actually chose to live with the People! He'd met the Wise One by then but had not seen her do anything that was unusual, so she did not stand out to him. He couldn't believe she and Untuk-na were married. Untuk-na was Mol and so much taller!

The women were surprised that the man had not had any part of his body frozen black. They examined his boots and were very impressed. His boots had tough elephant skin on the bottom that curled up about as long as a thumb on the outside of the boot, adding some waterproofing. The boots were fully lined inside with winter caribou, the hollow hairs of which provided excellent insulation. The boots had thick deer hide with fur left on covering the outside. There was a ring of caribou fur that went from the inside of the top of the boot like a cuff to the outside of the boot and hung down about a hand's length on the outside of the top of the boot. It could be raised to extend the top of the boots, when white rain piled up too deep for the tops of the boots. The People had never seen caribou or felt its luxurious softness, but the Mol had seen it from time to time on their high mountain cousins' garments or boots.

When it came time at the men's council, the stranger was asked to tell the story of how he came to be where they found him.

He began, "I am Kipotuilak of the men of the Altay in the High Sunset Mountains. My father is chief. I am the second son. I chose to go to the sea to travel to lands beyond where the sun rises. I wanted to learn to build boats for travel, see what else is on this earth, meet different people, and learn their ways. I have seen much. The earth is huge. No one could see it all. This was my third trip. I returned from the land beyond where the sun rises and traveled for more than five full moons on the salt waters before we were returned to our shore this time."

"The land we go to beyond where the sun rises is warm. Much warmer than here all year. It is lovely land, and often I've thought of making that my home. The people are kind and I like their food. There is much fruit that grows on trees and shrubs, and it can be picked as you walk by it. Life is much easier. But I have a wife here, and I have an obligation to her. That's why I have the bag. There is much in the bag for her and for our children."

"Building boats is fascinating. The boats are very big and they go well on the sea. When you help build, you can sometimes take a trip to the land beyond where the sun rises, and they will let you return here, when the boat makes its return. I have done this three times. My wife tells me this is my last travel across the salt sea. I don't know whether that is what will be. Time will tell."

At this point Manak-na wanted desperately to talk to the stranger someplace other than at the men's council. He was hanging on every word the stranger spoke. The man was living the life he wanted to live. He was so close to the place where he could easily leave for the sea. A path even went there! But what about Domur? He heard the man mention his wife, but she did not sound happy about his adventures.

Domur had been watching Manak-na, not Kipotuilak, while the man spoke. She knew this would be wood for the fire that burned in her husband's belly. Her belly sank further at each word the man spoke. She knew Manak-na would love to help build a great boat, and to go to sea on such a boat would be the biggest dream he could have. Domur did not know that Ki'ti had already made it known that the path on which the man was found led to the sea.

The men's council ended and people readied themselves for sleep. Domur didn't know whether to address the sea adventure or leave it alone. For this night she decided she would not introduce it. Manak-na finally came to their sleeping place and quickly fell asleep. He brought no words, just a brief hug.

Ki'ti was fascinated to think on the size of the earth. To know there was a great sea that took more than five moons to cross left her breathless. She could not imagine spending five moons on a boat. She thought that even a big boat would become painfully small in that length of time. At the same time, the idea of such a large body of water left her pondering the small size of a human in comparison. Wisdom cared about them. She *knew* that. How, she contemplated, could Wisdom even find them to care about them? How could Wisdom care about all those created People, Minguat, and Mol across the face of the earth all at the same time? Were there others that she didn't know about besides People, Minguat, or Mol on the other side of the salt sea—or, on this side?

Ki'ti considered the sand on a riverbank. A person must be to Wisdom like a single grain of sand on all the riverbanks and seashores of the earth. She had always felt small compared to other people, but now she felt far smaller. Wisdom, on the other hand, seemed larger and more fantastic to her than ever. She realized that she was comparing Wisdom to the People and there was no comparison. Wisdom could care about endless numbers of beings because Wisdom was Wisdom. Wisdom could find that grain of sand that was Ki'ti and Wisdom could find the People, even if they were not all grouped together. She was grateful that Wisdom was so immense and utterly other than they were. The bigger and more different Wisdom was, the safer she felt entrusting herself and her People to Wisdom. She was awed by the love she found in Wisdom. Her mind web spun as she drifted to sleep.

When Wisdom restored color to the land in a great light of yellow and orange, the cave became energized. The sun was shining outside. The gray was gone. The world outside the cave would be sparkling. There was a distinct eagerness to see the new day.

Kipotuilak was up and dressed. He seemed to feel good again and when Manak-na saw him, he appeared to be getting ready to leave.

"Are you leaving?" Manak-na asked him. He had hurried to reach the man before he left. Manak-na had not even combed through his hair.

"I must get to my home before the mountain passes become too deep in white rain. I hope I haven't waited too long." He was bent over tying the mouth of the bag of gifts he carried to his family.

"You are sure that the boatbuilders need help and that they will provide passage to this land beyond the rising sun and return?"

"Yes, Manak-na of the People. Just ask for Pah. Tell him I sent you."

"I will do that. Thank you for your help."

"Wait until you have built boats, traveled to the land beyond the rising sun, and returned home before you thank me. You may find it's nothing to be thankful for."

"I am grateful for the opportunity," Manak-na insisted.

"Time will tell," Kipotuilak said while he examined his spears, not looking at Manak-na.

Ki'ti met Kipotuilak at the entryway. "I see you are leaving. Are you provisioned with food to get you to your destination?"

"Wise One, I have more than enough. Thank you for your generosity. I have found you a truly Wise One and your healer has special talents. May Wisdom give you great peace and may your time at the big lake be good. Just remember that to live there at the coldest part of the year, you must double all your winter garments. It is utterly cold there and fierce winds blow. Be well provisioned for you will not want to go outside in the wind and extreme cold."

Ki'ti put her hands on Kipotuilak's shoulders. "Go with Wisdom," she said. He smiled and walked outside and down the path to the main path below where he would turn toward the west and go to the high mountains.

Manak-na found Domur and sat beside her. "My wife, we must talk." Domur had known this conversation would come and had dreaded it.

"I have talked to Kipotuilak. The boatbuilders seek workers who will be given opportunities to travel to the land beyond the rising sun and back. I have wanted an adventure from the time I was young. Our children are grown. I know you don't want to go, that you will be well cared for here among those you love and who love you, that you are important to this group of people. I do love you, but I also want this adventure. Can you give me your farewell truthfully?"

Domur looked into his eyes. In some ways even at his age of thirty-nine he still had some ways of boyhood. "My husband, I do not want to give you a truthful farewell, but I know I must. You know this will cause me pain, and I know it, but for you to have the opportunity to live a part of what has been a dream for so long, I cannot withhold my true farewell wishes. Now, will you promise me two things?"

"What is your desire, my wife?"

"Promise me you will return safely, and that this will be the only time you will ask this of me."

"I promise," he said, believing that one adventure would suffice.

"When will you go?"

"When Wisdom has returned the color to the land after sucking it away tonight."

Domur was not surprised. She had expected that. He would have to do it quickly. For both their sakes.

Ki'ti passed Elemaea in the cave and asked, "Have you found an interest, Elemaea?"

"Yes," she replied with enthusiasm. "I am knapping spear points and making blades. I enjoy it very much."

Ki'ti smiled at her. "I am glad to hear that. Are you doing well?"

"Ekuktu-na said that I am doing well. He said my little hands are really good with the smaller blades and spear points. He says it takes years to become thoroughly skilled, but that I am learning fast and that my work is . . .," she sought the word, finally she remembered, "solid. What does solid mean?"

Ki'ti smiled at this child who was actually reflecting seriousness and caring that had been missing for so long. "My Dear One, it means very good."

"Does it sound like I'm fitting in? I want to fit in, and I really like making tools. It keeps my belly happy longer than anything I've ever done."

"Then, stay with it and when someone criticizes your work, don't fret. Learn from it. That is part of the learning process. Maybe you are fitting in, Elemaea. Maybe you are." Ki'ti continued on her way to check on Din. Elemaea watched her go, wishing they had more time. She put her thumb in her mouth.

Manak-na found a leather bag suitable for holding dried strips of meat. He dressed warmly and headed to the meat preparation cave where the jerky was stored. He knew that Kipotuilak had told him to prepare for twenty days of travel, so Manak-na knew how much meat to get. Kipotuilak had added a few days extra into his computation because Manak-na had a smaller stride than he had.

As soon as Yomuk realized what Manak-na was doing he raced to his uncle and asked whether he could join him. Absentmindedly, without reasoning out the entire situation, Manak-na told Yomuk that if his parents agreed to give him permission, he would allow him to accompany him. Manak-na was certain that Ki'ti and Untuk-na would withhold permission. Manak-na's statement to Yomuk was all the youth needed.

First, he tried his father, "Manak-na is going to build boats and travel to the land beyond the rising sun. Father, I wish to join him. He said that if you and mother agree to give me permission, he will take me. Will you agree?"

Untuk-na looked at his son. How bright and uncluttered were the mind webs of the young and carefree! "My son, you are not old enough."

"Father, I landed a killing strike on a live aurochs. I was stung by bees while gathering honey. I am not lazy and I don't look my age. I am more mature than many who are my age and some who are older."

Untuk-na considered what the boy was saying. He didn't want to crush his enthusiasm so he told him, "I will not give you permission unless your mother gives hers first." He did not think Ki'ti would let him go on such an adventure, even if Manak-na agreed.

Yomuk found his mother bringing up water gourds from the water source low in the home cave.

"Mother, I must ask your permission."

"For what, my son?"

"Manak-na is going to build boats and travel to the land beyond the rising sun. I wish to go with him. He said that if you and father agree, he will take me. Will you give me permission?"

"How will this adventure make you a better member of the People on your return?" she asked eyeing him on an angle.

"I do not know, mother, but I am certain that it will give me opportunities to do things that I would not otherwise have the chance to do. It will give me wider vision to understand how things on this earth are similar and different. It will make me a better hunter because I will see things more sharply and with better elements for reasoning."

Ki'ti was surprised at his thoughts. They were the optimistic thoughts of the young, but they carried more wisdom than thoughts of most youth his age. She also remembered that he was short with his father and with her, thinking that what they did was of lesser importance than hunters. She felt Tiriku at her left leg. She reached down and picked up the little puppy. She hugged him.

"And what did your father tell you?" she asked.

"He said he would not give me permission unless you gave yours first."

Ki'ti caught herself before she laughed out loud. So that was the way it was?

"Sit with me," Ki'ti said. She walked to her place at the men's council. He sat at the place for youth his age. Ki'ti bent her head downward to think without interruption. She sat for a long time. Yomuk was fascinated. She hadn't given him an instant negative. He wondered whether there was a chance.

She looked up. "Tell me what's the worst thing you could imagine happening while you are gone?"

He said, "I could die."

"Is that really the worst thing?"

He was worried that he'd made the wrong choice. He tried, "Manak-na could die." It occurred to him that Manak-na was his protector.

She returned her head to the downward position. His second choice was better than the first, she thought. She sat for a long time with her head down. She raised her head.

"You are about to learn a huge lesson, my son. Be very careful what you ask for, because it might be given to you. I give you permission as soon as I hear from Manak-na's mouth that he truly agreed to take you, if you have permission. You still need your father's permission."

Yomuk ran to Untuk-na. "Father," he said breathless and still in disbelief, "mother has given her permission. Will you give yours?"

"As soon as I verify what you've said, you'll have my permission." Untuk-na was certain that Manak-na had not really thought about taking Yomuk with him and had spoken without due reasoning. Nevertheless, he had said the words, of that Untuk-na was convinced. Why Ki'ti had said what she had, he had no idea, but he had committed, if she gave her approval.

He went to find her only to see her coming towards him. She smiled broadly.

"Why? My Dear One, why did you give him permission?"

Ki'ti took both his hands in hers. Then she let one loose so they could walk. "There is much that goes on in that young mind web of his. He almost worships Manak-na. He wants to be just like him. Manak-na is wonderful, but he's not perfect. Yomuk doesn't know that. At the same time, Yomuk denigrates both of us. It isn't something he flaunts, but he thinks it, and it colors his behavior. Manak-na enjoys the attention of Yomuk. I think it wise that both have some time together. I know that Manak-na will look out for Yomuk to the best of his ability. He loves his nephew. But having him along will also be a burden, one he agreed to, probably without careful thought. He may have assumed we'd never give him permission."

"I see what you're doing. I would never have thought to do that. But, then, you are the Wise One."

"I asked Yomuk what would be the worst thing that could happen."

"How did he respond?"

"His second answer was better than the first. The first was that he might die. The second was that Manak-na might die."

"The child has a good mind web."

"Yes, he does, but it has some significant flaws. This trip may correct some of those flaws. He will become homesick and will not be able to fix that. It won't happen right away. The adventure and newness will carry him along for a while. But after he's seen it all, he'll long for home and he has to face more than five moons on a boat once he has the opportunity to come home. He will not be allowed to be a child from the moment he leaves. That will come as a shock. He'll take it well at first. But he'll cry from time to time. He will learn much."

"You are beginning to make me wonder how many lessons you've taught me that I didn't know I was learning."

Ki'ti smiled. "You will verify what Yomuk said with Manak-na?"

"Yes. I will do that now." Untuk-na left her feeling unsettled but not confused. He was glad he was not Yomuk. The boy wanted to do great things. He was about to learn a great lesson. Untuk-na did not envy Yomuk—or Manak-na.

After Untuk-na and Manak-na talked, Manak-na realized he had taken on a responsibility that he had no intention of accepting. It was too late. Now he would have his adventure, but because he had not thought carefully earlier in the day, he had a huge burden—Yomuk.

Untuk-na gave Yomuk his own backpack. It was larger than Yomuk's. He told the boy he needed to get enough dried meat for twenty days. He suggested he find out from Manak-na how much that would be. So Yomuk thanked his father for the backpack and went to ask Manak-na how much meat was needed for twenty days. He also had enough presence of mind to find out what else he might need for the trek to the sea or beyond. Manak-na carefully told him what he was taking, checking to be sure the boy had it placed exactly in his mind web. He wouldn't want to have to give Yomuk what he carried for himself. Manak-na would not know that Likichi and Ki'ti would be putting things in Yomuk's backpack that Manak-na would enjoy with Yomuk as they traveled and when they arrived at the sea.

That night Ki'ti and Untuk-na, Manak-na and Domur, and Yomuk tossed and turned instead of enjoying restful sleep. Each entertained a multitude of thoughts, concerns, excitement, and sadness—a wide range of emotion.

When Wisdom returned color to the land, Manak-na and Yomuk dressed, ate, and put on their outerwear, attached their backpacks, and stood at the entryway while Ki'ti put her hands on their shoulders and said to each, "Go with Wisdom." Yomuk followed Manak-na down the hill without looking back. Domur turned away and began to fold up their sleeping mat and covers. Elemaea stared wide eyed. She had heard that Yomuk was leaving with Manak-na and did not understand why he would want to do that. They'd just spent a long time trekking. Why go again? She wanted to run to him to tell him she would miss him. She restrained herself. It all felt wrong, but she would remember to keep her mouth closed so that no one disapproved.

The white rain had melted so that it was only about the depth of a man's hand from heel to fingertip. Walking was much easier than it had been when they went to find the man who had collapsed on the path. They could walk at a normal stride and that made the trek pleasant.

After some time had passed, Manak-na told Yomuk that Kipotuilak had explained that the evergreen trees were not often found in this area. Travelers had put them in places to mark certain locations. Caves where travelers could camp were marked with evergreens. Other places that were important were marked with them. If they didn't wait until Wisdom sucked all the color from the land, they could find a place to sleep each night just by looking for evergreen trees. The trees were designed to be seen from the path. The path was concealed by white rain, but Kipotuilak's tracks left a rut to follow even though more white rain had fallen since they were made.

Each of them carried two spears. They had other tools in their backpacks. The day was warm and the trek went through beautiful land. They walked and ate jerky when they became hungry.

The two continued on towards the sea. They found the caves each night by searching for evergreens. They had seen no other travelers. By the fifteenth day Yomuk was beginning to show signs of restlessness. He was bored. He had not learned that just when one becomes bored on a trek, the perspective shifted to how close one was to the destination, not how far they'd traveled. What was in the past was in the past. They were so close to their destination. Before the day was over Manak-na would explain to Yomuk how to shift perspective so he did not become bored and, therefore, a nuisance.

In the evening of the eighteenth day they could see the sea in the distance. They had to decide whether to stop at the cave marked by evergreens or continue on. Yomuk wanted to continue on, but Manak-na decided it was time to stop. Entering the area in the light was better than in the dark. They entered the small cave and had some meat, put their sleeping skins and covers on the floor of the cave, and settled down to rest and sleep. They spoke little. Each was brimming with excitement. Sleep came quickly.

Chapter 3

Manak-na awakened and quietly went outside to make water, careful not to look towards the east. He wanted to save his view of the sea until he was actually headed there. He stood at the cave entryway and savored the morning air and the breeze. He could detect the hint of salt in the air. It had been a very long time since he'd smelled salt in the air. It took him back to his childhood. He broke off a small piece of woody material from a branch to pick his teeth. He felt to the bottom of his belly that this would be a good day—one to remember.

He went into the cave and took his comb from his backpack. He combed his hair, braided it tightly, folded it, and clasped it with a wide leather collar. The collar had two opposing holes. Manak-na had a wooden pin that he pushed through a hole, his hair, and the second hole. It held the collar in place. Yomuk was awake and had dressed and was combing his hair. Manak-na took a piece of jerky and bit off a piece. It was remarkably tasty. The People were very good at smoking meat. Some of the People felt they had come to hard times when they had to resort to their stores of dry meat. Not his People. The dry meat was as good as the other meat. At least he felt that way.

Yomuk was quiet this morning. He'd gone out and now reentered the cave. Manak-na was glad for the quiet. He was about to begin an adventure and he wanted to feel every moment of it. He drank some water from the gourd he'd filled last night. It was cool and slaked his thirst.

Yomuk let out a startled sound. Manak-na looked up. Yomuk was holding a rounded piece of food with what looked like blueberries in it. Manak-na began to salivate. Yomuk looked back inside his backpack and found another

and handed one to Manak-na. Someone had packed tasty treats in his backpack. The round balls had fallen from their wrapper and collected near the
bottom of his backpack.

"Thank you," his uncle said, forgetting about his reverie and the sea for a
moment and feeling truly grateful Yomuk shared.

"They're good!" Yomuk said with enthusiasm. "I thank whoever put these
in here," Yomuk said into the air.

Manak-na nodded to Yomuk and began to roll up his bedding. He tied
the roll to the top of his backpack. Yomuk did the same. It was time to put on
his warm outerwear, load his backpack, and head to the sea. Yomuk copied
what his uncle did.

The man and the youth stepped outside the cave, walked down the short
path, and turned onto the path to the sea. They could see the sea beyond
them extending far beyond where they could see. It was an amazing sight.
Yomuk had never seen the sea and he was dumbstruck. The largest water he'd
ever seen was the lake where the People used to fish from bamboo boats. He
knew just looking at the sea that the big lake to which his People headed was
not nearly as big as this sea. The size of the sea was a revelation to Yomuk.
They walked purposely in quiet each realizing that life was about to change
and not having any way to anticipate how significant that change might be.

The boatbuilding area was clear to them as they followed the path. It
was as if the path were built to end at the boatbuilders' place. Manak-na
wondered whether the giants had built boats in the same place. There were
people, some with tanned skin, who looked like Mol crossed with something
else but not People or Minguat, but no giants as far as he could tell. There
were some People and some Mol, maybe a few Minguat. Everyone seemed
to be very busy doing work that Manak-na didn't really understand. He felt
comfortable that whatever the work was, he and Yomuk could learn it. First,
he must find Pah.

The boatbuilding covered a huge area of land. There were piles of
bamboo and places where bamboo floated in the sea. There were neat stacks
of bamboo. On a slope there was what Manak-na thought were two boats
being built. He marveled at the size of them. They were made of bamboo that
curved upward in the front and back, and they were held together somehow.
He couldn't see detail at that distance. They were, he estimated, longer than
the bent tree house they had left to begin their trek. Yomuk was overcome
with the scene. He'd never seen any place so busy or so many people doing
things he didn't understand. He noticed that on the hillside there were build-

ings made from huge bamboo supports and covered with bamboo, which was covered again with what looked like skins, covered by dirt. The roof sloped slightly towards the sea. A few plants grew on the roof. It was a place of excitement to both Manak-na and Yomuk. There was so much going on at the same time. It made their heads spin.

Manak-na noticed a small hut in the midst of the boatbuilding activity, and he headed toward it. He guessed that the hut might be a place he could either find or ask for Pah. He cautioned Yomuk not to speak to anyone unless he was first asked to speak. Manak-na wanted to be the speaker and not have to worry about interruption. Yomuk agreed immediately. He was definitely in a situation where he had no idea what to say or how to act.

They arrived at the hut and Manak-na saw a man moving around inside. He waited to be recognized, and the person inside either didn't see him or postponed recognition. Manak-na couldn't tell which, or whether something else kept the man from communicating.

After more than a polite wait, Manak-na, said in the best Mol language he could, "I come from Kipotuilak to find Pah."

The man in the hut turned sharply. "I am Pah, who are you?"

"I am Manak-na and this is my nephew, Yomuk. We come to build boats, to travel to the land beyond the rising sun, and to return here together."

Pah studied them for a quite a while in silence. Then he said, "Go to the big bamboo structure on the hill over there." He pointed to the largest structure. "In the back on the north side are sleeping places. Put your backpacks on a sleeping place where no bedding is. Those places are not in use. Stop at the food table and eat. Do not avoid eating to hurry back. You will need to be well fed. Then, return here. Do you understand?

"Yes." Manak-na said.

Pah looked at Yomuk. "And do you understand?"

"Yes." Yomuk replied.

"When someone asks or tells you something here, it is important to acknowledge. Each must do it for himself. That way the person asking or telling knows you got the message. Understood?"

Manak-na said, "Yes."

Yomuk said, "Yes."

Manak-na and Yomuk turned and left for the bamboo structure.

People were rushing about carrying bamboo poles, rope, strips of leather, tools, and all looked as if an enraged rhino was chasing them. They moved fast, as if their lives depended on it. Manak-na tried to judge how they felt about what they were doing by their expressions, but most had flat expressions—no emotion shown at all. He assumed the men were absorbed in their work. Manak-na wondered whether he had expression on his face during a hunt.

He and Yomuk entered the bamboo structure to find sleeping places arranged at the north end. A big hearth was in the center of the structure and there was a hole for smoke to exit similar to what they had constructed for the bent tree structure they used to call home. There was a huge table filled with food. They found two vacant sleeping places next to each other at the far end of the structure. They put their backpacks and spears on the vacant sleeping places and headed to the food.

They brought their food bowls to the table, and they filled them from a table arrayed with a very large choice of food. They stood to eat—something they didn't do in the home cave. The food was remarkably good. Manak-na noticed an opening in the wall that appeared still to be enclosed. He walked through the narrow corridor and found the place where food was cooked. He had a feeling that he should leave the cooking area and he did quickly.

"Where did you go?" Yomuk asked.

"I think they cook the food there. Don't go there unless you are told it's permitted. It feels like a place where we should not be."

"I will remember."

"Good. Not bad food," Manak-na said raising the leg of fowl he was eating. "Well seasoned, different but well seasoned."

"Not bad." Yomuk thought it was good but chose to use Manak-na's negative, something Manak-na rarely used. Yomuk was learning this new place and how it worked, and he was noticing subtle differences in Manak-na.

Yomuk noticed that food bones apparently were placed in the hearth for burning. He dropped the remains of the leg he had devoured to burn there. Manak-na was pleased to see that Yomuk didn't wait to be told everything to do. He also placed his bones on the sticks on the hearth with the others. Apparently they had no dogs to help to use the bones. They looked to see what else they might want to eat. Manak-na took a piece of roast and Yomuk put some greens in his bowl along with some fish.

Yomuk looked at Manak-na seriously. "There are some different looking people here with light brown skin. Pah is one. What are they?"

Manak-na replied. "I really don't know. They look as if they work in the sun. My skin tanned when we lived far south from here. They are about the same color—a little darker. Even now, as cold as it is, they are going about with little clothing when it's barely the season of new leaves. Just remember from Wamumur and the stories, all of us are people regardless of what our physical characteristics are."

When they finished, they wiped their bowls and put them back in their backpacks. They returned to the hut in the area where the boatbuilding was taking place. Pah wasn't there. They waited.

Finally, Pah returned.

"We have good food, yes?" Pah asked.

"Yes," both Manak-na and Yomuk replied in unison.

"What do you do?" Pah asked.

"I am a hunter," Manak-na replied.

"I am learning to be a hunter," Yomuk replied and then added, "I have landed a kill strike on an aurochs."

Pah stood looking at them, resting his chin on his hand. Pah was not very tall. He was obviously strong. Muscles were visible everywhere. In the cold, he wore a leather like the Mol, hair trimmed like Yomuk with a headband, and a short, two shouldered tunic over it. He did not wear pants and a jacket. He was barefooted.

"Why are you here?"

Manak-na wondered what to say but did not hesitate. "I have longed for adventure since I was a child. I love to explore, to find new places, and to try to understand new ways of doing things. Then, I can bring them back to my People to let them know of differences in the world. Some may benefit us, if we choose to adopt them. Also, it is possible we may benefit those we meet."

Yomuk said, "I, too, long for adventure. I want to know what there is to know."

Pah continued studying them. Obviously the older one did not know the language well, but his use of the language was passable enough to communicate. He was smart. He'd learn the language fast. The younger one seemed fluent, but then he was Mol.

"For the rest of this daylight, both of you will be carrying bamboo to the salting pen. Then when the next daylight arrives, you will go with the hunters to hunt. That will be your job. When the boat below is ready, you will be part of the travel. When we land, you hunt for food for us. When we are at sea, you may be needed to row the boat from time to time. Do you understand?"

Both replied, "Yes."

"Do you have questions?"

"What does row the boat mean?" Manak-na asked.

"It means to hold a long stick that is flat on the far end, place it in the water that is too deep to touch the bottom. With the long stick, you push the water behind us. It takes much strength. When there is little wind, we need to row to move the boat through the water. Most of the people on the boat will row from time to time when we are in calm water. It is part of travel on a boat. It is hard work, but necessary. When called to row, you must respond. Some people use slaves to row. We find that makes too many mouths to feed. Our journeys are very long. Does that answer your question?"

Manak-na said, "Yes."

"Are there any more questions?"

Manak-na and Yomuk said together, "No." Neither felt they knew enough to ask any more questions.

"Follow me," Pah said.

They followed him through the boatbuilding space to a spot where bamboo logs were piled together, not neatly. Pah stopped there.

"Each of you take a pole and start walking downhill."

Manak-na and Yomuk each took the same two bamboo logs, one in each hand. Manak-na was in front and Yomuk behind. They accurately judged where they should stand to make the weight bearing most efficient and they began to move to the water.

"Stop!" Pah was fascinated.

"You automatically did this the most efficient way possible, each of you carrying an end of each pole, even though I told you each to take one. You have done this before?"

Manak-na looked at Pah. "Yes, we made small flat bamboo boats to fish the lake near us. It is easier to carry bamboo this way, especially when the bamboo has not been dried."

"Continue on," Pah said.

Manak-na realized Pah had tested them. He'd explain to Yomuk later that day while they transported logs. It might benefit Yomuk to know that Pah would test like that.

When they reached the water, they could see that an area had been set aside where bamboo logs were floating in the salt water. Manak-na was fascinated.

"Unload your logs into the pen," Pah said.

Manak-na and Yomuk put the logs into the pen.

"Any questions?" Pah asked.

"Why put them in salt water?" Manak-na asked.

"It kills any bugs or worms that might be in the bamboo," Pah answered. He was beginning to like this man who was not Mol. He asked smart questions briefly. He thought things out. It seems that Kipotuilak had done him a good service. He would remember.

"Before you walk back up to get another log from the pile these came from, come over here and get a log apiece from this pen."

Manak-na and Yomuk did as they were told.

"Now follow me to the place where these logs are stacked to dry."

Manak-na and Yomuk followed Pah up the hill to a place where the bamboo logs were stacked neatly with cross pieces of bamboo laid out to keep air spaces around the drying bamboo.

"Unload the salted logs here, Pah said, "and when you hear a drum beating, that means the work day is over. It will be time to eat. Finish what you're doing, and return to the bamboo structure for food."

Manak-na and Yomuk thought this arrangement was good for the purpose. They unloaded their bamboo logs and headed to the place to pick up more that needed to be penned in salt water. Pah watched them go. *These were superior additions,* he thought.

For the remainder of the day, Manak-na and Yomuk worked hard taking as many logs as possible to the salt water pen and bringing up as many from the other pen as possible. They finished transporting the salted logs long before they finished taking the logs down to be salted. They enjoyed the work even though it was tedious. When they heard the drum, it took a moment or two for them to realize that the drum meant the end of the work time and the beginning of food time. They had seen no places to wash up, so they washed their hands and faces in salt water and returned to the bamboo structure.

They smiled at the people in the bamboo structure, but few smiled back. Manak-na did not understand at all. Yomuk didn't notice. Each person got their own bowl for food, so Manak-na and Yomuk got theirs and went to the food table. The food from earlier had been removed and new food was on the table. It occurred to Manak-na that what hunters brought to the person who cooked is what got put on the table. It was interesting to him. He was beginning to understand a little of how this place worked. There were greens and he wondered whether hunters gathered them.

The food was wonderful. He thought that some of what was done with food here could contribute to what was done at home, but he'd need to learn what it was or figure it out.

Yomuk was just enjoying the whole experience of being in the strange structure, eating wonderful food and plenty of it, being around a lot of men who seemed to be smart at what they did. It was a wonderful adventure.

Manak-na was looking surreptitiously at the men wondering who was a hunter and who a boatbuilder, and whether there were people who did other things.

One man, a Minguat, with no hair came over to Manak-na and said, "One of you has placed your backpack on my sleeping place." He seemed enraged.

Manak-na studied him. "We were told to put our backpacks on sleeping places where there was no bedding. We did."

"I have no bedding!" the man sneered.

"He does, too!" another man shouted from the crowd.

Manak-na noticed earlier that there were plenty of unused sleeping places. But it struck him that the issue wasn't that he'd taken the man's sleeping place. He thought he was being bullied. So he said, "You have a choice. Either I move my sleeping place and you sleep with no bedding at all, or we have a fight right now and if I win you shut your mouth, and my sleeping place is where my backpack is, and if you win, I move."

The people in the bamboo structure were dumbstruck. They couldn't believe that Manak-na, who was shorter, was standing up to the bully. They gathered to see what would happen.

"We will fight!" the bully growled.

Yomuk had moved nearer the wall. He was frightened for Manak-na. Size clearly favored the bully.

The group of men in the bamboo structure encircled the two so they could see what was happening. At first, Manak-na easily dodged the man's wild swings. He could see that he fought from brute strength, not wisely. He continued to dodge the man, tiring him. Fighting after consuming a full meal was not wise. The group members could not understand what Manak-na was doing. Some were muttering about strange ways of fighting, seeming to think that Manak-na might be cowardly.

Once the bully had gotten himself tired and had gained false confidence, he continued to swing at Manak-na harder and harder. Sweat poured from the huge man. His face was bright red. Manak-na saw an opportunity and slammed his fist into the man's jaw, causing a tooth to detach and fall out, making a bloody mess. The bully was furious. As soon as he recovered from the shock of being injured, he came lunging at Manak-na who stepped quickly out of the way. The bully turned and fixed his eyes on Manak-na's head. He lunged, and Manak-na blocked the swing of the massive arm, and hit the man in the throat with his tight fist. The man fell to the ground gur-gling. He was clearly hurting, but he staggered to his feet one more time. Manak-na hit the man on the left temple. The bully fell to the floor and did not rise. Manak-na calmed his own breathing.

Manak-na turned toward Yomuk and said, "The fish is good. I think I'll have some more. You want some, too?" He gave the impression that the fight had been nothing to him.

Yomuk reasoned that they were playing a bit of a game, so he said, "Yes, Manak-na, that sounds good." Yomuk got both bowls and went to the table and handed Manak-na his bowl. Manak-na noticed the slight tremor in Yomuk's hands. The two acted as if nothing had happened.

After some time, the bully rose from the floor seemingly a little dazed. He went to his sleeping place, which was at the front of the sleeping places not the back, where Manak-na and Yomuk had put their backpacks. The bully lay down and covered himself with his own blankets. He would never again bully Manak-na, or Yomuk, for that matter, nor would he bully anyone if Manak-na were present.

Manak-na, and Yomuk through association, had gained full respect of the group of men among whom they would live. Yomuk would wait until Manak-na and he were alone to ask how Manak-na knew to do what he did. Yomuk would have apologized and moved his bed. He knew now that would have been the wrong thing to do, but he needed guidance on how to make decisions like Manak-na had made. He knew he had a lot to learn.

When Wisdom restored color to the land, a drum beat quickly and the men in the bamboo structure awakened. They went outside to the privy and returned to eat. Manak-na wondered when or whether they bathed. From the smell of it, they didn't.

"You're a good fighter," a man with tanned skin said to Manak-na.

"I do not like to fight," Manak-na replied.

"Then, I think you do not like bullies more than you dislike fighting."

For the first time since he'd arrived at the boatbuilding place, Manak-na laughed heartily.

"That, my friend, is a good observation. What's your name?" he asked.

"I am Komus. I come from the far north near the big lake."

"I am Manak-na. This is my nephew, Yomuk. My People are trekking toward the big lake."

"Why are you here?"

"I long for adventure. And you?"

"First, I was supposed to do what my father did. Build boats and travel the sea. But more importantly, I wanted a woman, whom I loved, and who loved me. Her father gave her to someone else. It broke our hearts to see each other constantly and know we could never be together, so I left when I was young."

"That is a sad story, my friend," Manak-na said.

"It is not so bad. I finally found a woman to love. She lives there and waits for me. She knew it would be this way from the beginning. She is a good woman."

Yomuk was drinking all the interaction in as if he were part of it.

"Have you traveled on the boat?" Manak-na asked.

"Many times. It is an amazing adventure but you have to be willing to work hard. Rowing is hard, but I enjoy it. It builds up great muscles." He showed his biceps.

"My nephew and I want the adventure once. That's why we're here."

Komus made an interesting face, as if he were studying Manak-na and Yomuk and, perhaps, didn't understand them. He said nothing. He wondered how anyone could leave the life of adventure in boats after only one adventure. Each trip had so much different about it.

Another two men came over and said, "Good fight."

Manak-na replied, "Fighting is never what I'd choose to do. But I will not be bullied."

"That's clear," one man said. "I am Rokuk from the south of here along the coast. I came here to avoid the Minguat who are infesting the area. Gurst, the man you fought, is Minguat, as you probably know."

"I hear you are hunters," the other man said. "When the drum beats, come with us and bring your weapons, rope, and field knives. I am Mogil."

"My name is Manak-na and this is my nephew, Yomuk."

The drum beat and Manak-na and Yomuk got their spears, rope, and field knives. They left the bamboo structure to join the hunters. Hunters made it clear that they bled the animal but did not bring back the gut to boatbuilders' camp. They needed to keep the bladder and the stomach. Upon their return, they should take animals to the back door of the bamboo structure, which they called home or the boatbuilders' camp. There were hooks to hang the meat on near the back door. The hunters said that a single drum beat from the cooks would draw men and women from the hillside area, people who skinned the meat and did initial butchering of it for the camp. They got to keep the skins and whatever meat the cooks rejected. They also got the leftovers for their service. Those people also brought greens and fruit to the cook. It was a good relationship the boatbuilders had with local people—relationships that had lasted for many lifetimes.

One of the hunters explained further. "When someone at camp needs a garment or boots, the people in the area would make them or get them from their supply. Those people would also take coconut fibers from the trunks of the plant to make ropes for the boats. They trade the coconut people skins for coconuts. The coconut people are peaceful Minguat to the south. Our people travel there in numbers of small boats along the coast to reach the coconut people."

Manak-na and Yomuk were storing all the new information in their mind webs for later use.

Manak-na and Yomuk trekked to the northwest for half a day with the group of hunters. Then the groups split up to enter different valleys. Manak-na and Yomuk decided to climb a hill to an elevated valley. Manak-na thought he'd detected some movement there, but wasn't certain.

When they reached the top both were very quiet. There was a deer at the top not far from a stand of trees. The wind blew behind the deer towards the trees.

"Follow me," Manak-na whispered. "Keep total quiet."

Yomuk nodded.

They crept to the trees, and, using the strategy that had worked with the aurochs, they let out bloodcurdling yells and raced from the trees and speared the animal. Manak-na's spear entered the heart and Yomuk's the lung. They checked the animal, and it had breathed its last. They removed their spears and pulled the body to the trees and tied rope to each rear leg. They pulled the rope over a tree limb on the tree on the right and the other over the limb on a tree to the left to raise the animal. They bled it.

Then, they turned the deer to hang from its fore legs. Manak-na pulled out his knife from its sheath and slit the animal from neck to anus and around. The intestines fell out in coils. Yomuk was making every effort at self control. His initial desire was to vomit.

"Yomuk," he asked, "Do you know how to grasp above the stomach so we can haul out the guts without leaking anything inside?"

"Yes." Yomuk was glad he had studied the procedure.

Yomuk cut above the top of the gut so he had plenty of tubing to turn over and over to prevent spilling. Manak-na trusted the youth to do what he said he could. He took care of the other end. Some of the entrails were on the ground, so Manak-na and Yomuk pulled the rest from the body. The smell still wasn't to Yomuk's liking, but he was not as nauseated as he'd been around the aurochs.

Yomuk pushed the stomach contents toward the intestine and tied off the intestine so he could harvest the bulging grouping of multiple stomachs.

The two men wiped the inside of the deer with wet grass from the treed area. They tied its legs around Yomuk's spear, threw the stomach grouping and bladder inside the deer, and began to head back to the boatbuilders' camp, as they'd learned the men called it. Each man had a portion of Yomuk's spear held just above his left shoulder.

When they descended the slope they'd recently climbed, and were walking on flat ground again, Yomuk asked his uncle, "How did you know to fight the Minguat with no hair?"

"Well, first, when something like that happens, you have to know whether you're dealing with a bully or someone rightly offended. When the bald man said he had no bedding, I remembered that Pah had said that everyone else had bedding. Then, a man in the bamboo structure said the man had bedding just before the fight. Which would you choose to believe?"

"Definitely, Pah. I'm not sure about the other man."

"That's what I thought. And then bullies tend to want to push others around. If they get by with that, they abuse them. The man seemed to want to fight. If I failed to fight, he'd find another reason to provoke me—or, worse—you. So I decided to get it over with. I hoped he was as unskilled in fighting as he was in knowing how to act towards others. You decide to fight when you cannot successfully avoid it."

"Why did you avoid him for so long?"

"What I wanted to do was to make him tire himself. He's a lot bigger than I am and he would tire faster. By continuing to swing at me and miss, he'd tire and he'd also become angered enough that his thinking would not be very clear. He'd leave himself wide open to attack, which he did. When I got a clear opening, I took it and gave it all I had."

"Well, now it looks like everyone wants to be your friend."

"Careful, Yomuk. They have simply sided with the winner. It takes a long time to know who your friends are. Be kind and thoughtful to all, but never assume a person is your friend until there is reason to believe so. Right now there's no reason to believe that they have done anything but decide to favor the winner of a stupid fight."

"Uncle, you are wise."

"Yomuk, you need very much to understand one thing. I am not wise, I am favored by Wisdom. I understand things from our stories and from listening to your mother and to Emaea and Wamumur, Wise Ones before your mother. I make decisions based on what I've learned from them, and, when I reason correctly, based on what I've learned from them, success follows."

Yomuk listened in silence and did not respond. He still thought hunters superior to Wise Ones. He was young and simplistic in his knowledge of how Wisdom affected life. For some People, it took life-threatening events to make the need known, and sometimes People died just as they grasped it. Some never understood. There was a story about that, but it didn't connect in the mind web of Yomuk.

"Yomuk, think on the story of Comargh-na and Elmindrid-na."

Yomuk remembered the names but he could not connect them to a story. He walked in silence wondering whether he really needed to know what Manak-na was telling him about one of his mother's stories.

After walking for quite a while, Manak-na said, "Once when I was young I made a fool of myself in front of Nanichak-na and all the hunters when I let it slip out that I thought Notempa in the Maknu-na and Rimlad story was a giant who exploded in anger, not a mountain that erupted. They corrected me and I spent many hours thinking on that story. If the elders hadn't really understood that story, all of us could have been buried in the ashfall—and you would not have been born. Taking the stories lightly can cause you to fail to have information that can prevent your death. Interesting, huh?"

Yomuk was suddenly more aware that he had a serious lack. He'd listened politely to the stories, but they were just stories told by his mother, not something life critical. He shifted the spear on his shoulder. It was getting heavy. They still had far to go.

As time passed, Yomuk couldn't shake Manak-na's comment. Maybe the stories were life critical. He asked, "Manak-na, what is the story of Comargh-na and Elmindrid-na? I cannot remember it."

"I can't do it from memory, but I can tell you what the story is about. Two hunters, Comargh-na and Elmindrid-na were heading to grassland to hunt deer. They ran into a bear. The bear stood and clicked its teeth, shook its head, and issued a frightening growl. Comargh-na reminded Elmindrid-na not to run but rather to stand still and to make him look larger by holding his arms out like the stories tell, but Elmindrid-na got frightened and ran as fast as he could away from the bear. Of course, the bear chased and killed him. While the bear ate his friend, Comargh-na returned home with little desire to hunt for the rest of that day. He grieved for his friend who wouldn't listen to the stories or to his wisdom from the stories that he shared while the bear growled."

Yomuk listened carefully to Manak-na. He understood the words and the need to listen to the wisdom of the stories, but he didn't make the connection that his mother was the People's treasured storyteller and his father's responsibility was to guard the treasured storyteller. He had fixed in his mind that his parents were somehow less than hunters—almost lazy—and that was the foundation upon which he placed the story of Comargh-na and Elmindrid-na. To him it was a life critical lesson in meeting with a bear. Yomuk was tall, looked like a young man, was responsible beyond his years, but he was, after all, only ten years old.

They continued on to the boatbuilders' camp. On the back of the building there was a door, and they carefully hung the deer on one of the hooks near the door. At that point they went inside through the door on the other side of the building to eat. The table was laden with food that looked and tasted wonderful. Each wondered whether to return to the hunt or what to do, so they prepared to return to the hunt.

On their way out, they saw Komus and Fengren returning with another deer. Komus stopped. "Manak-na," he said, "stay at the hunt until you have been successful or until darkness is about to come. Once you have brought meat, you do not return for more."

"What do you do with the extra time, once you've brought your kill?" Manak-na asked.

"You take logs to the salt water and bring up salted logs to stack them," Komus replied with a smile. "Oh, this is Fengren. You haven't met him yet. Fengren, this man who fought Gurst is Manak-na and Yomuk is his nephew."

Fengren nodded at them. Manak-na and Yomuk nodded at Fengren.

The two men took their kill to the back and Manak-na and Yomuk took their spears inside and placed them beside their sleeping places. They returned outside to meet the others who would also be taking logs to the salt water pens and bringing up others. Manak-na and Yomuk noticed that the logs this day went into the empty pen where they had removed the salted logs the day before. It became the salt water soaking pen for this day and the other became the salted log pen. Each day it shifted, so Manak-na concluded that it took overnight to salt the logs sufficiently to kill the pests inside. Yomuk understood the daily shift but neglected to tie that to the purpose of killing pests.

Day after day, as the weather became colder and colder, Manak-na and Yomuk followed the routine of hunting and, if finishing before the drum for the evening meal, moving bamboo logs. Surprisingly, one day Pah appeared at the boatbuilders' camp and asked for Manak-na and Yomuk. They came out to meet Pah.

"You called for us?" Manak-na asked.

"Yes. We have been having a bit of trouble with the boat. I'm wondering whether someone who knows nothing about boats might see something we don't. Maybe it would help to solve the problem we're having."

Manak-na was overwhelmed. He knew nothing about boatbuilding, but he certainly was willing to look. Yomuk assumed this was a normal thing that happened, so he just followed along.

Pah spoke in a quiet voice. "We are trying something new this time. Normally, we take two boats shaped somewhat like you see down there—bamboo logs attached into cylinders and pointed in front and back with both ends pulled upwards so they don't sink. But occasionally we lose one of the boats. This time we are trying to pull the two boats together into one boat with the two main boats we have now for sides. We are having trouble getting the idea to work. The old boats function well enough, but losing one is not good. When we get there, take a look. You'll see what we've been trying to do. There has to be a better way."

When they arrived, Manak-na examined the boats from top to bottom and from front to back. He was dumbfounded at the work involved. The bamboo was lashed together in bundles, which were interwoven with vines that laced individual logs together. Each bundle was coiled with a rope. The bundles were attached together with more vines and rope. A larger sized rope was wrapped as a coil from end to end as the bundles got merged. He realized what they were trying to do and spent no little time running many thoughts through his mind web. He appeared to be sitting atop one of the boats and doing nothing but staring out at the sea, but Pah realized he was deep in thought.

Finally, Manak-na climbed back down the boat. He met Pah on the ground. "I can tell you what I'd do to solve the problem. Only you will know whether it might work. I have no experience at all with this. First, I would cut down," he showed three fingers, "hardwood trees of equal height—trees that are strong but not very thick and about the length of," he showed ten fingers, "men. At the end of each log, I would cut a hole and peg the hole with a branch about as long as a man. I'd reinforce the peg with rope. I'd do that to all three logs, making sure that the pegs point in the same direction at each end of each log. Then I'd lay the logs on the structures you have now, with the pegs up and down. I'd add girth and length to the current boat structures, enclosing the logs. If tree wood is not appropriate, you could use bamboo in bundles, I suppose. When you've laid some bamboo bundles to add to the girth and length of what you have now, peg the logs on the inside edges of the old designed boats, so that they firmly hold the boats they are designed to hold and will not squeeze the space between the two boats. Each log has," he showed four fingers, "pegs one on either side of an old boat—all with pegs in the same direction on each log. Pegs should be placed up and down—perpendicular to the line of bamboo. It might help, after some bamboo bundles have been added above the logs, to use rope to loop over one of the tree projections outside the boat to loop over the tree projection on the other side of the log where it extends beyond the boat to add extra sturdiness. It would make lines all over but might add strength."

"Then, when the height above the bamboo flooring is just more than a man's height, I'd add another," he showed three fingers, "logs, done the same way. The lower logs could support bamboo flooring to store supplies in bamboo cases secured to the flooring. The upper logs could support bamboo flooring for the boat activity, whatever that is. Then those logs would be covered with bamboo bundles where they rise above the old boats, and you'd have a boat that is made of two boats with two floored spaces between them.

Pah looked up, clearly understanding what Manak-na had suggested. He thanked him for his thoughts. Manak-na and Yomuk returned to the hillside and began to carry logs to the salting pens and bring up salted logs. Yomuk was fascinated.

"Uncle, will they do what you said?" he asked.

"I do not know. He asked for my thoughts and I gave them. It was a way I could see to solve the problem. What he does with my thoughts is up to him. I am only guessing. I know nothing about building boats. It will be interesting to see what he does. Never expect anyone who asks for your thoughts to use them. Simply give the best you can and wait to see what happens. In this case he could ask," he showed ten fingers two times, "men the same question he asked me. It's possible that all of them would come up with something different. Whatever sounds best to him is what he'll do. It's what he *should* do."

Despite the cold weather, Manak-na could not stand not being able to bathe. Finally he asked Mogil, "Where do men bathe here? I fear getting lice."

"Some go to the salt water and go in unclothed. It's cold for that with the wind, and I don't feel clean from salt water. You can take a large scoop for water and go to the creek up the hill on the right and get someone, like Yomuk there, to scoop water over you until you're clean, or just go into the creek to bathe. It is cold, but you'll survive. That's what I do. Some of the men never bathe. I'm guessing you've smelled them?"

Manak-na smiled. "Yes."

Since there was plenty of time before the evening meal, Manak-na and Yomuk went to the creek and bathed in the frigid water. They shivered and dressed quickly, but they were invigorated and felt wonderfully clean. Each had brought a large skin to help keep them warm until they returned to the boatbuilders' camp. It came in handy over their heads and around their shoulders. Once at camp, each crouched near the hearth to warm up.

When Wisdom returned color to the land, Manak-na awakened before the drum. He wondered what had caused him to wake up, but could find nothing unusual. He lay there wondering whether this adventure had been wise. Instead of learning many new things quickly, he found he contributed as much as he gained. He wondered if Domur was doing well. He hoped the winter wasn't too bad. He thought about his children, Tuma and Mhank, and his grandchildren. So many uncertainties. It would not behoove him to think this way, he convinced himself. The drum sounded and he got up, his thoughts dissipating like a morning fog in strong sunlight and breeze.

Manak-na dressed and went outside. The morning was clear and there was a light wind. He remembered he was clean and he breathed deeply expecting his clean skin to breathe with him. He returned inside and food was already put out. He got his bowl and helped himself. This morning the food was outstanding. There was a tiny difference in the seasoning on the meat and there were blueberries. He would like to congratulate the cook, but it occurred to him that he'd never seen the cook.

He asked Rokuk, "Why do we never see the cook? This food is wonderful. I'd like to thank him."

"Hope you don't see him! A bear got him in the face. He can see and he has a nose, but his features are rearranged and he is terribly scarred. He hides from us, so don't press it."

"Do you ever see him?" Manak-na asked.

"Yes. I'm the only one. He is my cousin. And he does cook well."

Manak-na looked sincerely at the man, "If there is ever a time when you can tell him, please let him know that I really appreciate his cooking. It would be hard to work here if the food were not so good. Rokuk, is he connected to the people who live up the hill?"

Rokuk smiled. "Yes, Manak-na. They are my people. We are from a people distantly related to the Mol. They live to the west of the big lake.

Komus still makes contact with them. We are sea faring adventurers and have lived at the sea since time began. We all moved here from the far south. We lived on the sea coast north of here where it was very cold. We lived off seal, a food we love, and it keeps us healthy. When we split with those to the northwest, we moved here to continue with the sea. They moved further west. Komus's people are part of our people. They live east of the other group. When the bear on that hill to the north injured Mirk, he didn't want to have people looking at him. Our people already had an arrangement like now with the boatbuilders. The cook at that time was very old. The boatbuilders asked Mirk to learn to cook, so he could eventually take over from the old cook. It worked well. It solved two problems: we got a good cook and Mirk found a place he could work without being stared at. Mirk gets here before the drum in the morning and leaves after the drum in the evening. Sometimes he hears people talking about his food and it pleases him. I'll tell him what you said."

"You don't go to your people at the end of the day. Why?" Manak-na asked.

"If you are a boatbuilder, you must live here. It's part of the way things have been since time for boatbuilding began, and that is generations and generations and generations. I don't mind. My wife died giving birth to our first child. I didn't want another wife, so this life pleases me."

"Well, I'm glad you're here," Manak-na said, and he meant it.

The hunters dispersed for the day of hunting, and the boatbuilders returned to the edge of the sea. A few of them looked at Manak-na and wondered what manner of man he was. He had solved a problem they had worked to solve and for which they were unable to find any solution. And he'd never built a boat.

—◆—

The People had come to enjoy their temporary home. Food was abundant, caves were spacious, and they kept warm easily. Since the first white rainfall, there had been little more. Tiriku took off for the privy, and on his way back he heard a noise that he couldn't place. He curiously followed the sound, trying to learn the source. When he reached the level of the pond, he found the sound came from the north end, so he jumped through untrodden white rain to reach it. There he found a raven with a strange looking wing. The two animals stared at each other. Tiriku had no inclination to injure the bird. The bird took heart and rested quietly to see what would happen.

Tiriku turned and bounded over roots and fallen limbs to find Ki'ti. He reached the home cave and looked all around, and then used his nose to find what his eyes could not see. Her scent went down in the cave so he followed as quickly as he could.

"What are you doing little dog?" Ki'ti asked when she spotted him.

He had been trained not to bark unless strangers were around, so he made very quiet whining sounds and trotted up to the main level of the cave. He turned to see if Ki'ti followed. She didn't, so he kept repeating the pattern. Finally, she realized he wanted her to follow, so she did. Her curiosity was great. When she realized he wanted her to follow outside, she wasn't very happy to go out, but she put on her boots and warm outdoor clothing and followed. Tiriku led her. Untuk-na followed Ki'ti. They took the strange route beyond the pond and heard odd sounds.

"It's a raven," Untuk-na said.

Sure enough, Tiriku had led them straight to a young raven with a broken wing.

"You brought me here because the raven has a broken wing?" Ki'ti asked Tiriku.

Tiriku sat by the raven as if they were friends. Ki'ti didn't hesitate. Smiling at Tiriku, she lifted the raven into her arms and the raven remained calm. She turned and they went back to the home cave with the bird. Inside the cave the People were shocked to see Ki'ti arrive with a raven, but when they considered the dogs she'd had, they simply quieted and watched.

Elemaea saw the raven and raced over to her mother. "Is it hurt?" she asked.

"Yes," Ki'ti replied and smiled at Elemaea. "Would you go outside and find something that the raven can use as a perch?" she asked her small daughter.

Elemaea put on boots and her warm garments for outside. Maig, the son of Tita and Keemu, joined her to help. It was a beautiful day and they went first to the bone pile. Nothing seemed right so they walked the path to the first night cave and found a branch that had fallen in the wind. It was large enough to support a raven without tipping over. They removed a few limbs that were in the way and carried their find back to the home cave.

They stopped at the entryway to hang up their winter gear and then found Ki'ti. She showed them a spot at the back of the cave where they could put the limb. They had done well, and she told them so. The youngsters glowed with the praise. Ki'ti added, "When you next go outside, you might look for some moss to put under the perch. It could get messy there." The two looked at each other. They asked Likichi for a basket and left to find moss.

They filled the basket and carried it back, putting moss under the perch where the raven was likely to need it.

Ki'ti meanwhile had been working with the raven's wing. Finally, she asked for Likichi who was their healer. Likichi came over and felt the wing. She left and returned with leather strips that were fairly short and stiff and some other things, including honey. She had Ki'ti hold the wing in a specific way while she applied the stiff leather with honey and other pieces of softer leather to the bird. She folded the wing against the bird's body, tied it with soft leather strips, trying diligently to construct the support so that it could not come apart. She knew the wing should remain immobile for a time. The raven seemed patient through all this attention, but he kept watch over what they did. It also kept looking at Tiriku. Tiriku could not take his eyes off the raven.

When Likichi finally felt satisfied that she'd done her best for the raven, she handed the bird to Ki'ti, and Ki'ti put it on the perch. Likichi went to a place where she had many containers and herbs. She reached out for a small gourd. She went to the water gourds and put some water into the small gourd. She carried it to the raven.

"With all this attention, Raven," she said, "you should heal well and don't be a pest while you visit here." The bird turned his head sideways and looked at her.

"I know a thing about ravens," Likichi said sharply.

The raven made a really odd sound and sat there as if someone else had made the sound.

Likichi said, "I thought so. Behave yourself, Bird!"

The raven hopped off the perch and drank some water. Then it hopped back onto the perch and seemed satisfied. What astounded Ki'ti was that Tiriku curled up near the raven. He seemed to plan to remain there for some time.

As the evening meal was served, there was increased movement in the cave, and the raven moved around a little on its perch. After the evening meal, scraps were given to the dogs. Tiriku got his and Ki'ti watched as he brought it and held it out for the raven. She was astounded. The raven cocked its head, reached out carefully, and took the offered meat from Tiriku's mouth. Tiriku bounded back outside and found a piece of meat much smaller for himself, but it seemed to satisfy him. Untuk-na came over to Ki'ti, who said, "Did you see that?"

"I did. I cannot believe what my eyes have seen, but I did see it."

In another part of the cave Domur was busying herself with hand coverings she was making for Rish. She had found that keeping very busy was the best means to deal with the absence of Manak-na.

Just before they went to their sleeping place, Ki'ti and Untuk-na noticed that the raven had left the perch and was snuggled up to Tiriku. The vision of the two animals was one that Ki'ti seared into her mind web. It was to her utterly sweet. Never had she seen such a thing and she didn't expect ever to see one again, unless it was these two. She and Untuk-na snuggled into bed but before they closed their eyes, they took another peek at the two sleeping animals. Tiriku was curled like half a nest for the raven.

When Wisdom returned color to the land, Ki'ti and Untuk-na were up and had their sleeping materials rolled up and stored against the side of the cave. Ki'ti took a piece of jerky to Tiriku and told him to give it to the raven. That way, he would get his own food. Tiriku seemed to understand clearly, because he trotted over to the raven with the jerky and held it out to the bird. The raven again cocked its head and then took the jerky from the dog.

Then, Tiriku raced out of the cave to the privy and back. The raven was concerned when Tiriku left the cave. The raven hopped off the perch and headed to the entryway hopping fast along the ground. It looked a sight with a piece of soft rabbit fur wrapped around it and tied and tied. The fur on the raven made it look ragged. Nobody in the cave laughed, but several of the People watched it, fascinated. The raven looked outside and did not see the little dog. It saw other dogs that were not as favorably impressed with ravens, and the bird backed up, unsure what these dogs would do. Finally, it spotted a fast moving little dog and realized it was the dog it knew. The raven stood in the entryway and was greeted by the little dog licking its beak and head. The dog was ready to continue licking the raven, but the raven took its beak and nudged the dog along the neck. Then, the raven returned to its perch and jerky. Tiriku got his food at the entryway, ate, and then came inside to the raven.

Winter passed very much as winters had in their prior home of the cave and bent trees. The weather seemed no colder or warmer. The place was very suitable and meat was plentiful. They had also been able to dry many vegetables and fruits for the winter so they had good food in variety. They loved the place and some were not looking forward to the time when they'd leave.

As days passed, Likichi checked the raven to see if the wing had healed. She had to wipe off the sticky honey and extend the wing. The raven looked at her with what could only be called surprise. The wing healed beautifully. Tiriku came close and began to lick the honey residue off the wing. At first Likichi tried to push him away, but the raven seemed to want the attention from the dog and held out its wing, so Likichi left them alone. She had, after all, done what she was asked to do. She wondered now whether there would be two animals living in the cave. She didn't have to wait long for an answer. The raven hopped to the entryway. Tiriku followed. The raven went outside and hopped along the path for a moment. It tried out its wings and they worked. It swooped up into the air and came back down right next to Tiriku. Tiriku seemed to understand. It was time for the raven to go. The raven nudged Tiriku and then hopped a bit and took off to the skies, calling and calling. And then it was gone. Tiriku came into the cave, lay down near the perch and rested his head on his forepaws. He did not move his head. He seemed to know the raven was gone. For two days he remained waiting.

On the third day, Maig stopped Ki'ti and asked if she'd like him to remove the perch and clean the area of the raven's perch. She told him she would really appreciate it. As soon as the area was cleared and cleaned, Tiriku stopped his wait and began again to follow Ki'ti wherever she went in the cave.

Occasionally when Tiriku was outside, the sound of a raven above made the little dog search the sky. Not all raven calls affected him. When he responded, Ki'ti was certain that it was the voice of his friend. They also began to notice that certain sounds of ravens meant that there was something afoot in their area, usually an animal, but sometimes it was an eagle. It was as if the ravens were telling them something about their environment. When they heard the sound, they'd check the pathways to be sure the notice wasn't about a person.

One day as the weather warmed, they heard a raven call that announced something in their environment. Tiriku recognized the sound of his friend. Ki'ti and Untuk-na looked carefully and saw someone approaching from the west. It looked like Kipotuilak. Sure enough, the adventurer began the ascent to their cave. The raven flew over to Tiriku when the man started up the hill. The raven bounced its side right into Tiriku who licked the raven's beak and eye. The raven rolled over and Tiriku played gently with the bird. Then, when the traveler came closer, the raven hopped three times and took off with a raucous call.

Kipotuilak said he was heading back to the boatbuilders' camp. He just fit there so much better than with his people. Domur was devastated. She hoped that Manak-na would not be like this man. Kipotuilak asked if he could stay a night or two before heading on. The People at the cave were delighted.

That night he told about arriving home in the mountains. His wife was not really delighted to see him. She had been alone for so long that she had come close to another and preferred him. He left the bag he'd carried to her with her and the children and tried to fit in, but he just wanted to return to the boatbuilders' camp and take another sea voyage. He said he considered remaining on the other side of the water where it was warm and fruit was available everywhere.

When he left, Domur felt relief. Maybe the boatbuilders needed him more than they needed Manak-na. She thought how wonderful that would be, but she knew that Manak-na would be an asset to any who knew him, and she let her hope evaporate.

Elemaea had found her fit. Her spear points and blades were becoming exceptionally good and she loved knowing it. There was something calming about making them. She could feel the points in the rock and was convinced it was her job to free the points gently from their stone encasement. Ekuktu-na was delighted to work with her. She seemed to have an inherent sense of how to free the point from the rock. Ki'ti was delighted. She had worried about her daughter and to know that she was happy doing something that was so needed pleased Ki'ti enormously. What still worried Ki'ti was finding her successor.

As the days became warmer, Ki'ti and Nanichak-na spoke about moving north. It seemed time to begin to gather what they would take and prepare. The white rain was gone from their area, only the wet soil still remained, and when that was gone it would be time to start trekking. At the men's council they discussed it. They would start to prepare for the move.

Manak-na and Yomuk had found a deer and had brought it to the boatbuilders' camp. They were carrying two logs to the salting pen when they saw Pah.

"Halt a moment," Pah called out. "We will leave in ten days. You both will go, if you still wish to travel on the boat."

Manak-na realized Pah was asking a question. He answered, "I really wish to go."

Yomuk who had paid good attention said, "So do I."

"Then, when it's time, report to the boat when the drum sounds. Do not stop to eat. Bring your things with you."

"Will we have any other notice?"

"Yes," Pah replied, "I will tell you again the day before."

"Thank you," Manak-na said.

"I thank you also," Yomuk said.

"Wait until you are safely back here to thank me," Pah said.

Manak-na smiled.

Yomuk copied his uncle.

After Pah left, Manak-na told Yomuk not to talk to the others about the boat trip.

"Why?" Yomuk asked, surprised.

"Because I don't know who else is going. I don't know if some people, who worked here longer than we have, may want to go and not be chosen. It is wise to keep your own information to yourself."

"What if someone asks if we are going."

"Tell whoever it is that you hope to go. That is true."

"I see."

"I am very excited to know how a boat like this one feels on water like this," Manak-na said, feeling the excitement of youth.

"I, too, Uncle."

"A few days. Just a few days."

Time passed and when Wisdom returned color to the land, the men were up and dressed when someone came in the door. Manak-na was surprised to see Kipotuilak. All the men in the camp surrounded the traveler.

"Just couldn't leave you," he jested. The men were obviously glad to see him.

"What's Pah up to these days?" he asked looking at the boatbuilders.

"Seems like a trip is coming up pretty soon. We hunters have had to bring intestines for quite a while when we gut the beasts. Provisions have been loaded in waterproof gut bags and bladders, coconuts have been traded and loaded, and the boat is different this time. Two boats have been made into one very big one."

"I've got to see this boat after I get something to eat." Kipotuilak took his backpack and placed it and spears on a bed with no bedding at the far back of the camp. He took off his jacket and pulled out his bowl and began to find food that he wanted.

Manak-na hoped the appearance of Kipotuilak would not cancel his offer of the boat trip. He knew time would make all things clear, so he kept silent and waited. He ate and enjoyed the food. Yomuk had no such thoughts and was enjoying the morning, eager for the hunt.

When the drum sounded, Manak-na and Yomuk put on their warm clothing and gathered their spears and went outside. They headed off to the forest eager to find a deer and return early. They went northwest and before they had gone very far at all, they saw a deer. To get downwind of the deer would involve some maneuvering in the forest, but they were up to it.

Carefully they used the hunter's walk of silence and got downwind of the deer. Manak-na shouted and the two approached the deer at a dead run. The deer was startled long enough for them to get their spears set. The deer took off at a run spears and all. The two followed the deer looking at the ground when they lost sight of it. It had quite a run and lost a lot of blood. Finally, they caught up with it where it had fallen over.

"Well, we won't have to bleed this one," Manak-na said quietly.

"Why?" Yomuk asked.

"It bled so much as it ran that it drained the blood from it. It fell over when it was out of blood."

"That's amazing," his nephew said aloud as he thought it.

"Let's get this animal prepared and get back to the boatbuilders' camp," Manak-na said.

"Good!" Yomuk said with enthusiasm.

The two worked together well after all their practice. This time they retained the gut after pushing as much of the offal out as possible. They hung the deer and were soon on their way back to the boatbuilders' camp. They began to work on the bamboo salting.

Not long after they began transporting bamboo logs, Pah came over and stopped them. "We leave tomorrow. Be ready when the drum sounds. Do not eat. Just bring all your things and come to the boat. Your friend, Kipotuilak, will join us."

Manak-na smiled, "We'll be there."

Yomuk said, "Yes, we will."

Pah smiled back. He wondered whether they'd get sea sick. He wondered what they'd think of their first storm at sea. They had such an adventure ahead.

Chapter 4

Pah opened his eyes. His tiny sleeping place in the hut in the center of the boatbuilding place had cramped his left leg, and he slid to the floor to walk around, unkinking the muscles. He pulled on his tunic. His gray hair required little care. Pah hardly moved in his sleep. He smoothed his hair and put his headband on to hold it in place. He was very thin, often becoming so deep into his work that he forgot to eat. He was excited to see how the boat would do when it was released. They had dug a deep pit, and kept out much of the sea water by making an earthen dam. Today they'd dig out the dam and let water flood the boatbuilding dugout. Poles propped up the hulls. When the boat began to float, the props would be removed. How many times had he done this? Pah could not remember. Each time it was exciting, but this time, there was something new. He had changed the structure of the boat. This one was enormous. He was eager to know what that would mean to the overall function. They'd try out the boat just offshore and then he'd return to land to start another. Based on his partial day experience, the results of testing would determine whether he'd build single boats or one large one. He was convinced that a partial day was not enough experience, but testing the boats never showed what would really occur in unusually fast currents, rough seas, high wind, or contrary gods of the underwater. There were so many factors to consider. He wouldn't know for a certainty until the boat returned.

He recognized that he should eat, but he never hungered in the morning. Based on strict discipline and his practical nature, he went to the cookhouse part of the boatbuilders' camp and Mirk brought him a purple bowl filled with Pah's favorite foods from what was available. Mirk smiled his very crooked smile and Pah put his hand on the cook's shoulder and thanked him. He knew before he ate, that it would be wonderful food. He stood in the doorway looking out to sea. The day was perfect. A slight breeze came off the water, the sky was blue, and wave action was fairly gentle. Already men were digging the earthen dam away from the front of the boat. They had planned departure, knowing the tide would be exceptionally low and that would make the digging effort much easier. He deeply inhaled the salty air. Pah loved the sea. When he finished eating he wiped his purple bowl and hung it on a protrusion from the wall of the cookhouse where Mirk kept it. It was a shell from the sea. He prized the color and the feel of the bowl.

Pah walked down to the boat and stood, critically examining it in the sunlight. With Manak-na's suggestion on the hull connectors made from trees, there was a solid place for each of the two masts. The best mast maker had crafted them. The front mast was situated over the top front tree hull connector to the left of center, and the back mast was situated over the top middle tree hull connector to the right of center. There was a tight indentation to fit the bottom of each mast dug into the tree. When it was raised, the mast sank down into the indentation. Tight ropes fastened to the front and sides of the boat held the masts in place. To each mast was attached a perpendicular bamboo log to which the bottom of the sail was lashed. The women up the hill had woven the exceptional triangular sails from long sea grasses. An extra sail was folded and laid in the lower level, well tied to the flooring. In case weather made sailing unsafe, the masts would be laid down. There were two sails, one for each mast to propel the boat forward. When the wind was safe, both sails were unfurled and full sailing would move the boat smoothly through the water. When wind was very swift, the back sail could be furled so the boat would not go too fast on the water. When the seas were stormy and wind and waves were high, both sails would be furled, and the masts would be folded down and secured by rope. A center board between the two halves of the boat was placed on the lower level as a help to keep the boat moving in the desired direction. It could be lifted out or lowered to different levels to achieve the desired effect.

Pah went to the compound rudder, flat steering mechanisms on poles in the back of the boat that turned the boat. Because there were two hulls, Pah had insisted on a rudder apiece at the end of each hull. The rudder blade was an attachment to a pole made of wood wrapped by very thin rope so that the pole did not show very much. The design involved a rectangular blade structure that stood out from the pole to provide a large surface where the women had woven extremely tight sea grasses and layered the weaving multiple times so that it was awkward, but would push firmly against the water to steer the boat. It was layered for strength. At the top of the pole, there was a pegged part that rotated on a flat piece of stone. It held the rudder handle securely, and the peg prevented it from slipping down into the water. At the underside of the place on deck where the stone was attached, another peg had been hammered through the pole that held the rudder. That peg prevented the rudder from rising. The rudder handle, parallel to the deck, was pegged into the pole, and it was about as long as a man was tall. Wrapped ropes reinforced places where poles were pegged. Each hull had the same form of rudder. Ropes connected the rudder handles to keep them doing the same thing at the same time. They used their best rope for this function. They could not use rope that would shrink and relax significantly. When the water was too forceful for one person to hold the rudder, a second man would be called to push the second rudder handle. On the deck on both sides at the back of the boat, there were stones secured to the flooring. The stones had holes in them. When the boat was tracking well on the sea, a short pole could be inserted in the rock and that could be used to hold the rudder handles. The short poles had pegs above and below the floor to secure them from rising or falling. By securing rudder handles, it freed the person who would be steering the boat to do other things. The stones with the holes that fixed the rudder handles also served as anchors. Ropes threaded through the hole in the rocks and tied tightly at the end allowed other rocks to be added and the ropes were gently lowered to the sea floor and tied to the boat to hold the boat in place.

On the exterior of the hulls, ropes were tied to the bamboo for rowing. When there was a need to row, men would sit on the hull in designated places, tying themselves to the hull. Oars would also be tied to the boat on ropes about as long as a man was tall. By placing the ties at specific places on the boat and tying them to the oars where a short peg showed the place below which to tie the oar, the oars were able to be used in a synchronous pattern for efficiency and the ties tethered the oar. If a man lost his grip on an oar, it would not become detached from the boat. Near the oar tether there were rests built into the hull structure for the oars to provide leverage for rowing. They were strong branches with a forked end for resting the oar.

Pah examined all parts of the boat. He checked the supplies in the bottom level and the mat covered huts on either side of the masts on the top level. The huts were places for sleeping, to avoid the sun, or to warm up when it was cold. There was a cooking area outside the opening of the hut on the right side of the boat facing forward, and it was frequently used.

As the drum sounded, men from the boatbuilders' camp began to head either to the privy or to the boat. There was little discussion. When Manak-na and Yomuk reached the boat, Pah told them to take their things to the far back of the hut on the right side facing forward and tie them into the gut wrappers they'd find. The gut wrappers would keep their belongings dry. Along with gut wrappers there were coils of rope of various sizes. Pah told them to tie their spears to the ties at the top of the hut. The rope coils were all around the edges of the hut. Manak-na and Yomuk really didn't know the other men well, and their sleeping places would be very close. Each hut held fifteen men, but they alternated times for sleep. There was no level place. Manak-na wondered whether the rope coils would interfere with sleep, while he reminded himself that this was an adventure.

Water from the undammed barricade was filling the hole where the boat rested on logs. Yomuk stood on the edge of the hull, holding onto a rope, to watch the water swirl around the base of the boat. There were many little bubbles floating on the surface of the water. He was as excited as he'd ever been in his life. He couldn't believe that he and Manak-na were about to travel across this huge sea to a land where it was warm. He'd heard that there was much adventure between, including colder weather, storms, fog, huge waves, and sea monsters. Yomuk wondered whether there was such a thing as a sea monster. When the boat moved slightly, Yomuk grabbed another rope that was nearby to steady himself. The masts had been raised and ropes seemed to be everywhere. Manak-na did some foot shuffling to get his balance. His heart began to race with excitement. He had wanted an adventure for so long. Now he had one!

The dam's removal, creating a seawater backfill from the dam along with the incoming tide, would make the escape from the building hole work well. People, who were already seasoned seamen, were moving about the boat, aware of what was needed and what they should do. There was good-natured shouting. Manak-na and Yomuk went towards the back of the boat near the hut they shared and tried to stay out of the way of others. Manak-na saw many people digging he'd never seen before. He guessed they were men from the village up the hill. It was a lot of work to move all that dirt.

The boat was floating in its small pond. It was still trapped by some of the dam, but people were digging as fast as possible to open it up. Manak-na noticed some activity below him. He leaned over the back of the boat and found that men were pulling wooden logs out from under the boat. He had not noticed the boat was sitting on logs. *How much more was there that he didn't know?* he wondered. *Soon,* he expected, *he'd find out. After waiting so long to learn things he didn't know, he was about to have days and days of learning.*

Pah was all over the boat. It was leaving the building hole now and he wanted to know whether everything was functioning correctly. He checked the masts and the sails. He found one loop that hadn't been tied securely, and he called to Ralm to fix it. The man was there instantly and worked it carefully. Pah checked the fitting at the bottom of the mast and was pleased to see that the mast was well established. No problems there. He checked the decks and the tiller. The handle to move the rudder was new and he wondered how well it would survive the trip. It seemed to be working well. He moved it, finding it harder to move than he expected. He'd speak to Rokuk about having more than one man assigned to the rudders full time. He called the man over. Manak-na and Yomuk watched as Pah talked to Rokuk. It seemed that Rokuk would be responsible for much on the boat.

Pah took an oar and went to an exterior hull side and tried to seat himself on the bamboo hull. It worked. He tied himself and the oar to the ties already affixed to the boat. He seemed pleased with how that was working, but then that was not a new way of doing things—just separated by quite a long distance from one side to the other.

Pah called, "Rowers!"

Suddenly people were running all over the boat. They grabbed an oar from the tie on the sides of the huts and ran to the rowing places. Each seemed to know exactly where to go. Then a man whose name they didn't know began to use the Mol numbers to count. One … two, one … two. In synchronization with the count, the men rowed. Manak-na and Yomuk watched carefully, knowing they'd be called on to row sometime. The boat began to move slowly across the water, free of the boatbuilding hole. Out on the sea it moved, huge, seemingly proud and confident upon the water. It moved in ways that were new to Manak-na and Yomuk. The liquid environment was very different from their land environment.

"It's easier if you keep your knees bent," Manak-na said to Yomuk.

Yomuk tried it. Somehow it all felt so foreign. He kept his knees bent but didn't realize that he needed to rise and lower himself one leg at a time, so he just walked on stiff, bent legs as they took to the sea. Yomuk watched as the shore gained distance. He choked a little at thoughts of home.

Pah continued to move about the boat still checking and re-checking. He called on some of the men to unfurl the front sail. They did it so fast that Manak-na was dumbstruck. One moment there was no sail and then there was one. It was surprisingly beautiful to Manak-na. It moved his spirit as it moved. And the boat began to move. It wasn't fast, but it moved faster than the rowers could row. The rowers were told to remain seated but to pull up the oars. Pah called for the second sail to be unfurled. Then the boat began to move faster. Manak-na inhaled sharply. This was a wonder. It was alive! It was a way of using the wind to make a huge boat move. His heart was beating fast with amazement. These people were filled with a knowledge he'd never dreamed of—they'd taken what looked like great bird wings and fixed them to a boat to make it move. He was overwhelmed. He knew about poling boats. In the time it took to eat a meal, he'd learned about rowing and sailing. Manak-na felt that if he learned nothing else, his adventure already had great benefit. To the Mol on the boat, there was nothing unusual about what they were doing, nothing unusual at all except for the size of the boat.

Pah called Rokuk over. He told him to head to shore. Rokuk realized that it was time for him to take over. He was also excited to be directing this new experiment on the double hulled boat. He called for men to furl the back sail. He called to rowers. Using the rudder, he turned it to the right, which made the boat head towards the left. When the boat was still several boat lengths from shore, Pah waved farewell, and he dived off the boat into the sea. He swam fast toward shore. Then he stood on shore and watched as the boat headed north on the sea. He had taken these trips when he was younger. He was happy now to leave the traveling to the younger men and to spend his time boatbuilding.

Rokuk was delighted that they had a favorable wind for the first part of the trip. He told the men to tie up the oars to the huts, the chosen place to secure them when not used, and to take their sailing positions. Manak-na and Yomuk had no idea what a sailing position was so they headed toward Rokuk to find out.

"You want to know what your sailing positions are?" Rokuk asked with a smile.

"Yes," Manak-na and Yomuk replied in unison.

"Manak-na, I'll put you on the deck behind the back sail. If I call to furl the sail, you'll help Ralm. While you sit near him, ask what you need to do. He'll tell you, so you'll be ready."

Manak-na nodded.

"Yomuk, go to the back and sit by the hut. Piman controls the rudder right now. He'll need a helper, because it's hard to move the rudder. It's your job to help him. When you get back there, tell him you're his helper and do what he tells you."

"I will," Yomuk replied, remembering to acknowledge. He headed toward the back of the boat.

They traveled on and on. Sometimes land was visible on the right and sometimes the left, sometimes on both sides at the same time. The boat made creaking noises from the bamboo and other wood. Manak-na and Yomuk were having a wonderful time watching the scenery pass. The boat was floating gently on the sea and they enjoyed it all. When the sun was above, a young man walked through with a water bag and another came with meat sticks. They could have as much water and as many sticks as they wanted. They drank plenty of water, knowing that the meat sticks would draw water from their bodies. As the day lengthened, Manak-na and Yomuk began to feel the inactivity. Normally, they would have done much moving about by this time. They had been sitting for a long time. Yomuk had spent a little time with Piman adjusting the rudder, but that took little effort for the time they'd spent. The person who did the most moving about was Rokuk. He was obviously leader of the boat. They wondered where Kipotuilak was. He did not share their hut, so he must be in the other. Then Manak-na heard him speaking briefly at night while they were in the hut to sleep. It appeared that they'd see little of Kipotuilak. He worked at night.

When Wisdom began to suck color from the land and sea, the boat continued on. Rokuk called half the boatmen to sleep. The other half of the boatmen would sail through the night. Manak-na and Yomuk were called for the first sleep, as were Piman and Ralm. Different men took the rudder. The winds were calm and all was well.

Just before Wisdom raised the sun above the horizon, restoring color with an arc of brilliant rays of sunlight, the men were called to wake up to eat. When they finished eating, the other half of the group went to sleep. Manak-na found it unnatural that men could sleep when there was sunlight. He really hadn't thought about travel on a ship. In some ways, he supposed he'd thought that they would stop and all would sleep at night. It fascinated him that the boat could sail at night and Rokuk or someone else would know where they were going. He definitely felt untrained and incapable of understanding much of what was happening. He didn't feel comfortable in the role of a virtual child in knowledge of boat travel, so he began to ask questions.

Most people, he found, were more than willing to share. They found sharing their information with someone who really wanted to know to be refreshing.

At night it was cold on the boat. Wind off the water carrying moisture made it feel as if cold penetrated right through clothing. Many times, Manak-na was grateful that his sleeping time came at night. He could wrap his skins around him to keep off the chill. A few times he'd resort to putting on his season-of-cold-days pants and jacket just to sleep. Yomuk did so a bit more often. Sleeping wasn't exactly comfortable. With all the ropes coiled up, it wasn't possible to lie down straight anywhere. But, Manak-na would remind himself—this was part of the adventure.

One night after being on the water for many days, Yomuk awoke to the sound of thunder and raindrops falling on the woven roof. He could hear them hit but no water seemed to come into the hut. The boat, instead of gently rocking on the water, was tilting wildly from one side to the other. The creaking was intensified. Yomuk was frightened. He could see light through a few holes in the matting. Lightning was flashing, followed by more booms of thunder. He noticed that the others were sleeping and he didn't want to waken them. He took one of his skins and put it over his head, hoping to cut out some of the noise and flashing light. It didn't really help, and it removed some of the warmth from his legs. He fought the skins in the cramped space, finally getting his bedding into the form that normally helped him sleep, but he was too frightened for slumber. He did lie down and try to be quiet. With his fear and the rocking of the boat he felt a little nausea rising up. He curled up pulling his legs to his chest, but that still didn't help much. He listened to the sound of the thunder and noticed that it sounded farther and farther away. That gave him a sense of relief. Looking toward Manak-na, he wondered how anyone could sleep through the noise. Even the rocking seemed to decrease somewhat. He felt a little better, so he tried hard to return to sleep. After quite some time, he fell into a troubled sleep.

When Wisdom returned color to the land and sea with a clear sky, Yomuk asked Manak-na if he heard the storm during the night. Manak-na smiled. "I heard nothing," he replied. "I had a wonderful sleep and dreamed of going to places far away."

"Well, it scared me," Yomuk admitted. "The boat was moving up and down in large waves and I found that frightening. I almost rolled over on top of you but caught myself" he said looking at Manak-na. "You could see the sky light up through tiny holes in the matting over the hut. Thunder roared. The boat creaked louder."

"I guess, then, that you learned that a storm at sea rolls the boat around, makes it creak louder, and yet the storm abates, just like on land, and goes away. It's not something to fear."

"I wish I could calm myself as you seem to do. I am still stirred up about it."

When the men left the hut they had the morning meal and then relieved the men who had spent the night through the storm. Rokuk came over to the two of them and told them to sit. They sat and Rokuk handed each one a short piece of thin rope.

"Watch me tie this knot and then you tie one just like it," Rokuk said.

Each tried to tie the knot, but it seemed complicated and neither could do it on the first try. Rokuk demonstrated each step and had them follow. They were able to tie the knot correctly that time. Rokuk told them to try to do it by themselves and they were able to do it.

"Why this particular knot?" Manak-na asked.

"If we have a storm just a little stronger than last night, you will be told to tie up. When you hear that, you get a rope from the hut by your things and tie the rope around your waist. Then tie it to wherever you are working or sleeping on the boat. Tie it to the bamboo of the boat. If the sea becomes really rough—and last night was not really rough—you need to stay tied so you don't fall off the boat. In stormy weather it is not likely that if you fell off the boat anyone would know it happened. Even on a nice day, if you fell off the boat, it's unlikely we could find and save you. This boat doesn't really turn around. You must tie up if told, and you must use this knot. It won't come untied."

"Thank you," Manak-na said.

Immediately Yomuk followed with, "Yes, thank you."

"Did the storm wake either of you?" Rokuk asked.

"It waked me," Yomuk answered. "Everyone else was asleep and stayed asleep. I was frightened."

"Brace yourself, Yomuk," Rokuk said. "Out on the sea we can have lovely calm weather. Then the weather can cause a raging sea with high waves pounding the boat and winds that scream and blow so you can hear nothing else, as if they'd rip the very hut off the boat. It can be frightening, but realize the boat is built well and as long as you're tied on, when the storm abates, you'll be fine. Just don't tie yourself to the hut. Sometimes they do blow off. Tie yourself to the bamboo boat. Just realize that you are getting acquainted with the sea. It's not like land. The sea, however, is a wonderful place full of surprises. Look each day for the surprises and realize that you're as safe as you can be on this boat. Instead of letting yourself get frightened, pay attention to all around you all the time you're awake. You wanted an adventure, so Pah said. Enjoy all that happens as that—adventure."

Yomuk said, "Thank you Rokuk. I will put your words in my mind web and think on them. I will try, when I become frightened, to calm the fear and look around at what's happening, so I can enjoy this adventure and learn from it."

"Good," Rokuk responded. "Yomuk, how old are you?"

Yomuk was surprised. Nobody had asked his age. "I am," he showed ten fingers.

Rokuk grinned. "I thought so," he said. "You look older than you are and your behavior is mature for your age, but your fear was that of a boy. Be who you are, Yomuk. But you'll enjoy this adventure a lot more if you don't give in to fear, but rather look at what is happening and realize each time that you lived through what you feared. It will help you grow into a man."

Yomuk looked at the man. "Do you never become frightened on the boat?" he asked Rokuk.

"You remember how tall the boatbuilders' camp structure is?"

"Yes, I remember."

"Not often, but sometimes we have waves much more than four times that high. When that happens and the wind screams like a wild animal bigger than anything that grows on land, and the wave tops crash on the boat, sometimes, then, I get a little frightened. I've never been on a boat that a storm turned upside down. But I've always come out alive, so I have some fear, but it's not something that will paralyze me into a scared monkey. I have responsibilities and I see to them regardless of the weather—or my own fear."

"That's what you mean about being a man?"

"Exactly, Yomuk. Work through your fears and keep your mind web working well. Focus on responsibility. Do your work. In big storms your job is to make the rudder point us into the oncoming waves. That keeps us from flipping over. Piman will show you."

"I will do my best, Rokuk. Thank you."

Rokuk walked past him and touched his shoulder. Manak-na went to the area of the back sail and Yomuk went to the back of the hut near the rudder. Rain was gone and the sea was filled with waves and some wind, but it made the boat move more rapidly through the water. The creaking noises didn't seem so frightening to Yomuk. There was no longer any land to their right.

Ahead there was a large piece of land in the far distance. The sky was clear enough for them to see well.

Rokuk told Piman to change the direction of the rudder so the boat would begin to make a very slight right turn. Only one peg difference from where the peg was currently set would do. Yomuk came over to help and found that with the wave action and the wind the rudders were a little harder to move, but two of them could still do it. He returned to his place behind the hut to sit. He thought over and over the words of Rokuk. He had been frightened as a little child the night before. He was not ridiculed for his fear, but instead Rokuk had shown him a different way to approach fear. That was a new thought to him. Then he realized there was a story that he couldn't remember, but he seemed to think that the same subject was in one of his mother's stories. *Was there a story for everything?* he wondered.

Manak-na had listened to Rokuk. He was grateful that the man treated Yomuk so well. He could have been angered that he didn't know he had a youth on the boat, but that was not how he handled Yomuk. He handled the boy's fear very well. Manak-na thought Yomuk should have remembered a story that dealt with fear, but he realized that Yomuk was yet young and the stories probably hadn't made a big difference to him yet. There were several stories that dealt with fear. The story of Comargh-na and Elmindrid-na was one. They had just talked about that one. Of course, they were looking at a different aspect of the story when they talked about it. When they had time together he'd try to get Yomuk to organize the stories in his mind web, so when fear arose, he could look through his mind web and find the stories that dealt with fear and see what they'd tell him about the way to be wise. Suddenly, a sharp chill ran through Manak-na. He was thinking in terms of the mind web of the People. Perhaps, since Yomuk was part Mol, he had their scattered way of using his mind web. If that were the case, maybe he could help Yomuk organize some of his mind web and learn how to do it, so the information from the generations would be available to him. Manak-na couldn't imagine living safely without the stored information of the generations quickly available for guidance. He wondered whether the Mol who sailed to far lands were like the People, the inland Mol, or whether they used their mind webs differently yet. It would give him something to think about while he sat waiting to be available, if the sail were to be furled.

Two young men came through with food and water. Men all over the boat were ready for both. The boat sped toward the large land but it was clear they wouldn't stop there. They were heading out to sea where they could see no other land.

Once they moved away from land, the sea became somewhat more filled with waves a little higher and lower than what they'd experienced. They sped along. About high sun Manak-na was looking out at the horizon when a great spout of water rose off to the right side of the boat. It stank. Yomuk jumped up so he could see what caused the noise. Both saw the back of a huge creature in the water as it submerged leaving a great tail upright for a few moments. Manak-na and Yomuk looked at each other. No one else on the boat seemed surprised. Ralm, a man with skin colored a little darker than Pah's, explained to Manak-na that they had seen a whale. It was not a fish, because it had no gills. It breathed through nostrils on its head and that's what caused the spray. He told of encounters with the animals that sounded strange. The stories were of how these large animals occasionally helped people when their boats failed. He said whales sang. He told of dark colored whales, bluish ones, and white ones. The white ones were small. There was also a black and white whale, some of which had huge fins on their backs. They also had big teeth. Sometimes whales would hang in the water as if curious to observe the people on the boat.

Manak-na listened carefully. This Mol seemed to have a well organized mind web. He spoke in a coherent, sequential way. His description of the animals was well ordered. *What,* he wondered, *made the difference between the way he thought and used his mind web and the inland Mol, some of whom lived with his People now, used theirs?* He just couldn't understand. *Or was it that this man was not Mol or People or Minguat, but yet a different people.*

The animal they'd seen stayed around only briefly. Later a large number of fish literally flew by. Yomuk found the flying fish hilarious, and it caused him to giggle. Sometimes they'd land on the boat and the men on the boat would toss them back to the water. They were colorful and were so unlike anything they'd seen that Manak-na and Yomuk were fascinated. Manak-na got up and leaned over one of the hulls to stare into the salt water. Rokuk was beside him quickly.

"Any time you chose to lean over the side of the boat, Manak-na, you need to tie up. If you fell, it would be unlikely that we could rescue you. Safety is critical on the boat."

"I will remember," Manak-na said. "Thank you."

Realizing that he hadn't told Yomuk, Rokuk went to Yomuk and told him the same thing.

Manak-na thought a while about the information and how it had been delivered. He would have thought that information of a safety nature would be given before they put the boat in the water. He considered that this might be an example of how their mind webs differed. But then he thought about how children of the People were expected to watch to learn, not depend on direct teaching. But then no one had leaned over the side of the boat, so Manak-na couldn't learn that way. He thought of the style of hunting the People used. Direct teaching at the beginning of a hunt was an essential part of the way of learning for the young. It was designed to keep the young safe and avoid interference with hunters in an active hunt.

Ralm looked over at Manak-na. "Is it hard to learn what is required to sail in a boat? I've done it since I was a child. It seems to be part of me."

"I don't know the expectations like tying up before leaning over the edge of a boat. Are there other things I should know?"

Ralm thought for quite some time. "All I can think of right now is, if you are fishing, be sure not to hook a person on the boat."

"You fish from the boat?"

"Yes, when we tire of dried meat or just get bored. Sometimes we fish with hooks on lines and sometimes just with our hands. Sometimes as you saw with the flying fish, they join us. Flying fish provide many a serendipitous evening meal. We only gather fish when it looks as if we can cook the fish before the weather gets too bad for a fire on the boat. If the weather is nice, that doesn't mean we'll gather the flying fish for food. It's only if we decide they'd be good. Sometimes the flying fish are so small it's just too much work for a small amount of fish."

Manak-na found the idea of fishing and eating cooked fish on the boat convenient. This boat was wonderful in his eyes.

Behind the hut in the sunshine, Yomuk was drowsy. There was monotony about the boat ride. He hardly heard the boat creaking anymore, the sound joined other sounds he screened out. He still had edges of nausea when he remembered the storm he experienced that one night. Somehow he could not look at that as a great adventure. He realized that if storms arose with the same frequency at sea as they did on land, there would be many more, and Rokuk had made it clear that the storm he feared was but a small storm. He carried a seed of panic with him when he considered the larger storms. He hoped they wouldn't have one.

Wind picked up toward the time Wisdom would suck color from the land and sea. Ahead they could just make out a tiny island. Rokuk told Piman to make a change on the rudder and he did. They wanted to keep land to their left now. Yomuk helped Piman change the rudder. Yomuk considered the rudder. Whoever planned that part of the boat was clever, he was convinced. It was not something that anyone would have imagined easily. At least, he felt, he could not have. It would take a certain mind web to craft something like a rudder with the woven matting and the pegs in the pole along with the pegs in the stone holes to hold the rudder stick. Yomuk wished he had a mind web that could craft the ideas from which rudders sprang. He was thinking that these boatbuilders were on a level with superior hunters. He never thought there would be anyone other than hunters at that level of superiority. A flying fish landed beside his leg. Yomuk got up, picked up the fish, and tossed it behind the boat. He wanted to wash the fish slime off his hands. He didn't know how, so he wiped his hands on his leather tunic.

"Yomuk," Piman shouted, "There is a water bag hooked to that part of the hut." He pointed to the forward part of the hut.

Yomuk looked and saw it. He went over to the bag and lifted it down. He untied the neck and ran cold water over his hands. That felt a lot better. He shouted back to Piman, "Thank you!" Yomuk didn't mind meat from animals on his hands but fish slime bothered him.

The drum beat told the men that for the day boatmen it was time to sleep. Manak-na and Yomuk waited for their relief to arrive and then went to the hut. They had quite a bent over climb to reach the back of the hut. They made their beds, settled in, and prepared for sleep. With the rocking of the boat, both drifted off soon after finding a comfortable position.

When Manak-na arose the next day he emerged from the hut to see Rokuk, Piman, Ralm, Kipotuilak, and Skuku, the man who looked after the front sail in the day, looking to the east and then to the west, pointing, and discussing something very seriously. Manak-na was curious, but he said nothing. When the small group broke up, Ralm joined Manak-na.

"We have had a discussion. Do you see the reddish looking clouds?"

"Yes," Manak-na replied. "While Wisdom was returning color to the land and sea, the clouds did have a rosy hue."

"Those clouds normally mean that we will have a storm later. When I say storm, I mean one that is much more significant than the little one we had shortly after leaving the boatbuilding place. We know of a sheltered cove on one of the islands ahead. We were discussing whether to head for the cove or continue on as we are now, which would make us miss the cove. There is some question as to whether we can make the cove in time."

"What did you decide?" Manak-na asked.

"We decided to head for the cove. This boat is new design and construction. We think that we should avoid a terrible storm if at all possible. Now, help me get this sail unfurled so we can pick up some more speed."

The two men unrolled the sail and hooked it to the rope that would carry the top upwards. The wind caught and the speed increased. Manak-na loved to watch the two sails work together in the wind. They were like two wings of a bird seen from the side. The island ahead was the one with the cove. It came closer and closer as the day progressed. From the south and west and east clouds seemed to converge, ready to approach when they entered the cove.

Rokuk called for people to furl the sails and lower the masts and for others to row. Men ran to the huts and untied oars and quickly took their seats on the boat hulls. A man began the count in a voice that carried over the wind. Rokuk had come to the back of the boat near Piman. He and Piman turned the control of the rudder to the far right so that the boat would turn left. The boat entered the cove and turned to the left and then to the left again. Manak-na and Yomuk could see that the walls of the island would provide good shelter for the boat. When they approached land, Rokuk had men set out many anchors. Rokuk began a quick check of the boat. All seemed in order.

For some time nothing happened. Manak-na and Yomuk wondered what all the concern was. Maybe they misjudged the storm? While they waited, some men fished and caught white fish that they cooked for the evening meal. It tasted wonderful. Each man shared a coconut with another. It was a treat to have something other than dried meat for the evening meal. After the meal cleanup, men took empty bladders and water containers and put them where rain water would fall. They would collect them when full of rain water and stow them on the lower level of the boat, well tied so they did not leak or become contaminated by salt water.

As Wisdom sucked color from the land and sea, there were no stars visible. Clouds were circling about and rain had begun to fall. There was some lightning and thunder in the distance but nothing right overhead. When the drum beat, Manak-na and Yomuk went to the hut, got out of the rain, and prepared to sleep. Most of the men who worked at night had been told to go into the huts, so it was very crowded. None had slept long before the storm hit. Even in the cove, the boat was hit by winds and rocked hard. Fortunately, it was not tossed by the waves that would be running wild in the open sea or hit by waves crashing over them. By then Manak-na and Yomuk had learned that waves on the open sea could crash the boat from above. Both found that daunting. Anyone on deck without a tie up could be lost. It occurred to Manak-na that even people who had tied up could be washed off the boat, if the wave were strong enough to break the rope. With what he'd already seen, he believed there were waves strong enough to wash a tied up man off a boat. He would not share that thought with Yomuk.

The storm went on for several days. Yomuk realized what a small storm the first one was. He had learned to live with his fear of storms, because he had no other choice. Time in the cove gave him even more maturity. Certainly the first day he had experienced some panic, for the rocking was far greater than during the first storm. Lightning and thunder seemed to be everywhere at once. The noise of the storm did not stop. It shrieked louder than anything either of the People had ever heard. There was no way to avoid it. Even in the protected area, wind managed to enter through the tiny holes in the hut matting, making it cold inside where normally at night multiple sleeping bodies added warmth to the hut. They donned their season-of-cold-days pants not caring if they got wet. They added needed warmth.

During the day, Manak-na would strip off his clothing to tie up outside on the deck to watch the storm. He would lie on his back on the deck near the back sail looking up into the clouds. Securely tied to the boat, he felt safe. He listened to the loud boat creaking and the wind and men shouting. He imagined he was looking at the belly of a writhing beast in the clouds, a beast that threw noisy spears of fire at another writhing beast. It made him think of dragons in the sky. He was having an adventure! He was enthralled. He was also cold, but the cold seemed negligible compared to what he was seeing.

A few times Yomuk joined him to watch. He grew cold faster than Manak-na and had fear lurking in his belly. He'd soon return to the hut to dry off and dress in warmer clothing. Instead of finding a fascination in the clouds above, Yomuk was very grateful that the leaders of the boat had decided to go to the cove. He felt that what he was experiencing was about all he could take at this point. He recognized that there were storms worse than what he was experiencing and that edged his belly with panic. The panic subsided as he thought about the fact that no one else was concerned about the safety of the boat. Those who had been to sea would know. He hoped that if a storm came during the remainder of the travel that there would be a cove nearby to which they could flee.

One morning the drum sounded and as Manak-na and Yomuk awakened, they realized it was quiet. The wind was no longer blowing. They left the hut and went to the lower level where they used the sea off the back of the boat as their privy. The sky was blue and there were only a few white clouds passing by. Soon they'd leave the cove, they realized. It seemed to be a great day.

The mood on the boat was much improved. People occasionally smiled and there was an enthusiasm for moving the boat. After some of the men ate and drank water, they began to haul up the ropes with the anchors. The anchors were then returned to the tiller handle stake spots, and Rokuk called for rowers.

Manak-na asked whether he wanted them to row. Rokuk explained that he would tell them specifically when he wanted them to row. The others were experienced and the cove was a tight place. He didn't want any oars broken or confusion in the cove. He did actually thank Manak-na for offering.

They left the cove and traveled again on the open sea with a breezy and clear day. All of a sudden they began to see furry animals swimming in the sea. Not many, just a few at a time. Piman explained to Yomuk that they were seals. There were many varieties of seals and they had soft fur. It was warmer than fur of some other animals, such as deer. Some varieties were extremely soft. Men on the boat took some oddly shaped spears with ropes tied to them and threw spears at the seals. Sometimes they were successful. Ralm explained that the seals were a food source his people needed for good health. They would feast on seal that night.

Day after day after day they traveled along a series of mountains rising from the water. The mountains had no trees, but they were grassy. They saw some seals on the shore. It appeared that they might gather at some places to have their young. Yomuk was fascinated. They did spear a few more seals from the boat. Manak-na and Yomuk did not care for the seal, claiming it was too fishy, but the boatmen ate it. Those men with the darker skins divided up the livers. Manak-na and Yomuk enjoyed their meat sticks.

One day they sailed past an island where smoke was coming from the cone at the top of the hill. Manak-na knew immediately what that signified. Yomuk was not sure, so Manak-na explained that was a volcano and that the smoke from the top was not a good sign. It meant the volcano could explode and spew out rocks, liquid rocks, or ash—maybe all three.

They continued on, each day passing more and more islands. Sometimes a small storm would arise, but there was nothing like the big storm they weathered in the cove. As time passed, the islands became larger. One day they passed a large rock where there were brown animals bigger than seals. They proudly held their heads high on very thick necks and their whiskered faces looked like dogs, but they had tiny ears. Other rocks had seals perched upon them where they were resting from the sea. They spotted more of the big sea monsters with the spouts. The land and sea seemed more alive. The boat continued on, seemingly forever.

Rokuk stood near Manak-na one clear day and said, "Look at the mountains there, how they curve to the right. When we left the boatbuilding place, the sun rose on our right. As we passed the many islands, the sun rose straight ahead, and when we get to those mountains, the sun will rise on our left. What do you make of that?"

"I don't know what to think," Manak-na replied.

"It is how the earth lies. We traveled north until we turned right to follow the islands. Now we turn right again to travel south. We are about half way."

"If we're only half way, this land we live on is huge!"

"It is huge, Manak-na. I have traveled most of my life. I know that we could travel a lot further south. I have no idea how large the earth is."

"You say earth. Do you mean dirt when you say earth?"

"Not at all, Manak-na." Rokuk picked up a coconut. "See this coconut? It is round. The earth is like this coconut—not flat. When you look at the stars at night they look like flat round things, but instead they are like this coconut." Rokuk picked up a small stick of charcoal from the hearth. He marked an arc on the coconut showing roughly where they'd left heading north. He showed dots for the islands that went from the west to the east. Then he made land turn right to go to the south a far distance. "We will not go as far to the south as the middle of the coconut."

"How do you know that, Rokuk?"

"A sailing man knows it two ways: one is the sun. You get about equal sun and dark in the middle. You also get virtually no tide change at the middle."

"Rokuk, how do you know that?"

"The giant Mol left us that information. They traveled all over the earth. They studied the night sky for generations and generations and generations. They knew. We also have spent much of our lives on the sea. Didn't you stay at the cave where the paths cross?"

"Yes," Manak-na admitted.

"There is a place there where the giants studied the stars. They have circles around circles on the wall. That is the way we circle around the sun. The moon circles us and we circle the sun. There is at least one other earth that circles the sun. It is closer to the sun than we are. There are stars in the night sky that twinkle and dots of light in the night sky that don't twinkle. We live on one of the dots without a twinkle. The sun is fire. That's why it twinkles."

Manak-na was awed. He certainly knew that there were some objects in the sky that twinkled and some that didn't. He had never had anyone explain what the difference was. It struck him that, if the sun was fire—and it was hot enough to be fire—it would twinkle like fire at a distance, and that earth, this coconut-like thing they lived on, wouldn't twinkle, because it wasn't fire. He was overwhelmed with information. These people made boats and knew about the sky in ways he never dreamed of. What an opportunity he'd been given!

"Thank you, Rokuk. That is information I never heard, and it makes my mind web expand almost to bursting."

"We use the stars in the night sky to tell us where we are, and we use the sun in the day for the same purpose. You know the star that never moves?"

"Yes," Manak-na said.

"That star disappears if you live down here." Rokuk showed him the lower part of the earth on the coconut.

"Have you ever been that far?"

"No, but some of the people, who live where we're going, have been that far on land and on the sea."

Rokuk tossed Manak-na the coconut. "I've got to check the ties," he said and left.

Manak-na studied the coconut. He followed the way they'd traveled on the coconut. He could see the shoreline where they left and how they traveled between land areas. He could see the big land to the north where they turned off to follow the islands. He could see where the islands turned to land. He could see where they were! On a coconut called earth! A coconut that made circular paths around the sun! He yearned to share with Ki'ti. He would keep the coconut as a treasure. He put it in his gut wrapper in the hut.

More and more sea creatures floated by. Funny little furry faces with whiskers appeared on furry bodies floating on their backs. Some carried sea shells which they pounded with rocks. They could tell that the shells contained animals of some kind, and when the furry animals broke the shell with the rock, they had food. Yomuk couldn't take his eyes from the funny little floaters. They seemed to smile while they floated with their feet together sticking up. Some floaters had babies on their bellies. They floated in large groups.

Day after day they continued to travel. Occasionally when the winds became very calm, Manak-na and Yomuk would be assigned to row. They found at first that the work was tiring, but once they worked the muscles in their bodies, they enjoyed the effort. They were comparatively strong and each was put on a different side and they were placed at the end of the line of rowers so they didn't interfere with other rowers.

At the end of the session of rowing, Manak-na noticed a man shove against Kipotuilak, causing him to fall overboard. Kipotuilak swam rapidly to the boat. Rokuk saw it and called to the man who had pushed Kipotuilak. Manak-na and Ralm helped Kipotuilak climb aboard. As he got on board, Manak-na was surprised at how cold Kipotuilak was. The water, he reasoned, must pull out the warmth from a body quickly. Kipotuilak went quickly to his sleeping area and changed his clothing.

Manak-na could hear Rokuk tell the man who had caused Kipotuilak to fall overboard that if there were any other problems with him, he would send him overboard and refuse to let him return to the boat. He would not tolerate carelessness or intentional injury to another. All members of the boatmen were critically needed. He warned him that if anything happened to Kipotuilak he would be suspected and probably thrown overboard.

"But I was only trying to be playful," the man replied trying to excuse himself.

"If you wanted to play, you should have remained a child on shore," Rokuk said with asperity. "This is a boat where one lapse in proper thinking can result in death. Get rid of any ideas of play until you return to shore. If you find you need to play, don't return for another boat trip."

From what he'd seen, Manak-na could not tell whether the man intentionally tried to knock Kipotuilak off the boat or whether it was accidental in play as the man claimed. Whatever the case, he shared the incident with Yomuk and urged him to avoid that man at all costs.

Kipotuilak knew the man had intentionally shoved him overboard. He had a grudge against Kipotuilak ever since he'd lost a fight to him at the boat-builders' place one night. Kipotuilak hadn't caused the fight, but once forced into it, he fought with all he had. He had shown the other to be a coward. Kipotuilak would be much more watchful around the man now.

One morning just after Wisdom had quietly returned color to the land and sea, Rokuk called for the boat to head directly toward a large island they had been passing. They had been sailing through a series of islands that lined the larger land. It gave them adequate breeze and a respite from the sea. The boat stopped at a place designated by Rokuk and there was much activity getting the boat anchored and the masts tied down. Rokuk told Manak-na and Yomuk that it was time to hunt. They were delighted. They gathered their weapons and waited until they were told to head to the land. Yomuk's knife holder was a little worn, so he tied an extra piece of thin rope to it to hold it together for the hunt. Three groups of two would be going ashore, it seemed. They wore no clothing. Two were not hunters, because they had only one spear and some digging tools. Finally the signal was given and Manak-na and Yomuk watched the others get off the boat. They went to an end and climbed down a bamboo ladder. The water was just over their heads, but it was close to the land. Manak-na and Yomuk quickly decided to leave their clothing on the boat so they stayed dry. They tied their knife sheaths to a rope around their waists.

When they reached land following their short swim, Manak-na asked Yomuk, "Did you feel lighter in this salt water than in the lake?"

"I did!" Yomuk said with a smile. "There is much to learn on this adventure."

Manak-na and Yomuk went into the forest and began to climb a hill. The fragrance of chlorophyll was a taste of home and Yomuk emotionally choked up, severely missing home for a time. The dirt was another welcome scent. Mosses grew plentifully, soft on their feet. The day was beautiful and they were happy in the land environment. They were alert, looking for any sign of deer or other animals that could feed the boatmen. Yomuk pointed uphill spotting a small deer. In fact there were several of them.

Manak-na experienced his legs feeling as if he were still on the boat and the land was moving like water. It frightened him momentarily while he thought it might be an earthquake, but it didn't last long, and he continued the hunt with single minded purpose.

The two would try for two deer, each taking one. Silently, from downwind, they stalked their targets. They had chosen healthy young males. On a signal between themselves, they rushed their chosen deer at the same time. Both were successful. They quickly bled and gutted the animals and carried them both on their spears back to the boat. It had been almost too easy.

Suddenly from the brush a large bear huffed and came toward Yomuk, who stood as still as possible. Until it huffed, the men hadn't known it was there. Instead of charging, the large beast came slowly once it neared them. They guessed that the bear was intent on getting the deer more than them, but they wanted to keep the meat which lay on the ground at their feet. They knew the bear would fight them for it. Each slowly readied a spear and waited. Manak-na knew Yomuk had never fought a bear. He had been told how, but he'd had no practice. The bear continued toward Yomuk. Manak-na almost imperceptibly moved behind the bear. Just as the bear was about to attack Yomuk, Manak-na speared it in the lung from the back side. Yomuk speared the chest while the bear was turned to see what was attacking from behind. The bear swiped Manak-na's shoulder, and then fell, rolling downhill about two man lengths. Yomuk had continued to stab while the bear stood, so both lungs were gone, but the beast struggled fiercely on the ground until it finally gave up. The men looked at each other, faces filled with a combination of fear and triumph. The bear had been very big. They got their deer and continued to the boat. They'd find out whether Rokuk wanted the bear meat.

When they reached the boat, boatmen came down the ladder to help them with the meat. Manak-na and Yomuk had skinned and quartered it on shore to bring only the quarters aboard. They would hang the meat at the back of the upper deck. As soon as they hung it, they took it down. Birds went after the meat. The men took the hind quarters and hung them in the back of the hut on the right and the forequarters they hung in the back of the hut on the left.

As soon as Rokuk saw Manak-na's shoulder, he told him to sit and called to Mokul to take care of the shoulder. Mokul brought a container with many herbs and some liquids. He took a water bag and ran water over Manak-na's shoulder and cleaned it with a piece of soft leather followed by more water. He poured something on his shoulder that briefly tormented him like the stings of many bees. Then he took some salve made with honey and pasted it over the shoulder where the bear had scraped him. Wrapping his shoulder and chest with strips of soft leather followed that. Manak-na was grateful for Mokul's help. He knew that, left alone, a scrape like he got could cause sores that would be worse than the scrape. Sometimes people sickened from untreated openings into their skin; sometimes they died.

When asked about the bear, Rokuk refused it. According to Rokuk it was meat to eat only if you were starving. Manak-na liked bear meat, but he reasoned the meat would feed shore birds and the great birds he'd seen flying spirals in the air. It never occurred to him that he could have brought some on board for his personal consumption.

When the other men returned, some had water and some had green plants. The green plants made Yomuk salivate. He yearned for greens. He and the other men would thoroughly enjoy their deer meat when it was ready to eat. Rokuk liked to hang it for a few days before eating it. One of the men who brought the greens told Rokuk that there was a berry patch with ripe berries available where they got the greens. Rokuk pondered the information and then sent four men to pick the berries and put them in grass bags he supplied. Meanwhile, several men who had not gone ashore fished and caught several great fish for the evening meal. The berry pickers returned with four full bags of berries. The berries would protect the boatmen from the sailing sickness. Oranges, lemons, and limes were also effective for that purpose but they didn't grow that far north. Coconuts were not effective for preventing sailing sickness. After checking to be sure all were on the boat, Rokuk called out the order to bring up the anchors. When that was done and the stones had been placed in the back of the boat, Rokuk called the rowers, and slowly the boat backed out into the channel and they rowed southward.

Manak-na sat near Ralm and asked, "What are the people like where we are going?"

Ralm sat there for a moment thinking. "They're mostly Mol, if that's what you mean. There were also people like you long, long, long ago, but they have merged with the Mol, so the differences don't show very much any longer. At least that's what I've been told. There were fewer people like you to start. That was generations and generations and generations ago."

"Why do they stay there?"

"You'll see for yourself. It's warm there all year. For those who have difficulty with cold weather, it's an ideal place. Also, there is food that isn't available at home. There are fruits everywhere. You can walk along and pick one and eat it as you walk. People have branched out and they live in a variety of places. Some like to explore and they have traveled all over. Many of them died from a volcano a few years after they first arrived. They were covered deep in ash. Only two pairs of people survived, because they had chosen to live in a different place. Even so, they wanted to stay here. That was in the very beginning of the travel time. The land is vast. Once you pass the middle of the earth, the sky is different so you have to learn to navigate at night by a different set of stars."

Manak-na again was fascinated with how the mind of the Mol worked. He asked about people and heard about people, fruit, travel, a volcanic eruption, and the lower earth night sky. Manak-na had been trained to listen to the question and answer the specific question, not add other details. All he felt that he had discovered is that the people where he was going liked warm weather and were essentially Mol, but some of his People had been to this land. He wondered how.

"Ralm, can you tell me why you keep traveling from your home to where we're going and back again?"

Again, Ralm thought. Finally, he replied, "They are our people. If ever they want to come back here, we can bring them back."

Manak-na asked, "Have any ever asked to come back?"

"Not in my memory. They have been there for too many generations. But we like to know how they are, what they have learned there, and they learn from us. They are our people and we are theirs. I think we do this because we have done it for longer than memory. It also tells us about the earth we live on. It's just what we do."

While they talked, the cook brought the skin for boiling some of the greens. He set it up and then brought the greens they'd eat raw. He ran water over a bag of the berries. Manak-na hungered. Sometimes it was tough to sit by the cooking place. To have to smell the food and wait for a long time to eat required much patience.

That night the wait was worth it. They had fresh fish, cooked greens with some raw ones, and berries. It was delicious. They had enough fish to have more than they put on their bowls the first time. The same was true of the greens. Once they had taken berries, Rokuk put the container away for another meal.

For days and days they traveled south. They passed some rough water as the sea entered a very wide place that seemed to be a river or a huge cove, Manak-na could not tell which. They saw several whales. Things calmed down some when they reached the other side of the great opening.

Mokul had dutifully taken care of Manak-na's bear wound. Finally he removed the covering for the last time. The wound showed clearly, but it had healed well.

From the beginning of the trip to the present, Manak-na noticed that the temperature had warmed up greatly. At night he no longer pulled his covers over every inch of his body. Some nights he didn't even need a covering, but he used one anyway. More and more frequently he dreamed of Domur. He wondered how his wife was faring with him so far away. They had always been so close. He knew he'd hurt her when he left, but he thought she understood. So much he would have to share when he returned. He wondered whether Domur would want to hear what he'd seen and learned. He knew Ki'ti would. Manak-na drifted off to sleep.

Sometime in the night a storm came up. Winds began slowly and increased steadily. Men who ran the boat at night saw lightning and could hear thunder in the distance. One of them went to waken Rokuk. He insisted that in real storms he be awakened. The man quickly realized that this was a storm to respect. He ordered the lowering of the sails and masts. He told the boatmen to check their ties and then to check them again. He told them to anchor with long ties. That would give the boat some flexibility in the wind and waves. Rokuk went around the boat to check that everything was well tied down. He found some water containers that needed better tying. Otherwise, all seemed to be well done. He looked at the double hulled boat. This would be a real test, he believed. He told the first person in each hut to be certain that all the sleepers were tied up. They crept down their huts and waked each man to tell him a storm was getting near and to tie up. Panic entered the heart of Yomuk when he heard the news. He tried to place this storm to come as adventure, but he found it almost impossible. He kept checking his tie up. It irritated him that Manak-na had tied up, checked the tie up, and rolled over and resumed sleeping. *How could he sleep with a big storm approaching?* he wondered.

Winds rose and the boat twisted and slid down high waves creaking out deafening complaints. Lightning flashed and thunder roared. Yomuk sat curled up with his skin around his back and pulled forward. He shivered from fright, not cold. The noise was high and finally Manak-na awakened. When he saw Yomuk, he realized that the youth was terrified. *Part man, he was,* Manak-na thought, *and part boy.* He slid over and put his arms around Yomuk. Yomuk put his face into Manak-na's chest and wept. Finally, the warmth and security of Manak-na flowed into Yomuk. He calmed, stopped shivering, and tried to gain some strength to fight the fear that was troubling him. Manak-na moved back away from Yomuk. With Manak-na so close and seemingly unafraid, Yomuk had grown a seed of courage.

Just as his courage began to sprout, a wave covered the boat, causing the roof of the hut to hit Yomuk in the head. It startled him and Manak-na. Yomuk reached out and grabbed Manak-na's hand. Manak-na resisted the inclination to reach out again to the boy with his arms. If Yomuk was now satisfied with his hand, that was good. Yomuk worked hard to regain his seed of courage. It grew very slowly. He knew he'd survived being hit by a wave that came from above but did not ruin the boat. That helped his seed of courage grow a tiny leaf.

The storm began to abate when Wisdom began to return color to the land and sea. Rokuk realized that one anchor line was missing. It hadn't become untied; it had broken in the storm. It was good that they had more anchors and oars than they needed, but Rokuk felt that when they stopped next, they should look for more anchors—just in case.

Yomuk was sleepy when the drum sounded, but he was glad to be able to untie and get out of the hut. He and Manak-na looked at the boat and were surprised to see no damage except for one oar that had broken in half.

The storm had been fierce. Each ate eagerly and went to his sailing position. Monotonous travel would begin again. Yomuk realized that although the storms were very frightening, they did relieve the terrible boredom that came from sailing day after day with little change. He did still think, though, that he'd prefer total boredom. He wondered why Manak-na chose this adventure.

As days passed first one and another of the boatmen shed their clothing. Water was not good for leather, and the air was warm. It took a while before Manak-na and Yomuk shed their clothing. Once they'd done it, they were pleased and wondered why it took them so long.

Just before Wisdom began to suck color from the land and sea to shift it to vivid skies above, Manak-na noticed that there appeared to be a fire off to his left on the land. He asked Ralm if he thought it might be a camp fire or one started by lightning from a storm.

"I am certain there are a few people living in there. You never see them at the shoreline. Just a few tiny fires from time to time. I don't know where they come from or why they are here, but I've seen them for years. As we go farther south, you'll see more of them, maybe as many as one every six or seven days. There never seems to be a larger group of fires, just the occasional one. They could be our people adventuring or lost, or people from somewhere else."

"How sad it would be to be lost in all that forest alone."

"Unless you wanted to get away from people," Ralm added. "They may not be lost at all."

"Why would anyone want to be so alone?" Manak-na asked truly mystified.

"I don't really know, but I do know there are those who want to be alone and some who travel from place to place just to see what there is to see. I've only known one loner, personally. He never fit in anywhere, so he went off to the forest to be alone. We saw his fires off and on for years and years. Then either he died or he moved too far away for us to see the fires anymore."

The drum sounded and the men waited for their relief, then went below to relieve themselves, and went back up to the huts to sleep.

The People had prepared for the move and had been trekking for quite a long time. Each time they lost the path, they would build a cairn with one arm and a head. The arm pointed to the direction Manak-na and Yomuk would need to go to find them. They had made six cairns at this point. They had reached some hills and they moved a shorter distance daily. Along with the People there had been a raven that followed them. The raven, the People were certain, was the one that had the broken wing Tiriku found and Likichi healed. When they'd stop to camp, sometimes the raven would call to Tiriku and Tiriku would race to meet the raven. Tiriku would often go out in the evening and the bird would come down and spend a little time with the dog. It was as if they were great friends of different groups who saw each other only infrequently. Then, the bird would rise up and fly away.

Kai-na and Nanichak-na marveled at the path made so long ago by giants. Kai-na asked Nanichak-na, "How do you think the path has lasted so long?"

"I think it was used for a very long time. That would have made it hard, and that would make it so things did not grow on it easily. But you have to realize that some parts are just gone already. Without her spiritual guide leading her, Ki'ti would never be able to find the path once it disappears," the old man said and continued, "I wonder whether it has been such a long time since the giants were around. Suppose they were here more recently than we think."

"Now, I'd rather not think about that," Kai-na said quietly, his eyes darting around into the forest on either side. "I wouldn't like to see live ones!"

"Nor I," Nanichak-na agreed.

Some time passed and Kai-na asked the old man, "Have you seen any evergreens up here or anywhere on the path since we left the cave where the paths crossed?"

"No, Kai-na, and I have looked carefully. For some reason, if we see any, I'd like to stop to see what we might find. Look at that raven! That is the strangest thing. I enjoy watching it with Tiriku at night. Have you seen the other raven that flies a way back from ours? I think it's the mate of our raven."

"I haven't noticed, but I'll look for it."

The People reached the peak of the pass they were following. The downhill part of the path was wider and far more open. They could see a valley below with a small hill near the path at the far end. Beside the little hill there were some evergreens. The People were eager to reach the hill and it was nearing time for Wisdom to begin to suck color from the land. They reached the valley in a short time and in about the same length of time again they arrived at the hill. Kai-na and Grypchon-na went to the spruce trees and found a small cave behind them. The cave was not a natural cave, but it appeared to have been hammered into the hill, probably by the giants judging from the height of the ceiling. They wondered how they had made it, but there was little time to try to figure that out. They searched the cave carefully to determine whether it was useable for the night. It was. They called out for the People to come quickly, and two women, Ey and Minagle, came with brooms to sweep the cave.

Men checked the area and told the girls where to set up the dogs. This time Mona and Lakop had responsibility for the dogs. They unburdened them, got meat sticks for them, and went searching for a water source. Tongip-na saw them looking and told them that there was a creek beside the cave on the north side. The girls got the short, new watering containers made of aurochs stomach just for the dogs and filled them. The dogs were very thirsty. They showed the dogs where to relieve themselves. The girls went to the cave to see what else needed to be done.

Domur wasn't busy in the cave as she normally was. She sat upon her sleeping skins, tired and sad. She slumped and her shoulders sagged.

"What's the matter?" Likichi asked.

"I am just tired. I miss Manak-na so badly." There were unshed tears in her eyes.

Likichi sat on the skins beside her. She put her thin arm around her son's wife. "I, too, miss him, Domur. But we have things that need doing. You have to realize that he is on a very dangerous journey. He may or may not return. I have a son and a grandson on that journey. I hurt, missing them even as you do. You must fight letting the hurt eat you, my dear one. Keep busy and spread some of that love that aches to others who need it. Many of the little ones in big families often are overlooked. Find a place to spread your love, my dear. Love grows when spread. When you let something eat you, sometimes it makes your body ill. That would not be good. There is little cure for it. If it goes on and on, it can kill you.

"I'd think the cure would be the return of Manak-na," Domur said.

"No, my dear. That might just make his return such that he would find his wife nearing death with no hope to turn it around. That would make him feel guilty of something he should not feel guilty for."

"It would serve him right!" Domur replied grumpily.

"Domur, my dear, your mind web is already suffering from bitterness. You need to forgive him for wanting to have his adventure, unless you are perfect and never wanted something you shouldn't have. Manak-na did not understand that if he wanted to adventure he should not have joined. He has made a mistake that hurt you. You are compounding the problem by acting like a spoiled child. If Manak-na had died, you wouldn't be acting like you are. Who knows, maybe he *is* dead. Time will tell on that. Meanwhile, you need to pull yourself together. That starts with truly forgiving Manak-na for whatever you're holding against him. Forgive him fully, without condition. Do not allow yourself to dwell on his adventure. You'll see him *when* and *if* you see him. Until then, live. Get busy giving of yourself to others. There is great need here with all the little ones. Right now you're no good to anyone including yourself. Wake up before you make yourself so sick that you cannot turn it around. How would Tuma and Mhank feel without a mother, or Rish, Van, and Solu feel with no Izumo? Choose life instead of continuing the bitterness. That is all I have to say." She did a palm strike and left.

Domur had been chastised. It hurt, but she had to admit she deserved it. She had let herself think on selfish things, not what was good for the People. She had been distant. She had been bitter, feeding the flames of anger at having been hurt, and that was a trait she disliked in others. Now, she understood it better, but it didn't make it easier to get rid of it in herself or to tolerate it better in others. She thought about Manak-na dead. What good was her irritation to him, if he didn't even breathe? What good was it at all? She began to understand. Yes, she had been acting as a spoiled child. One who had been given so much that she expected more. She resolved to get rid of her bitterness. Likichi had told her the way—eliminate the bitterness, forgive totally. She had to hope and pray that Manak-na was alive and that he would return. That would be her way. Yes, she *had* to change. She *would* change herself. Alone, she did a palm strike. From a far part of the cave, Likichi saw it and smiled.

The People planned to remain at the hammered out cave for eight days. They rested up and enjoyed the company of each other. On the trek there was little time for talking unless you confined your words to the person next to you. Each of the People had time for bathing and cleaning their hair. The women and girls played with their hair or with the hair of another to make it attractive or stay out of the eyes. Ki'ti finally asked Likichi to use a tool to cut her hair so that when the wind blew it would not blow hair into her eyes. She knew her hair would be short and would require frequent cutting to keep it from her eyes. She had become very tired of having it in her face. Likichi had her lower her head so her face was parallel to the ground. Then Likichi cut her hair just so it could not reach her eyes. When Ki'ti raised her head, Likichi cut the rest to go with what she'd done to the front. Ki'ti was delighted. No longer did she have to braid her hair. She could simply run a comb through it and it was ready for the day. On the trek it would no longer get into her eyes. She wondered why it had taken her so long to have it cut.

While Ki'ti sat beside the creek with her feet in the water, Elemaea came to sit beside her.

"I like the way you have your hair cut," the young one said.

"Do you want yours cut, too?" Ki'ti asked knowing the answer already.

"No, thank you. What looks good on you might not look good on me."

"Oh, you're worried already about your appearance?" Ki'ti teased.

"Not really. Not yet." Elemaea stretched out with her head resting on Ki'ti's leg. She asked, "Where's Tiriku?"

"I think Raven flew by just a little while ago. I expect they are visiting somewhere."

"I love it that Tiriku has a raven friend."

"I've never seen anything quite like it. I think Raven realizes that Tiriku saved his life." Ki'ti fingered Elemaea's curly hair.

"I really am fitting in now, aren't I, Mother?"

"Do you really love working spear heads?"

"Yes. I can make things that are beautiful and have good usefulness. I do love it."

"Then, yes, I think you have fit in well, Elemaea. I approve you, my dear."

Elemaea's heart jumped at the word, approve. How long had she wanted to hear that word? She was relieved and joyful at the same time. Approved. It felt good! She lay with the sun on her face, looking into the clouds. Ki'ti stroked her curly hair. Tiriku bounded over and Raven landed right beside Ki'ti. Raven turned his head to one side and then the other looking at Elemaea. Then he let off a string of sounds that sounded for all in the world like a man laughing. Ki'ti and Elemaea laughed, too. Raven did a little dance and then took to the sky.

"What did he do that for?" Elemaea asked.

"I have no idea. It makes sense to a raven but to People, that's something else. I think it makes sense to Tiriku. Now, I must get up, Little Girl, to see what I can do before the evening meal this day."

"I need to do the same, but I know what I have to do. I'm trying to learn to make cores, but it's hard for me with the size hands I have."

"Well, do your best Little Girl."

"I will, Mother." Elemaea smiled and skipped back to the tool making place where she had been working with Ekuktu-na.

Mootmu-na and Arkan-na arrived at the camp with a deer hanging from their spears. They took the animal, which had been bled and gutted, to a nearby pond. They had to reach the center of the pond to submerge it fully.

To hold it down they placed rocks on top of the animal. Tomorrow they would cut it up.

"I told you not to do that," Amey shouted to Mootmu-na after observing the men with their kill. "We are leaving tomorrow."

"Then at the men's council, I'll ask to let us stay longer," he replied.

Amey snorted and turned her back and went into the cave. She saw Likichi and said, "My man has gone hunting again and has brought back a deer."

"Well, what's another day here?" she asked.

"I should think that before the time for cold days, we'd need to find our next place, and delays keep us from getting there in time for much hunting.

"Oh?" Likichi said.

Amey had no reply to that, so she got busy getting the water gourds filled. It was harder to do that when the water was not in the cave.

After the men's council that night, the People agreed that there would be no more hunting and that they would remain two more days at this camp. Ermol-na brought out his drum and for those who chose, there was dancing—for no reason at all.

—⁓—

For days the boat had passed land where an occasional small river entered the sea. They had just reached the mouth of a very large river. The waves were choppy and there were occasional whirlpools seen sometimes as the river entered the sea. Some of the men thought the sea was angered by the river, since it always seemed there were very choppy seas when they sailed by, and it was not pleasant. The men on the boat had long ago named the water Unpleasant River because of the nature of their passing every time. It was a landmark that made them realize that within two moons they should be at their destination. Since Wisdom had not returned color to the land or sea, Manak-na and Yomuk did not see the river, but they both heard the man call, "Unpleasant River … Unpleasant River … Unpleasant River." Rokuk got up and left the hut. He looked around and saw the Unpleasant River. *They were traveling well,* he thought.

A few minutes later the drum sounded. Rays of sunlight were rising and for a split second the rays seemed to bend to earth before arising and soaring to the sky. Soon Wisdom would return the color to the land and sea. Manak-na and Yomuk had to wait their turn, but they were eager to catch a glimpse of Unpleasant River. They were about half way across the mouth of the river when the men got outside the hut. They were impressed by the size of the river. This one was clearly a huge river mouth, not a cove or inlet. Way beyond the river they could see white topped mountains. They were huge. Despite the white on top, Manak-na realized they were volcanoes.

"Are those volcanoes live?" Manak-na asked Ralm.

"Yes. About thirty some years ago as we sailed through here, one of those peaks was erupting. Fortunately for us, the wind blew the dust from it eastward, missing us altogether. The dust blew at least four times higher than the height of the mountain. It was something to see!"

"I'm glad that nothing is happening there now. We experienced a horrible volcano that uprooted us from our home and chased us north about the same time you described for this one. When it blew, we made it to a cave where we lived through the winter and then moved farther north to get away from the ashfall." Manak-na's face reflected the tough time he'd experienced.

Ralm asked, "Is that the one far south of home that happened a long time ago?"

"It was definitely south of the boatbuilding camp. South and to the west."

"I heard about that volcano from some people sailing north to get away from it. They since moved farther south again. They said it had multiple spouts."

"It did, and it was awful. For the season of cold days we had to preserve meat from animals that had died in the ashfall. They smothered. But their meat kept us alive and we had a cave where water ran. We were safe from the devastation. Once ash fell, there was no way to survive unless you could get away from it somehow."

"You lived through it?"

"Well, I'm no dead person standing before you!" Manak-na teased.

"I'm just shocked that anyone lived through it!"

"We knew about some caves and trekked fast to reach the one we knew had water. Two other groups also made it to the cave. All of us knew that we had been spared death. We all lived in the cave with water and used the other cave for meat and skin preparation. As soon as the weather warmed, we trekked north far away to avoid any more eruptions like that. Some went east. We had to find a place where grass grew and animals browsed. Nothing lived in the ashfall. No birds sang, no creeks were visible, the ash subdued even the voices of children. When sound was made, it was dulled."

Manak-na remembered the silence. He was lost in the remembrance of the monochrome views and the silence. He thought briefly of Enut and Reemast buried there under the ash. He was glad to be alive. It was nice sailing weather and the sea had calmed once they passed Unpleasant River. Manak-na breathed deeply of the salty air. Life was good.

Days turned to days. Manak-na was fascinated to watch the phases of the moon. He knew that the day they passed Unpleasant River was a full moon. They needed two more full moons to reach their location. Manak-na could see on the faces of the boatmen that they were near. The boatmen would look at the land and then look at each other wordlessly but with raised eyebrows as if the land spoke to them.

Finally one day arrived that without explanation made Manak-na know that they were at their destination. He could see the beach, and all eyes were on it. Clearly there was a camp there, but it appeared that no people were to be seen.

Yomuk came to his side and asked, "Is something wrong? All morning people have been happy and now there is tension. I see no people at a place where you'd expect to see them. Do you understand?"

"No, I can see that the people on the boat seem troubled. There is something wrong, but I'm not at all certain what it is. We'll know soon enough, I think."

Rokuk seemed confused as to what to do. He didn't know whether there had been sickness or warfare or what, and he didn't want to lose any men trying to find an answer. There were no traces of smoke from hearth fires, no voices coming across the water, no sounds of birds. Just silence. He decided to anchor the boat offshore to watch the little place where his people lived. Perhaps they had gone to a hunting or fishing place and would return. He was too far out to permit someone to swim into shore. He just wanted to get an idea what was happening before trying to land anyone. They fished and caught enough for their evening meal. They ate quietly since most of the men were watching the land for signs of life. There was nothing.

The drum sounded and the men who slept at night waited their relief and then went to their places in the huts. Overhead the sky was blazing with light from dots that twinkled and those few that didn't. Manak-na would have enjoyed looking at the night sky longer, but it was time to sleep, so he did.

When Wisdom returned color to the land and sea, Manak-na and Yomuk went out and took another look at the place where they'd expected to be received by happy people. Rokuk was already calling to raise the anchors. He had decided to send a few men to the land to see what they could see.

He ordered the rowers and the rudder man to head for the beach. When they were in water much deeper than a man was tall, they let down the anchors and Mokul, Manak-na, and Ralm were sent to the camp. Carefully they checked the dwellings. The quiet was bothersome. When they reached the last dwelling, far from the beach and situated on a hill, they found a man who was very old and disabled from pain when he moved. The old man was startled to see them.

"Old Man, are you well?" Mokul asked.

The man spoke feebly, "I am old and have the stiff man sickness. But I live and all my people are dead."

"What happened?" Mokul asked gently.

"It was two days ago. I saw the tide sweep out very far. Fish were dancing on the sand. It was as if the god of the underwater was giving us fish. The people all raced to gather the fish, even the little ones. I could see from up here a huge wave rising up at sea. I called to them, but they couldn't hear. It moved fast and covered all the people out there gathering fish. It pulled them into the sea. None have returned. I cannot walk well. I am hungry. I have cried for my people until my eyes hurt."

"I am so sorry to hear your story, Old Man. We will try to help you. What is your name?"

"I am Tikarumusa from Aikot. This place is called Aikot."

"Tikarumusa, we will need to take you to our boat. We will head back home. We come here often. I don't remember seeing you."

"You have not seen me because I lived in the central part of this country until I became stiff. Since then my close relatives left me here because I could no longer travel. My relatives here have cared for me. Do you remember a man who wore a red dot on his forehead years ago? I saw some of you from time to time when you came here while I visited."

"Yes, I remember seeing a man with a red dot on his head," Ralm replied, wondering how they were going to get this man to the boat.

"That man was me in my younger days. I was the only man who by himself killed a mammoth. I wore the red dot because the people honored me that way. Now, look at what I have come to. And all my people here are gone. I have not been able to honor them."

Ralm looked at Manak-na. Neither of them knew what a mammoth was, but they didn't take time to listen. "Would you please go to the boat? Tell Rokuk what we have found and heard. Ask for people to help this man come to the boat and for people to come to pick fruit. I'll see what we can do to honor his people."

"I'd be glad to help," Manak-na said as he turned and left.

He ran to the water and splashed into it, climbed the ladder, and met Rokuk as soon as he boarded. He explained about the old man and the wave that washed out all the people who were gathering fish from the unusual low tide. Immediately, Rokuk sent six men to help the old man to get on the boat, sending the one stretcher they had. They could not abandon him. Then Rokuk sent another group to gather as much fruit as possible. He told them, if they could find baskets to hold the fruit in the dwellings on shore, to use them. He also told them to look for rope. He sent Piman and Yomuk to look for stones for anchors.

The men turned the corner from the hill and Rokuk could see the old man on the stretcher. He was terribly thin. Rokuk guessed that Mokul would know how to help the man eat and feel better. Rokuk could see the man's hands. They were twisted the way he'd seen some old people's hands twist. That meant the man lived life painfully, but otherwise he was probably healthy.

"What do you do to honor your people who have died?" Mokul asked.

"We need to burn their houses."

"Burn their houses?" Mokul wanted to be sure he got it right.

"Yes, the old man said in a voice showing much pain. It keeps the wandering souls from lingering and urges them to go to the place of death."

"I see," Mokul replied while others were setting fire to the houses. But he didn't see. These people were connected to them and they definitely stopped by on a continuous basis to be sure all was well, but the people had not been able to maintain closeness due to the brevity of the visits. Generations had passed since there was closeness. They had a connection, but the boatmen did not know the people for whom the old man grieved.

Mokul had the men turn the stretcher so that Tikarumusa could see the burning houses.

"Is that what you had in mind?" Mokul asked him.

"Yes. Thank you." The old man sank into himself.

Getting the stretcher out in the water while swimming was a little difficult but the stretcher almost floated. Men swam with it braced on their shoulders. The man in front swam a little like a frog while he held onto the handles in front of the stretcher. He could swim only with his legs. He'd put his head underwater and kick with his legs and then raise his head for air. When they reached the boat, the front stretcher grips were tied below their first tie and the whole thing, man and all were raised. The man had been tied tight to the stretcher. He moaned, but did not otherwise complain. They took his wet clothing and gave him a dry tunic. Then they helped him to some skins at the front of the hut on the left side of the boat.

The men from the boat found an abundance of fruit and used baskets to contain the fruit that they had found in the dwellings before they burned them. Piman and Yomuk did not have the same success. All they found was sand everywhere—no anchor stones.

By the evening meal, all were back on the boat and were enjoying fruit that Manak-na and Yomuk had never seen. It was delicious. They ignored some of the fish to fill their bellies with more fruit.

"Be careful, Manak-na and Yomuk," Rokuk said loudly, "if you eat too much fruit, you'll be hanging off the lower deck all day tomorrow."

Instantly Manak-na and Yomuk slowed down on the fruit. Neither had known it would make them evacuate their bowels frequently the next day, if they ate too much this evening. Rokuk talked to Ralm at the far end of the boat. He was unsure whether to try to contact another group on the land while looking for anchors or to leave directly for home. He and Ralm talked at length about either choice. In the end, Rokuk decided to send a group of men to try to find another group of people to report what had happened. He wanted someone to know of the tragedy and that Tikarumusa was in their care.

Manak-na was sitting next to Tikarumusa. He felt the old man's hand on his arm.

"Manak-na," he said, "This is for you." He handed Manak-na a pouch on a leather tie that hung around his neck. Inside the pouch was red ochre.

Manak-na took it and lowered his head. He looked inside the pouch inquisitively. He thanked Tikarumusa.

"You wear it like this," the man said and spit in his hand, moistened the red ochre with his first finger, and drew a straight line on a piece of bamboo. "The line goes across your cheek bone." He drew the line on each side of Manak-na's face. "Above the line there are dots. There are seven dots." He drew them on the bamboo and then on Manak-na's face. "You put this on every morning and take if off in the evening."

Manak-na wondered what the man was thinking. "Why?" he asked.

"Because it will save your life." The old man was very serious, but Manak-na could not understand.

"I do not understand," he admitted.

"The god of the underwater wants you. This sign prevents him from harming you."

"Then, when I get back home and arrive on land I won't need it any longer?"

"Young man," Tikarumusa said to Manak-na, "Do you know nothing of the gods? The god of the underwater is not confined to the sea. You wear this for the rest of your life or beware of the god of the underwater."

The drum sounded and Manak-na and Yomuk went to their sleeping area. Yomuk was not pleased to be going back across the sea. He did not care for boat travel. Manak-na found his way into the hut after washing his face.

"Uncle, what was that on your face?" Yomuk asked.

"I'll talk about it later." He needed to work it through his mind web before discussing it.

When Wisdom placed peach and gold into the clouds of the morning sky with dancing reflections in the water, the drum sounded and the night and day boatmen changed places. Rokuk had decided to send a group of men to the shore to find anchors and to make an attempt to locate a group of the people to let them know what had happened. He chose Ralm as the leader and Skuku, Mokul, Manak-na, and Kipotuilak.

The men left the boat carrying their clothing, backpacks with jerky, and a small water bag over their heads. Each had a spear that was stuck through the edges of the backpack to be held high to transport dry things through the water. On land they dressed and went to the far edge of the little grouping of dwellings, where some had seen paths leading away from the place. Ralm had asked Tikarumusa which would be the best path to choose and he said the best would be the one to the south. He said it would take half a day to reach the next group of people, who lived over the hill. He warned them to beware of poisonous snakes.

The men walked at a quick hunter's walk. If they could shorten the time, they would do that gladly. Except for Manak-na they all felt more at home on a boat than on strange land.

By high sun they had reached a pass through the hills. The day was beautiful and they had seen no snakes of any kind. Manak-na reached into his backpack for a piece of jerky. The idea became contagious as others decided to do the same thing. No one, however, slowed the trek progress. When they reached the top of the pass, they could see a valley below. The valley land was large and flat. It was filled with a wide variety of animals but mostly camels, horses, and an animal that looked like an elephant but was much bigger. They rested briefly, enjoyed water, and then moved on. The path they followed led them to the lower part of the valley and along the trees that were growing on the hills. Manak-na spotted the group of dwellings quickly and pointed it out to the others.

Ralm took the lead. They walked up to the living place and were greeted by hunters with spears.

"We have come from the home of Tikarumusa. We wish to speak to your chief."

The hunters said nothing but turned and a few walked in the lead position and others went behind the men and followed them.

Soon they saw little dwellings made in the style of those they'd seen at the shore, tree trunks cut down and buried in the soil with cross pieces to which had been tied long sea grass. The top the roof was cone shaped and long sea grasses in bundles were tied to that to keep rain out. The chief's dwelling was larger.

The chief came out. He wore a tunic made from bird feathers. The bird feathers were red, blue, green, and yellow. The colors were brilliant. He had hair trimmed like Yomuk and it seemed that he had glued the top with reddish clay similar to the color of the ochre Manak-na used to paint his face. The chief sat on a log in front of his dwelling. The men were told to sit on the little flat rocks that formed an arc before the chief. They were told to lay their spears at his feet. The hunters took positions on either side of the chief and behind the men. Curious people came to look at the strangers.

The chief said, "Speak."

Ralm said, "We have come on the boat to the people at the edge of the water at Aikot. When we arrived, there appeared to be no one there. Finally, we found Tikarumusa. He told of how the sea withdrew very far and all the people went to gather fish that were flopping on the sand. He could not join them. Then he saw a huge wave rising up at sea. He yelled to the people, but they could not hear him. The wave crashed over all the people and took them off into sea. He is the only one left. Right now he is on the boat, so he could be cared for."

The chief was visibly disturbed by the news. "Tikarumusa is my father. We must follow you to bring him here. We will care for him."

Ralm said, "In some storms we lost some anchors. We need to find replacements. We need stones that are flat on opposing sides so we can make holes in the center to tie rope through. Can you tell us where to find stones like that?"

The chief talked to a few of the hunters. Manak-na had difficulty following since they spoke language similar to the Mol but with different ways of saying the words. They spoke much slower than the boatmen or the inland Mol. The chief told Ralm that near the pass that went through the hills there were stones like they sought. He'd have the hunters go with them to get

Tikarumusa. They would carry the stones to the boat. He made eye contact with a hunter who left to gather five more hunters along with himself. Then the chief looked down at the ground.

Eventually he raised his head and looked right into the eyes of Manak-na. "We have a prophecy. Do you understand?"

Manak-na looked bewildered. Ralm translated, "He said they have a prophecy, and he asked if you understood."

"I don't understand. Why are they telling me?"

Ralm asked the chief, who responded, "Our bird man was told by the spirits that a man would come who is of the people of old—people whose heads are like his." He pointed to Manak-na. "My daughter was told not to join with any man, but when this man came, she was to go with him to his people, because there is something she must do there. She might as well go with you, for she is worthless here. She simply waits and waits. I think her waiting is over. Look at her head. It is somewhat like his."

Ralm explained to Manak-na what he'd been told. Manak-na was shocked. Not only did he have to care for Yomuk, but now there was a girl to join them? He was wise enough not to respond negatively or in shock. He looked at Ralm and said quietly, "Tell him that, if that's what he wants, I will take her to my People."

Ralm told the chief. The chief thanked Manak-na. Manak-na lowered his head to the chief. The chief said something to one of the hunters who left and returned with a girl who seemed to be about eight years old. She was very beautiful. Her hair was golden red, spiraled it appeared, though it was not properly combed out, and her eyes looked as green as jade. Her skin was extremely pale. She wore a skirt made of long grass. She looked like People, but she was extraordinarily thin. She gave one look at Manak-na and walked toward him and kneeled placing her head on her hands on the sand beside him. Manak-na had no idea what to do.

Ralm quietly told her to rise and to be seated. She did, just behind Manak-na. She bent her legs and sat on her heels. Her hands were placed on her upper leg. She looked down. Not only was it clear that she knew her wait was over, but also she realized that Manak-na was the one who would take her. Ralm knew Manak-na would take responsibility for her seriously, but on the boat, Rokuk and Ralm would have a responsibility keeping the boatmen focused on what they were supposed to do. A girl on a boat was not a good thing. Frankly, he thought, it would be far better to take the old man, but he did not have a choice.

Hunters arrived and appeared ready to make the return trip with the men. They carried no food or water, but they did have a stretcher. The boatmen filled their water bladders. The chief thanked them for coming with the news. He thanked Manak-na, specifically, for taking the girl, Ahna. They left, trekking faster than they had on their way earlier. The girl carried nothing with her, not even food or water. She trekked dutifully right on the heels of Manak-na. She said nothing. Manak-na wondered whether she felt pain to leave her home for someplace across the water that she had never seen. Maybe she liked adventure? Maybe there was something at home she didn't like? There was no hug between the chief and her. He felt it was very unusual—somehow all wrong.

At the place where they found rocks, Kipotuilak pointed out snake after snake.

"How can you find them so easily, Kipotuilak?" Manak-na asked.

"Smell," he replied.

"Smell? Can you smell them?" Ralm asked incredulously.

"Yes. They smell musty," Kipotuilak said.

"You've got a better nose than I have!" Ralm responded.

While the men had trekked to find other people and anchors, Rokuk had been joined by Piman to swim under the boat to evaluate the hull lashings and the rudder to be sure that all was ready for the voyage home. They knew that land would not be so accessible on the return trip, so all needed to be in good shape. They tied a few straps around the bamboo hulls, not because they saw problems but because they wanted to forestall any that might originate at sea. Piman tried very hard to find any problem with the rudders, but could see nothing at all. They appeared to be working well and the weaving was holding up well, looking like it had their day of departure from home. They pulled off a few trailers of kelp that had been snagged on the bottom of the boat and looked like long ribbons of leather.

The other men arrived back at the boat and exchanged Tikarumusa for Ahna, much to Rokuk's displeasure, although he tried not to show it. All were surprised when Ahna and Tikarumusa hugged. He was her grandfather and it was clear there was love between them, something far different from what appeared at her home with her father. Tikarumusa had told the men which way to go to find his people, knowing they'd find Ahna. To have turned north they'd have found some of his people even quicker, but they'd have missed Ahna. Somehow Tikarumusa knew Manak-na was the person who was supposed to take Ahna to her new home.

On the boat the men thought nothing of their nakedness even with the girl on board. Rokuk told Manak-na to keep the girl with him unless it was stormy. During storms, regardless of the time of day, she was to be tied up next to their sleeping places to keep her out of the way. The men prepared to make the boat ready to depart for home. Ahna was told to sit behind the back sail to wait for Manak-na to join her. She did. Ralm made it totally clear to Rokuk that the idea of the girl had not been Manak-na's, and that to the contrary, he wasn't interested at all, but had no choice. Rokuk snorted though he knew Ralm told the truth. He just didn't want a girl aboard.

The sailing was uneventful. When the drum sounded, Manak-na took Ahna to the lower level and showed her where to relieve herself. Then they went to the upper level and the hut where they were to sleep. Manak-na stopped by the water container long enough to wash off the design from his face. He didn't know what to think of Tikarumusa's warning about the god of the underwater. He could think of no other reason the old man would have painted his face. Yomuk had been trying to get a look at the girl ever since she boarded, but Piman had kept him very busy at the back of the boat before and after the departure. He'd given him tools to use to start chipping the anchor stone to make a hole in the center. He'd had no time to look around. That's what Piman wanted, but he could not control Yomuk's being so close to her during sleep.

Chapter 5

Stars twinkled crystal clear in a dark sky over gentle waves on the sea where single celled organisms below lit the water around the boat with their light making ability. It was a wondrous sight for the night boatmen. Manak-na, Yomuk, and Ahna were set for sleep. From somewhere Rokuk had brought Manak-na a sleeping skin and a soft fur cover for Ahna. Manak-na thanked him greatly. Otherwise he and Yomuk would have had to share, and their covers barely kept them warm when the weather became cold. Yomuk wanted to talk to Ahna, but Manak-na made it clear it was time for sleep. He positioned himself between Yomuk and Ahna. The girl had never had such soft sleeping covers. The soft furry skin was made from many gray pelts sewed together. She wrapped herself in them and wondered what this new life would be. Manak-na wondered what he'd gotten himself into. Yomuk was fascinated with the girl who was so close and so far away.

When Wisdom returned blues, gold, and very rosy peach to the sky, the drum sounded. Manak-na, Yomuk, and Ahna got up, went to the lower level, and came back up. They washed their hands and faces at the water container on the huts, careful to check to be sure there were no people below who might be soaked. The boat floated well, but the design was one in which the water upon which they floated ran right through the boat. Water hitting the top of the boat never collected, but instead ran straight through to the sea. For that reason, they had to check the lower level before pouring water atop the boat for fear of soaking someone on the lower level. The advantage was that when waves crashed above them in great storms, the water never collected inside the boat but rather ran through, returning to sea quickly. They went to their assigned places where Manak-na painted his face. Ahna appeared happy but very quiet. Manak-na had a piece of thin rope. He showed her how to tie the special knot that would not come apart. He noticed she learned very quickly. He explained to her about the tie up, but thought she might not understand him well enough, so he asked Ralm to tell her when to tie up. Ahna understood.

Manak-na looked seriously at Ralm. "Is the color of the sky telling us that we will have a great storm? It has a reddish color."

"I've discussed it with Rokuk and Piman. We will be paying attention, but none of us thinks this is a prediction of a great storm. The wind is wrong and there are no clouds or haziness anywhere on the horizon. I think it is just a rosy day," Ralm said with a smile.

"Thank you for the good news, Ralm. That relieves my belly."

Ralm laughed and Manak-na joined him.

Ahna had understood the conversation. She realized that Manak-na's speech revealed that he didn't normally speak the language. She wondered what he spoke. When it became quiet she asked him about his language, saying, "It will be important for me to learn your language. Will you teach me?"

It had not occurred to Manak-na that he needed to teach Ahna his language. He told her, "I will begin to speak my language to you. Try at first just to listen to what I say. See if the situation helps make sense of the words. I will repeat what I've said. Then I will say it once in your language. I am not good at the language of the boatmen, and your language is somewhat different from theirs. When you think you've understood some of my language, start to use it. I will correct you if you make errors."

"Thank you, Manak-na," Ahna said in her sweet slow voice. Then a few minutes later she said, "Do you have any understanding of why I am supposed to go to your people?"

Manak-na shook his head. He said in the language of the People, "I have no idea."

Ahna looked at him. "You have no idea," she said. "What means *no idea*?"

Manak-na was shocked that she was trying the language so soon. She'd been quiet as a mouse up to this point. He said in the Mol language, "*No idea* means I don't have a place in my mind web where I can find that information. I store information or ideas in my mind web. Later when I want the information or idea I think through my mind web to find it. I did not know that your father would ask us to take you, or that I was supposed to take you to my People."

"Our bird man said it not long after I was born."

"What is your bird man?" Manak-na asked.

"He is the one who talks to the spirits. The one who told what would become of me is walking the spirit paths now."

"So you had no one to ask?" Manak-na tried to be sympathetic despite the fact that he was already responsible for Yomuk and was irritated to have to be responsible for another youth.

"Yes. By the time I was old enough to know what questions I had, he was walking spirit paths," Ahna said. "You have no idea," she added in the language of the People.

"Good!" Manak-na said.

The day progressed and food was served. Yomuk joined Manak-na and Ahna to eat by the back sail. He and Ahna smiled at each other shyly.

"Are you having success hammering holes in the anchors?" Manak-na asked in the language of the People.

Yomuk was surprised that he used their language, and he replied, "Slowly. I have completed," he showed two fingers, "only."

Manak-na looked at him with a smile. "It should make the time pass faster than just sitting there."

Yomuk lowered his head. Then he said, "Why are we speaking in the language of the People?"

"Because, Ahna has to learn it. It will be easier for her, if she arrives already speaking some of it."

"I see," Yomuk replied. "Why is she wearing that grass skirt?"

"It must be the clothing of her people. She should have a leather tunic."

"I don't sew. You don't have time to put one together."

While Manak-na and Yomuk talked, Ahna watched how they talked. She listened to try to make sense of any words, but did not have success. She could hear *you* and *I*, but that was about all she could understand. They had her full attention. She noted they spoke quickly. She also noticed that they seemed to care a great deal about each other. *They had a lot of information passing between them,* she thought, *information that was not spoken but was understood because they cared about each other. Bodies spoke when words did not,* she knew all too well.

The high sun meal finished and the two men returned to work. Manak-na saw Rokuk and went to him. He asked how the sailing was going, and Rokuk said that things seemed to be doing well. He asked him how he was doing with Ahna. Manak-na came as close to rolling his eyes as he would allow himself. He replied, "Well enough, I suppose. I had no plans nor desire for this," he said looking at Ahna. "Now I have a girl, wearing an awful garment that has mold in it, and I need to teach her to speak my language, be sure that she and Yomuk don't get too close, and participate in the adventure of a lifetime.

"Do you want me to put Yomuk in the other hut at night?" Rokuk asked.

"Thank you, but no. When I get back we have to find the People and that will mean days and days of trekking. They have to learn to be together."

"Do you want a tunic that I think will fit her?"

"You have one on the boat?" Manak-na was astonished.

"I have many things on the boat. Just a moment." Rokuk went down to the lower level. He reappeared with a gut wrapped garment. It was a two shouldered tunic and it appeared never to have been worn. Rokuk said, "This is for your girl."

"Thank you. That will get the mold out of my nose and make her appearance not so extraordinary. I appreciate this from the bottom of my belly. Do you want the gut wrapping?"

"No, tell her to use it to wrap the garment to keep it dry when we have a great storm, high seas, or she has to walk through deep water," Rokuk said as he walked away.

Manak-na went to Ahna and reached for her hand. He took her to the lower level. He tried to remove her skirt and couldn't figure out how to do it. So he told her to take it off and throw it behind the boat. At first Ahna was not pleased at all. The men might be on the boat unclothed, but she did not want to be naked. Manak-na pulled the leather tunic from the gut wrapper and she understood what was happening, so she took the skirt off and tossed it behind the boat. Manak-na was horrified to see how thin she was. Her ribs had given him a clue. Her bones stuck out sharply. She reminded him of the starving Minguat when they met following the ashfall. Her head looked like People, but her body didn't. He would try to get her to eat a lot more than she was eating. He put the tunic over her head and slipped it on her. It was a little large, but it would do. It came down just below her knees. It would last her a long time. He told her when she saw Rokuk to thank him. She understood because he was using her language. Because it was a little wide for someone so thin, Manak-na took the practice knot tying rope she had in her hand, circled it around her waist, and tied it. It helped the garment stay put and not move around her body so much.

Ahna was overwhelmed. She'd never had any clothing like this. Where she'd lived was hot. Her people wore little. They did not have anything so soft. The leather of the tunic was extremely soft. She would want to take very good care of it, so it would last a long time. Manak-na told her what Rokuk had said about wrapping it when water was present.

Rokuk told Ralm to unfurl the back sail. Manak-na and he untied a few ropes and Ralm pulled the sail up. The boat caught more wind and sped over the waves.

When Manak-na sat down, Rokuk came over and told Manak-na to get his coconut. Manak-na didn't know that Rokuk knew he still had it, but he got up to get it. While he was gone, Ahna said to Rokuk, "Thank you for the tunic. It is beautiful and wonderfully soft."

He smiled at her. "It was for my wife. She died before I could give it to her. Take good care of it. It will last well. Try to avoid getting it wet. If it rains, go to your sleeping place and stay dry. If water comes in take it off and wrap it in the gut wrapper."

"I will," she replied.

Manak-na came back out with the coconut, handing it to Rokuk. In the middle of the sea Rokuk put dots on the coconut using a piece of charcoal.

"Look, here, Manak-na," Rokuk said. "See these dots?"

"Yes."

"These dots are islands. They are in almost a straight line, not an arc as the islands in the far north. If we take proper aim, we will go either just south or just north of them. Then it's a straight sail home. Usually the wind takes us right by these islands. If we hit a big storm we could be anywhere. This time of year there are great storms in this part of the sea. We'll have to hope we miss them. The good thing about them is that they can cut our trip very short because they can blow us homeward with great strength. They can also blow us to the south, but that's rare."

"Where's the first part of our journey?" Manak-na asked fascinated.

Rokuk smiled. "I'll add the rest of what I know. This is where we built the boat. We went north and then east following these arched islands. Then we turned south and came down this very long land. The people who lived there tell me that the land goes on this east side of the sea about as far down that way as to where we began our southern turn." Rokuk drew the lines as well as he remembered. "There you have it. Oh, wait. There is a great land south of the land where we build boats on the west side of the sea. It has a long shoreline. We were once blown there during a very bad storm. It was below the belt on the earth because for a long time we could not see the star that never moves." Rokuk's coconut was surprisingly accurate. He measured not in distance but rather in average time it took to go from one place to another.

Now Manak-na had a visual reference to their route home. He was fascinated to know the information Rokuk shared. What a wonder this coconut was! What a wonder it was to sail with people who knew where they were and how to get home over such vast distance. He hoped they didn't hit a great storm.

Ahna had not been part of the discussion, but she had heard it. It was, after all, in her language. She wanted to know more. At home she would never have asked, but somehow, she believed, this might be different.

"Will you show me?" she asked in her language.

Manak-na sat beside her. He held the coconut. He spoke in the language of the People. "This is where we left," he said. He put his finger on the boat-builders' place and traced his finger north. "We traveled up this way past this big land. We passed these islands. We came down by this distant land to the place where you lived. We stopped. We met Tikarumusa and you and your people. We returned to the boat. We sail towards these islands and then home."

Ahna looked into his eyes and pointed to the dots. "Islands?"

"Good, Ahna. Those are islands."

She pointed to the larger places, "Land?" she asked.

"Yes. Good, Ahna."

Ahna touched the bamboo boat and held her arms outstretched to describe the boat. "Boat?" she asked.

"Yes. That is good, Ahna."

She smiled a great smile. She was learning. It wasn't so hard. She had made Manak-na happy that she was learning. She could tell from his words and how he acted. She knew that he really didn't want to have taken her on the boat. He tried to cover up how he felt, but she knew. To work hard to learn his language was her way to try to make him less resistant to accepting her. She knew her people didn't want her. She hoped that despite Manak-na's reactions on the boat, he would take her to a people who would accept her. Finally, he was pleased with something she did. It was a good day! Manak-na took the coconut back to its place in the hut and he returned with his comb. He sat next to Ahna. He showed her the comb. "Comb," he said.

She repeated the word, but she seemed to have little sense of what the comb's use was.

Manak-na told her to sit in front of him. She complied. He began to comb her hair. There were many tangles in her hair and combing through them was hard on her. Sometimes the pain was terrible. She shed a few tears as he combed through her hair, but she did not cry out or try to fight him. He pulled all of her hair back and braided it. He bit off a piece of thin rope at the end and tied that around the bottom of the braid. He hoped that the braid would keep the tangles controlled. If she would be part of the People, she had to comb her hair, bathe, and pick her teeth. He would not take a dirty, uncombed, child with food in her teeth to his People. What would they think of him? He had not often had to comb the hair of children. Domur had always done that. Domur! Thoughts of her sliced pain through his belly. He missed her sorely.

Aside from the boat travel, Ahna was experiencing life she'd never known. Manak-na and Rokuk were kind to her. As one who the bird man had said was destined to leave, she'd become an afterthought to her people. They had dismissed her when they realized from the bird man that she would not remain with them. Her father called her good-for-nothing, as if he felt she had *chosen* to desert them. She was given the least of food. She was always wary and feared making a mistake. A small mistake could result in a rough strike from any adult and some who were between child and adult. Little love was ever shown her, while it was lavished on her siblings. She wished for more for herself, but she loved her siblings. Often she was charged with watching the little ones. She enjoyed the task. The little ones did not treat her badly. It kept her from total despair. She had come to look forward to the time when the bird man's prophecy would come true—someone would come for her. In her daydreams, whoever came would take her to a place where she would be part of a happy life. She looked at her hands. They were clean. She put her whole hands on the skirt of the tunic. She ran them over the soft leather. It was such an unbelievable experience. Sometimes she wondered whether she dreamed. Something so soft on her! It seemed impossible.

Lost in a daydream, Ahna unintentionally let out a shout when a flying fish landed beside her foot. She had never seen such a fish and it startled her. She looked at the lovely colors it displayed, but she moved away from it instinctively. Instantly many others joined it. She was considering that fish don't fly; birds fly. It was confusing her. Manak-na was on the lower level. Yomuk went to her and saw the flying fish. He smiled. He picked up the fish and tossed them back to the sea. Then he went to the water container and began to run water over his hands. Ahna saw what he was doing and was there quickly to pour the water over both his hands.

"Thank you," he said in the language of the People.

"You are welcome, Yomuk," she replied. "What was that?"

"Flying fish," he said in his language.

Ahna looked at him with lack of understanding showing on her face.

Yomuk put out to the side both his arms and twisted slowly to one side and then another. He flapped his arms, "Flying," he said. Ahna understood. She repeated the word.

Then Yomuk put both hands together, finger tips to finger tips. He made his hands move from left to right in a snake-like manner. He said, "Fish." Ahna got it. She repeated fish and then added the words together, "Flying fish!" Then she laughed. For some reason the idea of flying fish struck her as hilarious, and she enjoyed the laugh. Yomuk joined her, but for the life of him, he had no idea why he was laughing. He returned to his work hammering holes in anchors, wondering about the beautiful girl that would be People.

The endless array of days blurred. Time at sea did not seem so clear cut to Manak-na as it did on land. He asked Rokuk, "Have we passed the time of one moon to the same moon? I forgot to check the phase of the moon when we left."

"Yes, Manak-na, we are not quite a third of the way to our destination. This has been a good trip but not very fast. I usually feel that we are much closer to home than we are when we reach the islands in the middle of the voyage. We should be getting some speed soon."

"What do you mean?" Manak-na asked.

"See those clouds down there? They are the edge of a big storm. I don't think we will be hit with the full fury of the storm, but I expect the edges of it to speed us northwest toward the middle islands I showed you."

"Then we could get some tie up weather?"

"Yes, definitely. You've never seen the full fury of a storm. I hope you never do."

"I do also, and I assure you that Yomuk doesn't want to see one." Both men laughed.

The rest of the day they experienced mildly increasing wind speed. By the time of the evening meal, Yomuk was becoming alarmed, but he had a motive to try to hide his feelings. That motive was to appear manly in Ahna's eyes. He wasn't sure how much to eat, but he ate his normal amount of food, because he didn't want to appear afraid. Manak-na was noticing Yomuk and was recognizing the conflicts that he could see on his nephew's face.

Wisdom began to suck color from the sea. Stars that they used to guide them would be obscured this night by the fast approaching clouds. The drum sounded. Manak-na, Yomuk, and Ahna went to the lower level to relieve themselves, and then they went to the upper level. Manak-na washed the ochre off his face. When they entered the hut, Rokuk told them, "Tie up. You may not need it now, but you will later."

They reached the back of the hut and each tied up. Manak-na checked Ahna's tie up.

"Ahna, this is not done well. It's too loose around the bamboo. For tonight I will tie up for you, but this is something you have to master. A single tie up can determine whether you live or die at sea."

Ahna was chagrined that she had not done well, but she was overcome that Manak-na cared enough about her to do the tie up for her. She watched carefully. She put her basic sleeping skin on the floor of the boat and covered up with the soft, warm covering Rokuk had given her. The short dense hair was so soft!

"Manak-na," she asked, "Is this soft cover one that Rokuk had for his wife?" She had used the Mol language because the words were ones she didn't know.

Manak-na looked in her direction in the dark. "What made you think that?"

"When I thanked him for the tunic, he told me it was to have been for his wife, but she didn't live to wear it."

"Ahna, I don't know, but I think it best not to ask him."

"I won't. It was very kind of him to share with me."

"I agree. Now, let's get some sleep."

The day boatmen got sleep while the wind rose. It wasn't terribly blustery, but the back sail did have to be lowered and tied up. They were making good progress with the current and wind in one sail. Yomuk slept restlessly. He kept waiting for the wind to blow frighteningly wild. Yomuk slept through the worst of the storm.

Wisdom restored color to the sea. When the drum sounded and the men and Ahna untied and went outside, they could see that they still had some wind but it wasn't terrible. Ahna felt the need to hold onto something so as not to lose her footing. She had never seen the sea so choppy.

She looked at Manak-na who happened at the time to be looking at her. "I am afraid the sea spray is getting on the tunic. Rokuk told me to keep it dry. I must relieve myself. Then should I return to the hut inside?"

"Stay beside me and I'll find you a place to be. For safety you might tie up. And you need to do a good job of it."

"I will, Manak-na."

They got to the upper level and Rokuk met them. "I have put together a lean-to at the seat by the back sail. Ahna can tie up there for the day."

"Thank you," Ahna said quickly, followed immediately afterwards by Manak-na's expression of gratitude.

Rokuk showed them the little lean-to he'd made. It was a bin from the lower level turned upside down and lashed to the boat where the bamboo strips made a seat for Ralm, Manak-na, and Ahna behind the back sail. It was designed to be waterproof by the women who made the bins for the boats. They did expert weaving of grasses for the boats. Manak-na noticed that the lean-to was well tied to the boat—maybe even over-tied. It had a rolled grass mat that tied to the front of the lean-to. It was a cover for the bin, and Ahna could lower it, if she chose to. It would keep out most of the sea spray. The bottom had been a side of the bin, so the lean-to was essentially floored with waterproofed matting. Ahna would not be hit by water splashing up from below. Rokuk handed her a hairless skin that was soft and told her to wrap herself up in the skin while she was in the little hut. When she left the lean-to she was to fold the skin, put it in the gut wrapper, and tie it to the lean-to, so it would be protected from water. Ahna went into the lean-to where the wrapper had been tied to the side wall. There was good room for her, but Manak-na would not have fit into the place. She tied up carefully to the bamboo log just outside the lean-to.

Yomuk was fascinated that Rokuk was taking such effort for Ahna. He had watched the man set up the lean-to. He had really tied the structure to the boat, seemingly lost in thought.

Ralm knew Rokuk's story. Ralm had been at sea. He knew Rokuk's wife was going to have a baby when he left on one of the trips. He had found a tunic and wonderful sleeping skins, one made of chinchilla, from animals far, far south of Aikot, the place they stopped on the side of the water where the sun rose. They had been given to him as a gift. He had put them in empty gut skins to carry to his wife. He was devastated when he returned home to find that his wife had died giving birth to their daughter. His daughter had lived, and for years he resented her and was glad that his work involved sailing, so he didn't have to be around her. His mother took care of the girl. She grew up not really knowing her father. Somehow Ahna softened him and he thought he might look for his daughter when he reached his destination. He had seen what rejection did to a child who had no part in the reason she was rejected. He felt guilty. Ralm hoped he would follow through with his daughter when they returned home. The girl was introverted in much the same way Ahna was.

"Land! Land! Land!" Skuku called as loud as possible. His voice was deep and resonant. It carried well even in some wind.

Manak-na and Yomuk looked as far as they could along the horizon. Finally, Manak-na saw the top of a mountain and then another to the north of them. He wondered whether Rokuk would have them stop. Ralm told him, "We'll stop for water. There is nothing to hunt here except lizards and birds."

Ralm was right. As they neared, Rokuk told the boatmen that they would stop for water and then they'd continue to sail. Their stop was very brief and Manak-na and Yomuk stayed aboard the boat while they were there. The men knew exactly where to go to get water. They made several trips back and forth with water and to fill all the containers on the boat. Then they counted all the men aboard and resumed their travel, delighted to be at the middle islands.

Days blurred into days and more days. The boat kept heading towards their destination with little concern about storms. They passed island after island until finally there were no more islands visible. The only thing that kept Ahna from total boredom was that now she was learning faster and faster the language of the People. Manak-na had finally told her that when speaking to him or Yomuk she was to use only the language of the People.

Just before Wisdom lit the sky with brilliant rays of gold against a light blue sky, the drum sounded early and as soon as the exchange was finished, Rokuk gave out the tie up order. Ahna tied up in the lean-to and Manak-na checked to be sure she had done well. She had. Then he tied himself to the boat beside the lean-to. Yomuk had tied up in the back of the boat so he could help with the rudder. Everyone had tied up carefully, or so they thought.

Waves increased in size and great storm clouds began arriving from the south. Rokuk ordered lowering the back mast and sail. Manak-na and Ralm furled the sail and tied it down along with the mast. A few hours later, Rokuk ordered the lowering of the front sail and mast. It was done and he checked to be sure that it was done well. The bamboo and wood were creaking in protest from the twisting in the waves. Rokuk was busy checking and rechecking everything. He knew they were in for a great storm. Manak-na seemed to understand from the way Rokuk was acting. There was tension but apparently no real fear among the boatmen. Ahna lowered the rolled entry cover of her lean-to about half way. She wanted to see out but she also wanted to keep water out. She noticed that Rokuk was not tied up to the boat. She could see the rope dangling behind him as he walked.

The boat was hit by stronger wind and the waves were growing as big as any they'd seen on this trip. Rokuk could no longer deliver orders, because he could not be heard. Still he kept checking the boat. He went below to check the stowed bins. He had forgotten to check the covers to be sure they were well tied up. They were.

The storm hit with a fury that frightened Yomuk and Manak-na. Alone in her lean-to with the front flap secured all the way down Ahna was not frightened. She knew nothing about sailing and when the boat was wildly elevated on one side, it did not mean anything to her. In the tiny bin, she was not tossed around. Even the huge, ear-splitting cracking sound did not cause her to fear. When a wave came over the boat, it meant nothing to her. Besides, Manak-na was right outside. She could see his arm holding onto the bamboo of the boat right in front of her lean-to. Once she heard him shout out a word she didn't know. The word was "Wisdom!" During the whole of the lighted part of the day, the boat bobbed erratically in the wind and wild waves. Instead of sunlight, it appeared to be twilight to dark with frequent snatches of lightening flashing and thunder roaring above the roar of the wind and complaints of the boat. Waves the size of mountains would raise them up and they would slide down the other side as if in a great valley. Once in a while a huge wave top would crash upon them, making it hard to breathe until the wave washed back to the sea.

By the time Wisdom was about to start sucking color from the sea, the winds were dying down. Yomuk was exhausted. Both day and night boatmen worked the rudders together through the storm, trying to keep the front of the boat pointed toward oncoming waves. Yomuk had no time to fear—work took everything he had. Wave height was no longer as tall as big hills. They waited for Rokuk to give the order to untie the forward mast. Wisdom had changed the color of the sea to black, but still no order from Rokuk. Ralm became very uneasy. He told Manak-na to remain where he was. Ralm went through the boat systematically. He looked everywhere for Rokuk. He could not find the man anywhere. He began to sob near the point on the right front of the boat. He *knew*. Rokuk had been so busy checking the boat that he had either forgotten to tie up, or, worse, he had intentionally not tied up. Whichever the case, and he'd never know, Rokuk was gone. Ralm was now in charge of the boat. It would be his responsibility to get them home. He certainly knew how, but without his lifelong friend, it would be so difficult.

He returned to his spot near the back sail. "Manak-na, Rokuk is gone."

"What do you mean *gone*," Manak-na asked, not able to accept the fact that Rokuk might have been washed overboard.

"He has gone to the sea." Ralm was weeping. "I must get myself together to take over. I really ache for my friend. It is almost too much to bear."

"I understand, Ralm, but you have lives that depend on you now. You need to exchange the boatmen for night and turn over the responsibility to the night boatmen. Then, you need to find a way to sleep."

Inside the lean-to Ahna heard the conversation. She had not cried in her memory. Tears pent up from years slipped down the side of her face. She had cared for Rokuk. He had been so kind to her. Now, he was gone. It was too quick. Ralm beat the drum and called the untie order. The men were all on the top level at the same time. Ralm told them what had happened and that he was now responsible for getting them home safely. He turned the night responsibility over to Skuku. Manak-na went to the lean-to where Ahna was crouched. She rolled the cover all the way up and tied it. She came outside.

"I guess you heard."

"Yes, I heard," she affirmed, though her face covered with tears would have answered the question.

She untied and wound the rope around her arm. She and Manak-na headed to the lower level. They relieved themselves and returned to the upper level where she held the water container while Manak-na washed the ochre off his face. Yomuk was already in his sleeping area. They joined him quietly.

Manak-na asked, "You heard about Rokuk?"

"Yes. Of all the people on the boat, I can't believe we are missing *him*."

"He was traveling all over the boat not tied up," Ahna said.

"Ahna, are you sure?"

"Yes. Should I have told him?"

"No, Ahna, it's not your responsibility. He probably untied to go check something and meant to tie up again. I thought maybe his tie line broke."

"I only know what I saw before I lowered the front of the lean-to all the way down."

"Then he may or may not have been tied up. He could have tied up after you saw him untied. We'll probably never know."

They tried to find a comfortable place to sleep. The storm had sapped energy from each one of them for different reasons. They needed sleep. Ahna drifted off quickly. Manak-na wondered about Rokuk until he finally fell to sleep. The time had been short, but Manak-na had a friend in Rokuk. He grieved.

Yomuk lay there wide eyed. He had experienced a fierce storm at sea and had lived through it. He had been on the upper level when waves broke on the boat. He and Piman and the others worked the rudders occasionally during the storm. He had seen the boat travel up the side of unbelievably monstrous waves. He expected to die. Terror hurt his belly. He wasn't sure he'd ever want an adventure again. He was terribly homesick. He was glad they'd found Ahna. He really liked her. Now, he was certain he'd be glad to be a hunter to stay with the People. Without question he wanted no more sea adventures—ever. Finally, he, too, succumbed to the need for sleep.

When Wisdom brought light again to the sea, the boatmen discovered the source of the great cracking noise. When the boat had twisted in the big waves, one of the cross-piece logs at the bottom had split in the middle. It was a longitudinal split and it had not broken through, but it was a big split. No wonder that the noise was so loud.

The boat sailed with both sails for days and days. No more storms threatened. It seemed that they were endlessly at sea with no land visible for uncountable days. The boatmen and Manak-na, Yomuk, and Ahna experienced boredom, not even relieved by the occasional flying fish. One day turned into another.

"Land! Land! Land!" one of the night boatmen shouted just before Wisdom brought a crystal clear blue sky to the sea.

Ralm heard it and realized he had to get up. He didn't know how long he'd slept. He exited the hut and took a look for himself. Sure enough, there was land ahead.

"Head for the land," he said to the night rudder man.

He walked forward to the front of the hut. He watched for hours as they approached the island. *They could hunt,* he thought, *if this were the right island.* They could use some fresh meat and fruit.

He saw that they were approaching the big island from the southeast. He knew there were no sheltering coves, but the weather was fine and he had no concerns about approaching and anchoring on the sea side. He called for the sails to be furled and he shifted to rowers as they got close to the island. The beautiful beaches were composed of fine sand and ancient volcanic rocks. It made for a scenic, if somewhat treacherous, place to anchor.

Manak-na and Yomuk were sent to shore to hunt. Ahna remained on the boat watched over by Ralm. He alone knew why the girl had touched the heart of Rokuk. She occasionally looked like the man's wife. He would take good care of her—for her sake and Rokuk's.

Manak-na and Yomuk climbed the slope that was nearest to them. They carried two spears and their knives. The two moved as quickly as possible. Sitting on the boat had made them lose some of the strength they had before the trip.

Yomuk pointed out a couple of deer, the barking deer of short stature. Manak-na suggested they wait to see if they could find anything larger. Those animals were only as tall as his forearm was long. As they progressed up the hill, Manak-na looked down over a protruding rock and saw a larger animal herd where many of them were ruminating. Their horns were cone shaped and not branched. They grew straight upon the heads, curving only slightly backwards. They were about as tall as the waist of a man from the ground. Their coat was a dark shade of tan with yellow spots in the area of the head. The animals had very short tails. Neither Manak-na nor Yomuk had ever seen these animals, so they did not know what to expect of behavior. Both selected a resting animal. They would try to surprise it. At Manak-na's signal, the two went after their selected animal. Manak-na got his but Yomuk's began to run away before he could spear it. He was frustrated and threw his spear at the animal. He wounded the deer's front leg. He raced to the animal and managed the kill while the animal was struggling.

The two men took the deer and bled them. They gutted them and left the guts lying where they were. They tied the front and back legs together on each animal. They threaded their spears through the legs of the animals and carried them down the hill and towards the boat. The two saw men gathering fruit and water below. The fruit would taste good! They went to the water's edge and began their butchering. The meat would hang in the huts for a few days and then they would enjoy great feasts.

From habit the men skinned the animals, keeping the skin whole. They left it on the ground, not having any women who worked skins on the boat. When they took the first quarters of meat to the boat, Yomuk asked Ahna whether she knew how to work skins.

She looked down uncomfortable at the thought of disappointing him. "I have no idea," she replied.

Manak-na remembered when he taught her the words, "I have no idea," and realized she equated it with "I don't know." They'd deal with that later when he'd had time to figure out how to explain it.

When all the fruit, meat, and water they could carry had been loaded aboard, they rowed out and around the northernmost part of the island and on toward their destination in the north. The boatmen all knew the shoreline where they traveled. This was part of their land. There was an almost festive air on the boat. The person who felt the festive air acutely was Ahna.

When the evening meal was served, men carried meat sticks, lychee fruit, and the apple-like lembu fruit serving all the boatmen and Ahna. The sweetness of the lychee fruit with its lovely red skin was the favorite of all on the boat. Ahna was surprised when she was told she could have one of each. She had never been given such food! She had had no food bowl, so Manak-na had fashioned one for her from a half coconut. It was one of her treasured possessions. She leaned over the food bowl to avoid dripping the fruit on her tunic.

Slowly, Wisdom removed the color from the sea and land, while the drum beat told the boatmen that it was time to change places. Before going into the hut, Ahna stood looking to the southwest. The sunset was deep hued and lovely. It reminded her of her long ago home, but she did not long for it. She was now adventuring, and she delighted in it. Somewhere before long would be a place where she would fit. She had no understanding at all how—only the certainty that it would be.

The People had left the carved out cave. When they left, they couldn't fail to notice the call of Raven who seemed to chide them for leaving. Raven did not fly away. Instead he followed with his mate. Ki'ti wondered whether he was interrupted in raising his young. She felt sad about any disruption she may have caused the birds, but the People needed to find a place to stay for the winter, and the place they last occupied was not adequate. She considered also that Raven did not need to follow.

They had been trekking for moons. All were tired, when a hill across a small valley displayed a sign, evergreen trees, graceful pines, visible against the background of the hill. The People rested while Sum-na, Tongip-na, and Ekuktu-na went to see what the pines marked, if anything. The trail up to them was somewhat difficult to find. There was a cliff under them.

Sum-na located the trail and they climbed up. There was a natural cave there. Sum-na listened carefully. He thought he could hear water, but he was unsure and, without a torch, he wasn't going deep into the cave. The other two men arrived and only Tongip-na could hear what Sum-na was hearing. They made a small torch and went to explore. There were remains of something that had been eaten by an animal, but the cave had no odor of animal presence as it would if one habitually lived there. They saw some tools lying about and hearths, used a very long time ago. The ceiling like the others was very high. A smoke hole was open at the top. There were numbers of rooms, and down at the very bottom was water. Tongip-na tasted the water. It was good. They all enjoyed slaking their thirst.

Tongip-na went outside. He looked to see if he could find a meat preparation cave. Usually where there was one cave, there were others. Sum-na and

Ekuktu-na came to help look. Finally, Ekuktu-na stumbled on one that had been hidden by some evergreen rhododendron bushes. The bushes actually blocked the entrance. Sum-na returned to the first cave and retrieved the torch they had left in a hearth. They entered the second cave and found it ideally suited to serve for meat preparation. It, too, had running water.

Sum-na offered to return to the People to call them to the caves. The other two men fully explored the second cave. Ekuktu-na noticed that there were pines above the place where they had explored the caves. He decided to have a look. He climbed up the unused path and reached the place where once again, he was surprised by what looked like a structure made of rocks from which to examine the night sky from high placed windows. It also had a clear view back to where they had been. He became more and more convinced that these places served several functions. Two of them must have been to examine the night sky and to communicate somehow with others at a distance. He wondered what other purposes they may have had. He returned to the cave where they'd probably live through the winter. From there he could see the People trekking towards the cave. Soon they'd be sweeping the caves and packing in their supplies. Until then he chose to rest against an old tree the trunk which first grew horizontally from the hillside and then straight up.

Soon enough the People arrived and it was quiet no longer. Women were sweeping both caves, enabled to see in the dark by the torches the men had set up to light the interior. The youth were busy searching windfall logs for hearth fires and the girls had set up a perimeter for the dogs. Other young men had been digging out a human privy away from the cave. When setting up a cave, there was always a flurry of activity. A few women had already started a hearth fire for cooking and had a spit set up over it for roasts they had been carrying. There were aurochs roasts. They had been cut into pieces which would cook faster on several spits than the whole roast on a single spit. A single spit would likely have broken with a full roast on it. Some girls were searching for greens, while hunters were assessing the safety of the area from predatory or poisonous wildlife. Overhead the sound of Raven added to the din.

Tiriku went down to the flat land below. Raven saw him and flew down while his mate sat in a tree nearby watching. Tiriku nuzzled the bird, and Raven used his head and beak to touch Tiriku on his neck and chest. Raven lay on the ground on his back and Tiriku took his forepaw and arched it above the bird's belly, but did not touch the bird. He nudged its wing with his nose. Raven got up and hopped about as if dancing. Tiriku danced back and forth with exaggeratedly lowered forepaws. Then he'd stand still and twist his head from side to side. Raven would cock his head. What or whether they communicated anything People could understand was not clear, but they did display happiness in a long friendship. There was no doubt of that. Tiriku returned to the cave and Raven left.

Ki'ti had already agreed that this cave would be good for the winter. They had seen deer in the little valley and some had been seen on the hillsides. Meat was available. They were almost at the season of colorful leaves, so there was time to prepare for winter. It seemed good. Ki'ti was tired. She looked over and noticed that Domur had gathered several small children and was teaching them to sing children's songs. There was Rish, Yosh, Lag, Solu, Phelen, Olmot, and Kuma. Domur had their attention. The fatigue drained from Ki'ti at the sight. How she had worried about Domur. Something had changed her seemingly overnight. It was wonderful. Out of the corner of her eyes, Ki'ti could see her own hair. She would need to get Likichi to trim if for her. It had grown a lot since she had her cut it. She loved having it cut short.

Likichi looked around. Already it looked like People had been living in the place for some time. The walls were edged with sleeping mats and skins; the hearth was alight with a fire cooking the evening meal; the weapons were placed neatly by the entryway; winter clothing was folded and stored in the next room waiting for cold weather; gourds were filled with water for drinking or cooking; Domur had children singing, which caused Likichi to smile; life was good. It would be even better, she thought, if her son and grandson returned soon.

Nanichak-na listened to Ekuktu-na tell about the building of stone blocks above them that made an observation place. He was fascinated with the building by Mol giants of long ago. He asked if there were other evergreen marked places around. No one had stood out in the valley to observe. Ekuktu-na was curious, so he went down the path to the valley and looked up. Sure enough there was another, or maybe two more sets of evergreens. He rejoined the men and they climbed to the place Ekuktu-na pointed out. Again, in this place there was a flat surface on which had been placed objects—some were familiar to the People, and some were not. Ki'ti had suggested these were offerings to Wisdom, but the men wondered about whether Mol giants had any knowledge of Wisdom. They doubted it. Of course, they recognized, People could have occupied these caves after the giants. They had not, however, encountered any People north of where they lived. Maybe the Mol giants left them to honor a god they worshipped. They still felt, no matter what, it would be best if the People left the things untroubled. They would discuss it at the men's council.

Ekuktu-na remembered the other place that might be a cave. He pointed that out to the men and they followed him to the place where he thought he might find another. The entrance was very small and it was covered by tenacious growth of some old evergreen rhododendron shrubs grown tight together, shrubs that did not want to be removed. It was hard work just getting to the entrance. They had to cut down most of the blocking limbs. Finally, they broke through. Once inside, it was so dark that they just could not see. They decided to make a quick torch. Sum-na put one together. He took the torch to the home cave and lit it from the hearth fire. He returned to the cave and stepped inside. All three men gasped. The walls were painted in much the same manner they had seen in the land where they lived so long after the ashfall.

The paintings were breathtaking. There was what appeared to be one of the People. Men who looked like Mol surrounded him. It appeared that they were giving him gifts. He looked very, very old. There was the old man again. One of his outstretched arms was a perch for a raven; the other held a walking stick. In another place there was the old man again, and this time he stood with his foot on the neck of a man who appeared to be Mol with darker colored skin. In another there was a woman with the old man, and they appeared to love each other. Painted much smaller were many other figures that looked like People. The old man had white hair and wore a tunic that was down to his ankles. Atop the tunic was a long rectangular shape that had a slit for the man's head to stick through. It was cut open down the front and tied at the waist. The old man had an exceptionally long beard and long hair. In another place there was a huge slab covered with every kind of food imaginable, and he ate from it. The three men looked at each other dumbfounded.

"I think it's time to get ready for the evening meal and talk to Ki'ti about coming here to see what she thinks of this," Ekuktu-na said. He did a loud palm strike, joined by Sum-na and Nanichak-na.

"I couldn't agree more. I don't think we can imagine what this represents or communicates," Nanichak-na admitted, "And for some reason I really want to get out of here."

The three men went back down the hill to the home cave.

There were times, Nanichak-na thought, *when one was far more comfortable not exploring to pursue things that made no sense. Narrow boundaries were safe, less stressful. Sometimes ignorance was wonderful.* Nanichak-na wandered over to his sleeping bundle. He unrolled it and set up his place for the night. He sat on the soft cover and rested his legs. He was tired and his muscles were aching. His aged joints had taken a beating on these treks.

The call for the evening meal went out. The -na hunters gathered and Ki'ti joined them at the end of the line, just after Untuk-na. They were talking animatedly. Nanichak-na wandered over and took his place just in front of Untuk-na. He was hungry. When the two stopped talking, Nanichak-na told them about the strange cave with the pictures. He asked Ki'ti to go there the next day to look at them and to tell them what she thought. She agreed.

Domur and Minagle were discussing the greens. They tasted fresh and good. They expected that someone had put some meat in the cooking water to flavor them. They discussed the new cave and how wonderful it appeared to be. Sum-na told them about the strange cave they had found. The two women were surprised. Paintings again. They wanted to see them. Sum-na expected that everyone would want to see them.

Wisdom brought up a covering of clouds at the same time that the color left the land. No stars or bright moon illuminated the darkness. The People had gone to their sleeping places. Calm fell over them and the fires were allowed to remain low for the night. Guy-na and Arkan-na were taking the night watch, since this was a new occupancy. The dogs were just inside the entryway. They had circled and found places on the ground that seemed to appeal to them. The men chuckled as the dogs rearranged themselves. It seemed to them that the dogs got up, moved in circles, and then lay down, always returning to the exact place they'd vacated, as if it might be different after making the circle.

Grypchon-na was experiencing some significant pain. Likichi had used every herb she could think to try to relieve his pain. He was just stiff. She massaged him, and that made him feel better on a very temporary basis. She had given him some herbs for pain this evening and he seemed to feel some relief. They both knew his condition might be permanent. Some old people got this stiffness. She wished he hadn't, but he had. All that was possible was to try to relieve it. She knew of no cure.

Ki'ti watched the flames from the nearby hearth make shadows dance on the ceiling. She thought that Elemaea had made significant change. No longer was she the impulsive child she had been, instead she was contributing to the People some excellent work in her spear point making. Ki'ti was grateful that she had settled down and was not only fitting into the group but also fitting in well. It was great joy to her to see her daughter thriving.

It was a different feeling she had for her son. She missed him sorely, but she still had the conviction that it was necessary for him to learn from the adventure. What he needed to learn, specifically, she didn't know. She only knew that he had an idea that hunters were somehow superior People, and he needed to reassess that idea. All were equally People. -Na indicated a superior hunter, not person. It didn't mean the -na hunter was superior to other hunters personally, just more seasoned and mature. The People would no longer be the People, if *some* thought better of themselves than others, or if even *one* thought he was better than others. It was a concept totally foreign to Wisdom.

When Wisdom restored color to the land the cloud covering had moved away. People waked up and began their morning meal. Some gathered around Sum-na, Ekuktu-na, and Nanichak-na. Ki'ti was there and Lamul-na. Hahami-na and Untuk-na had joined, along with Tongip-na. They left for the strange painted cave. Tiriku was at Ki'ti's heels. They didn't have far to go up the hill. Those who hadn't seen it before noticed the structure made from stones. It seemed something out of place or time to them.

Ki'ti could see the place where the rhododendron bushes had been cut down at the entrance. She noticed there were still some tiny leaves at the base of the bushes. She hoped they had strength to grow back. She entered the cave after the men had gone inside with torches. She was overwhelmed at first, not by the pictures which were beautifully done but left one to wonder why they were there, but rather by the intense feeling that the People should not be there. In logic she had no reason to think they should not be there, but the feeling was with her.

Ki'ti pushed past the pictures. Untuk-na had a torch and he followed Ki'ti. She found a break in the wall and went through it. Untuk-na had to squeeze through. It was awkward. There was a musty smell. Once inside, he saw what Ki'ti had found. Facing him, sitting on a seat with a back carved from the wall of the cave was a mummy. There was no question that this mummy was the one depicted in the pictures on the wall. He even had traces of long white hair and a beard. He was a good bit taller than People, but he was clearly People. He exhibited no trace of mixing. There were things laid out on the floor all around him. She wondered at the sight. The oppression was increased. She knew that there was some spiritual attempt to reach her, but she was not at all certain that she wanted to allow herself to be reached. She called silently to Wisdom to protect her from contact. She kept hearing from memory what Wamumur had said so long ago, "You NEVER need to know what happened in another time or place." What appeared to her was that one of the People had allowed himself to think more of himself than of others, and others had agreed to it. Then the man gained power and when he died, he was given this mummy burial as someone special. It appeared to be the opposite of what she wanted her son to learn. Somehow she was convinced it had to do with the structure that had been built from rocks. Did the man who was now a mummy have information gained from the structure that he used to make him powerful? She wondered how such an awful social stratification could have happened. She did not want this to be something that the People would see as good.

She looked at Untuk-na with an expression on her face of pain. She told him that she needed to understand more and that she would let the spirits talk to her. She asked him to call Wisdom if she appeared to be in distress. Untuk-na was frightened, but he agreed. He wished Manak-na were there with him.

Ki'ti sat on the ground facing the mummy. She saw the mummy gain flesh but remain immobile. It said to her, "How dare you invade my place!"

"It's a cave, nothing more," she replied with more force than Untuk-na knew she had.

"It is my burial cave! You have invaded it! This place is sacred!" the old man screamed.

"You were just a man. You are not Wisdom. You should have been buried in the earth so you could return to Wisdom. Yet you sit here as if you're still walking this land."

"I am Wisdom. I am worshipped as Wisdom. The Wisdom you speak of is not real."

"You have misled yourself, Old Man. You are not wise. You speak nonsense." She did a palm strike.

The mummy shouted at her, "I am Wisdom!"

"You speak foolishness, Old Man. You have made yourself appear to have flesh again, but the truth is that you are a pile of dust that has the appearance of what used to be and is no more. I am from a time much later than you. You are nothing and will stay nothing until you are buried in the soil. Then you can return to the true Wisdom."

"You know nothing!"

"I know Wisdom, Old Man, and you are not Wisdom. Wisdom is not puffed up. You are. Wisdom does not need all this. You do—to keep fooling yourself."

Untuk-na was listening to a one-sided conversation. So far there appeared to be nothing serious occurring. He watched carefully. He was aware that some of the People were listening beyond the crack through which they had entered this part of the cave. The People knew better than to interrupt something like this.

"I am not fooling myself. You are here now. You speak out of turn. You are in the presence of Wisdom, and I am not pleased."

"You are nothing but a foolish old man," Ki'ti said firmly. "I do not fear you. You have a mummified body that sits in a cave year after year when you could be with Wisdom. That is nonsense."

"I should have your head cut off!"

"Old man, you have been dead for a very long time. There are none of your people here. You are totally alone. You can order nothing. You speak arrogant, empty words just like you did when you were alive. What ate your soul?"

"Get out!" the mummy screamed.

"I will leave when I am ready. Not before." Ki'ti was standing up to this spirit in stronger ways than Untuk-na knew she could. He was unable to see anything change with the mummy, which Ki'ti must be seeing. He was definitely curious about what was happening.

"Get out! Leave! You have no permission to be here." The mummy was beside itself with rage.

"Not until I have buried you and removed all the pictures from the walls," Ki'ti said. "Then you will no longer remain here. You will go where you belong."

The mummy screamed horrible screams. Ki'ti disconnected from the spiritual world of the mummy. She asked the men at the crack to bring tools to bury the mummy. They were a little troubled, but they acted quickly on her request. They returned and squeezed through the opening to dig a pit.

"Wait," Ki'ti said, "I think we should remove him from this cave for burial outside as we bury our own. This man is People."

Some of the men went quickly outside and began to dig a pit. The land was filled with tree roots, and it was too difficult. They returned to Ki'ti and told her.

"Can you dig on the flat land down there? His body could be taken from here and moved."

"It could fall apart," Tongip-na said.

"It doesn't matter," Ki'ti said firmly. "He must be buried outside."

A few men went quickly to the valley floor and away from any path. On the other side of the valley, they began to dig. Others had brought a skin to transport the mummy. They had a difficult time getting it out of the cave and it did not come in one piece. They wrapped up the remains and tied it tightly to a stretcher. They carried it down the path and to the valley. The men placed it in hole in the ground. Once the dirt covered the mummy and rocks had been placed on top, they returned to the cave. Ki'ti had been specific about destroying the pictures. They were fantastic pictures and the men felt badly about destroying the art of it, but Ki'ti said it must go. They sensed it had something awful connected to it, and they saw the man with his foot on the neck of someone. They carefully destroyed all of the art work.

At the men's council that night, Ki'ti explained to the People, "We went to a cave uphill. In that cave were beautiful paintings of a man who was doing things that were not right. He was a chief who was evil. He was People and he was tall. He wanted others to worship him as if he were Wisdom."

People all over the cave gasped. The idea was foreign and totally repellant.

"He needed to be buried, so he could go to Wisdom. Wisdom will deal with his sickness. I have decided that we will do a proper burial story by his grave tomorrow at high sun. I have asked the hunters to destroy the paintings. They were amazing but what they showed was evil. It is now gone. For People to go to look on evil paintings could contaminate the mind web with evil thoughts and keep the evil of this mummy going on and on for years. It has ended. I am asking that Wisdom will destroy the ideas from the paintings from the mind webs of those who saw them—including mine. That is all I have to say."

At high sun the next day, all the People gathered at the grave site of the mummy. Ki'ti stood there solemn, wondering what had happened to the old man. She began the graveside ritual of the People:

"In the beginning, Wisdom made the world. He made it by speaking. His words created. He spoke the water and the land into existence, the night and day, the plants that grow in the dirt, and the animals that live on the dirt, and those that live in the water and in the air. Then he went to the navel of the earth. There he found good red soil and started to form it into a shape with his hands. He made it to look a little like himself. Then he inhaled the good air and breathed it into the mouth of the man he created. The man came to life. Then he took some of the clay left from the man and he made woman. He inhaled and breathed life into her. Wisdom created a feast. He killed an aurochs, skinned it, made clothing for the man and woman from the aurochs, and then roasted the aurochs for the feast. The man and the woman watched carefully and quietly to see how he killed the aurochs, how he skinned it, how he made clothing from its skin, and how he roasted it. They paid good attention and they were able to survive by doing what they had seen done."

"The People were special and Wisdom pronounced that the man was to treat the land and the water and the animals and the woman the way he wanted to be treated—good. And the same was true of the woman. And it went well for a long time. But Wisdom hadn't made the People of stone. He had made them of dirt, knowing that they shouldn't have lives that would go on too long for they might get prideful and forget Wisdom. That is good because People should not be without Wisdom. They would die."

"That is why the People return to Wisdom when they die. They are placed in the earth and Wisdom knows. When Wisdom hears of a death of the People, Wisdom waits until the grave is filled back. He waits until it is dark. Then he causes the earth to pull on the spirit of the dead to draw that person's spirit back through the dirt of the earth to the navel from which all People came, the navel of the earth where the red clay for making the first man was. The dead spirits depart for the navel of Wisdom. That is where they reside for all time. All People's bodies return to the dirt. But their spirit, that essence of the person made by the One Who Made Us, is pulled back to Wisdom in the place where first man was made, and Wisdom keeps all those he chooses with him there, safe and loved. There is a cycle Wisdom made: a cycle from the navel to the navel. He keeps the spirits of those whom he chooses and he destroys those whom he hates. Wisdom hates those who hate him, those who ignore him, those who would be hurtful to him or the land or water or to those living things Wisdom made including People."

In silence the People returned to their chores. It had been an odd burial. No one had spoken a word about the dead man. What could they say? He lived in a long forgotten past and he seemed to have been very evil.

Ki'ti remained sitting for a long time on a log near the grave with Tiriku right beside her feet. Something bothered her, but she couldn't pin it down. She felt fear for Manak-na and Yomuk. Little could she guess that while she felt that fear, they were experiencing a storm unlike any they had seen. Finally, Ki'ti said, "Wisdom, protect Manak-na and Yomuk. Thank you."

Later, startled by a fluttering noise, she stared towards the north. Untuk-na shared the log on which she sat, but he was not right next to her. Ki'ti was very tired, but wasn't ready to climb the hill to the cave. Suddenly, they saw ravens land. The ravens formed an irregular circle. They seemed intent on harassing a raven that was with them and about which they had circled. They pecked at it without doing it harm, but the raven was frightened. Ki'ti hoped it was not their raven. The others continued to peck at it and they seemed to be talking one by one. One or several would rush the raven and then appear to peck it. Ravens in the circle seemed to cheer on ravens that pecked at the raven in the center or chat among themselves. The birds were very noisy. The bird in the center appeared accused of something. It had feathers askew, and Ki'ti wondered whether it had indeed been pecked hard by some of the birds. Some others hopped up to it shrieking.

Ki'ti and Untuk-na were startled when Raven flew from the sky and landed right beside Tiriku. The bird cocked its head from side to side using first one eye and then the next to scrutinize Ki'ti and Untuk-na. It was as if Raven wondered why they were there. Raven brushed against Tiriku and flew off. Momentarily the thought passed through Ki'ti's mind web that the bird wanted them to know he was not involved in the activity of the other ravens.

The whole ring of ravens began to hop towards the single raven. Finally, the raven that appeared to have been accused took flight. Others followed screeching at it. It flew as high and fast as it could. Ki'ti was certain that the raven would not return to the area where these ravens lived. But what had happened? She wondered, *what could a raven do to make a whole group of ravens reject it?* Untuk-na took her by both hands. He pulled her up. He knew she needed sleep, even if she'd forgotten.

―✐―

The boat was nearing home. An inlet had been dug but was dammed. They would have to dig out the dam and wait for a high tide before the boat could enter. A new double hulled boat was sitting in an adjacent area. Boatbuilders raced to the shore when they saw the boat returning. It was a time of rejoicing for the safe return. There would be feasting.

Manak-na had talked to Ralm about getting cold weather clothing made for Ahna. They would be leaving to find his People and she would not survive without cold weather clothes and boots. Ralm had explained that all that was needed was to ask the women on the hill. He'd accompany Manak-na and Ahna to the village after he finished up at the shore. He told Manak-na they might already have some things available. They did that service in exchange for the hunting the boatbuilders did for them. Manak-na told him he'd also need a backpack for her. Ralm assured him that the backpack would be part of what would be supplied. He told him that meat sticks would also be provided to each one. Manak-na was very grateful.

They spent some time saying farewell to people they knew. Later that day, Manak-na, Ahna, Yomuk, and Ralm went to the village on the hill. Ralm explained what was needed.

"We have what you need," a very thin, gray haired woman told Ralm. "This is the girl?" she asked.

"Yes," Ralm said.

The old woman went to another part of the building in which they were standing. The building wasn't a place where people lived. Manak-na had no clear idea what the purpose of the building was but it appeared to be a place where clothing and other things were kept so they were available when needed. It seemed to fill a storage function for clothing, backpacks, boots, head coverings, boat sails and rudders, strips of leather and rope, and things unfamiliar to him. These items were kept in the way that their meat storage worked for keeping meat available when needed. It struck him as a great idea to have needed items made in advance of need and ready for use.

She returned with a number of items and a backpack. She tried the garments on Ahna. Ahna had never had any foot coverings and they felt very strange. She did not reject them, she just watched. She had to learn how these garments worked, so she paid good attention. The pants were a little long but with the boots on, they were fine. The heavy, long jacket was fur lined and had fur cuffs. There were hand coverings made of fur lined skins. The head covering was fur and it draped around the shoulders to a length longer than Manak-na's hand. It tied in front. The material was heavy. Ahna wondered what type of weather required all this heavy clothing.

Manak-na thanked the old woman. She seemed surprised at his outpouring of gratitude. She told him that they had appreciated his hunting. He bowed his head.

Ahna thanked the woman. The woman reached out and hugged her. Ahna returned the hug, but she could not understand the behavior of these people. They were so different from what she knew. She was amazed at the clothing. She guessed she was going to a place where it would be very cold. Just wearing the heavy clothes for a few minutes made her sweat profusely.

Ralm suggested they remain that night and depart the next day. Manak-na thanked the man, told him he wanted to say farewell to Pah, but then wanted to depart. He had far to go.

They went to find Pah and he tried to encourage them to stay, but Manak-na was firm. They would leave. Ahna was struggling under the weight of the backpack. Manak-na already had her bedding tied to his backpack along with his. They were all weighted down. Finally they left the boat-building place and began to walk up the hill. Manak-na had decided to stay in the cave where they slept the night just before arriving at the boatbuilders' place. It would take about half a day to reach it.

Ahna did not complain. Her load was heavy for her, but she had no intention of saying anything that would be of a negative nature. She felt truly grateful for all that had been done for her. Ever since Manak-na had taken her, People were caring about her for what felt like the first time in her life.

After much uphill struggling, the three reached the first cave. Manak-na checked for snakes and spiders and beckoned them inside. They went in and laid down their burdens and took time for meat sticks and water. Wisdom was sucking color from the land, so they finished the meal and got out their bedding and prepared for sleep. They slept well.

When Wisdom restored color to the land, they ate, packed up, and left heading for the place where the paths crossed. Manak-na was convinced it would take more than two double hands of days to reach the place. Ahna definitely slowed them, or, he wondered, were they just not in very good shape after sitting so much on the boat? It was easier to blame Ahna than face the fact that they were not in the hunter shape they had been before the trip. But Manak-na wouldn't let himself live with a lie, and finally he realized that he and Yomuk were grateful for the extra time they were taking. They were no longer in good hunter shape.

They plodded on until they found a place for each night. Occasionally Manak-na or Yomuk speared something for the evening meal. Manak-na usually cooked the food, since neither of the others had been taught. Manak-na decided that the time for them to learn was the present, so he began instructing them. He explained the meat sticks as useful for their designated purpose, food in the absence of fresh food. Ahna learned to look for specific greens and Manak-na showed her how to cook them in a bladder he'd taken from a deer Yomuk had killed. The greens and water were placed in a bag which was hung on a tripod. Hot rocks from the fire were dropped into the bag using folded leather or sticks to pick up the hot rocks. The hot rocks warmed the greens. Manak-na talked to her about local snakes and showed her some of them and where they stayed during the day and at night. Not knowing the plants in this place, she was told not to deviate from what they had previously picked. She was very careful.

When they reached the place where the paths crossed, it was too early in the day to stop. They turned north on the path, and finally saw the cairn with the arm pointing north. They knew that was a sign for them, and they followed knowing they might see more of those. They did. When they reached a place where dirt covered the path, another cairn pointed the way. Manak-na speared a black, long nosed boar that he found in the hills. They had a great time eating that night. They slept in lean-tos in the valley. The meat they hadn't eaten the night before was tied high in a tree across the valley from where they were. They could hear other animals trying to get it as they drowsed. Manak-na had the first watch and Yomuk had the second. Animals left them alone.

The next day foretold the pattern of many more. They walked and walked. The cairns were clear for giving directions whenever the path was covered. All three of them were increasing in strength. Yomuk had taken some of the clothing for Ahna and put it in his backpack to ease her load. Manak-na was impressed. Ahna was relieved.

They had fresh food almost every night. What wasn't eaten at night was eaten the next day. Rarely did they need meat sticks. Meat sticks, or jerky, from the Mol was palatable, but it wasn't as good as the jerky prepared by the People in Manak-na's and Yomuk's opinions. Ahna was grateful still for food regardless of how it tasted.

As they had felt on the boat, day faded into day with little to change the pattern. They continued north, surprised at how far the People had come, yet bored at the seemingly endless sameness of the place. As they continued on, one day a raven kept sweeping over them and screeching with great force. As they continued, suddenly Ahna said, "What is that? Do you hear people?"

Manak-na said, "I hear nothing but a noisy raven."

Yomuk said, "I can hear something. It is very faint." The raven was flying about making sounds that varied and suddenly in the pauses Manak-na could hear People. "We have finally arrived," he announced, standing a little straighter.

People came flooding down the hill. Domur was in front. She had heard the raven and hoped it meant what she wanted it to mean. Her hope was rewarded. She raced down the hill and the two hugged. She looked at her husband's face and wondered about the face painting. Her fingers found the scars on Manak-na's back and she knew she'd find out about that later when it was time for sleep. All were shocked to see three People when they only expected two. But no one was displeased. There were hugs and People took their burdens and carried them up the hill. It was nearing time for the evening meal and the excitement created so much noise in the home cave that the sounds were almost deafening. Likichi shouted for the noise to decrease. An instant hush fell over the People. -Na hunters were called to get their food. Ki'ti realized that Ahna would have no way to know the way of the People, so she went to her side and told her to follow her. She asked where the girl's food bowl was. She looked for her backpack and saw it in the cave toward the end. She went to get it and returned to Ki'ti. Ki'ti looked at the bowl.

"Manak-na did this?" she asked.

"Yes," Ahna said with pride.

"We'll get you another," Ki'ti said.

"No, please, that is the first thing I ever owned in my life. I treasure it."

Ki'ti looked at the girl. She reminded her of herself. "It's okay," she said, "Nobody will take it from you. It's just that our bowls are better. Why don't you keep yours and use one of ours."

That seemed reasonable, so Ahna took her bowl back to the backpack and Ki'ti gave her another.

"After you get your food, Ahna, find me and sit with me," Ki'ti said. "I want you at the men's council after we eat."

"I will," was all that Ahna could think to say. She knew if she'd ever approached the men's council at her home, she'd have been beaten severely. It would take her a long time to understand these People.

Domur and Manak-na walked outside together. She asked, "What is the face painting?"

"Ahna's grandfather believed that the god of the underwater wants to hurt me. He gave me this bag of ochre and showed me how to paint this to protect me from the god of the underwater."

"But you are not near water now."

"He assured me that the god of the underwater is not constrained by the water."

"Oh?" was all Domur could think to say.

The evening meal was finished. Ki'ti showed Ahna how to clean her bowl and where to put it. She showed her how to recognize it again. Then she took her to the place where the men's council met. Ki'ti took her seat and Tiriku came over and sat beside her and then stretched out. Ahna was astonished.

"I do have a dog," Ki'ti explained to Ahna.

Ahna suddenly realized that Ki'ti had the leadership seat at the men's council. She did not understand at all. She grew up in a place where women had no leadership function.

Manak-na made eye contact with Ki'ti. She nodded to him.

Manak-na said, "We went to the land of the boatbuilders. There we hunted while the boatbuilders finished the boat. The boat was huge with two sections called hulls. Hulls are made from binding bamboo logs together to make it almost solid. Six trees, three at the lower level and three at the top holds the hulls together. It creaks. There is a mast in the center of the front two top logs. A mast is a pole to pull up the sail, a wind catcher. The mast is made from a log. The mast holds a flat mat of grasses carefully woven together in ways I do not understand. That's the sail. It catches the wind and that makes the boat move through the water. It is an inspirational thing to see. It's as if the boat has two bird wings of brownish green that make it speed over the water. On the back of the boat is something called a rudder. There are two of them. This makes it possible for a man to make the boat move in the direction he chooses. The front and back of the hull is pulled upwards. It's much narrower at the end point than in the middle. I will draw this tomorrow so you can see what it looked like."

"We live on a huge thing called earth. This coconut has a drawing of where we went. If anyone is interested I'll show you how the coconut shows this. I treasure this coconut, because it shows our entire voyage. When we reached the land where the sun rises, we found this girl. Her name is Ahna. Their bird man had given a prophecy about her just after she was born. He told that People would come for her to take her to a different place where there was something she was supposed to do. After her people heard that she would leave, she was treated poorly. It was as if they thought she had rejected them. She was just a child! She is still a child. She managed to survive in spite of little food and being struck for anything they felt she did wrong—or for no reason at all."

"On our voyage home, Ahna, Yomuk, and I experienced a terrible storm. Waves on the water were as high as these hills, if not higher. Sometimes the storm would stand the boat on end. It frightened us, except for Ahna who didn't know what to expect from a boat on water. One man was taken by a wave. Some waves crashed over us. We were tied to the boat. There were things we've never seen. There are fish that fly. When they land in the boat, you have to throw them back to the sea or keep them to cook for the evening meal. There are monster animals called whales. They are large to enormous.

They can be as long as it is from this cave to the valley below. They breathe through nostrils instead of gills. When they breathe out, it makes a steamy spout that looks a little like a volcano exploding, and it all smells awful. We have had an interesting time, but it is good to be home."

When Manak-na stopped talking everyone was looking at him gaping. He had tossed out so many ideas at once that they were having trouble assimilating. Manak-na desperately wanted to talk about his adventure, but he had tossed out the information in ways he'd seen the Mol do, and it frustrated him, because even he recognized it. There was no way his People could put all the information together and make sense of it. Even Ki'ti was staring at him, unsure what to say.

Ki'ti looked at Yomuk. "Do you want to add anything?"

"Manak-na did a good job of telling the adventure," Yomuk said.

Ki'ti looked at him. *Maybe he did a good job for you. You were there. For us, it's confusing,* she thought, but she didn't say it out loud.

Ki'ti looked at Ahna. "Is there anything you'd like to say?"

Ahna was stupefied that she'd be asked a question, but she recovered quickly and said slowly as one learning a language, "I am glad to be here. I do not know why I am supposed to be here. Do you?" Her green eyes pierced Ki'ti's blue ones. She was searching, and Ki'ti understood.

Ki'ti looked at the little girl. Little Girl? The two words that came together almost took her breath. Surely this couldn't be the one to replace her? She said, "I am not certain why you are here, Ahna. We are glad you are here, and no one will hurt you. In time we will know why you are here. Do not spend time in worry. Just enjoy life here."

Manak-na noticed the peculiar expression on Ki'ti's face as she tried to answer Ahna's question. Then it occurred to him that the girl might be Ki'ti's replacement the People so desperately needed. It also occurred to him Ki'ti might be thinking the same thing. He was glad he didn't suspect that on the trip. He'd have been even more frightened on the ship in the storm, if he'd thought for an instant that Ahna was Ki'ti's replacement.

The meeting ended and People began to unroll their sleeping skins. Ki'ti wondered whether Ahna had sleeping skins. She asked Manak-na. He wanted to go to Domur, but he answered that she did. Ki'ti asked him to send Ahna to her.

Before he could reach Domur, he told Ahna to go to the Wise One, the one who led the meeting. She did, but suddenly she was frightened.

Ki'ti noticed and she asked, "What is troubling you?"

"Manak-na said you are the Wise One. Are you like our bird man?"

"Little One," Ki'ti said, "I am a storykeeper and storyteller. I do not know anything about your bird man. You have no cause to fear me."

"I feared the bird man, because he told that I had to go away, and my people hated me for that."

"People here will not hate you. You are just a little girl," Ki'ti said. *There were the words again,* she thought. She was looking into an exquisitely beautiful face, Ki'ti realized. It looked like Manak-na might have braided her hair.

Ki'ti continued, "Get your things and bring them here. You will sleep right here." That meant she was to sleep next to the Wise One, not Manak-na. She dutifully did as she was told. On her return she unrolled her sleeping skins and sat. Ki'ti motioned for her to come to her.

"Sit before me," she said. She had a comb in her hand. Anxiety rose in Ahna's belly, but she was silent. Ki'ti untied the braid and began to separate the pieces. She ran her fingers through the hair. Fortunately there were not many tangles.

"Has Manak-na been fixing your hair?" she asked.

"Yes. At first I had many tangles. He got them out."

"I'm sure he did, and not too gently either."

"True," Ahna said, allowing herself to smile a little.

Ki'ti laughed out loud. "His wife did the hair of his children. He has had little experience." Ki'ti began to comb the girl's hair. Ki'ti did not like the look of the braid down the girl's back. She loved the color of Ahna's spiraled hair. She was trying to decide what would be a good way to fix the hair when Elemaea arrived.

"Mother, let me fix her hair," she asked.

Ki'ti handed her the comb.

"I'll fix it better than Manak-na did it," Elemaea said leaning over Ahna's shoulder and looking into Ahna's face.

Ahna laughed. It was good to see someone near her age. She was the Wise One's daughter. Ahna stored the information. She remained still.

Elemaea began to work on Ahna's hair. "My hair spirals too, but not as tight as yours," Elemaea said. She continued to work with it. "You have a lot of hair and the color is beautiful."

"Thank you," Ahna replied.

"I'm glad you got to come here. This is a good place for you. People here are kind and helpful. I'm Elemaea."

"I am glad to be here, Elemaea."

Ki'ti was watching Elemaea. She was pleased to see how her daughter was treating this new person. She had definitely matured.

Elemaea took some hair from the front and sides of Ahna's head and pulled it back together at the top. She took the little leather piece that had tied the braid and tied the hair at the back of Ahna's head with it. It rested gently on her combed out curly hair that fell to her waist. She leaned around Ahna and looked into her face. "What do you think, Mother?"

Ki'ti looked into Ahna's lovely face. She thought Elemaea's work was an improvement and said so. "She needs someone to teach her how to fix her own hair. Will you do it?" Ki'ti asked.

"I'd be glad to, Mother. Ahna, you get to sleep next to me. That's great! It's like having a sister. I've never had a sister. Yomuk is my brother."

"He is a good young man," Ahna said. "He worked hard on the boat and he hunts well. I am eight years old. How old are you?"

"I am the same age as you," Elemaea said.

"Girls, you must stop talking now and go to sleep."

"I love you Mother and Father," Elemaea said.

"I love you, too, my daughter, and Ahna I have a soft spot in my belly for you."

Untuk-na said, "I, too."

"Thank you," Ahna said. She covered up with her soft sleeping skin and went to sleep.

When Wisdom brought color back to the land, the People waked up from their slumber and began their chores. The morning meal was served quickly, the sky was clear, and there was a bit of a chill in the air, as if to push the People to get on with their preparations for the season of cold days. White rain had fallen overnight.

Ki'ti and Untuk-na met Manak-na at the entryway. Manak-na had his coconut with him in a grass bag. Ki'ti and Untuk-na were eager to know more about it. They dressed in warm clothing and left to climb to the rock structure up the hill.

Once inside, Untuk-na and Manak-na began a small hearth fire for warmth. Manak-na began to pull the coconut from the bag and said, "The Mol boatbuilder who directed the boat taught me things we do not know. He used this coconut to show our travel. The coconut is like the earth we live on. We do not live on something flat but rather something like this coconut that has depth and is all the way around. When you look at the night sky, some of the points of light up there twinkle; others do not. We live on a point of light that does not twinkle. Twinkling means the stars are of fire. That's why we get warm from the sun. The heat travels a long way to warm us. Our earth is not of fire or we'd be consumed." Untuk-na and Ki'ti were seated to either side of Manak-na looking at the coconut.

Manak-na put his left index finger on the place where the boatbuilders were. "We started here with the building of a boat. It was huge compared to our boats. It was made of bamboo. The interesting part is that they soaked the bamboo in salt water to kill any bugs or worms in the wood. It would appear that it takes a full day to do that. We didn't build the boat. We hunted so the boatbuilders and we could eat."

Manak-na moved his finger up the coconut from the boatbuilders' place. "We traveled through islands here to this large piece of land. Then we turned eastward to follow these islands that form an arc up north. The place was colder than where boats were built, but not so cold that we had to put on season-of-cold-days clothing by the time we got there. It's also windy. We followed the land around this turn so we headed south. It took us so long to take this trip. I thought we'd never arrive! And we didn't go even half way down the coconut. There is land that goes far down south from there. Once you pass the middle of the coconut going south you cannot see the star that never moves. There are different stars there. As we moved southward, it got warmer and warmer. Where Ahna lived it was horribly hot. Hotter than where we lived before Baambas and the need to flee the volcano. The sand near the middle of the earth would burn feet. We moved our feet quickly to avoid the sting of the heat of the sand."

Manak-na moved his finger across the coconut trying to show the sea but not to mess up the islands. "All across here is sea. It takes about four moons or more to cross it. In the middle there is a line of islands. You can get water there. There is nothing for us to hunt there, unless we wanted to eat lizards or birds. We had two storms. The first one shoved us toward these islands when we'd had little wind to make the sails work to pull the boat along. After all these islands we had the huge storm which pushed us toward this big island. We lost a man in the storm. We hunted on this island successfully. Shortly after we left that island, we were back to the boatbuilders' place."

"I learned that the earth rotates around the sun like the moon rotates around us here on earth. Let me look at these walls. Yes, here is one. See this dot where there are circles around it? The sun is in the center. It twinkles. Around the sun there are sources of light like us that don't twinkle. Of the non-twinklers we are not the closest to the sun. There is one and may be two between the sun and us. There may be some farther out than we are. So when you look at the night sky you can see twinklers. Some of them are circled by non-twinklers that also show as light in the night sky." Manak-na used his right first finger to trace a circle around the point. "Those circles around the point are the paths the non-twinklers take around the twinkler. I think that is fascinating. And, I think, that is what that drawing or painting means when you see it."

Manak-na found a flat surface on the rock. He picked up a stone and another stone that had a pointed end. He began to tap on the stone with the pointed end using the first stone he'd picked up. Little by little he tried to incise the boat with sail on the stone of the structure using the pointed part of the tool he'd chosen. He described what he was doing as he went along. "This is the hull on the right side, if you're looking forward. This is the left side of the hull," he said chipping out the part that could be seen if standing on land or in the water. "See how the fronts here are narrower than the middle part and how they are pulled upward? The same is true for the back of the boat." He chipped out a single mast. Out from the single mast was a bamboo crosspiece to which the sail was attached at the bottom. He chipped out the sail unfurled. "I only made one mast," he ran his index finger up the mast, "and one sail," he said pointing to the sail, tracing the triangle with his finger. "There are two masts and two sails. One behind the other. You can see how they'd look like bird wings."

Ki'ti and Untuk-na understood. It was massive information for them, but they understood. They needed time to think on it, but they did not doubt that Manak-na had gotten the information correct and was sharing it accurately. They had experienced what he had, a huge mind web expanding lesson. It didn't have any immediate effect on the People, but it did give them a different perspective.

Ki'ti said, "Manak-na, these people must have mind webs that are way beyond ours in knowledge."

Manak-na replied, "I really don't think so. You wouldn't be able to tell whether one of these boatmen or boatbuilders was an inland Mol who never saw a boat or a sea Mol. And there are those who are People and those who seem a little different. They both seem to have learned to make boats together and use the boats to travel widely, but they claim to have been doing this since time began. Their knowledge is limited to building and sailing boats. If they heard you tell your stories, Ki'ti, they would be as amazed at the power of your mind web as you are of theirs. So, no, I just think that somewhere in the long past, they learned to make boats for the sea and used them. Some of their people long, long ago wanted to live on the other side of the water where it is warm all the time, and they found a way to do that and to continue to connect to the people on this side. They are interesting people but no different from people we already know."

Ki'ti listened carefully to the words of Manak-na. She realized he had already been using his mind web to come to the conclusions he expressed. She considered his words wise. She lowered her head to him. Manak-na was surprised at the gesture, and he returned it. Untuk-na was fascinated with the information and the way it was presented. He, too, thought Manak-na wise.

Back at the home cave, Ahna was feeling the cold severely, even inside the cave. She shivered occasionally and lingered by the hearths, sometimes wrapped in a skin. Likichi noticed. Even though Manak-na had been seeing that Ahna ate a lot more than she was accustomed to, she still was terribly thin. With extremely little body fat, she chilled quickly. Likichi called her over. She measured her feet, legs, and her upper body. Then she let her go. Later that day she brought Ahna some in-the-cave boots that went over her knees and a jacket to wear in the cave. She explained that the boots were not ones to wear outside. She had brought boots for outside wear when she arrived. The jacket had fur left on the skin. Ahna was overcome. People were so kind to her. She threw her arms around Likichi and hugged her.

"Thank you for your kindness," Ahna told her.

Likichi was startled but hugged Ahna back. "You're welcome, Ahna." As she turned to her chores, Likichi felt warmth grow for this little child, who had been taken on such a long trip after having a tough childhood.

The days wore on. Without going outside, Ahna stood near the entryway and watched as more white rain fell. She had never seen anything like it, and it was beautiful to her. Her boots and her jacket kept her warm, so that she no longer shivered. She was excited because she heard that this night the stories would begin. She was eager to hear the People's stories.

Chapter 6

Story time was a special time for the People. After the evening meal they gathered in the largest part of the cave and awaited the first story of the year. They had to wait for the cleanup following their meal. All chores had to be finished before they began so there would be no interruption. There was no men's council that evening. Finally, quiet began to settle among the People. Ahna was sitting in the back next to Yomuk and Elemaea. She was eager to hear the story. Yomuk was trying to avoid showing boredom. Suddenly, he remembered that it would be to his benefit to listen carefully to the stories, because, according to Manak-na, they taught him what he needed to learn to have Wisdom's advantage in life critical situations. He looked up and noticed Manak-na was looking at him with a very stern look on his face. All his thoughts of Ahna dissolved as he set himself to listen.

Ki'ti began, "This is a new story. It is one that I chose for the People from the travel of Manak-na and Yomuk. It tells of something they learned in Aikot, the land where Ahna came from, far, far away, where the sun rises first from the land to the sea."

"There was an old man called Tikarumusa who was severely disabled with the stiffness disease. He was an old man who lived on a hill up from the sea. One day his people became very excited. They saw the tide going out. The tide is a change in the level where the water touches the shore. They lived where they have very little change in tides. This tide went out fast enough that it stranded fish on the wet sand. Fish were flopping all over the sand."

"His people got very excited and all of them, regardless of age, ran down to the sand to gather the gifts from their god of the underwater. Fish were everywhere and the people expected to feast. From his place on the hill, Tikarumusa stood to look out. He saw the people gathering fish. Far out to sea he could see a huge wave forming. He called and called to his people to warn them. He could not run to them, and they could not hear him. Tikarumusa hurt in his belly as he watched the huge wave come to cover all his people and to take them off to sea, not sparing a single one. He was left alone."

"Tikarumusa lay on his sleeping skins. He wept for his people and himself. He thought he would die there. Instead, Wisdom brought the boat that Manak-na and Yomuk had traveled on for their adventure. Men from the boat found the old man. They took the old man to the boat where he was later exchanged for Ahna, so he could remain with his son's people who lived inland. There he would be cared for."

"What is important to put in your mind web for this story is that if you ever are at the sea shore and observe the sea rushing out, no matter what you see on the sand, run the opposite way so that a monster wave will not take you to drown in the sea."

There was a hush in the cave. This was one of those lessons to remember for life, Yomuk realized. *How many stories were there, that told life critical lessons?* Yomuk wondered. Sitting next to him, Ahna wondered at hearing a story from her land in this cave with the People. She had listened carefully to Ki'ti's story and marked it word by word.

Ki'ti continued, "We have another story from Manak-na and Yomuk's adventure. This one tells us how Wisdom arranged the earth in the sky. We think of earth in terms of the dirt on the ground. This story requires that you expand that word. Earth means the entire place where we live. Our earth floats in the blackness that surrounds us."

The People looked at each other. There was a realization that this was meaningful information, but already they had trouble trying to understand "living in blackness," so they paid very close attention.

"This is a coconut from the adventure. Manak-na told that the Mol got coconuts from sea people on this side of the sea to take on their travel. A man named Rokuk taught Manak-na that the earth we live on is like the coconut. It is not flat but instead it is all round like this coconut. It swims in darkness, just as the points of light in the sky we see at night swim in darkness. When Wisdom brings sun is when darkness is dispelled to light."

"In the sky there are many points of light. Each looks like a flat circle, but instead it is round like this coconut. Some twinkle and some don't. The ones that twinkle are like our sun. They are of fire. That's why the sun brings warmth and light. The ones that don't twinkle are like our earth. If the earth twinkled, it would be of fire and we'd be consumed. So we can live, because we're on a non-twinkler."

"Suns warm their non-twinklers. The non-twinklers like our earth rotate around their sun. The sun warms the earth, like the hearth fire warms the meat that turns over it on the spit. We are not the only non-twinkler that rotates around our sun. There is at least one more, and there may be two between the sun and our earth. And we have a moon that rotates around us. When you go into the stone building above us and you see on the wall a point with circles around it, you are seeing the sun as the center point. The circles show the paths of the earths that rotate around the sun. Those who made that stone building knew about that. That's why they put the point and the circles there."

"Rokuk drew on the coconut the place where they left for their voyage. He showed lands and islands. Islands have water surrounding all sides. He showed the great sea and the land where Ahna lived far, far, far away. There is very much about the earth that we do not know. A few other things we do know. At the middle of the earth, it is very hot. At the middle of the earth, sand will burn your feet. Light and dark are about equal there. Tides change very little. The closer you get to the top and bottom of the earth, the colder it gets. If you go south past the middle of the earth you can no longer see the star that never moves."

"Imagine how fantastic Wisdom is to have created all this. What a way to expand your mind web—to look at the sky and to see so much created by Wisdom! How can it be that Wisdom has warmth in the belly for us? So vast is the creation that it is a wonder that Wisdom knows where we are. But Wisdom does. And that's the joy and the mystery of it."

Ki'ti had stopped. She had completely transported the People through the story to night skies and stars and what now were called earths. She tied it to Wisdom's creation. Knowledge swirled in their thoughts. Those thoughts were busy settling into the mind webs of the People. Ahna was overwhelmed. She'd had a lesson on land and islands from Manak-na on the boat. This story helped her to put it all together and she marked it word for word. She wondered about Wisdom. *Was it Wisdom who told the bird man she'd need to be brought here?* She wondered.

In the silence that followed People quietly went to their sleeping skins and prepared for sleep. The cave was incredibly quiet. It was as if each were still tied up in the stories and didn't want to break the silence. Yomuk was moved. He'd heard his mother's stories all his life, but they'd never had the profound effect they had this night. He berated himself, thinking that, perhaps, in the past he just hadn't truly listened. He realized that one story had a definite, immediate, life critical message. The other taught of Wisdom's otherness and how the sky works. Both were burned into his mind web. It occurred to him that never had he considered categories of the stories or their purposes. He had not put them in memory in any orderly way.

Ahna lay quiet covered with the furry skin Rokuk had given her. She thought those close to her were asleep. She kept coming close to something in memory, and then it would fade. She continued trying to recall the thing that kept escaping her. She closed her eyes and suddenly she remembered. During the storm, she'd heard Manak-na shout, "Wisdom!" He was calling to this creator, the one who made everything. He was calling in the midst of the horrible storm for help from Wisdom? What enlightenment! Was it possible when things went badly to call to this Wisdom for help to turn things to right? Would someone, who was big enough to make everything, care about her in this strange place? It sounded like Ki'ti thought so. How she wished she'd known about Wisdom long ago. She began to whisper to Wisdom. Ki'ti almost moved, but she caught herself and remained still, listening.

"Wherever you are Wisdom, I have never imagined such love. Thank you for bringing me here to these People who know you. I want to know you. My belly longs to be filled with you. I want to know Wisdom's People. I want to be part of this People."

Suddenly Ahna was flooded with warmth that she'd never known. As if a tiny voice from under the ground—or maybe far off from a star—spoke, she heard words of comfort. "I am with you, my Ahna. I have been with you since before you were born. I shall be with you until you die, when I draw you to me." That part Ki'ti did not hear, but she did hear, "Thank you Wisdom from the bottom of my belly. I am your grateful servant."

Ki'ti let the pent up tears flow. How could this child know Wisdom from what she'd lived through? How could her belly so clearly cling to Wisdom, about whom she'd just learned the tiniest part? Yet, there was no doubt about her sincerity. She wasn't doing this for effect. Ki'ti had struggled to hear her. This child, new to them, was naturally drawn to Wisdom with an attitude that some adults never attained. Again, Ki'ti wondered, *Is she my replacement?*

Untuk-na had also heard the prayer and the words of gratitude. He felt certain that Ki'ti would be training this child. Ahna definitely had something special about her. Time would show him whether his thoughts had merit.

When Wisdom returned color to the land, Tiriku ran outside. He raced down the path that led to the valley. His friend had returned and was calling in the early morning. Ki'ti and Untuk-na had gone out and lingered to watch the tiny dog greet his friend in the white rain that lay on the ground. Raven landed near Tiriku. They embraced as they always did, Tiriku nuzzled and licked Raven. Raven used his beak and head to touch Tiriku's chest, neck, and head. Raven hopped a dance that Tiriku appeared to try to emulate by lowering his front legs and moving from side to side in awkward leaps. It caused Ki'ti and Untuk-na to chuckle. Tiriku finally stopped and lay on his side on the ground panting. Raven began at Tiriku's back and slid his body back to back against Tiriku, both animals with heads thrown back, until they were nose to beak. They lay there without moving for quite some time. Then, they got up and shook themselves out, as if they hadn't really snuggled together. It caused more giggles from above. Raven made some strange noises that sounded a bit like gurgling and took off in flight. He swooped down over Tiriku and then was off to be about his day. Tiriku scampered up to the cave to find something to eat.

Yomuk and Ahna had dressed warmly and walked down to the valley. Once there, Ahna asked, "Tell me about Wisdom, please."

"Oh, Ahna," Yomuk replied, "I am not the one to ask. Ask Mother. She knows. She is the Wise One. She talks to Wisdom."

Ahna asked, "Can you not talk to Wisdom?"

"I just don't, because I don't know Wisdom well."

Ahna was confused. Knowing that Wisdom cared so much about the People, she could not understand why anyone wouldn't be pursuing Wisdom to learn as much as possible. She had heard Manak-na call to Wisdom in the storm. If he did that, surely he talked to Wisdom

"Do you not want to know Wisdom well?" Ahna asked.

"I feel off balance when I think about Wisdom. I think I need to know more. I plan to listen to the stories with much more attention this year. I have been bored in the past. When Mother told the stories my mind wandered off to other things. Manak-na made it clear to me that there are life critical stories, and that I need to know what they tell of how to survive tough situations—like the story about your people who got devoured by the wave."

"So you put off things until you are forced to do them?" Ahna looked directly into his eyes trying to understand.

Yomuk stood with his hand on the limb of a tree. He was running through his mind web. "Well, Ahna, you could say that. I should be more mature than I am. Once I thought I was more mature than People my age, but now I realize I was fooling myself. There are things I should have been pursuing that I just never thought about."

"And nobody struck you for delaying?"

"No!" The very idea caused Yomuk to recoil. "Here each young person has a duty to observe older People. We learn to do by observing. We are discouraged from asking questions and are encouraged to figure out things for ourselves. We have a responsibility to grow our mind webs so that we can reason well. A little one will sometimes be jerked back away from a cliff, but usually that isn't necessary. As children we may be struck for being mean spirited—little else. As a child, Mother was beaten severely. Occasionally, we are taught directly, but not often. We are allowed to ask questions once we have exhausted all the possibilities of our mind webs."

"What caused your mother to be beaten?" Ahna asked horrified. *These gentle People beat their Wise One?*

"She was being taught to be the next Wise One. She had seen a green bag that belonged to a man found dead and mummified in a cave. Mother knew that in another cave a mother and her two children were sick and waited for the man to bring curing herbs. Of course, they were long dead. Those Minguat who like to make war killed the man. The man's spirit or an evil spirit talked to Mother. She understood from that spirit that the family and the man were not rested in death, because he didn't get the green bag filled with the herbs to them. Mother was just a little child at the time, and she couldn't easily sort out whether the man lived and his family lived or whether they were all dead. She just was driven to get the green bag to the man's wife and children for him. None of the people from that other time had been buried. But then, they looked like Mol. Mol don't always bury their dead. So Mother took the bag to the dead family in the mountains alone without telling anyone. The spirit showed her how to get there. She had to travel a good distance to do that, and she did it while Wisdom sucked the color from the land. Three hunters went to find her. They said they'd never have found her, if she hadn't made a small fire just outside the entry to the cave. It took them a long time to find the path to the cave. And the spirit led Mother right to it."

"Why was she beaten?" Ahna was still aghast.

"She had asked the Wise One to take the bag to the wife of the man in the cave. The Wise One told her that they would not. That should have been the end of it. She disobeyed. The Wise One didn't know she was being influenced by spirits—she was just compelled by the spirit or spirits to get that bag to its intended destination. Mother didn't know she was being influenced by the world of spirits, but even not knowing would not protect her from punishment. She disobeyed. Not much is required of the People, but disobedience is not tolerated among us. When Mother did what she did, she also put the lives of herself and three hunters at risk. She had not considered the risk, because that spirit compelled her. Her disobedience was the reason for punishment. Obedience is very important to the People."

"Now I understand. I suppose that means that if spirits talk to you, you'd better be very careful."

"According to the old Wise One, there is never a need for someone in this time to communicate with someone from another time. If it happens, you call on Wisdom to make it go away. Unless you know how to deal with spirits, you stay far away from them and their influence. Now, Mother understands how to protect herself, so occasionally she will talk to these dead people, but it is not something she wishes to do. Like the man up the hill. She talked to him. He was evil. She saw to it that he was buried, and the paintings that gave wrong spirited ideas were destroyed."

"What if *Wisdom* talked to you?" Ahna had heard that small voice that filled her with joy when she prayed. Was that a spirit? Was that safe?

"Ahna, on that you'd better talk to Mother."

"We were raised so differently."

"What do you mean, Ahna?"

"My people hated me from the time I was born and the bird man said I would leave. If I did anything wrong they struck me. If I did anything they thought was very wrong, they'd beat me. If I cried out in pain, they beat me more. I could be beaten and never know why."

"Tell me they didn't do anything else."

"You mean like give me too little to eat?"

"Oh, Ahna!"

"It wasn't all bad. Sometimes they'd have me take care of the little children. I loved them and they seemed to love me back. It was what got me through. That, and my hope that the person who came for me would take me to a place where people were kind. I never lost my hope. And I have been rewarded. The People are more than kind, they also love."

"I love you, Ahna."

"I know."

"What do you mean, you know? I haven't told you until now."

"Yomuk, you say things by what you do as loud as by what you say—sometimes louder. I can understand both. Remember when the flying fish scared me? You came over and tossed the fish back to the sea. That was a loving gesture."

Yomuk was jarred. He wondered what else he'd done. What had she seen that he didn't know was being observed? He needed to watch his actions?

As if understanding his thoughts, Ahna said, "Don't try to watch every move you make and everything you do. I learned to watch what people do and say to keep from being struck or beaten as a little child. Most people wouldn't notice that there is something alike or different in what people say and do. I just learned to do it. If I have disturbed you, I am so sorry."

"You have nothing to be sorry for. You are just so small and for someone small to think these things, it certainly shatters my idea of myself that I'm more mature than People my age."

"Why would it matter to you whether you are more mature, equally mature, or less mature than People your age?"

"I was making another error, Ahna, one my Mother would greatly disapprove. I like to think in some ways I'm better than others."

"But Wisdom, from what I've heard, doesn't think that. Wisdom would see all as equal."

"I realize that. I just have a wrong thought that needs to be removed and replaced with a right one."

Ahna laughed her lovely laugh, not at him but more at his incongruity of thought. "Well, Yomuk, nobody can do that but you! You are making part of yourself something not real except in your imaginings."

"So true, Ahna. So very true. What is true—even simple—isn't always easy."

In the home cave, sitting on their rolled up sleeping materials, Domur and Manak-na were talking about the bear experience. She took another good look at the scars.

"Whoever did this healing did very well," she admitted. She traced the scars gently.

"It was a man on the boat. He seemed to know what herbs and liquids did what. He used something that stung like many bees."

"You'd have given your life to spare Yomuk, wouldn't you?"

"I will truly say, I don't know. I was not fully tested. Yomuk and I both fought. We were intent on killing the bear. Until testing, I'm not sure anyone can say unequivocally what they will or will not do. It was never fully a question for him or me. There was no time to think. We just relied on the training we'd had and did our best."

"Are you thinking to return to adventuring?" Domur asked, certain that she didn't want to hear the answer.

"I wish I could answer, my Dearest, but I don't know. The storm at sea was one of the most awful experiences I ever had and I'm not sure what to make of the travel they do by boat. I can say I'm not at all sure I'd want to take *that* trip again. Another adventure might appeal to me. Right now, it's too soon. I just want to be here with you."

"Manak-na I love you. When you left, I felt my life ended. I wondered why I continued to breathe. Likichi pointed out that I was not living and that by becoming bitter and unforgiving towards you, I was making my own body sick. She frightened me by telling me that if I failed to forgive and start living, I could make myself sick to death. She reminded me of our children and grandchildren. She waked me up. At that point I decided that, if and when you choose to adventure, it is something that you have a right to do, and I should not be bitter if you choose to do that. I also learned that I have a life here with the People whether you are here or not. Does that mean I love you less? No. It means I love you more, because I fully give you freedom. It also means I have a place here with you as your wife, and that I have a place here without you as one of the People. Both are important." She did a palm strike.

"I don't know what to say, Domur."

"There is nothing to say. You've said it already. Right now you want to be here. That is fine. In the future, if you want adventure, I will not try to hold you against your will or make you feel guilt that you shouldn't feel. If the time ever comes that I feel the need to have a husband who does not adventure, then I will simply renounce our joining and join another."

"You would do that?" Manak asked shocked. The thought had never entered his mind web. He felt off balance as if he might be falling feet over head through the blackness that surrounds the suns and earths.

"As you said, Manak-na, right now, I just want to be with you." Domur was in earnest, there was no attempt to be coy. She simply stated fact.

"But there is no one with whom you share an age who is not already joined," he reasoned.

"That is true today. Who knows what or whom tomorrow will bring?"

Manak-na was shaken. It had never occurred to him that Domur might leave *him*. They had always been so close. What if he adventured to return to find that she was joined to another? Kipotuilak had lost his wife for the same reason. Could he live with that? What made him think that her waiting and waiting for him was appropriate? All his certainties fell apart as a hearth log that has smoldered for too long, holding its form, finally collapsing in a single act to ashy formlessness. He put his arm around Domur and the two sat together in silence. All that needed to be said had been said—maybe more. He asked himself whether he put his arm around her from love or to protect her or to hang onto a lifeline. He couldn't answer his own question. *A huge storm at sea held nothing to compare with the terror of the life critical situation in which he found himself,* he thought. There was no story for it.

In the back of the cave, Gumokut, Flinee, Lolmeg, and Maylue were deep in discussion not for the first time about returning to their Mol home they'd left without really thinking carefully. They felt that they really didn't fit into this group and they remained homesick.

"I really miss our people," Maylue said for more times than she could count.

"But it's getting to the cold time of the year. White rain has already fallen. Can we make it back without freezing?" Flinee questioned.

"We have warm clothing to protect us. Lolmeg and I have hunted in the very cold. When you're active, you stay warm. Aside from that we can move a lot faster without children and old people to slow us down. We know the way." Gumokut sneered.

"I want to share the giants with our people. They should be able to visit them to see what we've seen." Lolmeg added.

"Can you imagine Gnomuth's face when he sees those giants?" Flinee said laughing.

"The Chief probably couldn't get up there," Gumokut said. "He's pretty old now."

"We could do what Kai-na did. Hold up a head!" Lolmeg said with a laugh.

"You shouldn't laugh about something like that," Maylue said. "That was one of our dead."

"Well, Maylue, the dead giant wouldn't know, now would he?"

"We should have respect for the dead," Flinee said. Her hands were on her shoulders as if somehow she could protect herself from thoughts around her.

"Why?" Gumokut taunted. "They cannot do anything to us."

"Because they are *our* ancestors," Flinee argued.

"Look at us now. We're fighting among ourselves. We need to get back to our own people where there was no constant moving and little irritants making us unsettled," Lolmeg snorted with an air of authority, mocking the People with an exaggerated palm strike.

"I agree," Gumokut said, using the palm strike.

"When would we leave?" Maylue asked.

"I say we leave at daylight," Lolmeg replied.

"Is there agreement?" Gumokut asked.

Each one nodded affirmative.

"We will not mention it until the men's council. Agreed?"

Each nodded affirmative.

Outside, Ki'ti and Untuk-na were wrapped in warm clothing and boots and had climbed to the stone building. It was a clear, crisp day, almost cloudless. The deciduous leaves were almost gone, but the poignant scent of evergreens added a reminder of chlorophyll to the clean air. The footing was a little slippery but not dangerous.

"I was astonished to hear Ahna pray," Untuk-na said as they entered the stone structure.

Ki'ti sat on a squared off rock. "I was, too. How could someone who just met Wisdom have such faith?"

"From what I hear, she's had a very difficult life, but it hasn't made her hard. Instead it's made her live on hope. Hope is tied to faith, if I understand correctly." Untuk-na sat close beside her on the rock.

"I agree with you Untuk-na. It's as though Wisdom has always been with her, just beyond her grasp until now."

"I'll ask the question we want answered, 'Is she the one?'"

"Oh, my Love, I hope so. If she's my replacement, I will stop one worry I've had for years. I wondered whether Yomuk might be the replacement, but time has shown that to be a false hope. Then, suddenly this little girl appears and the very idea of Little Girl springs out of the past and virtually strikes me. She was told she would be brought to a People because she had something to do. Do you remember how Wamumur became the Wise One?"

"What do you mean, Ki'ti?"

"He had been stolen from his People far to the west. The People carried him along with them to the south and to the east. He was from somewhere far away and he was brought with the People where he became their Wise One. There is, I'm trying to say, a tradition for this." Ki'ti was tracing a spiral on the rock structure wall. First she'd start at the center point and move outward, and then she'd start at the outer edge and move back in. Untuk-na was intrigued with her tracing.

"I think she's your replacement, Ki'ti. It all fits together."

"Time will tell, my Dear One. I will know when I see evidence that she has been given the memory."

"What do you mean?"

"Wisdom gives the capacity to hold in memory all the stories. I couldn't do that on my own. It's like a gift from Wisdom, though I didn't see it as a gift when it was given to me." Ki'ti did a palm strike. "You see, right now, Ahna is hearing the stories for the first time. It will take some time for her to begin to be able to tell them word for word. If she begins to tell them word for word, then, we will know she has not only the belly for Wisdom but also the gift of memory from Wisdom. Right now all we know is that clearly she has a belly for Wisdom."

"Now, I understand." Untuk-na grinned and did a palm strike. Ki'ti joined him with a palm strike.

"We know what the circles around the point are now." Untuk-na said.

"Yes. I had thought," Ki'ti replied, "at first, that the point surrounded by circles was a ripple like you'd get if you tossed a pebble into water. Manak-na's explanation showed it moves very differently."

"You saw movement in the drawing? To me it was just a drawing. What do you think of the spiral?" Untuk asked looking at the symbols on the wall.

"First, it makes me think of Elemaea's and Ahna's hair, she laughed. "But there's more to it. I can easily see that, unlike the point with the circles, the spiral more clearly implies movement. There is a going to a point or beginning at a point and moving outward, like life. But what these people who did this meant—I have no understanding. All this appears to have something to do with the sky. I look at it and see life because of the movement implied in the spiral. Maybe the sky and life are not different? I do not understand."

"What it says to me is that the whole sky—everything, including us on earth started at a point. There was a point for the sky, a point for the earth, a point for this tree, a point for Tiriku, a point for me, and a point for you. Each goes through changes and changes to this widest point, and then it begins to retrace itself to the point. At the point is where all the great energy for each begins and where it ends. I also see it useful in looking at a single life. It could show the most enormous sky and the tiniest form of life." Untuk-na felt awkward sharing his thoughts.

"Untuk-na, are you saying that you think all we see out there will ultimately end? That's horrifying to contemplate! We know from Wisdom that death is but another beginning of forever, a life outside of time or seasons, days and nights, years. We remain as spirits. But for all that we see to end—

that's beyond the scope of my mind web. It would be something to fear." That all things visible might end was a new thought to Ki'ti, and she was trying to make sense of it in her mind web. The very idea of an end to all things created was beyond her comprehension.

"Well, look at us," Untuk-na said. "Wisdom created all that is out there—and us. We were born and we die. We are given energy and we live until it runs out. Why wouldn't it be the same for out there? But, yes, I can see that the point of the spiral might show our entrance into time, our birth. A star might have a created birth and an eventual death—its own spiral. Then when we return to the point, the point disappears and we are outside of time in this forever? You told me that Wisdom does not live in time. Is it possible that what we see with earth eyes is time, and what we cannot see, without spirit eyes, is forever?" Untuk-na was excited to be discussing these things. He felt alive, invigorated, and challenged.

"I think there are rules for being in time. Time implies a beginning and end. Wisdom is forever—outside of time—and the rules that apply to us do not apply to Wisdom. I think that I'm at the edge of understanding something. Ever since Manak-na returned with his information about the earth, my mind web has been overworked," Ki'ti said. "You have just greatly expanded it again. Untuk-na I will have to think on these things."

"Ah, Ki'ti. I thank Wisdom daily that I met you. I would take nothing for this life we share. Gathering this information makes music for my mind web to dance to. It's like food for the belly of a starving person. I love to learn and to entertain new thoughts!" He did another palm strike.

"You're going to make your hand swell," Ki'ti laughed about the multiple palm strikes.

"Right now I am just filled with newness. It's good, and I won't do another palm strike. It is good to do them, for they make statements, wonderful statements for which there are no words or the words would take too long."

"I know," Ki'ti said seriously, "They're going to stop being used. Palm strikes may have their own spiral. But there is such expression available with them. I shall sorrow when they're not used any longer." Ki'ti gently coughed. The two headed back to the cave.

Back inside the cave, Manak-na and Tongip-na were having a heated discussion.

"It's just time that you stop the finger showing and give words to the numbers. Didn't the boatmen find it odd that you had no words for numbers?"

"If they did, they never said so," Manak-na said with a little irritation.

"Well," Tongip-na said with his hands on his hips, "it's time. You understand Mol numbers when we say them. You must have understood the boatmen."

"I understood them, and they understood me. I don't see a problem." Manak-na sat down on his rolled sleeping skins.

"Your use of our language is very good since you've been with the boatmen, but you still use numbers with your hands instead of the numbers you know. You are so smart! I want other people to see you and know how smart you are."

"My using hands or numbers in your language doesn't tell anyone else whether I am smart." Manak-na was irritated. "Besides, when we do numbers, we use" he showed five fingers on each hand "while you only use" he showed four fingers. "I like our way of doing it better."

"Manak-na, there is no reason not to give your numbers a name and still use them in words. You could use our numbers and then add the two extra ones you use for thumbs. You could count: one, two, three, four, five, six, seven, eight, and then the next number could be what?"

Manak-na looked at him with a frown. "Nine."

Tongip-na followed, "And the last one, would be what?"

"Ten," Manak-na said, beginning to wonder whether it didn't, after all, make sense to change their finger count to words. Sometimes they had to interrupt their talking to lay some burden down before continuing a conversation to show a number instead of saying it. He hadn't questioned it. It was simply what they did.

Tongip-na touched an index finger to a thumb and said, "Nine." And then he touched the other index finger to the other thumb and said, "Ten. I can learn this quickly. Almost all of us speak both languages to some extent now. It would be easy to make this shift from fingers to words."

"We will discuss it at the men's council," Manak-na said.

Tongip-na lowered his head. He thought that finally his constant chipping away at Manak-na's resistance had been successful.

Manak-na thought about making the shift also. He was very aware that the Mol had a verbal way of counting but it didn't go as far as theirs. To count three tens, Manak-na knew, would require the Mol language statement of "four—two—three—four—five—six." Manak-na reasoned that there would need to be a number for two tens, and three tens and so on for the language of the People. He also realized that there would need to be a number for ten tens. That would keep the numbers clear. But using a count of ten definitely counted farther than the Mol's numbers. To count to their highest number they would be counting to eight eights. They'd go through the process to eight—two—three—four—five—six—seven—eight. They could count to six tens plus four. The People could count at least to ten tens. If they gave the number ten tens an additional ten tens, a name of two ten tens, then they could count to ten ten tens. That number was staggering to contemplate.

In another part of the cave, Elemaea had finished making spear points and was trying to chip out a core, but she just couldn't master the larger work.

"Elemaea, you are pushing yourself to do what your hands are not yet ready to do," Ekuktu-na said calmly. "I know you want full mastery, but your body is not ready yet, for your hands are too small. You already do excellent work with the spear points, so why not forget the cores for now and work on knives."

Elemaea looked up, surprised. "I thought knives were harder to do than cores."

"Not really. You'll have to learn to attach them to the antler points we have in the storage area, but I think you could work them well. I'm thinking there would be many uses for smaller knives. Women might use them for making garments or cutting off a smaller piece of meat. You could create something that doesn't already exist."

Elemaea was fascinated at the idea of doing something that had not yet been done. She didn't see the subtle effort Ekuktu-na was making to get her to shift focus from the larger item to a smaller one that would be best suited to her small hands. Eventually her hands would grow, but he wanted her to stay interested in what she was doing, not continue to want to do what she wasn't ready to do. He went to the storage area and returned with some supplies for making the blade. Elemaea was delighted for the challenge and the change in object.

The women almost had the evening meal ready. The call went out. People began to gather to eat. Wisdom was sucking the color from the land and it was getting cold enough outside to require head and hand coverings for comfort when going out.

There was variety in food available. Root vegetables were cooked with greens they had dried, and the meat was from a variety of deer, aurochs, and jerky. They ate and cleaned up, hoping the men's council would be brief, because they were eager for stories.

The men's council began. Gumokut looked at Ki'ti for the signal to speak. She said, "Gumokut, please go ahead."

Gumokut began, "Lolmeg, Flinee, and Maylue and I have talked at length about a return to our people. We think we came on this trek without enough thought. We did not expect to miss our people so severely. In the morning we plan to return to our home. That is all I have to say."

Everyone was shocked.

"You are sure you'd not prefer to stay until the season of new leaves?" Ki'ti asked with concern.

"Yes. We are young and strong and can move quickly. We can find the way since we have already made the trip. We would like to fill our backpacks with jerky."

"Of course," Ki'ti said. There were murmurings all around. If they would make the trip there was no way to prevent them, but it was a dangerous trek they planned. Unwise at this time of the year.

Ki'ti noticed that Ermi-na was looking at her with a desire to speak. She nodded towards him.

"I have studied for a long time the words Manak-na brought about the earth circling the sun. There is much circling in the sky with the non-twin-klers circling the suns and the moon circling the earth. I find that there must be one other circling." He paused, checking to see that others were following his reasoning. "I see that the earth must turn in circles as it rotates around the sun. My reasoning is this. You compared the earth once to meat on a spit where the sun was the hearth. If the meat on the spit is not turned, one side will be burnt while the other side is uncooked. So the earth must spin in its rotation around the sun to keep the whole earth warm and not burnt on one side and cold on the other. When it spins us towards the sun it is day and when it spins us away from the sun it is night. And that makes me know why it seems that the sun circles around the earth, which we used to think. If the earth spins, it would make it look like the sun circles the earth—when it doesn't. Also, we know the moon does not spin like the earth, because we always see the same side of it even when we see it in daylight."

For a long time there was silence everywhere except for the hearth fires. Manak-na went silently to his belongings and pulled out the coconut. He placed more wood on the fire. He held the coconut up so the fire light shone on it. Slowly he turned the coconut while looking at the part of the coconut where Rokuk's drawing was.

Manak-na didn't wait for Ki'ti to give him permission to speak. He was too excited. "Ermi-na, that's brilliant! Anyone want to look at what happens here?" He asked the council and the larger group.

Because of where they sat, many People saw what Manak-na had seen. Several People wanted a better view, and they went to stand behind Manak-na to view what he saw. He showed them how the light and dark of night and day were visible on the coconut as the earth turned. Most People had no idea what was so exciting about light on a coconut, but for those who did, they were astounded. One of the most excited men was Nanichak-na. Silently, he thanked Wisdom that he was able to learn these things before it was time for him to die. All in Wisdom's creation seemed in motion, sometimes rotating, sometimes spinning, and sometimes doing both at the same time. Yomuk understood, but it was not an exciting revelation to him. To Elemaea it was delightful information. To Ahna it was as if more mystery were unveiled. It gave her insight into the night sky. *Since Wisdom made the twinklers and the non-twinklers, and Wisdom made them spin and rotate, didn't that say something about Wisdom?* she wondered. But what did it say? That life involved motion? That answer was beyond her. Her life had changed so fast and with so much more depth.

Tongip-na sought Ki'ti's attention.

"Tongip-na, please speak," Ki'ti said when the People had returned to sitting quietly.

"Manak-na and I were talking earlier about counting. The People use fingers to display numbers. We use words. The People use thumbs as well as fingers to count. We use only fingers without the thumbs. When People speak but need to display a number, sometimes they have to lay down a spear or something else just to display the number. Having a spoken number makes that effort unnecessary. Also, there is some difficulty understanding the numbers. When the People show two hands twice, that means a different number from what we mean when we say two eights or two—two—three—four—five—six—seven—eight. In our way of counting, we'd have fewer for a double number than the People would have for a double number. We need to develop a standard way of counting so we understand the count better."

The People and the former Mol understood the problem. They lived with it.

Hahami-na looked at Ki'ti for a nod to speak.

"Hahami-na, please speak," Ki'ti said.

"This is something I've done for a long time. I use vertical lines for counts and a horizontal line for nothing. None of our numbering ways provide for the lack of something. Let's say that we hunt for five days. On day one we return with three kills. I would mark three vertical lines on a branch or piece of wood. The next day we return with one kill. I would mark one vertical line under the three vertical lines. The next day we return with no kills. I would mark one *horizontal* line under the one vertical line. The next day we return with four kills. I would mark four vertical lines under the horizontal line. The final day we return with two kills. I'd mark two vertical lines under the four vertical lines. My lines show a true count of the number of kills and the number of hunting trips. My horizontal line is called zero. It represents the first little finger on our hands. I draw vertical lines to represent the other fingers."

Manak-na waited for recognition from Ki'ti. When he got it, he said, "This could be a very exciting improvement in our counting. I will suggest that Hahami-na, Tongip-na and any others who are interested gather tomorrow to see if we can work out a plan for use of numbers that will be standard for all of us with a consideration of using the zero that Hahami-na has used."

"Do all approve?" Ki'ti asked.

All the People nodded approval.

"Are there others who would like to join this planning group?" Ki'ti asked. Her mind web was spinning. There was suddenly so much to learn.

Slamika-na, Untuk-na, and Sum-na indicated they would like to join.

"Very well," Ki'ti said. "Are there other things to bring to the council?"

The People looked down. No one sought Ki'ti's nod to speak.

"The council ends," Ki'ti said quietly with many thoughts in her mind web.

"We will have a story shortly," Ki'ti said. She knew that there would be some desire to chat after such significant issues had been brought to the council. She would give them time to change to readiness for a story. A few People left for the privy; some put little sleeping children on their sleeping skins and covered them for the night; some got water to drink. A couple got a skin to put around their shoulders. Some went to the Mol to express concern for their travel in the season of cold days. They feared the Mol might not survive the journey.

When the People re-gathered, Ki'ti began.

"This is a very, very old story. It is the story of Kukuk-na and Timkut-na. Timkut-na and Kukuk-na were hunters. They had trekked far looking for meat to feed the People. It was a time of drought and meat was not easy to find."

"The men went to places where they had known deer to gather. There were none. They went to places where trees grew in groves providing shade from the sun for animals. There were no animals there. They went to the highlands where they'd found grazers. There were none. They went to the lowlands and found nothing. Hunger was everywhere, but they were determined that they would not let their People starve, if they could help it."

"Kukuk-na and Timkut-na were exhausted. They looked for a place to sleep. Wisdom was sucking color from the land fast. Below them was a grove of trees and they stumbled towards it. Timkut-na was the first to arrive. He noticed a spring that had not dried up. He kneeled and began to drink, for his thirst was great. Suddenly he felt a hit on his hand. A serpent had been harboring in the grass beside him, and it bit his hand. He noticed it was a cobra. He cursed himself for being so careless. Kukuk-na arrived. He saw what had happened, and Timkut-na showed him the direction the cobra had gone. Kukuk-na found the snake and killed it. He looked for others and found none. There was no cure for the bite. Either Timkut-na would live or die."

"Kukuk-na tried to make a lean-to from what was available. He helped Timkut-na put out his sleeping skins so he could lie down. He made a fire. He handed Timkut-na a piece of jerky, but the hunter declined. He wasn't hungry. Kukuk-na ate it. Timkut-na's hand was beginning to hurt severely. He became nauseated and vomited, but there was nothing in his stomach to get rid of but a little water. His eyelids were drooping and his hand and arm were swelling. He was in obvious pain. Kukuk-na was agonizing over his friend. He kept the fire going and watched over Timkut-na carefully. Timkut-na slept fitfully. When Wisdom restored color to the land, Kukuk-na saw that Timkut-na was struggling to breathe. He saw him breathe his last."

"Kukuk-na took the digging tool Timkut-na carried in his backpack and dug the best he could to bury his friend. When he had him in the hole and covered by dirt, he still needed to find more dirt to cover him. He did not want any animal to dig the man up. Slowly he brought more dirt and covered the body. Then he found rocks and covered the mound. In the distance he heard what sounded like voices. He thought it was just his being alone and starving that caused him to hear things that weren't there."

"Kukuk-na sat by the lean-to and wept. He wept because his People hungered. He wept because there were no animals to feed his People. He wept because he and Timkut-na were starving. He wept because Timkut-na died. He wept because he was alone."

"The voices came closer. Kukuk-na didn't notice. It was two hunters from his People. They had found meat. They came to call the hunters home."

"This story is the reason we always check thoroughly for snakes and spiders when we look at a place to camp or live. Even if you are terribly tired, you must look to be certain that the place you are planning to stay is free of harmful living things. Timkut-na died because his thirst was more important than his safety."

The cave was totally quiet except for the cracking of the fire. People got up slowly and headed for their sleeping skins and covers.

When Wisdom returned color to the land, Gumokut, Flinee, Lolmeg, and Maylue were at the entryway evaluating for the last time the things they carried with them. They had season-of-cold-days garments, including head and hand coverings. They had good sleeping skins and covers. They had a good supply of dried meat and some boar intestines filled with rendered fat, tiny bits of seasoned meat, and some dried blueberries—all of which had been well mixed. Tongip-na and Untuk-na were up, saying their farewells and asking to have messages delivered to certain people back there. Ki'ti stood at the entryway. As they moved towards the outside, she put her hands on their shoulders and said, "Go with Wisdom."

Flinee hugged Ki'ti tight and said, "Always stay with Wisdom."

Ki'ti smiled. "I shall," she replied. Ki'ti watched them until they disappeared from sight in the valley. She had sorrowful feelings. She was troubled that not all or any might make it home.

The men who would gather to plan a better use of numbers had decided to put on their warm garments to go to the stone structure up the hill to avoid the noise of the cave. There they would build a small fire to stay warm. Untuk-na had asked Nanichak-na and Arkan-na to watch over Ki'ti while he was gone. They agreed.

The men went up the hill as they got ready, not all at once. Tongip-na and Untuk-na were the first up there, and they gathered what wood they could find on the way up to avoid depleting the pile of wood they gathered for the home cave. They knocked off as much white rain as possible to reduce the smoke it would make. Untuk-na had brought the ember and some mosses to get the fire started.

When all had assembled, Manak-na began by summarizing the three different approaches to counting they had. Most of the People were curious, eager to learn more about Hahami-na's approach.

Hahami-na marked on the wall with a piece of charcoal:

He put his left little finger on the top horizontal line. "This is zero," he said. Then, he put his left finger next to the little finger on the vertical line next to it and said, "This is the count for this one." Then he put his middle finger on the next vertical line and said, "This is the count for this finger." He then showed that he had a finger and thumb to represent all the marks on the first line, including zero.

"For the second and following lines, you have a vertical line and a horizontal line for the little finger. You would need names for all the lines but a single name for each of the vertical and horizontal lines when they are used together." Hahami-na looked around to see whether the People understood.

Tongip-na said, "Then, if we use the numbers in my language it would be zero, one, two, three, four, five, six, seven, eight, and the number Manak-na gave yesterday, nine."

Hahami-na nodded, glad that someone understood.

"This is confusing me," Sum-na said.

"What's confusing?" Tongip-na asked.

"I just don't understand why this is better than what we do now."

"Have any of you who use fingers for numbers ever had to lay a burden down to show the number? Naming the numbers frees your hands," Tongip-na tried to explain.

Slamika-na said, "To me it's confusing because the numbers on the side seem to grow as you go down.

"They don't seem to, they do get larger, because the numbers get larger." Tongip-na could see it all so clearly. He couldn't understand why anyone had difficulty.

Patiently, Hahami-na went through the numbers again.

"So, if I understand," Untuk-na said, "The bottom line, where it shows three vertical lines and a horizontal line, is what we would show as three full hands?"

"That's exactly right!" Hahami-na exclaimed with relief. Some were getting the idea.

"Why wouldn't it be the whole of the bottom line?" Slamika-na asked.

"It's because of the zero," Hahami-na explained.

"Oh, now I understand," Sum-na said. "What was the name of the number on the far right of the top line?"

Manak-na said, "Nine."

"I can say the first line," Sum-na said. "Tell me if I'm right. Zero, one, two, three, four, five, six, seven, eight, nine."

"That's right."

Sum-na continued, "What name will we give the number that is a single vertical line and a horizontal line?"

Hahami-na said, "Ten." He remembered the numbers Manak-na used when he explained his approach to counting mixed with Tongip-na's.

"You've already named these, haven't you?" Tongip-na asked Hahami-na.

Hahami-na lowered his head. "I've been thinking about this for a very long time. Ever since I learned the names for the Mol numbers. Yes, I have names for the numbers."

"Will you tell us your names and point to the number on the wall?" Slamika-na asked. He really wanted to hear the names of all of them.

Hahami-na started with the first line, "Zero, one, two, three, four, five, six, seven, eight, nine." Then he pointed to the next line, "Ten, eleven, twelve, thirteen, fourteen, fifteen, sixteen, seventeen, eighteen, nineteen." Then he went to the next line, "Twenty, twenty-one, twenty-two, twenty-three, twenty-four, twenty-five, twenty-six, twenty-seven, twenty-eight, twenty-nine." Then he went to the next line, "Thirty, thirty-one, thirty-two, thirty-three, thirty-four, thirty-five, thirty-six, thirty-seven, thirty-eight, thirty-nine."

"After the second line, it's easy," Slamika-na said. Why did you give all the second line numbers different names?

"I don't know. That's just what I did." Hahami-na looked confused. "I didn't really mean to share this, just use it because it was easier for me."

"Hahami-na," Untuk-na asked, "If you wanted to show ten tens, what would the number be?"

Hahami-na pointed to one-zero. "Ten," he said and then pointed to the next line, "twenty, thirty," then he pointed to space under the lines he'd drawn, "forty, fifty, sixty, seventy, eighty, ninety, one hundred. Ten tens is one hundred."

"You left out the first line, Hahami-na," Tongip-na said.

"That is because I was counting by ten numbers to reach ten tens."

"Oh, I understand!" Tongip-na exclaimed. "Why did you keep this to yourself? This is wonderful."

"It is very useful. I agree with Tongip-na," Manak-na said. "I propose that we use this as a means for counting by all of us. I suggest that Tongip-na or Hahami-na propose it at the men's council."

Hahami-na spoke quickly, "Let Tongip-na do it. He can speak better at meetings than I can."

"I'll do it, but first I want to stay here long enough to learn the names of the numbers to one hundred."

"Wait," Sum-na said. "Is it difficult to count to one hundred tens?"

Hahami-na looked up. "No, it's not hard. You simply say, one hundred and one and then go throught the numbers saying one hundred in front of each number. Then, two hundred and one and two hundred and two, and so on. Then three hundred and one, four hundred and one, five hundred and one, and six hundred and one, seven hundred and one, eight hundred and one, nine-hundred and one. One hundred tens is one thousand."

"I, too, want to stay to learn all the numbers to one thousand!" Slamika-na said enthusiastically.

"I'll stay here as long as it takes," Hahami-na offered.

The men stayed there until they could all count in words to one hundred, and by hundreds to one thousand. After using the numbers to learn, it became familiar to them. They liked it. It was a combination of counting from the People and the former Mol with the zero from Hahami-na. It was something new made by the new People. They could see uses for it. They could count by tens! They could envision doubles and triples. Two hundred compared to eight hundred gave them a good sense of number comparison. Eleven enemy warriors gave them a good sense of the relationship to their twenty. Three coconuts were heavier than one. Hahami-na's spoken approach to counting made sense. It was orderly. It gave them a convenience for comparison.

Just before the men left, Untuk-na said, "I would like to say something to Wisdom before we leave. I think what we have just done is awesome."

All the men nodded assent.

"Wisdom," Untuk-na said, "Thank you for being with Hahami-na and making it possible for him to develop the numbers in a way we can use them for our benefit. Thank you for encouraging him to share. This should make a big difference in our lives to use this new way of looking at numbers. Help us to use it well."

Hahami-na blushed at the thought of being used by Wisdom to bring something so special to his People. He lowered his head. The men extinguished the fire and returned to the home cave.

Tiriku came rushing into the home cave. He was twirling in circles and pawing his muzzle. Ki'ti was alarmed and picked up the dog and carried him to Likichi.

"Something is wrong!" she called to Likichi the moment she found her.

Likichi took Tiriku and put him on the ground so she could observe.

"Pick him up and open his mouth, so I can see inside," Likichi told Ki'ti.

Ki'ti picked up her dog, put him on one of the rocks in the home cave, and opened his mouth.

Likichi looked inside. She reached her fingers into the dog's throat, making him gag, but she continued until she had a good grasp on the bone she'd seen in Tiriku's throat. She pulled it out. A little blood was on one end of the bone.

"There you are, Wise One. He had a bone stuck in his throat."

Ki'ti impulsively hugged Likichi. "Thank you so much. I had no idea what was wrong with him."

"You're welcome," Likichi said with a smile. "He'll be fine now."

Still outside, Manak-na struggled. He had seen Domur as his anchor, one who kept him from being blown about by life's winds. The idea that his adventuring might cause her to renounce their joining and enable her to join with another was an idea that had never crossed his mind web. She could, he reasoned, even choose to do that if he were not adventuring. He climbed to the top of the hill. It was slippery. As he crested the hill, he had a magnificent view, but he hardly saw it. He went down the other side of the hill and, when he thought he had gone far enough, he let out a scream of agony meant only for his ears.

He lay there in the white rain. How could he attend a meeting to plan rationally the People's new approach to numbers just a while ago and be so emotionally ripped and torn at another moment. *Is my rational mind web split from my emotional belly?* he asked himself. *How can I be two separate beings, one who functions well and the other who is like the jelly fish we saw in the salt water. How can this be? Am I no longer whole?*

As he lay there he realized he had to choose in the future between Domur and adventuring. Both made him feel wonderful—a real man. Both had rewards, but different ones. Unless Domur joined him in adventuring, the only choice was Domur or adventuring. He realized by her words that he had hurt Domur terribly. He wondered whether she would get over that hurt as he healed from the bear swipe. But then he'd had curing herbs and liquid for the bear swipe. What curing herb was there for someone hurt by desertion. It galled him to realize that his adventure was a desertion of his wife. What had he done?

Manak-na sat up. He realized he was getting his garments damp and that would stiffen them. He rose to his feet. Suddenly, he realized that he might not need to choose between Domur and adventuring. She might choose another just because of the hurt he caused her. His situation might be more life critical than he guessed. It hit him for the first time. He was thinking of himself only. For so many years he had thought of others first. When he was free from raising children and the trek was in progress, he'd seen himself free from all encumbrance and free to adventure. Free of the People. But had he thought of Domur and her needs and feelings? He had not! He had hardened his belly to her needs and feelings. He had thought only of his own. What a wretch he had become. No wonder Domur thought of another who would stay by her. Someone who could see beyond himself! Manak-na threw himself to the ground and screamed again, this time at himself.

A raven flew to a tree just above Manak-na, and it screamed at him and hopped around on the branch. It twisted its head and made strange sounds. More ravens arrived and made odd sounds that he felt were meant for him. It made him uneasy somehow that birds seemed to be chiding him. After all, wasn't he made a little better than birds? A raven flew down and landed near him but beyond his reach. It blasted him with a scream that sounded much like his own.

Manak-na looked straight up. "Wisdom, I have wronged my wife and you. Please forgive me. I must ask Domur to forgive me. But how can I do that if I ever plan to adventure again?"

He was silent for a long time. He spoke aloud, "I see what you have shown me, Wisdom. Truly an adventurer should not join with anyone. It is not for me to wait to see what I choose sometime in the future. I already chose Domur. Once I did that, I should not have given myself permission to adventure and hurt her by desertion. Either I should have remained with her or taken her with me. What was I thinking? I made a commitment to her when we joined. I have become truly a wretch. Yet adventure draws me almost irresistably."

Again he was silent. His reason and his emotions engaged in war within him. He lay on the ground forgetting about the white rain, his garments, and the raven that kept hopping around nearby. Somehow he had reasoned that his putting others first for so long earned him a time of freedom from the People—as if he had acquired a time to do whatever he wanted whenever he wanted. That was not a teaching of Wisdom, he realized. Not only had he deserted Domur, but also he had deserted his People, as if they were a burden he had put up with. He really didn't feel that way. He loved his People. How had he split himself so sharply? And finally, he remembered Wamumur so often saying to others, "You have permitted yourself to believe a lie." He reasoned that he had done just that. Now, in the woods where no one could hear him, he had to make a decision. Did he want Domur or adventure? One choice was appropriate, right, consistent with Wisdom. The other choice was selfish, wrong, and not consistent with Wisdom. He knew what he should choose. Could he? His contact with the white rain had made the ochre on his face streak, but he didn't know.

Manak-na was no longer willing to lie to himself. He was unwilling to return to the home cave until he had made a decision he could live with. He raised himself from the ground and began to walk through the woods. The ravens followed quietly, watching. He saw a deer and his hunter instinct urged him to take the deer, but he was too tuned to himself to bother though he carried his spear as all hunters did when out of the dwelling place.

He climbed the next hill. Atop the hill was an odd standing rock arrangement. He'd have thought that trees would have grown to disguise this place, for it clearly had not been used for a long time. Instead, the ground showed no sign of vegetation under the white rain, and the rocks were arranged clearly by people of old. While in the past, such a find would have interested him, it made little impact except to cause him to wonder why trees hadn't grown there. He touched a standing rock and noticed it had been carved, but he didn't study it. Just as he was about to go down the far side of that hill, Manak-na realized that Wisdom was rapidly swallowing color from the land. He needed to return to the cave. They would be discussing the new approach to numbering at the men's council. He had not reached a conclusion, but he had to return. He still had no knowledge that the red ochre had lost its shape and streaked the side of his face.

As quickly as he could, he retraced the path he'd left in the white rain. He arrived back at the home cave just as the evening meal was being served. He had little hunger. Tongip-na raised an eyebrow when their eyes met, but he said nothing. Manak-na sat next to Domur and her closeness pricked him in strange ways. He wondered whether she knew he was battling himself.

The men's council began that evening with a shout from Song, who had been sitting quietly beside her closest friend, Minal. Song looked horrified at her outburst.

"Song, what is it?" Ki'ti asked.

"I'm sorry. I didn't mean to disrupt the meeting. I just got kicked from the inside and it was a surprise."

"Are you injured?" Ki'ti asked.

Likichi interrupted, "She was kicked by the child she will have."

Song let out another sound, much softer.

Likichi looked at Song, "It kicked again. Get used to it."

Humko-na, who was sitting across the fire from Song, was looking at his wife. He was delighted to know that he and Song would have a baby. He could hardly suppress the smile of joy on his face. She noticed.

Ki'ti said, "I think we can begin." She looked around and Tongip-na caught her attention. She nodded towards him.

"Several of us met today to plan a new way for all the People to use numbers. We now have one that is made from a combination of all the ways of counting, but forming an orderly approach created by Hahami-na. The new approach will incorporate the zero that Hahami-na uses. Zero just means nothing or lack of something. Numbers mean how much or how many, so it stands to reason that the place to start is zero, or nothing. It is too new to try to teach at this meeting. We will take small groups of the People this season of cold days to teach. Once we've taught all the People, we can start to use it."

Ki'ti looked around. She waited for anyone to make eye contact for permission to speak. No one did.

Ki'ti said, "Because there are no other speakers, this meeting ends. We will have a story shortly.

People moved around, chatted briefly, and then reassembled.

Ki'ti began:

"This story is not old. It is something many of us knew about. For that reason names will not be used. There was a young man living among us who was Other. Another more proper name for Other is Minguat. He came with us when we left the cave in the ashfall and moved north. He talked to a young man who left the cave in the ashfall with the Minguat for the coast, where the Minguat were all killed except for four of them. The man who lived among us had a secret. His secret was he thought Minguat were better than People or Mol for that matter."

"He had not reasoned well, and the young man he talked to tried to reason with him to no avail. The young men had no idea that above them on the rock walk beside a big tree the Wise One was hearing the conversation. The Wise One was horrified. He shared what he heard with older men who were related to the young men."

"They decided to have some of the People disguise themselves and hide in the bushes by the lake. The men got themselves hidden and then the relatives of the young men took them to the lake. They had them sit on a log on the shore with their backs to the men."

"They asked them about their conversation and found that what the Wise One had told them was true. There was one young man who was arrogant and thought the People were nothing compared to the Minguat. The men of the Minguat told the young men to stand and to look into the bushes behind them. They did. They saw nothing. Finally, three of the People stood. It startled the young men. They had not seen them. In fact, the older men hadn't been able to see them either, for they were very well hidden."

"The older Minguat asked the young men how superior they were, if they couldn't see men on the hill behind them, whose spears could have ended their lives. The arrogant young man had no answer, except to repeat that he believed Minguat were superior."

"The Wise One, then, made a statement that all who lived with them were People. It was what he genuinely believed—that changes on the exterior were just minor differences for all were essentially the same. There were no Minguat or Mol. All were People. And all People were equal, none better or worse than another. He said that anyone not wanting to be People must leave when Wisdom returned color to the land the next day."

"Two of the Minguat left. They left in the dark. When Wisdom returned color to the land, one of the Minguat crawled back to the place where the People lived. A bear had attacked her and the arrogant man fought the bear and was killed. The woman died that day. They buried her but did not go for the young man's body, because the bear was eating it."

"The Wise One was right. All of us, whether we look alike or not, are one People. No one is better or worse than another. We have some differences, but they are nothing special. If I have black hair and yours is brown, it makes neither one of us better than the other. That is how we came to live as we do—all of us with our differences are one People. And with that came real blessings from Wisdom. For the Minguat and the Mol, they found Wisdom. For the People, we found that adding to us those who looked different added a better ability for us to have live births, and the children who were born were all delightfully beautiful."

In the hearth light in the cave Minagle and Sum-na squeezed hands. Each had lost a spouse that night long ago. In time they came together. Their pain had been replaced with happiness.

Ki'ti had finished. She looked around. Clearly, this story still moved People, especially those who were involved in the story. People quietly got up and went to their sleeping places. Those who lived through the story felt that the story had great merit and stayed as a constant reminder that Wisdom saw all as equal. Yomuk had heard the story all his life, but it had never made as significant an impact as it did this evening. His desire to be better than others was blasphemous. He was horrified.

When Wisdom with chill returned color to the land and glowing peachy color to the clouds, edged by the color of yellow metal, many of the People watched from the home cave entrance the change in color finding a type of nourishment in the beauty of it. Ahna and Elemaea sat at the morning meal chatting.

"What do you mean 'fitting in?'" Ahna asked, twirling her finger in a front piece of her hair.

"Every one of the People has something that is unique to them that they do. Some make garments; some hunt; some cook; some get water from the lower part of the home cave. There are many things People do. I talked to Mother because I couldn't fit in. She told me what to do. I ended up making spear points and knives."

"I need to find a place to fit in, then?"

"Yes. You are the right age for that search."

"What do I do?"

"Talk to Mother about it. That's the best thing I can suggest."

After all the morning meal had been cleared away, Ahna found Ki'ti and went to where she sat on her rolled up sleeping skins.

"What is it?" Ki'ti asked.

"I need to fit in. Elemaea said to talk to you."

Ki'ti sighed. *Now was the time,* she thought, but if this were not her replacement, it would make her sad. She said, "Sit here beside me, Ahna."

Ahna sat, wondering what would be her guidance to fitting in.

Ki'ti said, "Ahna, tell me the story I told about Tikarumusa."

Ahna was startled. She sat there thinking, and then she began.

"This is a new story. It is one that the Wise One chose for the People from the travel of Manak-na and Yomuk. It tells of something they learned in Aikot, the land where I came from, far, far away, where the sun rises first from the land to the sea."

"There was an old man called Tikarumusa who was severely disabled with the stiffness disease. He was an old man who lived on a hill up from the sea. One day his people became very excited. They saw the tide going out. The tide is a change in the level where the water touches the shore. They lived where they have very little change in tides. This tide went out fast enough that it stranded fish on the wet sand. Fish were flopping all over the sand."

"His people got very excited and all of them, regardless of age, ran down to the sand to gather the gifts from their god of the underwater. Fish were everywhere and the people expected to feast. From his place on the hill, Tikarumusa stood to look out. He saw the people gathering fish. Far out to sea he could see a huge wave forming. He called and called to his people to warn them. He could not run to them, and they could not hear him. Tikarumusa hurt in his belly as he watched the huge wave come to cover all his people and to take them off to sea, not sparing a single one. He was left alone."

"Tikarumusa lay on his sleeping skins. He wept for his people and himself. He thought he would die there. Instead, Wisdom brought the boat that Manak-na and Yomuk had traveled on for their adventure. Men from the boat found the old man. They took the old man to the boat where he was later exchanged for me, so he could remain with his people and be cared for."

"What's important to put in your mind web for this story is that if you ever are at the sea shore and observe the sea rushing out, no matter what you see on the sand, run the opposite way so that a monster wave will not take you to drown in the sea."

Ki'ti was so excited that she could hardly contain herself, but years of self-discipline had taught her self control. Not only had Ahna remembered the story, but she had done it perfectly. She smiled for a moment thinking how Wamumur felt when he asked her to do the same thing—and she did.

Ki'ti said, "Now tell me the story about Kukuk-na and Timkut-na."

Again, Ahna spent a time in thought. Then she began. Again she told the story perfectly.

Ki'ti was silent for a long time. She looked at Ahna whose eyes looked directly into hers.

"My Dear," Ki'ti said. "You have a hard path to fitting in. Wisdom has selected you to be our next Wise One. You will have to learn what I know, so you can serve the People for Wisdom and do it wisely."

"I what?" Ahna said timidly. Surely, she didn't hear Ki'ti correctly.

Ki'ti looked with compassion on the little child who had just joined the People and wanted to fit in. "The truth, Ahna, is that Wisdom knew I needed a replacement. Wisdom searched and found you. That is why you came here. But it will not make your life easy. You will have to follow me and learn how to be Wise One. You've never had much time to play. Well, you don't have any time for play beginning now. Someday, when I know that it's time, you'll become the next Wise One. I thought when I was young like you, that I had a choice in this matter. Try to understand right now—you have no choice. When Wisdom decides something in our lives, we cannot change it."

"Wise One, I am not worthy."

"Don't start that. You don't decide whether you are worthy. Wisdom has chosen you. That's the end of it. Today I shall adopt you as my daughter. You will call me Mother. You will no longer roam as you choose. All day every day you will stay by my side, unless I give you freedom. Do you understand?"

"You really mean this, don't you?" Ahna had extreme difficulty trying to take in the words of the Wise One.

"Yes, Ahna, from the bottom of my belly I mean this. I also know what it is to have your childhood cut short, but it doesn't sound like you ever had one."

"I am ready to do what you have me do. I have found Wisdom here, and I am Wisdom's servant. I will obey to the best of my ability." Her sincerity was cutting into Ki'ti's belly. She looked up and silently thanked Wisdom.

"After Wisdom sucks color from the land, I intend to notify the People during the men's council that we have another Wise One. Realize from that point your every move will be watched. You will not be permitted to go to the privy alone, but must have a hunter accompany you. The reason is that you are now a treasure to the People. You must be protected."

"I am comfortable being Wisdom's servant. Being a treasure of any kind is something I am not comfortable with." Ahna was trying to get Ki'ti to understand.

"Ahna, Wisdom doesn't care whether you are comfortable. You have been chosen. Do you want to know how I know?"

"Yes," Ahna replied almost in a whisper.

"I heard your prayer to Wisdom when you were newly arrived here, and I realized you have a belly for Wisdom. So I wondered whether you would be my replacement. There is one other element that qualifies you for my replacement. It is your memory in your mind web that enables your retelling the stories perfectly. You cannot do that unless Wisdom puts the memory in your mind web. I just tested you. You told the stories perfectly. You are my replacement."

"Won't your children want to be your replacement?" Ahna remained dumbfounded.

"My Dear, I don't think anyone *wants* to be Wise One. It is a job with little freedom. They will not envy you."

"What does freedom mean?" Ahna asked.

"It means being able to do what you want to do, when you want to do it. It comes with many conditions for normal people, but for Wise Ones, there is no freedom. You are available to the People any time they have a need."

"I guess I'll not miss what I've never had."

"We'll see about that," Ki'ti said smiling. She thought about her days at the same age learning the stories. There was no time to play, and she missed it. Maybe Ahna's words were correct. Maybe if you never played, you wouldn't miss it.

Chapter 7

Wind breezed through the entryway blowing ice crystals from the trees, as Wisdom restored vivid blue, gold, orange, and yellow colors to the land. The season of cold days was brutal, colder than any the People remembered. They were convinced that Manak-na was right about the farther north they went the colder it would become. Several of them had qualms about going to the big lake if it was much farther north. There was plenty of food available in this place—dried meat and plants from warmer days fed them well, as their storage attested—but while hunting fresh meat was certainly possible because wildlife abounded, it was becoming very difficult, if not impossible, as a result of the depth of the white rain on the ground. Never had they lived where snow lay for long times at a depth over the knees of the People.

Nanichak-na struggled to sit up. The light from Wisdom's return of color to the land caused him to waken. He was dizzy. A wet spot on his tunic made him realize he'd drooled profusely in his sleep. He lay there, not sure whether he sickened. The old man tried to rise again and the same dizziness overpowered him. He got tough with himself and tried to force himself to rise, but he found his left arm was not cooperating. With all his might, Nanichak-na pushed himself up with the other arm. He tried to stand and fell to the ground with a moan, calling attention to his difficulty. He was always reluctant to call attention to himself—it was not manly. The old man wanted to handle his problem himself. It was all so confusing. His dizziness turned to darkness followed by a pinpoint of light that seemed to grow and grow.

Likichi hurried to his side. One look at Nanichak-na's face told her what she didn't want to know. He had died! There had been no warning, no signs.

One moment he was with them, aged but doing very well, and the next he was gone to Wisdom. She sat beside him and cradled his wrinkled face in her lap. Gently she closed his eyes. Blanagah, teary eyed, brought her a damp cloth, and Likichi washed his face. Nanichak-na gone? She couldn't believe it! He'd been like Wamumur, one who was always there, a permanent person, functioning well right to the end. What would life be without him? Blanagah brought a large bowl filled with water for the cleaning of the body. Hahami-na knelt at his father's side and lifted his lifeless, gnarled hand to his own face. His grief was silent; his heart, broken. *No one ever had a better father,* he thought.

Slamika-na, Ermi-na, Sum-na, and Guy-na volunteered to dig the grave. Slamika-na went to Hahami-na and asked whether he'd chosen a place. He was having trouble speaking from the emotion he felt in the loss of his grandfather.

"I hadn't even thought about it. I trust you will find a good place. Thank you for your help. I haven't the strength I used to have."

"We're glad to help," he said. "Izumu," using the special word for grandfather or male elder, "was a very special person, a treasure to us all." Slamika-na managed to get the words out of his clenched throat.

The men dressed warmly and left with a few spears for safety, brooms to sweep the white rain away, and several bone and stone tools for digging carried in a couple of bags. Each would truly miss Nanichak-na. When they reached the bottom of the hill, they began to search the flat land for a place to put the body of Nanichak-na. They did not want it near the place where the evil man had been buried across the small valley. They decided on a place where a few ginkgo trees grew together at the base of the hill. Ginkgo trees were relatively rare in these hills. They began to sweep the white rain. It was mid-thigh on the original People. They realized they needed to sweep a large area, much larger than what they'd need for a grave. There would be many People for the graveside ritual. They shouldn't stand in deep white rain.

The white rain was light and swept well. Ermi-na went to the base of the path that led downhill and began to sweep the white rain from side to side, making a walkway to the site they'd chosen. White rain crystals became airborne again and sparkled in the sunlight. He took a moment to watch the sparkling crystals. He considered it would be a delightful experience if it weren't caused by such sadness. Then he turned his thoughts to the fact that Nanichak-na never had to go through age related problems. He was hearty until the end. Ermi-na felt that was good for Nanichak-na. It didn't help reduce the pain he already felt from missing his friend, however.

Sum-na, Guy-na, and Slamika-na had already discovered that the very top of the ground was frozen. Each used an adze to chop through the frozen ground where the grave would be. Once through the frozen ground, the digging was normal. The dug vegetation and dirt stained the white rain. The men noticed but said nothing as if such thoughts were unworthy. When they finished the grave digging, they asked about stones. Ermi-na suggested they go to the place where they'd removed the body of the evil one and take the stones they'd created when they destroyed the evil pictures.

"Would that desecrate the grave of our special friend?" Guy-na asked.

Slamika-na looked up, surprised at the question. "That man is buried and his paintings destroyed. The rocks have no power. I see no reason not to use them. If it makes you feel better, I'll ask the Wise One."

Guy-na said, "On our way to gather the stones, Slamika-na, please ask her. I'd feel better about it if she says it's good to use them."

The men picked up their tools and left to return them to the home cave so they could gather the needed stones. Since the ones they had in mind were in a cave, it wouldn't be difficult. Slamika-na sought the Wise One in the home cave. He found her sitting with Ahna going over stories.

Ki'ti looked at Slamika-na standing in his outside clothing, rosy cheeked, and dripping. She nodded.

"We have dug the grave for Izumu's body. We wondered whether it would be a desecration to use the stones we made, when we broke up the painting in the cave of the evil man. Those stones are easily available, but we don't want to do wrong by Nanichak-na. I don't see that the rocks have any power, but you would know best."

Ki'ti smiled at Slamika-na. "It was good for you men to be so considerate. I agree with you. The rocks that were broken from the wall have no power. Feel free to use them. It will put them to good purpose." Slamika-na lowered his head, turned, and went back outside.

Ahna had watched the interaction carefully. She was uncertain how Ki'ti arrived at her answer. She asked.

Ki'ti put her arm around Ahna. "In the cave of the evil man there were paintings. They showed a person who had made himself strong by having great power over others. It showed evil things, things People would not see as right. But, I had those paintings destroyed. I did that because when People see something evil, they can begin to conceive that what they see is good, right, or at least acceptable for no other reason than it is there. It can help People come to believe a lie. It makes People question what they know to be good or right.

It fogs the mind web by planting foreign seeds of wrong ideas. We can think up plenty of wrong all by ourselves, without getting help from evil paintings. For anyone to have power over another—that is not Wisdom's way. So the paintings were destroyed to prevent them from tempting our People. When the paintings were on the wall, they had no actual power except to influence others to think that what's wrong was right or, worse, to think things they'd never think. Now the paintings are utterly destroyed and they have no power to influence anything. They're just stones. Do you understand?"

"Yes, Wise One, I do understand. I also know what it is for people to have great power over others. It is not good."

"Let's continue," Ki'ti led Ahna back to the storytelling.

Slamika-na reached the cave of the evil man and assured the men there that the stones were just stones now, and there would be no desecration to Nanichak-na's grave to use those stones. Each man placed several stones in leather bags and began to carry them downhill to the grave site. Guy-na slipped and landed on his back. He was unhurt and the men gently laughed at the sight of him on his back on the white rain. He also laughed. It was a good release. He gathered the spilled rocks and continued on to deposit them at the grave site.

When all was in order at the grave site, the men returned to the home cave. Slamika-na and Sum-na volunteered to carry Nanichak-na's body to the grave site. The People in the home cave all began to dress in season-of-cold-days garments for the graveside ritual in the cold. Even Grypchon-na, whose joints caused him great pain, would make the trip to the grave. Tongip-na and Ekuktu-na would help him on the hill.

They all gathered. The ritual saying what the deceased meant to them had begun. Tiriku sitting next to Ki'ti moved slightly. Ki'ti looked at the dog. He was looking up. Her eyes followed his. Sitting above them in the branches of a gingko tree was Raven. For once, Raven was silent. His mate flew to his side, and she was also silent. When the ring of People had finished their comments, Ki'ti turned to Ahna and said, "Ahna, tell the story." It had not been planned, but Ki'ti's mind web had traced back to a different time when she had told the story at the grave side of Enut. She knew Ahna could do it.

Ahna was stunned, but she recovered well, and she began the old story. As Ki'ti listened, she heard just what she expected, Ahna told the story perfectly. Ki'ti was so pleased with her. Ki'ti knew that Nanichak-na would have been happy. She also knew she couldn't have told the story without breaking down. Her Great Hunter gone. The pain was too much.

Quietly all returned to the home cave. There were no flowers, nothing to add to the grave of this special man. Manak-na stopped. He returned to the site. He reached into his little bag of ochre, which he'd already used to paint his face that morning, and he put some of it on Nanichak-na's forehead. Raven and his mate watched from their perch. Manak-na returned to the home cave. The men who dug the grave returned with tools to fill it in and put stones atop the site. Raven and his mate saw all that the men were doing. When the men left, Raven made an odd sound and flew off with his mate.

Manak-na took off his outer wear and joined Domur on the rolled sleeping skins.

"I heard what you did. That was thoughtful," Domur told him. "Manak-na," she said, "How do you make the ochre you have? It's not in its natural form."

"I don't know. Tikarumusa didn't tell me that—only to be sure to use it daily."

"Do you know where any is locally? I'm asking because your supply is getting very small."

"I did see some atop the next hill to the west. It's in an area where there are some odd stones and nothing grows there."

"Do I want to ask what you were doing over there?" Domur inquired.

"My Dear One, I wrestled with myself when I realized I'd deserted you." He put his arm around her shoulder. "Honestly, I hadn't realized what it was doing to you when I left—I was following a childhood dream of my own. My mind web saw only Manak-na and his wants, in the same way that a hyena focuses on an opportunistic feast from the scent of a carcass upwind." His belly knotted up with this outpouring of his thoughts. "I loathed myself when I understood the full impact of my actions, and yet I still felt drawn to explore and adventure. Somehow I felt it was my turn to do what I wanted." He thought how empty that sounded, withdrew his arm from her shoulders, and picked at his thumb nail, looking down at his hand, not at her.

"On the other side of the mountain, where no one would hear or know, I fought with myself. I realized there on the other side of the mountain that my true choice had been to adventure or join. We joined before I knew about that choice, but I would not have chosen adventure then. Because of my ignorance at that time, I didn't realize I had cut off my own choice to adventure. Our joining brought me great happiness and made me feel such a man. But the childhood dream of adventure never left." He'd made his cuticle at the side of his thumb nail bleed, so he stuck the thumb in his mouth for a moment.

"I experienced my childhood dream by deserting you. I knew down deep inside that my leaving hurt you, but I had no idea how much pain it caused. I closed my mind web to it." His thumb continued to bleed and he put pressure on it. "I regret that. I am so sorry to have hurt you. I wish I could say I regret the adventure, but that would be a lie. It opened my mind web to so many things I didn't know. It, too, made me feel such a man." He checked the bleeding and it seemed to have stopped.

He looked briefly right into her eyes. "My mind web opened my understanding when I finally realized that adventure had become to me as another woman. It was as if I had you and another for wives. Then I knew I went against nature. A male swan would not have two females! A man of the People would not have two wives! I purposed not to return from the other side of the hill, until I could decide which path to follow in the future." He noticed the bleeding had started up again, so he put more pressure on the thumb.

"Have I reached a decision? No." He pressed harder than he intended. "It's not that I fail to recognize what is Wisdom's way or right or good for you and me or the People—I do. What is not easy is choosing what's right and meaning it for the rest of my life. Making change either way is extremely difficult—for I have known both." His head was lowered. He looked into her eyes again. "Some knowledge is not good."

Domur saw the contortions his face made. She felt for him in his agony. Obviously, he ached over the dilemma he had created for himself. "Manak-na, I take what I have from you a day at a time. I do not worry about tomorrow. Whatever occurs is what occurs. I will live my life and love every day I have. That has brought me peace. It has even brought me joy. I think you should go to that hill when you can and gather some ochre rocks. We need to learn how to turn it from rock to paint. Yours feels mixed with something like clay or fat or wax. I know it has been ground to a fine powder. It'll take time to figure out what to do with it. If you bring me rocks, I'll try to make some for you. But, Manak-na, you know better than to go alone. Promise you'll get someone to go with you."

He reached for her hands, which she gave him willingly. "I promise." He lowered his head.

Domur didn't try to understand what she couldn't understand. She continued to take Manak-na at his word. At this time he wanted to be there, she mused. She had lost trust that he would remain. She would not let that fact fester into frustration. She turned loose of it and truly enjoyed each day and what came with it. Deep down Domur knew that Manak-na loved her.

It would be easier in some ways, if he were infatuated with another woman. But Domur couldn't compete with adventure without making Manak-na feel deep guilt, and she refused to do that. It would solve nothing, and it would make her an irascible person, she thought. She realized that Manak-na wrestled fiercely with the issue. The conflict was hurting him. She had nothing but time to see what would happen and either way, she knew now, she'd still have a productive and happy life regardless of his choice. She got up to see what the excitement at the other side of the cave was all about.

Elemaea had made several women's knives. It was her first try and she thought they might be helpful to the women who made things from skins. These knives were much smaller than the men's knives. Elemaea had laid out numbers of the knives and women were free to take one, use it, and tell Elemaea how well it worked or what could be done to improve it. Domur picked up a knife. She and Minagle examined it together.

"Not only does it look useful, it's really beautiful," Minagle said.

"It fits my hand perfectly and seems to be very strong," Domur added.

Manak-na stopped by dressed for outdoors, carrying a broom, spear, and an adz. He told Domur that he and Kai-na would try to get some ochre. They were leaving now. From his small backpack hung two grass bags to carry the ochre rocks back to the home cave.

She smiled and wished them well.

"What was that about?" Minagle asked.

"Manak-na is running low on ochre, and he knows where to find more. He's going to get some. I told him I'd try to make some like what he carries. It has been prepared some way. We'll have to figure it out."

"Why does he paint his face?" Minagle asked.

"When he was on the other side of the earth, Ahna's grandfather told him to paint his face that way every day and wash it off at night. He said the god of the underwater wants to hurt Manak-na, and this would protect him."

"Well, we're pretty far from the sea."

"Manak-na told me the old man told him that the god of the underwater can leave the water for land."

"Manak-na believes this?"

"He seems to. At least he doesn't want to tempt the god of the underwater to hurt him." Domur ran her finger gently over the cutting side of the knife. It was sharp!

"We don't have a god of the underwater," Minagle stated the obvious.

"I don't know whether Manak-na has thought this through. I simply know that he does this ritual daily. I'm willing to help if it comforts him."

Hahami-na and Mootmu-na were sitting by the home cave fire warming up after the cold of being outside. Hahami-na asked, "Does it seem strange to you that in all this travel we have become aware of only a group of Minguat practicing war, Kipotuilak, the Mol who lives to the west but travels by boat on the sea, and the boatbuilders, whom we haven't seen? Where are the people?"

"I, too, have wondered. We are no threat, so there's no need to hide from us. We'd see signs of human life if it were there. Even now young hunters still climb to the tallest peaks looking for smoke from hearth fires at night. I just see a great human emptiness on this land. The land has food available and many places to live. We see evidence of life here from giants long ago, not people of today." Mootmu-na frowned.

"I wonder about the cold. Do you suppose, since it gets colder the farther north we go, that humans decided it was too cold?"

Mootmu-na frowned again. "Who can say? I do find it strange and limiting. Young girls will be restricted to the young boys of this group as they grow into maturity."

"That's true," Hahami-na agreed. "I remember Kipotuilak telling us that at the big lake you have to double your winter outerwear to stay warm. It must be very difficult to hunt there in winter, if it's possible at all. With deeper white rain and two sets of clothing—I'd rather rely on meat sticks in the season of cold days than to try to hunt."

"I have begun to question whether we should keep going that far." Mootmu-na was concerned about the effect it would have on the People to keep going to the big lake only to have to turn around and trek back many miles. "I think this is something to bring up at council."

"I agree with you, Mootmu-na. It's time to discuss whether to continue north."

To the west Manak-na and Kai-na had made it to the second hill. They were sweeping the white rain aside when Kai-na signaled for silence. Soundlessly an animal they'd never seen stepped upon an outcropping downhill from the men. Each tried hard to guess what the animal was. Its back was about as high off the ground as the men's chests. It had paired antlers that came forward a short distance and went back a much greater distance. It was a proud animal surveying the valley below.

"It has the furry skin that I have seen occasionally at the place of the Mol. The fur is soft!" Manak-na said.

"I don't want to go for it; do you?" Kai-na asked.

"Yes. I would love for Domur to have one of those for a sleeping skin. I'll try to throw my spear, but it'll be a chance in one thousand!" Manak-na said, using the new numbers.

"I'll help." Kai-na said raising his spear.

The two men quietly took their spears and stood at the edge of the hilltop. Manak-na nodded to Kai-na who then released his spear in a mighty thrust through the air. Manak-na's spear followed a split second later. Both spears found their target, which caused both men to look at each other in disbelief. They slid downhill to finish off the animal. The two men bled the animal, gutted it, and tied the feet together so they could carry it to the meat preparation cave on the spears. They did not choose to keep the entrails. Before heading back, they stopped to sweep the ground to locate the ochre, chip off enough to fill Manak-na's bags full, and gather their tools and the animal to head back.

The white rain was deep and both men labored to carry the meat home. They had to take high steps to get through the white rain without expending the energy it took to drag their feet through it. As it was, they were partly dragging the animal. Raven watched unnoticed from the tree tops. As soon as Raven felt comfortable with the distance the men made from the kill site, he swooped down and feasted on the discarded animal guts. He'd stop to fly to his mate and they would feast together. Not much escaped Raven's notice.

Somewhat winded, Manak-na said, "I finally remember what animal this is. It's a caribou."

"A what?" Kai-na asked. He had a little difficulty hearing through his fur head covering.

"Caribou," Manak-na shouted.

"It's soft!" Kai-na shouted back.

When they neared the cave, Mootmu-na and Tongip-na came to meet them.

"I thought you went for ochre," Tongip-na teased.

"Well, Kai-na saw this caribou and didn't want it, but I did. It will make Domur a great sleeping skin!"

"Let me feel that," Mootmu-na said.

Manak-na and Kai-na remained still so the other men could feel the softness of the caribou.

"Where did you find this?" Tongip-na asked.

"On the other side of the second hill over from ours. Off to the west. We were atop the hill and it climbed to an outcrop just below us. I'm eager to know what the meat tastes like."

Manak-na pushed his head covering back a little.

"Why don't you two let us take it to the meat preparation cave and you can rest from your trek. We'll take good care of it. And the skin's for Domur for a sleeping skin?"

Manak-na nodded affirmatively. Manak-na and Kai-na let the men take it. Both were still somewhat short of breath. They headed into the home cave where they removed their clothing designed for outside wear and came to a hearth to warm up. Domur arrived curious as to whether they'd found ochre.

"I have the ochre," Manak-na said, "and thanks to help from Kai-na, you'll have a caribou sleeping skin. It's very soft."

Domur smiled and took the bags of ochre. It was heavier than she expected. The men had made the trip worthwhile by filling the two bags full. She went to the area where tools used primarily by women were stored. She found a stone bowl and a crushing stone. She carried them to her place near the hearth. She took a small piece of the ochre and put it into the stone bowl and began to crush the stone. It would take her a while to make powder of it. She asked Manak-na to let her have a small piece of the ball in the bag he carried to paint his face. He pulled the leather strip over his head and handed her the whole pouch. She kneaded the ball trying to discover what besides ochre it contained. She smelled it. She tasted it. Then she carefully put the ball back into the pouch and she continued to grind the ochre to powder. She continued grinding until she could put a tiny amount of the powder on her finger and blow it off. It felt very finely ground. Domur added a little water and stirred the mixture. It certainly made a wet colored mixture, but Manak-na's wasn't wet. In fact he spit on it to moisten it just before using it.

Domur went to the container of rendered animal fat. She let the water mixture settle and then poured off the clear water she'd mixed with the ochre. She added a tiny amount of the rendered fat. It made the mixture workable, but wasn't exactly what she had in mind. Domur cleaned out the stone bowl and ground more stone. Again, to turn the stone to powder took a very long time. The evening meal was announced, so Domur had to abandon her work until they finished eating. The ochre experiment was fascinating to her. It captured her mind web. She could hardly wait to return to it.

The men's council was called and the People took their places. A hush came upon them. Ki'ti looked up to see whether anyone was making eye contact for permission to speak. Mootmu-na looked directly into Ki'ti's eyes. She nodded.

Mootmu-na began. "Today Hahami-na and I discussed two things. First, we talked about the lack of other humans in this huge territory we've explored. We've seen very few other people here. Night after night we send people to search for fires and we never see any. Even though we have many people, far more than at any other time in our history, we do not have enough to continue on without meeting other people to keep our joining safe. This is not an immediate problem, but if things continue as they are, it will be a problem in the future. The second thing we discussed is whether it is wise to continue to the big lake. Kipotuilak told us that it is severely cold there in the season of cold days. Cold enough to require double sets of garments designed for outside wear. We tried to guess how that would be to walk. How anyone would hunt in two sets of outside garments seems impossible to imagine. And the white rain would be deeper. As it is here, it's difficult to walk in this depth of white rain. Manak-na has told us that the farther north we go the colder it gets. My question is whether it is wise to continue on. This is a seemingly good place to live. We are distant from the boatbuilder people, but there *are* people there. That is all I have to say."

Grypchon-na laughed and looked at Ki'ti. "It would definitely be to my personal best interest to remain here! Cold is not good with this stiffness of old age. Neither is trekking."

Arkan-na looked at Ki'ti. She nodded.

"I reason that most of us are tired of trekking. It is hard to feel so impermanent. I suppose I wonder whether Wisdom plans for us to go to the big lake or whether it is just the direction that is important. If it's just the direction, I'd agree with Mootmu-na and Grypchon-na. Staying here is a good plan."

Lamul-na got Ki'ti's attention. She nodded.

"What do you say about Wisdom's plan, Ki'ti?"

Ki'ti looked startled. Normally, no one asked questions of her directly at council. "We knew we needed to leave the last permanent place we lived because of the earthquakes. The south was not possible—it is a land of nothing but volcanic ash. The east held warrior Minguat. The west was Mol territory. That left north for us. Wisdom never specified that we were to go all the way to the big lake. I think the idea of the lake captivated us when we heard of it. No one knew how cold it got in the season of cold days. Wisdom guided us on the path made by the Mol giants, because that is where we decided to go. I agree that we have traveled very far, and that it is colder and colder each winter. I, too, am troubled by the lack of people and the very idea of having to wear double season-of-cold-days garments to survive outside in winter. I want what is best for our People. What do the rest of you say?"

The men began one by one to indicate that they wanted to stay. Once the men had their say the women were polled. They, too, wanted to stay. Everyone liked the place where they were living. Not one voice was raised to leave for the big lake.

Secretly, Ki'ti was well pleased. She, too, was tired of the trekking. It drained her physically, for it required better breathing than she had. She looked up. "Are there any other issues to bring to the council?" The council members all looked down. "Then, the meeting is over for this night. There will not be a story. The stories will continue tomorrow." Ki'ti was tired. The meeting issues were a surprise to her and the outcome surprised her even more. So much had happened so fast in the lives of this little group of People that there was a great need to slow down and take stock of the changes. Ki'ti remained sitting at her place at the council as thoughts raced through the fibers of her mind web. Mootmu-na was so good to have raised the issues he raised. He spoke what all others had thought but not expressed. It would be good for Grypchon-na to be able to live without the trekking.

Untuk-na approached Ki'ti so she could see him and not be startled. He realized she was lost in thought. "My Wise One, he said gently, it is time you slept. You have been overtired for a long time. It is not good. Come," he said extending his two hands to help her up. She put her small hands into his and smiled her special smile for him.

"Tonight, my dearest Untuk-na, I wish we had places set aside on the hill where special time could be taken in private. I also wish I had the energy for it."

"There are places on the hill, Ki'ti. When you are fully rested I'll take you there."

"There are places there?" She laughed gently. She began to wonder where she'd been. Normally she'd have known about the private places. Her life had been too busy to think about the normal things in life.

Untuk-na prepared the sleeping place. Ki'ti snuggled down in the skins. Tiriku slipped under the covers at her feet. Untuk-na knelt beside her and brought his body beside hers. He put his arm around her and pulled her close. They kissed and Ki'ti closed her eyes in sleep.

Wisdom brought clouds and white rain to the hills and valleys, no color to the land—just black and white. The clatter and busy morning meal preparation awakened Untuk-na. He was surprised that Ki'ti still slept. He cupped her shoulder and tried to awaken her. Slowly she opened her eyes. Untuk-na realized that Ki'ti had slept through the night and was not refreshed. He told her to remain where she was. Ki'ti was jarred slightly. Untuk-na rarely told her what to do. He had done this clearly and decisively. She did not argue. She was very tired. She had dreamed and she was struggling to separate from the dream.

Likichi came to Ki'ti. "What is it?" Ki'ti asked. She moaned when she saw that Likichi had brought the container they used when someone couldn't make it to the privy.

Likichi looked at Ki'ti, loving her dearly. She helped her use the container and then lie back down on the sleeping skins. "You are exhausted. You need rest. You will now rest."

Ki'ti had no energy to use for arguing. She just lay there. Tiriku stretched under the sleeping skins and pulled himself so that his eyes just escaped the covers. He realized instantly that something was different this morning. He raced outside and returned to see what was happening with Ki'ti.

Untuk-na returned with Ki'ti's bowl of food. She indicated she wasn't hungry, but he insisted she eat. Ki'ti sat up. She ate part of the food. Untuk-na insisted she finish it. Ki'ti wanted to argue, but she didn't have the energy for it. She ate. The dream hung over her like a morning mountain mist. She tried to remember it, but recovery proved futile.

She looked at Untuk-na when she finished. "I have been pushing to do what was necessary to teach Ahna, to be sure that all was well with the People, to plan for the next trek, and to live my life available to all. I am tired. Last night I realized I could relax. I haven't felt that since we started this trek. I guess I took the idea of relaxing to the extreme, I am just so tired."

"Well, Ki'ti," he said, "Likichi and I have talked. We are going to move our sleeping skins near the hearth over there, so you'll stay warm. You are going to rest for as many fingers of days as I have on one hand. If you still are tired, then you will have another hand of days to rest. Do not fight me. The People depend on you. You must rest. Likichi and I will see that you do. There is nothing that needs your immediate attention. Nothing!"

Untuk-na braced for a fight. Instead, Ki'ti lay back down and murmured, "Let me know when you want to move the sleeping skins." She shut her eyes. She slept.

Likichi and Untuk-na worked quickly to prepare the area for the move to the warmth of the hearth. The People were watching carefully to be sure that their Wise One was well. Untuk-na spoke to the entire group telling them that Ki'ti had been carrying a lot of physical, emotional, and spiritual weight from the time the trek began. He told them that finally, when the decision was made to remain at this place, she put her burden down and could admit to the extreme fatigue she felt. Rest would cure the fatigue. She just needed a great amount of rest. He urged People to check with Likichi if they had any problems that needed to be solved while the Wise One rested.

Likichi had swept the area and Untuk-na picked up the sleeping Ki'ti and carried her along with sleeping skins to the location near the hearth. Tiriku snuggled against Ki'ti's side outside the coverings once the sleeping area was set up. It was too warm for him to be under the skins.

Domur awakened to the excitement of the challenge again to make the replacement ochre ball for Manak-na to use for face painting. She noticed the change surrounding the Wise One, but realized there was nothing she could do to help there. First, there was the necessity of the morning meal. When all that had been accomplished and her duties were finished, she gathered the rock bowl, the grinder stone, the bag of ochre, and returned to the hearth side to work on grinding the stone to powder. This time she planned to grind much more powder and put some aside once it was finely ground. Her plan was to make a large supply of powder and experiment with substances to bind it into a malleable, cohesive material that could be formed into a ball such as Manak-na carried in his pouch. She began to grind the tiny stones of ochre into powder. Minagle came over to sit by her. Minagle was making some hand coverings from deer skins.

"Are you happy to be staying here instead of continuing farther north?" Minagle asked her.

Domur looked up at her friend with a beaming smile. "Of course. I am ready for a good, long stop to establish ourselves in a land where there are no people threats and we are free to hunt to meet our needs. The constant trekking is hard on everyone. I'm so glad someone finally brought it up."

"I am, too, but I could never have done it." Minagle was not comfortable with the idea of presenting ideas when she didn't have any sense how they'd be received.

Song joined her mother and Domur, lowering herself carefully. "I'm glad I won't be having a baby on a trek," she said inserting herself into the conversation, knowing she'd be welcome.

Minagle put her arm around Song. "How are you doing?" she asked.

"I'm doing well, Mother. And Humko-na is so excited!" Song was radiating happiness as she caressed her belly.

Manak-na, Arkan-na, Ekuktu-na, and Lamul-na went to the meat prepa-ration cave to check the small smoking fire for the meat taken by Manak-na and Kai-na the previous day. On their way they swept the path. Already there was a wonderful savor of fresh meat from the cave. It was a great day, not-withstanding the clouds and white rain falling. Most of the men no longer dreaded the white rain. They had garments to keep them warm, and it seemed a natural part of their lives—except when the snow depth grew too great to walk easily. Some looked forward to the briskly clean air it brought; some, to the way it smoothed sharp edges and lay upon tree branches, giving a dif-ferent, yet pleasing, look to their surroundings. They worked well together and shared the same views that Minagle and Domur had just moments before—they were pleased to be remaining in this place. They began to look at the meat preparation cave differently, with a sense of ownership.

Lamk-na, Tongip-na, and Slamika-na took brooms and went out to clear a path to the valley below. They knew it would be necessary to repeat the process after the white rain stopped falling, but letting it pile up made the task much more difficult. They also chose to clear paths to the stone structure where the Mol giants had chipped symbols into the stones and to the caves associated with the evil man. They enjoyed working together in the white rain.

When they began sweeping uphill, Lamk-na said, "We've got to rename these caves. To continue referring to a cave as belonging to an evil one leaves a fog of bad feeling over what is now our real home. That evil one is gone and so are his evil ways."

"I agree. Why don't you bring it up at the men's council," Slamika-na suggested.

"I'll do that tonight. We will have one, even with the Wise One not feeling well?"

"I'm sure of it," Tongip-na said. "We are a People, not ever dependent on a single individual. The Wise One will hear us. I expect she will be glad to know we continue the council. She said there would be a story tonight. I wonder whether Ahna will tell it."

"Time will tell," Slamika-na added. "This is a very exciting time to be alive. There is so much new surrounding us. So much to learn. I am glad that we have such a great group of People. It is good. What is this?" Slamika-na had looked at the edge of a window in the stone building. There was a shiny piece of gold metal placed there. Slamika-na took a rock to the window, climbed up on it, and looked at the ledge. Where he couldn't see from the ground, he now saw a shiny rock, a piece of animal fur, and a black raven feather. He laughed and turned to face the others. "It seems that Raven has decided to deposit his treasures here. This is what he has put here: a piece of gold, a rock, fur, and a feather." He showed each item as he named it. Then, he carefully replaced the items on the ledge. He placed the piece of gold on the feather to keep it from blowing away.

"We are a strange People," Tongip-na said with a chuckle. "Our Wise One has a dog, and the dog has a raven."

"I like it," Lamk-na said, leaning on his broom.

"I, too," both others added.

They had finished sweeping paths, so they returned to the home cave.

When Wisdom dimmed the light and turned outside to darkness while white rain continued to fall, the evening meal was being served. Untuk-na carried food to Ki'ti and insisted she eat. She had slept most of the day. She wasn't hungry, having slept so much, but she ate what Untuk-na brought her without arguing. She knew she had to regain the strength which seemed to have flowed out of her when she found she could relax. If sleeping and eating when she wasn't hungry was the way to do that, so be it. She had asked Ahna to tell a story that night, one of her own choosing. Ahna spent the day preparing. Yomuk came over while she was working on the story and she had to tell him to leave her alone to do what she must do. Yomuk was hurt but he left her alone.

Yomuk had found Ahna irresistible from the day he first saw her. He wanted her for his wife, though that decision was premature, he knew. Nevertheless he sought her out at every opportunity. She lived in his belly, where emotions resided, and he treasured every time he could be near her. It hurt when he was rebuffed. He couldn't see himself as a nuisance.

After the evening meal, the men's council gathered without Ki'ti, though she could hear well anything that was said. She forced herself to stay awake so she wouldn't miss anything. Grypchon-na led the council. He looked around and saw that Lamk-na was looking at him. He nodded to Lamk-na.

"Some of us went to sweep white rain from the paths today. While we were doing that, we came to look at this place as our home, not just a temporary place to live. It concerns us that we have connected the evil man to the cave. We would like to rename the caves—other than the home cave and meat preparation cave—so that they are ours and reflect us, not someone who did evil here long ago." He looked at Grypchon-na.

Grypchon-na looked around to see who else was looking at his face. He nodded to Arkan-na.

"I think that is a great idea, Lamk-na. I have already tended to think of the stone structure as the observation place. That seems to be its purpose. We could also use it for that purpose if we brought stones to make it so we gained the elevation around the wall where we need to look out." He looked back at Grypchon-na.

On her sleeping skins, warm and resting, Ki'ti smiled contentedly. Her People were continuing on as they would have if she'd been there. How grateful she was that they did not totally depend on her. She mused that Wamumur must have had similar feelings from time to time.

Grypchon-na looked around. He nodded towards Lai-na.

Lai-na said, "The cave where the evil man was could be repurposed. Before we can give it a new name, we should have an idea of what use to put it." He looked back at Grypchon-na.

Grypchon-na noticed Manak-na looking at him. He nodded toward Manak-na.

Manak-na began, "When we returned from the boat trip, we stopped at a place Ralm showed us. Ahna needed garments to fit her for our trek to find you. There was a large room at their living area on the hillside by the sea. It was made from bamboo and was so tightly constructed that no rain could enter. Inside were places where they kept garments, backpacks, season-of-cold-days boots and season-of-warm-nights foot coverings, sleeping skins, all manner of things. They made them in advance of need. They stored them in that building as we store meat. Since we plan to live here, I suggest we use at least part of that cave to store things we can make in advance of need, so that when a need arises, we can go there to meet the need."

This novel idea caught everyone unprepared. They took the time to run it through their mind webs.

Lamul-na looked at Grypchon-na. Grypchon-na nodded.

"I approve and, if we choose to do that, we could call it the storage cave." He looked back at Grypchon-na.

Grypchon-na looked around. He nodded to Ermol-na.

Ermol-na said, "I also approve. And storage cave seems a good name. I also like the name observation place. I would ask whether there are disapprovals." He looked back at Grypchon-na.

Grypchon-na asked whether there were disapprovals. All the adults looked down, showing no disapprovals. "Now," Grypchon-na said, "we have an observation place and a storage cave." He did a palm strike. The People did palm strikes all around. Ki'ti lay on her sleeping skins smiling.

Grypchon-na looked around. The People had lowered their heads, showing that the issues had been covered for that evening.

"That is the end of the council. We will take a few minutes and then Ahna will tell a story."

When the People reassembled, Ahna began:

"This is one of our oldest stories—the story of Chopinuka-na and Miroan. They were young and had just joined. It was the time after the eruption of Poquatelka, a great volcano far to the south where it is always warm. The People left just before the eruption, and they had recently returned to find that their homes had been spared ashfall. Chopinuka-na and Miroan had taken many trips to the river before the eruption. It was a special place to them. It was there that they first realized they loved each other. It was the place where they decided to join."

"One day Chopinuka-na asked Miroan to walk with him to the river to their special place. She was happy to walk with him. They left on a beautiful, clear, warm day, thinking to swim in the water. When they reached the river they were surprised. The trees on either side of the river showed where the water had rushed down from the volcano. Dirt showed the level of the water as it raced down the hills. Only the upper third of the trees was above the dirty water line. They were shocked at the silt along the river bank. Things were different now. Their beautiful river appeared to have been drowned in silt." Their once sparkling river was covered with silt, peeking through only in spots to show running river water below. Tree trunks lay sideways in the river bed. The bright colors they remembered were turned to a grayish clay color.

"Hand in hand Chopinuka-na and Miroan walked along the river bank on the soft silt listening to the water race by hurrying to its destiny. They were astonished at the smoothness of the silt. They had never seen the river run so fast. Suddenly, Miroan's right leg, the one closest to the river was thigh deep in water that was running fast under the silt. She made a sound that Chopinuka-na heard. He pulled her hard to free her, and they headed directly for land, continuing to hold each other's hand. Away from the river bank they stretched out on the land, and Chopinuka-na asked her about her experience."

"She told him she had walked on solid land until suddenly it liquefied instantly under her right foot. It became wetter than any quicksand they'd ever known. She explained how her leg was caught in rushing water under the silt, rushing fast enough to pull her leg sharply backwards. She assured him that if he hadn't pulled her out, she'd be gone. She told him that it was clear to her that volcanoes could make quicksand alongside rivers that drained land following an eruption. It clearly frightened her. No longer would they walk along rivers that had served to let water flow from volcanic events. They returned home to warn the People."

Yomuk realized he was hearing another story that contained a life critical lesson. He carefully placed it in a spot to be remembered in his mind web. He reflected that he had not seen any volcanic peaks nearby, but then he reasoned that he might see some in the future. Whatever the case, he needed to know the information the story contained, not just eliminate it for lack of immediate relevance.

The gathering dispersed for sleep. Ahna stopped by to see Ki'ti.

"I approve, my Ahna. Thank you. While I rest, you must be prepared to tell the stories at night. You will do that?"

"Of course, Wise One." Ahna was happy to do whatever she could do for this kind woman.

"Ahna, what did I tell you to call me?" Ki'ti asked.

"I'm sorry, Mother."

"That's better, my Dear One. Now, sleep."

"I will," Ahna replied while unrolling her sleeping skins.

"That was a great story, Ahna," Elemaea said as she unrolled her sleeping skins.

"Thank you, my Sister," Ahna replied.

Elemaea walked on her knees to Ahna and hugged her. "I'm so glad you're here."

Ahna smiled. "I'm so glad to be here."

"Settle down, you two," Untuk-na said quietly.

The girls complied.

The darkness suddenly erupted into light and a loud noise, followed by a jolt and explosion. Hunters leapt from their sleeping skins and raced to the home cave opening. Down in the small valley, they could see fire from a hole in the earth. Manak-na, Kai-na, Slamika-na and Lamk-na were all dressing as fast as possible, taking torches, and descending to see what had happened below. A noise above them caused caution. A streak from the sky brought another crash, much smaller, to the valley floor. Things were falling from the sky!

The hunters reached the largest hole in the ground—some three feet deep. There was a glowing hot rock in the hole. Slamika-na went to the place where the one they saw fall had come to rest. It too was a rock but much smaller than the first one. The men looked up. There was another, but it was off to the side of them.

"These are falling stars," Manak-na shouted, realizing what they were seeing.

"These must be tiny compared to real stars!" Slamika-na shouted back.

"Think what damage a real star could do!" Kai-na shouted.

"I think we should return to the cave in case others fall nearby. We can look again tomorrow," Lamk-na shouted.

The others nodded and all headed back to the cave as quickly as possible. With all the white rain out there, the fires from the falling stars weren't going to cause a fire problem for them.

When they reached the cave, the People wanted to know what happened. Kai-na explained that falling stars had hit the ground down in the valley. The People could see them in the light of day. Slowly the People in the home cave returned to sleep.

When Wisdom returned color to the land, the pines seemed to glow bright green in the light outside the cave. Down below Kai-na could see a hole in the white rain where there was blackness inside and a considerable amount of dirt thrown up on top of the white rain. Having been down there the night before, he couldn't wait to see what light would show. Quickly he began to put on his garments for outside wear. Slamika-na touched him on the shoulder from behind.

"Why not wait until those of us who eat can accompany you?" he asked.

"I'm just so eager to see," Kai-na answered standing there in his outside pants.

"It's not going anywhere. Let me bring you your bowl. I know you're excited. So am I. To walk around in all that white rain, food will help."

"Very well," Kai-na replied.

Mitrak was there with his bowl of food for the morning meal. Kai-na smiled at his wife. He brushed a strand of hair from her face and she smiled back. He took the bowl and she ran her hand along his arm, keeping her eyes on his.

"I love you," he said quietly.

"And I, you," she whispered back. She turned away to attend to other things.

Soon men gathered to see what had fallen in the night. At the site of the larger rock, they noticed the way it had been pocked and how part was apparently burned. It certainly had made a deep hole in the ground, throwing up buried dirt and grasses in the process. It was still slightly warm.

They saw that there were other holes in the white rain and the rocks in them were considerably smaller. To realize that falling stars left these wrinkled burned rocks was shocking. They had literally thought falling stars were stars that were falling. It expanded their mind webs to take on this new information. Small rocks could make the streaks in the night sky from these rocks! Some of them had seen it done. Knowledge was increasing almost daily! Manak-na picked up one of the rocks that was of medium size. He was shocked at the weight of it.

"What do you plan to do with the rock?" Kai-na asked.

"Share it with Ki'ti. Eventually she'll see the large one, but I can take her this one and she won't be tempted to come down here right now."

"I see," Kai-na said. He hadn't thought what it would mean to Ki'ti to have to stay on her sleeping skins while the People could examine falling stars. Manak-na would know.

Up in the home cave, Untuk-na and Yomuk were having a serious talk near Ki'ti. They thought she slept. She was not sleeping.

"I owe you and Mother an apology," the young man said. "You see, when I left for the adventure, I thought that hunters were somehow more important or more special than People with other functions. I guess it was because of the -na designation—I'm not sure. But I snubbed you and Mother as not knowing what hunters knew. I hadn't learned that you'd been a great hunter among the Mol. I thought Mother just dreamed up stories to pass the time of the season of cold days. The problem is that I didn't think. I saw what I wanted to see. I wanted to have superior status among the People, and I didn't realize that such a thing is contrary to the People."

"You did what the old Wise One, Wamumur, would have called believe a lie."

"Yes, Father. I did. I was responsible at an early age. People seemed pleased with me that I'd matured beyond my years. I thought that made me special somehow. I gloried in it. I felt it made me better somehow than others."

"You really weren't listening to the stories your Mother tells, were you?"

"No. Manak-na got after me on the adventure for not listening to the stories. He said they contain life critical wisdom."

"What did you make of the chiding Ki'ti gave to those who teased Humko-na about the snake and Song?"

"I didn't see the application to myself, because I hadn't teased Humko-na."

"Oh, my son. You were so far from truth." Untuk-na silently groaned for his son. How could he have been so blind and deaf? "What do you think of taking adventures?"

"That is for others—not me! I was sometimes so frightened on the boat that I wept. So many times I thought I would die on the water. After I began to get an idea of the error of my thinking, I worried that I wouldn't make it home in time to give an apology to you and Mother. Do you think Mother will accept my apology?"

"Why don't you ask her?" Untuk-na asked.

"There is no need. I have heard you. You have my acceptance of your apology, Yomuk." Ki'ti turned over on the sleeping skins to face her husband and son. Her face was expressionless. Her belly was rejoicing. Finally, he had learned what she knew he needed to know.

The three noticed Manak-na walking over in his outside garments. He held something out to Ki'ti.

"What is this, my Brother?" she asked.

"Last night falling stars came over the valley. Didn't you hear the explosion?"

"I suppose I did, but I didn't know what it was. It wasn't an earthquake?"

"No. It was several falling stars that landed nearby or right in our little valley. There is a huge one, but I couldn't carry it up here. I thought you might like to see what a falling star really is. I don't think falling stars are actually falling *stars*."

"I see what you mean, she said feeling the rock."

"You can see the little indentations that the big one also has. You can see where it was burnt from the fire that it trailed behind it."

Ki'ti laughed, "Manak means strong rock. My name means falling star but now I realize it means falling tiny rock."

Manak-na, Untuk-na, and Yomuk enjoyed the laugh. They were all fascinated. They'd seen falling stars for years.

To hold something that flew with a brilliant tail of fire expanded Ki'ti's mind web again. She looked mainly at Manak-na and Untuk-na but included Yomuk, "What is the cause of all this learning so fast and clumped together in time. What do you make of it?"

"I find it the most exciting time of my life," Untuk-na said unequivocally.

"It makes me feel so alive. I savor it." Manak-na realized he was dripping, so he turned towards the entryway to put his season-of-cold-days garments on their peg. He wanted to share with Domur.

Ki'ti turned to Yomuk. "My son, take this stone to share with Grypchon-na. He cannot easily go to the valley to see for himself. Explain what Manak-na explained to us. Then, bring the rock back."

"I will. Thank you, Mother."

"Why thank me?" Ki'ti asked.

"First, for accepting my apology. Second, for giving me this to do," he said looking at the rock and back at her.

Ki'ti smiled.

Manak-na sat beside Domur and marveled at what she'd done. She had ground the ochre rock to a fine powder and put it into a gut container. He was astonished that she'd ground so much. She'd almost finished one of the bags he'd filled. Seeing her doing that for him under the circumstances warmed his belly and tore it all at the same time. He felt so undeserving.

"You've been very busy," he said.

"So have you. What do you make of the rocks?" she asked.

"They're just burnt rocks that have traveled through the night sky to land in our valley. They are bent into odd shapes and have burn marks on them. They're heavier than you might think from the size of them."

"Are they anything to fear?"

"I don't think so. It isn't like they fall every night."

"That's good. I'm adding some oil to this powder. Can you bring me some birch resin?"

"Of course," he replied and got quickly to his feet. They both knew he'd have to go to the meat preparation cave to get it. "That may be just what you need. Now that you mention it, when I smelled my ochre ball, I think that's an odor I detected but couldn't place."

"I hope so," she said.

When Manak-na returned with a small container of birch resin, he was surprised to find the powder transformed into a ball mixed with oil. Having left his outside garments on the peg, he sat next to Domur and watched while she added some of the resin to the ball. She kept mashing the ball and folding it on itself and mashing and folding until she finally squeezed it into a ball.

"See if this feels right," she asked.

Manak-na took the ball and broke off a small piece. He spit on it to make the substance suitable for painting. He painted his line and dots on his leg. Sure enough. It worked! Domur had replicated his painting ochre ball. Manak-na threw his arms around her and hugged her, knocking over the resin container. Domur broke free and turned the resin container upright, so that nothing spilled, and then hugged Manak-na again.

"Come take a walk with me," he asked huskily. "I know a little cave that isn't too far."

She smiled, got up, and went to put on her garments for outside wear. She carried the birch resin container to the home cave entrance. They could take it back to the meat preparation cave on their walk.

At the entryway they met Lamul-na who offered to carry the birch resin to the meat preparation cave because that's where he was heading. Domur thanked him and handed him the container.

She and Manak-na went outside and she started to walk the path to the meat preparation cave. There was a special cave in that direction. He pulled her hand the other direction up the hill.

"What's up here?" she asked. This was a surprise.

"This is the new cave and it's filled with some really great skins. It's back in the earth, so it's warmer."

They arrived at the cave with the log out front that they would place in the upright position that signaled the cave was occupied.

"I would never have seen this!" she said.

The two climbed into the cave where there was just enough height to stand stooped over, but standing wasn't what they had in mind. Each hungered for the other, and they wasted no time before feasting.

Back in the cave, Ki'ti was coughing. Likichi brought her a gut container that she could cough the foamy substance into. The coughing didn't help her fatigue. Tiriku worried over the coughing as if somehow he could help, but just couldn't figure out how. Likichi brought some additional skins and propped her sleeping skins over them so that she rested with her chest and head elevated.

"How long will it take to get over this?" Ki'ti asked petulantly.

"Wise One, you have to rest your body, mind web, and spirit together. You're barely resting your body. Oh, it looks like you're resting it, but it's primed to leap up at a moment's notice. It's important for you to give in to the rest. I'm surprised you stayed in the skins when the men went to see the falling stars last night. Your mind web and spirit are still running."

Ki'ti laughed. "You're right. Last night after the explosion Untuk-na made it clear he'd sit on me if I tried to go outside to see what was happening. Am I that difficult?"

Likichi smiled at her daughter. She still thought of her as her daughter even though Emaea had adopted her while she was a child. "To answer your question in one word, yes."

"I deserve that," Ki'ti replied.

"There are times, my Dear, that you remain Little Girl. By failing to rest properly, you postpone your recovery."

Ki'ti moaned. She wondered how to give in to rest and make her mind web and spirit stop working. She had no idea.

Later when Untuk-na stopped by, Ki'ti asked him to carve out a little of the cave side to make a shelf on the wall behind her. He asked what she had in mind.

"I'd like to have a small shelf to place things set aside for Wisdom. I'd like to put special things there like the stone that Manak-na brought.

"What about the little owl that was Wamumur's?" As soon as he said the words, both looked at each other in surprise. "That should have been given to Ahna, shouldn't it?" Untuk-na asked her.

"Yes. Do you have it on you?"

"Of course. I keep it tied to my waist band." Untuk-na pulled the little pouch from his waist band.

"Ahna," Ki'ti called.

Ahna appeared swiftly and seated herself on Ki'ti's sleeping skins.

"Ahna, do you know what is around my neck?" Ki'ti asked.

"A skin pouch."

"Do you know what's in it?" Ki'ti asked.

"No." Ahna was wondering what was the point of all the questions.

Ki'ti pulled the pouch on its leather strip over her head. She opened it and showed the little owl to Ahna. She showed her how to see the owl. Ahna was fascinated.

Years and years and years ago, a man named Torkiz, who was related to Wamumur, the Wise One before me, made these owls. Torkiz lived far, far, far away to the west. Torkiz's People chased him away from them, but they kept the owls. Torkiz traveled to the place where we used to live before we moved here. The man had made many owls but left with only three. One owl lives with the Mol back where we used to live. It is broken. This one is mine. It belonged to Ilea, the Mol woman Torkiz loved. Untuk-na has been carrying the one that Wamumur wore, keeping it for the Wise One who follows me. It is yours. Untuk-na showed her the pouch he carried. He reached into it, withdrew the owl, and showed it to her. He laid it on her hand. Ahna looked at the shining yellow rock carved to look like an owl. The way it captured light sent chills all over her. To have entrusted to her something so lovely was beyond her comprehension. She looked at Ki'ti and Untuk-na with tears in her eyes. Untuk-na picked up the owl from Ahna's hand and put it back into the pouch. He slipped the leather looped strap which was threaded through the circular pouch over Ahna's head. Ki'ti put her owl back into the pouch and put the looped strap over her head.

"It's yours now," Ki'ti said. "Take good care of it."

"I will," Ahna whispered. She was overwhelmed and feared she might cry. The change from where she was born to where she was now was so large that often she would wait to awaken from a dream to find someone about ready to strike her for laziness or some other reason. The weight of the soft little pouch against her neck made her realize that this was not a dream. Perhaps she had cause to thank the bird man. For years she'd wished he'd never spoken about her leaving. She would have been treated better, if her people had thought she wasn't planning to reject them based on the bird man's statement that she'd leave. But the bird man must have known somehow that she had to be here to keep and tell the stories. What a wonderful life she had now. But sometimes, deep down inside, she wondered whether it would last. Was it just too good to last? Did she really deserve this? She knew time would make all things clear. She returned to repeating the stories.

Meeka and Liho sought Elemaea and found her at the back of the cave coming up from gathering gourds of water. "You're just the one we seek," Meeka said smiling.

"What can I do for you?" Elemaea said returning the smile.

"It's what you've done for us." Liho said. "The knives are wonderful. I've used mine for cutting skins into patterns for hand coverings, slicing vegetables for stews, and cutting meat for portions for the evening meals. They are well suited to our tasks. I want to thank you for making my work easier."

"Oh, I'm so glad you like them. I enjoy making them so much."

"You do great work and your knives are also beautiful," Meeka added.

"I have to admit, I look through the supplies to find the stones that are the prettiest for the women's knives." Elemaea lowered her head.

"Well, for me it makes any task easier when the tool I use is so attractive," Liho said.

"Is there anything I can do to make the knives better for you?" Elemaea asked.

"Not for me, Elemaea, they are great just as they are," Meeka replied.

"I agree with Meeka," Liho said.

"Thank you both for letting me know. If you find any way I can improve them, please let me know. Also, if they chip off and you need them sharpened, let me know."

Elemaea turned and headed towards the far corner where she and Ekuktu-na worked the tools. On her way Smosh stopped her.

"Elemaea, I've broken my spear tip. Can you fix me a new one and put it back on the spear before tomorrow?"

She looked at him surprised. "Let me see the spear."

He handed it to her. She examined it carefully and then looked at him sharply. "What happened to this spear tip?" she asked.

Smosh, twice her age, lowered his head to her. "I dropped it," he admitted.

"I'd try to get it finished by tomorrow, if it were repairable. I can't just repair this spear tip. You need a new one. Soon you'll need a new shaft for this spear."

"How can you tell?" he asked with surprise.

"See this little line right here?" She showed him a tiny line barely visible on the shaft.

"Yes. But it's really faint."

"It is. That doesn't mean it's good. You could spear a large animal and when you go to withdraw your spear for reuse, you could find that this faint little line is a wide crack and your spear would be worthless. You should replace it before the season of new leaves. I'll be glad to remount a tip when you have a new shaft."

"Thank you, Elemaea. You've taught me something today."

Elemaea looked at him with a small smile. Sometimes she wondered about hunters. *If I'd been a hunter,* she thought, *I'd be constantly checking the soundness of my weapons.*

Shukmu, Smosh, Elet, and Cam gathered at the entryway to dress warmly, get their spears, and head towards the valley. Smosh borrowed his father's spear. Lai-na was willing to lend it, warning him in pleasantry not to drop it. The young men had bags of snares and were dressing in their season-of-cold-days garments ready to set snares for small animals. They had seen many rabbit tracks at the edges of the valley and they wanted to see how successful they could be with snares in the white rain. When they reached the lower part of the hill, Shukmu and Elet went to the north and Cam and Smosh went to the south. They hoped for great success.

Ki'ti lay on her sleeping skins. She had finally reached a state of full relaxation. Likichi had noticed and told her so.

"I feel like a bag of rocks that has just been emptied."

"That is good. Now, hopefully, your body can find the means to heal itself."

"What has my body been doing while I lay here?" Ki'ti asked thinking her body had been healing.

"You've been fighting yourself, best I can tell."

"What?" Ki'ti raised herself up on her elbows.

"You've been telling yourself you should be doing this and that, instead of relaxing so your body can heal itself."

"You mean to tell me that in order to get back on my feet, I have to feel like an emptied sack of rocks and not be concerned about other things?"

"That's what I've tried to tell you since your collapse." Likichi was enjoying finally being able to reach Ki'ti.

"How long must I be like an emptied sack of rocks?

"Until I tell you you're free to get up."

Ki'ti lay back on the skins. Likichi left and Untuk-na came over to her.

"You've done a great job of making that shelf, Untuk-na. Will you put the falling star on it, please?"

Untuk-na took the stone from her and put it on the shelf.

"You look like you're finally resting," he said as he sat beside her.

"Likichi just told me that this is how I must rest to heal."

"Good. I'm glad you finally can see that."

"How is it that this is something everyone seems to know except for me?"

"You're just too hard headed, Little Girl," he whispered teasing.

She lifted herself back up.

"No, none of that!" he said recognizing her attempt to fight the term Little Girl. "You just keep resting. We do need you, you know." He leaned over her with a wicked smile. "And there's a cave I want to introduce you to."

She put her arms around his neck and kissed him. She determined to work at resting and then laughed as she realized how incongruous her thoughts were.

"Why are you laughing?" Untuk-na asked.

"It just crossed my mind that I should really work at resting. Just some incongruity, Untuk-na."

"I'll say. Just rest. Empty out all those thoughts." He got up and headed to the entryway. His heart was filled with Ki'ti. How it hurt him to see her struggling to rest. How eager he was for her to return to good health. He put it in his mind web that never again could he allow her to push herself to the point she had. Responsibility didn't show. It couldn't be weighed, but the weight she carried in responsibility, he thought, more than equaled any weight he carried on treks. Work that others did with their hands never exceeded the work she did in her mind web and spirit, but what other People did and what she did differed in what there was to show visibly for it. He was beginning to see what she carried. Yomuk had thought they were lazy. He like others was blind to what she did and the load she carried. Yomuk wasn't the only blind one. Untuk-na berated himself for his own blindness.

Wisdom was sucking color from the land, not that there was much color out there. Light was giving sway to darkness in the black and white of the outside environment. The young men who set the snares were back and the home cave hummed with desire for the evening meal. Ki'ti had actually fallen to sleep. Tiriku curled into an arc between her shoulder and head.

Untuk-na got his food bowl and Ki'ti's. He was unsure whether to wake her, but when he sat on their sleeping skins, she opened her eyes.

"I must have fallen asleep," she said slightly groggy.

"That's when you heal yourself," he replied. "Sit up. You have good food here."

She tasted it. "What is this?" she asked surprised.

"Kai-na and Manak-na took a caribou. Manak-na wanted the skin for Domur's sleeping skins. This is caribou."

She took a bite and chewed thoughtfully. "It's really good meat," she said with some enthusiasm.

"I agree," Untuk-na said smiling. It was the first time since she had collapsed that she had been enthusiastic about food.

"I like it a lot. I haven't seen a caribou. Where are they?"

"That one was high in the hills."

"Oh," she said.

"More white rain!" someone shouted and a few went to look. Huge flakes were falling like feathers windborne from a plucked goose. It was an awesome sight for those who took the time to look.

"Wonder what that'll do to our snares," Elet mused.

"Will we ever hunt again?" another said from somewhere in the home cave.

"Maybe it's just a light one," another added.

Little conversations were occurring all over. It was a good evening.

"Excuse me," the voice of Grypchon-na silenced all. "Tonight there will be no council meeting for there is nothing to discuss. There will be a story after cleanup."

Likichi brought Ki'ti a cup of chamomile tea. It wasn't one that Ki'ti favored, but she drank it. Untuk-na rearranged the sleeping skins and Ki'ti settled back comfortably to rest. Very quickly she was asleep.

Ahna wondered whether her choice of story was a good one, but then she realized any one of the stories was a good one. People gathered and Ahna said in a good strong voice, "This is an old story. It is the story of Moraka-na and Pekutla-na."

"Long ago far south from here, Moraka-na and Pekutla-na were planning to cut down a tree to place over a river so they could reach the other side by walking over the tree trunk. A large tree grew by the river bank and they chose that one. They had their hand axes and knew it would take much effort to cut that one down. Other People came to help chop. They used a variety of tools to cut down the tree."

"They had learned how to chop the tree down to make it fall in the direction they wanted. They made the wedge and continued on making it larger, for the tree was very thick. If they were successful the tree would fall across the river from bank to bank. For days the People worked to chop the tree down. From time to time, men would put their hands high on the tree and push in the desired direction of the fall. It continued to hold."

"Moraka-na got up one morning and said that he thought the tree would fall that day. He urged all those who watched the chopping to stay out of the way. He even said they should stay far enough away that, if it fell in a different direction, they should be safe."

"The People trusted the hunters that were chopping away at the tree making the wedge larger and larger. Suddenly, the tree made an explosive sound and fell away from the river opposite to where they expected it to fall. It twisted on its fall and frightened the People terribly. A man named Amatlen-na was trapped under the tree where he died. The tree was so thick the man was never seen again. The People could not understand what happened."

"Finally two men from the Mol came by and they showed the People what happened that awful day. The men showed the People that they had chopped down a left handed tree. If you put your hand on a tree, with your thumbs up, the bark makes lines that go either like the fingers on a right hand or the fingers on a left hand. Left handed trees don't fall like right handed trees—they are unpredictable. They went to the river and showed the People how the bark went to the left up the tree, not to the right."

"The People decided to test the Mol's tree knowledge. They found another large tree downstream from the left handed tree that fell the wrong way. This was a right handed tree. They spent days cutting down the large right handed tree. Again the People came to help the cutters and to watch. All were careful to stay out of the way of the fall, whichever way it might fall. This time when one of the People pushed the trunk of the large tree, it fell exactly the way it was supposed to fall—from one side of the river to the other."

"From that time, when People plan to cut down a tree, they will check to be sure that they are cutting down a right handed tree."

Ahna watched the children after the story. They held up their hands and their parents would help them see what way the bark on a right handed tree would grow and how it would grow on a left handed tree.

Hearth fires were dying down. It was time for sleep. Quietly People headed for their sleeping skins.

Days passed in the black and white world of the season of cold days. Over time Ki'ti began to recover from her exhaustion and was finally released from forced rest by Likichi. She was terribly weak from disuse of her muscles, but she was relieved to be able to participate in cave life actively. She was grateful to Ahna for telling the stories at night. She'd listened, delighting that the girl had done so well. She told her later she approved.

Ki'ti had been having recurring dreams while she'd been resting. She kept seeing people from the north near the big lake, people with darker skins and brown eyes, people a little different from those she recognized—but people nevertheless. They were well nourished and their faces were rounded. They were living there where it was very cold, and they seemed to be thriving. She also saw them travel in her dreams to the place where the boatbuilders lived. *Were the boatbuilders a little different?* she wondered. Certainly Kipotuilak looked like the Mol, but a little different. She put in her mind web to ask Manak-na about the boatbuilders. She wanted to know what they looked like. The People knew the Minguat, the Mol, and themselves. Were there other humans that looked a little different? Maybe where people lived made a difference in how they looked? She was fascinated.

Manak-na, Yomuk, Sum-na, Tongip-na, and Lamk-na had been hammering out squared off stones to line the observation place wall so the People could see out by standing on the elevated stones. They used the wall in the storage cave for the source of the stones to take to the observation place. They hoped to learn how to use the observation place once they could look outside easily. They worked carefully trying to make the stones as squared off as possible with their tools. They needed only two more stones to complete the work. Getting the stones from the storage cave to the observation place was difficult. They used an aurochs skin to slide the stone and it took ten men to pull the skin to the observation place. They hoped they wouldn't destroy more than one skin to do the job. Then at each end of the elevated stones, they would add steps made from more stones to get to the elevated level without having to climb up. The men still marveled at the height of giants who could, no doubt, look out the windows without the elevated stones.

In the meat preparation cave, women who worked the skins were just finishing up the caribou sleeping skin that Manak-na wanted for Domur. All were impressed with the wonderful softness of the fur. They knew Domur would love it. Some of the women had already decided they would ask their hunter husband to get one for them.

Domur had finished the red ochre balls for Manak-na and had taken the extra ones to the storage cave, each wrapped in a leather pouch with a looped leather strip to go over Manak-na's head. A nice place had been set up for things made in advance of need in the back of the cave. Men who were carving out stones for the observation place were cautioned to be careful not to harm the items women had placed in the storage cave. The men had used old leather for covering the stored items. They would sweep the cave thoroughly when they were finished. All worked diligently glad to know that they had a home at last.

Frakja-na, Humko-na, and Hupu had left early with spears to see if they could find more caribou. The People really liked the meat and they knew women would want the skins. They knew the one Manak-na and Kai-na had taken was located to the west, so they headed in that direction walking with great difficulty through the deep white rain over the hills and down the other side. Fortunately the white rain was dry and when kicked, it littered the air with crystals. By high sun, they gathered to eat some jerky and drink some water. Even though it was cold enough to require head and hand coverings, they sweat profusely from their effort in walking through the white rain. Despite the sweat, they knew better than to cool themselves down by opening their season-of-cold-days garments to the air.

Downhill near the valley, Elet, Cam, Shukmu, and Smosh checked the snares again. This time there were four rabbits. The rabbits were all white. The young men gathered them and reset the snares. They met at the path uphill and took the rabbits to the meat preparation cave. They each cleaned one, skinned it, and deboned the meat. They'd carry the meat to the cave for cooking stews or soups and the skins were given to the women who worked them in the meat preparation cave.

The hunters on the hill to the west realized that soon Wisdom would be darkening their black and white world. They needed to retrace their steps. As they turned, Hupu silently held up his arm and lowered it, pointing to a valley to the northeast. There a large herd of caribou gathered. They wanted to hunt, but they knew it was too late. They would have to return another day. It was time to return to the home cave. They had four hills to cross. They were glad that the white rain marked their trail, and they were happy to know that there were many caribou and where they were.

Men returned to the home cave from the observation place. Manak-na noticed that Ki'ti was walking around.

"Wise One, you're better," he said with enthusiasm, certain that she wouldn't be walking around unless Likichi had told her she was well enough.

"Yes, I am better. When you have some time, I would like to talk to you."

"How about now?"

"After you see Domur, my Brother. First things should be first."

"Thank you for the reminder," he said and hurried off to find Domur.

He found her in the place she usually worked near the hearth. He sat beside her and asked about her day. She told him that Ermi-na had brought something from the meat preparation cave and he'd said for Manak-na to find him when he returned.

Manak-na told her he'd be right back. He found Ermi-na who showed him the rolled skin that was the caribou Manak-na wanted for Domur. It was finished. Manak-na went to look at the skin. He unrolled it. Domur in the other part of the cave was trying to keep herself from looking, since she had figured out why Ermi-na wanted to see Manak-na. Manak-na was delighted. The skin was worked exceptionally well. It was soft and he rolled it back up, thanked Ermi-na, and carried it to Domur.

"This is a gift to you to show that I hold you in my belly with great love," Manak-na said with joy.

Domur kneeled down and unrolled the skin. She could not believe how soft the fur was and how well the women had worked the skin. It was an object of great beauty. Unshed tears filled her eyes. Manak-na sat beside her. She sat beside the skin and reached for Manak-na's hands. "It is beautiful," she said, wishing there were words more appropriate to express how she felt. "Thank you for this wonderful gift." Unashamedly, her tears escaped the rims of her eyes.

"Domur, I just wish there were words to tell you how special you are to me." Manak-na had a lump in his throat and was loath to free his tears publicly. He stared around at the ceiling trying to regain emotional control.

Domur knew him. She whispered to him, "We'll enjoy this tonight. Please roll it back up. It's almost time to eat." She knew if she gave him something to do he'd recover his self control faster. She loved him and wanted to ease him. He loved her for knowing what to do. They went to the line to fill their bowls. On the way he told her that the Wise One wanted to talk to him.

He wondered if she knew why. She told him she had no idea, but she suggested he seek her out after eating.

When they finished eating, Manak-na went to find Ki'ti.

"Is now a good time?" he asked.

"Of course," she replied. Manak-na sat down near Untuk-na. He was curious.

"I have had many dreams while getting better. One dream recurs and that is why I want to talk to you. You see, my Brother, it has concerned me and some others here that there are so few People. In my dream I continue to see People to the north of us, some near a big lake, that I think may be the big lake we were going to find. These People are not People, Mol, or Minguat. They have darker skins, brown eyes, and brown hair. They do not look terribly different, but they have their unique characteristics as the People, Mol, and Minguat do. They are definitely people as we all are."

"What do you want to know, Wise One?" he asked.

"Tell me about the boatbuilders. Were they strictly Mol like Kipotuilak, or were there differences?"

Manak-na went to his mind web and methodically walked through memory. He pictured Pah and the boatbuilders, especially those he thought were Mol who lived on the hill. He pictured Ralm and Rokuk and the woman who outfitted Ahna. He remembered Komus, who lived near the big lake. After examining his memory, he put together what Ki'ti wanted to know.

"Wise One, the boatbuilders are mixed somewhat. On the hill there is a group of people I first assumed were Mol. When I think about them, I remember they were darker of skin color than any Mol, Minguat, and People I've ever seen. But their skin is not so dark as to call great attention to it. They all had brown eyes. They had some characteristics that differ from ours and the Mol and Minguat. Their brows were more like ours with less heaviness above the eyes than we or the Mol have. They have rounded faces as if they eat very well. Their hair is fine like ours. They were not as tall as the Mol, more our height. There are some Mol working there like Kipotuilak and some Minguat like Gurst and Skuku. There were a couple of our People. All spoke the language of the Mol. It's strange that you ask, because I've learned not to see the differences and I've had to work hard to make my memory call them up. I've learned we are all People."

"I'm glad you see that way, my Brother. I am also glad you have made it clear to me that it's possible that there is yet another group of humans in this land, although they are far from us."

"My Sister," Manak-na said, "you do not ask questions for no reason. What has your dream foretold?"

"I am not sure. What I know for certain now is that there are others alive out here. We are not alone. There may be great distance between us, but we are not alone. I think that when the time comes that we need to find others with whom to join, there is an option to the north or possibly with the boat-builders. They are different from us, but that has never been a barrier, and I see no reason for it to become one now."

"So you have answered the question the men who search the night skies have asked when they see no hearth fire smoke. There are others out there, just too far away for us to see."

"I think so, Manak-na. I think so."

"One of the boatbuilders is named Komus. His people live near the big lake. He does have the look of the different people who live on the hill above the boatbuilders. From time to time he journeys to see his people."

"I wonder whether he follows the giant's path. If he does, he'll come right past here."

"That's true. If he does, I'll introduce him."

"I'd like to meet anyone you met at the boatbuilders, Manak-na. He'd be welcome."

"I was sure of that," he said. Manak-na stood. I think the council is about to begin. "Are you presiding?" he asked Ki'ti.

"No, my effort today has tired me out. I will listen from my sleeping skins. Thank you, Manak-na. Oh, Manak-na."

He looked at her.

"We have been too long without naming the new -na hunters. It needs to take place."

"I will see to it tonight, Wise One." He replied. To himself, he thought, *Always formality. My little sister has been sick and I have to treat her with some distance as Wise One.*

The council met. Frakja-na got the nod from Grypchon-na and he told about their hunt for caribou. He told of Hupu's find just as it became too late to hunt. He shared the information that a large herd of caribou was four hills from them in the valley. He shared their desire to return to hunt them, and asked whether others might go with them. The decision was made to make the hunt a significant one on the next cloudless day. Everyone liked the meat and there were women already interested in the skin.

Manak-na looked directly at Grypchon-na.

Grypchon-na nodded.

"I call the following People: Patah, son of Hahami-na and Blanagah; Mhank, son of Manak-na and Domur; Meeluf, Halmi, and Shukmu, sons of Minagle and Sum-na; Yomuk, son of the Wise One and Untuk-na; Ekoy and Smig, sons of Ekuktu-na and Wamumal; Hupu and Koi, sons of Lamul-na and Meeka; Keemu, son of Olintak and Slamika-na; Bun, Mingugno, and Kal, sons of Lamk-na and Liho; Trokug, son of Ermi-na and Shmyukuk; Smosh and Alkomut, sons of Lai-na and Inst; Cam, Elet, and Truto, sons of Tongip-na and Aryna."

The men walked to Manak-na who stood in the center of the council circle.

"We regret taking so long to make this pronouncement. As of this moment all are -na hunters. Congratulations, men." The men lowered their heads and quietly returned to their seats.

Without a thought people began to do palm strikes. There was nothing but silence except for the crackling hearth fires and the palm strikes. As they began, the palm strikes ended.

Ahna told the story of Maknu-na and Rimlad. Then, the home cave settled down for the night. Domur and Manak-na delighted in the caribou skin.

Chapter 8

Ki'ti had been up and steadily gaining strength, but she continued to cough. Having been so terribly fatigued, which was her main concern, she thought little of the cough. From time to time she'd produce a lot of phlegm, and she'd spit it up. It lacked color, so both she and Likichi were not worried. What they both found comforting is that Ki'ti improved daily. She was presiding at the council meetings again and telling stories at night. People came to her with problems for her help to resolve. It was as if the heart of the People was beating well again.

When Wisdom brought a brilliant golden morning to the black and white world of the season of cold days, twenty-five hunters had already left for the fourth mountain to the west. They were eager to hunt the caribou and bring home meat to smoke and skins the women wanted. The distance was great for the conditions. The white rain was over the knees of the People except the Mol. Walking was difficult. The Mol hunters went first to break down the path for those who followed, but regardless of where a hunter was in line, walking was not easy. They tried to follow the trail left by those who had gone before, but wind had partially covered their tracks. Travel was much easier for the two ravens that followed the hunters. They were as expectant as the hunters. The ravens had seen the spears, and they recognized hunt behavior. Their bellies would be well fed. They flew silently just behind the hunters, resting on trees to observe the men who traveled so slowly below them.

Despite the difficulties, the hunters were eager for the hunt. It had been so long since they had really feasted on fresh meat. The white rain had kept them close to the home cave. They were beginning to realize that they could function in the white rain, though it was tougher. It was invigorating to be back on a real hunt. The men did not talk much, afraid that their voices might precede them in the quiet woodland, alerting the caribou. As they began the climb up the fourth hill, there was a tension sprouting from their expectation. Tongip-na reached the top first, and was surprised when he did not see a herd of caribou anywhere. Manak-na hurried to the top and looked down. He could see where they had been—not where they were. The hunters descended to the place where the caribou had been. Quickly they spotted the trails left by the caribou as they moved to another place. The hunters followed, not believing the numbers of animals inferred from their trails. It was spectacular!

It was almost high sun when the hunters found the herd. They had crossed another hill and many caribou were ruminating below. Hunters began to make signs that showed their plan. The ravens watched silently from above. The birds would not warn the caribou of the hunters, since it would not benefit them to do that. They just observed in silence, waiting, eager to share in the hunters' profits. They had a role to play just as the hunters did to assure success.

The hunters spread out. They used trees to block them from sight, but some of the hunters wondered whether these animals had ever seen one of the People. If they had never seen a person, they would have no reason to fear, some thought. When a grouping of caribou was surrounded, hunters swiftly began to spear the animals. Many hunters were able to spear more than one caribou. The animals were not frightened of the People, until they understood what was happening. Then they bolted.

Twenty-five hunters participated; twenty-nine caribou were taken. It was a phenomenal hunt. They bled and gutted the animals as quickly as possible and then readied them for transport on their spears. The odor of animal gut and iron from blood hung in the air. Some hunter pairs carried two caribou suspended by their legs from the spears that the men held on their shoulders from man to man. Walking was awkward, but it could be done and was more efficient than leaving animals and having to return to them later. The excited ravens hopped back and forth on tree limbs ruffling their feathers and hopping again, wishing the hunters would take their animals and go, so they could feast undisturbed on the entrails. The men said little. More was communicated by facial gestures—gestures that made it clear that the men were very well pleased, even a bit shocked, by the success of the hunt. The men had a long distance to return home. They were as eager as the ravens were to get started.

Back at the home cave, Song had begun labor. She had been at it for hours. Humko-na was on the hunt and was not aware that he might soon be a father. Likichi hovered, watching. Ki'ti watched from a distance where she worked with Ahna.

The cave was busy. Domur had gathered the little children and was encouraging them to sing. She taught the little ones a song she'd made to help them learn to count from zero to nine. Ermol-na had joined them and brought his drum. Domur taught them to dance in place to the song, and Ermol-na supplied the rhythm. Some of the adults found themselves humming to the music or dancing little steps. The song was also helping adults to learn the numbers. There was an air of joy despite the cold keeping most people inside the home cave. Something wonderful had happened when the People knew they had a permanent home. There was renewed optimism, happiness, increasing activity to make improvements in their way of living.

Ki'ti was sitting with Ahna discussing their day's work.

"Does Wisdom have some aspects of People?" Ahna asked.

"You've got it turned around. We have some aspects of Wisdom. Wisdom is not like us; we are a tiny bit like Wisdom."

"But you can begin to know Wisdom in a similar way as you begin to know a person?"

"Yes. You are thinking to communicate with Wisdom as you would with me or another person."

"Yes. How do you come to know Wisdom, Wise One, uh, Mother?" Ahna asked.

"As you become more and more familiar with the stories, they will tell you about Wisdom. You'll learn from our life and the stories what you need to know about Wisdom. On our travel from where we used to live when the earthquakes made us move, Wisdom led us, because often the path was not clear. Wisdom led us by making a bright light. I didn't realize that only I could see that light. We didn't need more than one person to see it. But Wisdom always knew where the path was. From the story of Maknu-na and Rimlad, you learn that Wisdom provides and protects. They were trying to survive a volcano—not Baambas—a different volcano. It was before Baambas. Wisdom let the volcano explode when they were by a lake. Maknu-na and Rimlad submerged in the lake, and they breathed through reeds until the worst of the eruption was over."

"So while I practice the stories, I need to look for what they tell me about Wisdom?"

"Yes. That way you come to know Wisdom better. You discover who he is, how he relates to the People, what to expect from what he's done. You find Wisdom yourself directly when he reveals himself to you. I could tell you that Wisdom leads, defends, sees all, and is all powerful. Those are just words. They have no real meaning to you until you start to see them for yourself. Then, the words have more depth of meaning."

"There are some People who don't know Wisdom."

"That is true. They know about Wisdom. They may know, for example, that Wisdom protects, but they have no direct experience calling to Wisdom for protection and receiving it. When they do, then, they have a fuller sense of who Wisdom is."

"You can talk with Wisdom, can you not Mother?"

"Yes, that is possible. If you can communicate with Wisdom, that is good. Sometimes Wisdom wants you to know something directly. Then you may hear that small voice. You've heard it, haven't you?"

"I have. I didn't know where it was coming from that night in the cave when I was still new to the People. I wondered whether it was under the ground or from a star far away."

Ki'ti laughed a genuine lovely laugh. It startled Ahna, but it was not derisive or a social fake laugh. Ki'ti put her arm around Ahna. "Wisdom is not made of the earth as we are. Wisdom is spirit. Wisdom is with you and us always. We sometimes forget that Wisdom is present. Wisdom never forgets. Because Wisdom is spirit, to talk with Wisdom you must talk through your spirit even though you speak physically or in your mind web. You communicate spirit to spirit. When you heard that voice that night, you heard it with the ears of your spirit."

Ahna looked at Ki'ti in wonder.

"I want you to understand that the spirit world exists. There are good spirits and evil spirits. They are not made of flesh, bones, and blood as we are. Many years ago I listened to an evil spirit that told me to take the green bag from our home to deliver it to the family of the man who was murdered on his way to take it to his sick wife and children. I did not understand that there was a spirit world and a tangible world. The Wise One made it totally clear that there is NEVER a reason to listen to spirits. But that is different when you listen to Wisdom. Wisdom will never have you do something that is against Wisdom's teaching. When I took the green bag to the man's family, I overlooked the fact that Wisdom would never permit one to be disobedient to a parent—to go roaming alone in the wild land at night to take a bag to dead people. Wise One had told me that we would not return the bag. I listened to the spirit or spirits instead of him. That was dangerous to me and to the hunters who came after me. I'm telling you this, so what happened to me won't happen to you. I didn't know about spirits then. I was so new to learning to become Wise One. I know about them now. I know that I must teach you so that you do not become oppressed or possessed by one, as I did. Because you are open to Wisdom, you are also open to evil spirits. You must learn."

"What must I do, Mother?"

"First, when you encounter a spirit, do not just listen without protecting yourself. Call on Wisdom to protect you immediately. If the spirit is of Wisdom, it will not flee when you call on Wisdom. Some spirits will tell you that you don't need to call on Wisdom. That's when you definitely need to call on Wisdom. Ask Wisdom to remove the spirit, if it's not from Wisdom. Wisdom cannot remove Wisdom. Do you understand?"

"I think so. You're thinking that evil spirits tend to come after people who can communicate with Wisdom?"

"I am certain of it."

"Then, it's like trying to run off with someone who belongs elsewhere, like the man who was taken and became Wise One before you; only it's a spiritual running off, not a physical taking?"

"You understand well, my Ahna."

"So I must be wary lest an evil spirit cause me to listen to wrong things."

"Yes, Ahna, or *do* wrong things. That's what I did. I believed wrong things that I heard from a spirit, and I acted on them through disobedience to my Wise One. I thought the spirit who had me take the green bag to the man's family was the man himself. The Wise One told me that it was probably an evil spirit pretending to be that dead man. When I talked to the evil spirit in the cave here, I don't know whether it was the unburied man or an evil spirit. It didn't matter. I learned that the man was evil and needed to be buried to enable his spirit to go to Wisdom. So we buried him on the other side of the valley below."

"I understand. And if I hear an evil spirit, what do I do?"

"You tell it to go away, and immediately call on Wisdom. You are not as strong as evil spirits, but with Wisdom you can be stronger. You're safe. Never idly listen to one. Only listen to Wisdom or Wisdom's messenger, Kimseaka."

"I was so surprised when I realized that not everyone wants to pursue Wisdom. Wisdom is amazing, but even that word is not good enough to describe Wisdom," Ahna said.

"I find for whatever reason that only one to three of the People at any one time know Wisdom as we are talking about knowing Wisdom. They know what Wisdom expects, but they do not talk to Wisdom except in prayer, when they're in great need and remember to call on Wisdom. I do not know why this is true. When Wamumur and Emaea and I were together, the three of us were close to Wisdom. Nobody else was. Each of us in our own way communicated with Wisdom. Untuk-na has pursued the knowledge of Wisdom but not the spirit of Wisdom. His knowledge is vast. I love him for it. I think each of us has a means of talking with Wisdom. Maybe it only becomes active when there is a need for communication. I don't know. Maybe in you and me it becomes more active because of the stories, because we are used by Wisdom to communicate to the People." Ki'ti began to cough. She took the little container she used to cough into and cleared her air passage.

Ahna was concerned. She didn't like Ki'ti's cough at all. "Do you want some water?" she asked.

"That would be good," Ki'ti replied winded.

Ahna went to the place where filled gourds were placed for drinking. She brought one to Ki'ti who used it and coughed some more. She seemed to have coughed clear the mucous after drinking the water.

"Now, let's go over that last story again," Ki'ti told the young girl.

Wisdom had removed all the color from the land by the time the men had returned. Those who hadn't hunted had already enjoyed the evening meal. The world of the hunters that evening was black and white as they threaded their way exhausted to the meat preparation cave. Their way was lit by moonlight from a bright full moon. Men, who hadn't hunted, heard them arrive and went to the meat preparation cave to help get the meat ready. They were astounded when they saw what the hunters had taken. They suggested the hunters go to the home cave and have their evening meal and then return to the meat preparation cave to help with the abundant meat harvest. The men who hadn't hunted would get started on the preparation. The hunters were grateful for the chance to eat and rest a little before continuing. Gladly they left for the home cave.

Humko-na heard about Song and forgot he was tired or hungry. Likichi brought him a bowl of food to eat while he visited with Song. He would not be going to the meat preparation cave that night.

Manak-na got his food bowl and went to sit beside Domur. "Did you have a good day, my Dear?" he asked.

Domur smiled. "Yes," she replied. "I had the children today and taught them a song I made to help them learn their numbers. Ermol-na brought the drum and we made a song and dance of it. They are doing well. I think some adults are learning it that way too," she said with a slight smile.

"I think that's great. I am so proud of what you do with the children. Your spirit of motherhood is wonderful."

"I hear you had quite a hunt today."

"We took twenty-nine caribou. I think they have never seen People."

"That's a lot of meat. No wonder all the men who weren't on the hunt left to help out. And aren't you tired?"

"I am tired, but after I eat and get a little rested, I have to return. We may be at the meat preparation all night."

"Oh, Manak-na, that's a very long time."

"It is, but we have to make good the hunt so the People get the full benefit, and the caribou will not have died needlessly. We must make the best of every life we've taken."

"I know. I just look at you and you look so tired."

"I'll recover in a few days." He touched the side of her face with the back of his hand. His fingers toyed with a strand of hair that had fallen to the side of her face. He was greatly aroused. "Will you go with me to the cave quickly?" he asked huskily not specifying which cave.

"Of course," she replied on her feet and heading for the pegs where their outside garments were hung.

They went to the nicer, newer cave and spent a short and very powerful time there enjoying each other in frenzy. Then Domur returned to the home cave and Manak-na headed to the meat preparation cave.

Song let out a stifled cry, and her baby was born.

"He's a boy!" Likichi announced. She thought how much better it was in childbirth, when People join with Minguat or Mol.

Song and Humko-na called the baby boy Mikanu.

Days merged into other days as white rain melted. Often men would go out without securing the fronts of their jackets or putting on head or hand coverings. The season was changing. There was a slight smell of mold on the dirt as ice rotted to melt water, making their land a bit swampy until the earth absorbed all the melt.

Yomuk-na came running into the home cave, breathless, yet shouting, "Come, hunters, you must see!"

He had their attention so he turned and began to go back outside. "It's the caribou. They are leaving."

Yomuk-na definitely had their attention.

"Come to the observation place," he said breathlessly and left at a run.

When the hunters arrived at the observation place, they saw Yomuk-na standing on the observation platform so he could see from the window. They joined him and far in the distance they could see what had astounded the young man. A whole hillside moved with the bodies of caribou as if the hill were heaving with maggots. The animals moved with purpose, not fear. Hunters could tell that much from their observation place.

"They are migrating," Mootmu-na said. "I wonder how far they go."

"What's migrating?" Yomuk-na asked.

"They live in these hills in the winter and go north to some other place in the spring and summer, probably to places where they have their young and food is plentiful. It's too soon for them to have their young yet." Mootmu-na said.

"How'd you know about migrations?" Yomuk-na asked, fascinated.

"I have lived a long time, Yomuk-na," Mootmu-na said. "You've seen the huge bison. In some places they migrate like this. Some of the elephants migrate."

"How marvelous this is! They will return?" Yomuk-na asked.

Mootmu-na turned to face the young man. "Yes, I trust in it. They should return in the season of colorful leaves. It's the way of such animals. Someday someone will look out this same window to see them running this way. It's good we live near them in winter."

"Why is that?" Yomuk-na asked.

"Because we get their better winter coats," the old man said with a smile. "In summer their coats will be losing fur and the wonderful softness will decrease to shorter fur that is not as soft."

The hunters found that what Mootmu-na predicted happened just as he said it would. Mootmu-na was, unfortunately, not there to see it. He and Amey had taken a season-of-warm-nights walk through the forest and encountered a sow bear with cubs. She killed both of them quickly on the hillside. Tongip-na and his sons Cam-na and Elet-na had been hunting nearby and heard them shouting. By the time they reached the site, both Mootmu-na and Amey were dead, but the men managed to get the bodies away from the bear while she tended her cubs. They took the bodies back for burial. Everyone in the cave was horrified. It had been a long time since bears had killed people. Mootmu-na and Amey were older, but it seemed premature to all that they died. Seenaha was weeping over the bodies, and Likichi had to move her out of the way in order for the other women to clean the bodies in preparation for burial. There was no shame in weeping and there was a cave full of People with tearful faces. Mootmu-na and Amey's sons took care of the burial site near Nanichak-na's grave. They gathered rocks from the storage cave and the Wise One told the story.

A few years later in the season of new leaves, Seenaha lost her left foot. She had been bitten by a snake and had recovered, but her foot, where the bite occurred, festered and went to black rot. The foot was removed, skin sewed together, and the stump was seared to prevent infection. She wore a cylindrical covering for her foot that was padded with thick, soft fur from a caribou. That made it possible for her to walk on the end of her leg. It was carefully constructed to add the height back so that her hips were balanced to keep her spine straight. She used a stick to help for balance. She was very glad they were finished trekking but she felt deformed and ugly following the event. Trokug-na, her husband, saw her as strong and a real fighter, not seeing anything ugly at all. Eventually, she would listen to him, but at first, she withdrew and experienced some significant depression.

Yomuk-na continued to yearn intensely for Ahna. He noticed clearly that his feelings were not returned in kind. He discussed what he saw as a problem with Untuk-na and Manak-na. Both told him the same thing. It was not a problem—not something to fix. There was no way to make her change her mind web—he needed to look elsewhere. Yomuk-na's belly was ripped at the very idea. Both men also had realized that for quite some time Meta had been looking at Yomuk-na with caribou eyes. He should stop to take a look at Meta, both independently suggested. Both Manak-na and Untuk-na were surprised that Yomuk-na hadn't noticed Meta's interest.

After he began to recover from the pain of the fact that there was little chance that he'd ever win Ahna, Yomuk-na began to take a look at Meta. Once he did, he quickly saw what the men had told him was true. Meta did flirt with him. She was very attractive and he enjoyed the attention she gave him. When they'd walk the paths in their new home land, she made him feel strong and smart and good looking. She made him feel like a man. He liked that a lot. It was a new feeling. He was learning to care very much for her. They spent much time together to enjoy getting to know one another better. The more they were together the closer they became. In time they became even more special to each other.

Elemaea had continued to work on tools that were like the ones the men made, but smaller, for use by the women. She was very successful. She and

Patah-na, Hahami-na and Blanagah's son, had become attracted. Patah-na was about twice her age, and he was physically fit and exceptionally good looking. He was very strong, a great young hunter, and also tender and gentle. He found Elemaea fascinating with her skill in tool making. She was touched that he'd found her interesting. The two took time to be together like Meta and Yomuk. They were forming a bond that would last a lifetime.

Manak-na found Domur sitting on the tree that grew sideways from the hill. She was gazing over the valley watching Tiriku and Raven visit below. She loved to see Raven slide along the grassy lowland running his head along the side of Tiriku and then snuggling close, back to back, heads thrown back, beak to muzzle. To her it was precious. The two animals almost always did their little dance where Tiriku would leap and lower his forelegs, putting his head on a level with Raven while his butt was in the air. Raven would hop and hop turning his head from side to side and making odd noises. Tiriku was getting old and grizzled about the head, but he and his friend would spend time together often, never seeming to tire of it. Manak-na stood beside Domur and watched the animals below.

"Domur," he finally said. "I want you to know that I can finally say without equivocation that I will not adventure again. I will do what I should have done and stay with you. I have never loved you less because I left; I just did not at that time understand what I was doing to you. I was thinking only of myself. I love you. I think you know that. I had to know that I could say this truly and mean it forever, before I could commit to these words."

"You really do mean that?"

"Yes, I do. Until one of us dies, we will no longer have a long separation. I have a responsibility to you and to the People and to Wisdom. I will honor that responsibility and do what's right. I only regret it took so long for me to be able to commit to do what's right. I have known what's right for a long time. Doing it was hard. I found myself doing what Ki'ti did as a child, when she made cracks to hide in to avoid doing what she should. And I gave her such a terrible time for doing that."

"Yes, you did!"

"Should I go to her with an apology?"

"Do what your belly and your mind web tell you is wise." Domur's counsel placed the decision firmly back on him.

"I'll do it. It's only right. I'd like to get right for the wrongs I've done."

"When you scolded Ki'ti, you changed her into an obedient girl who would become Wise One. You have to know that. It wasn't wrong."

"I never credited my actions with that."

"Well, that's how everyone else including the Wise Ones saw it." Domur put her soft and gentle hand on Manak-na's shoulder. They smiled at each other. Each was glad that the decision Manak-na had wrestled with for so long had been made.

Time moved quickly and the season of warm nights was upon the land. The People had found a lake bed nearby. It seemed to have been used by the giants long ago. They tried to discover how the giants had made it hold water. Finally, they decided that they must have laid tough skins in the bottom of the lake bed and covered them with sand. They tried the same thing and after years of white rain accumulation, the lake had begun to fill in and hold water. As it was, they could store meat in the water there, because the water level was finally deep enough. Their home place was continuing to improve with the passing of time.

It had been ten years since the People had trekked to the north. Ki'ti was forty one. More People had joined: Elemaea and Patah-na, Yomuk-na and Meta, Ahna and Cam-na, Smosh-na and Tin. More People had gone to Wisdom: Grypchon-na, Flayk, and the youngsters, Luko and Gratu, who were killed by hyenas, when they wandered unaware near a big cat's kill site.

This new day dawned with great color. It was well into the season of new leaves, white rain had gone, and the ground had dried out. Tiriku walked with a bit of a limp. He was almost white faced from age, but he still shared visits with Raven—both doing their dance and snuggling. Ki'ti was standing at the cave's entryway. Tiriku sat beside her. Down below there were two ravens flying and squawking the sound that someone or something was entering their area. The ravens still alerted the People to changes in their environment. Manak-na and Untuk-na went to the entryway to learn the cause of the noise. In a short length of time, they could see a man with a great backpack. He was walking the path. To Manak-na there was something about the man, something familiar. Then he realized what seemed familiar and he began to run downhill. Ki'ti glanced at Untuk-na with a question. Untuk-na returned the question.

When Manak-na reached the ground level, he called to the man, "Komus, is that you?"

The man stopped and stood very still looking at the one who had just come from the hillside. He had called his name. "I am Komus," he shouted back.

"Komus, I am Manak-na from the voyage to the other side of the water."

Komus understood. The People Manak-na described must have stopped short of going to the big lake and decided to live in the caves marked by the evergreens. Komus knew the evil one oppressed this particular set of caves, and he normally hurried past the place. He walked to meet Manak-na, not believing they could live there with contentment. Other People were coming down the hill slowly to meet the newcomer.

Manak-na invited Komus to come to the cave to meet his People. Komus agreed with no little trepidation. Manak-na helped carry some of his things other than his backpack. At the entryway, Manak-na introduced him to the Wise One. Those who were not busy with some activity and were able to take the time gathered at the council space to talk with the traveler. Likichi served some tea and the man settled himself comfortably on some of his skins.

Manak-na made introductions all around. Then, Komus began to speak.

"I will never know why Pah sent me that day to hunt rather than build the boat. Sometimes he just did that. It was a nice day, blue sky, no clouds. Pah came into the boatbuilders' place while we ate the morning meal. He told me and two others to hunt and chose three hunters to work on the boat. He was very definite about it. Of course, we did what Pah told us to do. I was halfway up the hill and for some reason I turned to look back."

"Manak-na, do you remember the story Tikarumusa told us about the water that went way out leaving fish flapping on shore and then came back and carried all his people away?"

Manak-na nodded, not sure he wanted to hear anything else. "We have made it one of our winter stories," Manak-na said.

"Water went far from shore leaving wet sand exposed with flapping sea creatures. Just as Tikarumusa had said so many years ago, there was a wave forming way out at sea. You could see it—it was incredibly tall! That wave raced into the shore so fast. It was even higher than the village and beyond. We watched from the hillside. It crashed over the boat we were building, over the boatbuilders' place, even beyond the top of the place where people lived on the hill. The waves took everything. There is nothing left." The man's voice was breaking, and it was clear to all that he was still quite shaken from the event. His eyes were wide with fright, as if he'd witnessed the event anew. Those of us who had been sent to hunt were all that was left. We searched for a few days for the bodies of the people we'd known. Nothing. The sea took it all. They are all gone. And so is everything they built."

"I am so sorry to hear that. People I knew also. Pah gone. It seems impossible. Even Gurst gone."

Komus laughed a nervous laugh. "Even he," he said. Gurst had been a bully, but no one wanted to see him drowned.

Manak-na said, "I guess that will be the end of the connection with the people from the other side of the water." Manak-na thought about that connection severed just from a single wave. If Ahna ever wanted to return, it would be impossible now.

Komus looked up. "For the love of all the gods," he said, "I had forgotten about *them*."

"And won't there be a boat returning from the other side?" Manak-na asked.

Komus thought for a while. "Yes. You're right. They will certainly wonder what happened. The wave was so high that it left nothing. There is not a single dwelling where the people on the hill lived. Absolutely nothing. When that boat returns, those people will be terribly confused."

"Which crew will be returning?" Manak-na asked.

"Rahm's crew just left. Most of them are those you know. The other crew had recently returned."

"What will Rahm's boatmen do when they return?"

"I have no idea. I suppose they could travel to the other side of the water, if the boat is holding well. They have no real home on either side of the water. Their home is the boat, and the boat will not last."

"I am guessing you're returning to your people past the big lake?" Manak-na asked.

"Yes. My days at sea are over. I return to my people. I might return to meet Rahm's boat to tell them what happened. Do you mind if I remain here for a few days to rest?" He looked at Ki'ti, since there appeared to be no chief.

Ki'ti looked at the tired, upset man. "You are welcome here until you are ready to continue your trek, Komus."

Komus looked at Ki'ti, the small woman who had been introduced as Wise One. "Thank you, Wise One. I need the rest."

Ki'ti asked Likichi to show him where to put his backpack and sleeping skins when he was ready.

"Wise One," Komus continued. "There is no longer a feeling of evil here. What happened?" Komus had feared coming to the cave from his past feelings when just walking past the place on the level ground below.

"There was an evil man in another cave up here. He was dead, but the evil was present. We buried him on the other side of the level ground below us. He had paintings that showed evil things and we totally destroyed those images. Since then, the evil has left here."

"It is good, Wise One."

"Thank you, Komus," Ki'ti replied.

Likichi showed the man where to put his things, and he returned to the place where Manak-na, Domur, Minagle, Hahami-na, Tongip-na, Slamika-na, Untuk-na, Ki'ti, and Ahna sat. Likichi had fixed him more tea, this time with a mild sedative included. She gave the others additional tea also.

As they talked, Komus complained that he was exceptionally tired. He couldn't understand why he'd be so tired so early in the day. People suggested he nap until he felt rested. He set out his sleeping skins in a different place in the cave, where Likichi showed him. It would be quieter there during the day. She knew the man needed rest. He still had traces of shock from the event, as if he kept reliving it.

Domur was fascinated with the color of the man's skin. She asked Manak-na, "Did all the people at the boatbuilders' place have skin the color of Komus's skin?"

"Most did, but there were some Minguat, People, and Mol who worked there. I think that there are at least four groups of people: People, Minguat, Mol, and Komus's people. I think that where people live has something to do with what they look like. There seems to be a connection between the people of Komus and the boatbuilders. Komus looks like most of the boatbuilders. They have added other groups as we have. I think that across this huge earth, there must be other groups of people who have some characteristics that vary from ours. The people on the other side of the sea that we saw were originally Mol and People. They still show characteristics of Mol and People, but they're a little different. But then, Rokuk said they've been going there since time began, so there could have been some changes caused by mixing with other peoples during that time. Perhaps, there are additional other people on the far side of the sea—maybe even on this side."

"They can all join?" Domur asked.

"I'm sure they can all join. Like Wamumur said long ago—all are People!"

"He has a long way to go to his home—alone." Domur wondered how people traveled alone. It seemed so lonely.

"He'll do fine, Domur." Manak-na asked Ahna, "On the other side of the sea are there people who look different from us and the Mol and the Minguat?"

"There are a few people with darker skins like Komus has. Only his skin isn't really dark. I have seen two men whose skins were very dark brown, almost black."

"I've heard of that," Hahami-na said. "Some traders talked of that when we lived far to the south before Baambas. I see little difference in the color of Komus's skin and ours, compared to what the traders told us."

"What a fascinating earth we must have. I wonder if people come in other colors," Tongip-na said.

"You mean green or blue?" Aryna said as she made herself part of the group, sitting next to her husband, Tongip-na.

Everyone laughed gently. "Blue is reserved for those who don't get enough air," Likichi said from the side.

Again there was light laughter.

Domur heard something unusual. She got up and went to stand at the entryway. She could see a raven in a tree just outside the entryway bouncing on a limb with a feather in its beak.

"Wise One," Domur called into the home cave, "I think you should take a look at this."

Ki'ti came to the entryway and saw the raven. She knew it wasn't Raven, but was unsure whether it was his mate or another bird. The raven seemed to recognize her. It flew to land on a tree limb closer to Ki'ti. Tiriku walked over to see what was happening and saw the bird. He seemed anxious. The raven dropped the feather down to Tiriku. He sniffed it and whined. Tiriku looked at the raven. He started down the pathway. The raven flew just ahead of Tiriku. Manak-na and Domur followed Tiriku. Ki'ti watched from the entryway. The raven flew across the flat land below. Tiriku followed with some urgency. Manak-na and Domur continued to follow. Ki'ti picked up the feather from the ground. Somehow she knew that Raven had gone to Wisdom. Ki'ti felt chilled suddenly. The feather was one of *his* feathers. Her belly was ripping for their loss and more so for Tiriku's loss. Ki'ti took the feather and laid in on the ledge she'd gotten Untuk-na to make for special things. Then she returned to watch.

The raven flew to a tree where there was a large nest. The People had never seen Raven's nest. Now they knew where it was. The raven swooped down to land on a low branch of a birch tree. Tiriku climbed up the side of the hill with some difficulty to the place where the bird was perched. It was making a moaning sound. Tiriku detected the scent of his Raven before he saw the body. It lay on the earth appearing to sleep on its back. Tiriku knew the bird wasn't sleeping. He went over to it and nudged it with his nose. The life clearly was gone from Raven. He looked up at Raven's mate. He lay on the ground next to Raven and slid his body against the bird's, doing to Raven what the bird had done to Tiriku for years. Then he snuggled next to it, back to back, with his head thrown back. Habitually, each animal would move its head way back so that they were muzzle to beak. Raven's head was limp on his neck. Tiriku knew it wasn't the same. Finally, he whined and stood up. He barked sharply at Manak-na and Domur.

"Are we supposed to bury Raven?" Domur asked.

"Sure looks like it," Manak-na replied, not believing what he was watching.

Domur went to pick up Raven. "I'll find out," she said.

Domur held the bird next to her chest. Both Tiriku and Raven's mate seemed to approve. "I think you'd better get a hole dug and a couple of stones quickly," she said. She began to walk towards the place where the People were buried while Manak-na hurried for digging tools and a couple of rocks. Both Raven's mate and Tiriku went straight to the burial site. Manak-na went rapidly to the place where the tools were kept. He was joined by Untuk-na and Lamk-na. They dug a hole for Raven and placed him in it. Ki'ti didn't know what to do about the story. What she did was to do what she'd done when they buried her dogs. She provided the eulogy. While she spoke, Tiriku sat beside her. Then the men covered the bird's body with dirt and stones. The Raven's mate sat rigidly in the tree above watching everything. She had been with Raven when they buried People. She knew what was happening. Ki'ti looked up at the Raven's mate. "I'm so sorry for you," she said, and the bird seemed to understand and then flew away. Tiriku stretched out next to Raven's grave. Ki'ti tried to get him to come with her but he refused. She let him remain while she tried to control the lump in her throat. He was taking the loss very hard, she thought. Tiriku's refusal to leave was not an issue of disobedience, she could tell, but rather it seemed one of loyalty. Ki'ti's belly ripped apart for Tiriku.

Later after the evening meal, Ki'ti noticed that Tiriku still had not returned. She was worried. She asked Yomuk-na to go down to see if he could get him to come up. He should eat and be with others.

Yomuk-na went down to the burial site. There was Tiriku lying beside the grave of Raven. His muzzle was placed between his front paws. He lay on his belly with his feet extended behind him. Yomuk-na and Meta cried to see the little dog in his grief. They tried to lift him to carry him away but he growled. Yomuk-na let go of the dog. He didn't want to get bit. They went back and explained to Ki'ti that Tiriku wasn't ready to come home. She agreed it was best to leave him there then. She did ask them to carry some meat sticks to the dog.

The men's council was about to begin. Ki'ti planned to have the time to let all the members of the cave meet Komus. Komus seemed to be somewhat rested and was eager to meet the People of Manak-na. The council meeting lasted a long time that night as the People asked Komus about the big lake and his people. Komus confirmed what Kipotuilak had said—in the season of cold days, they wore double outside garments.

After much talking, Aryna asked, "Komus, how far is it from here to the big lake?"

Komus thought for a few minutes. They had no way to measure distance, so they used time as the measure for distance. "If you're a hunter and have no young children or old people, and you're willing to live on jerky, it takes about a moon."

She continued, "And after you get to the big lake area, how much longer does it take for you to reach your people?"

"About two moons if you're without children and old people and live on jerky—unless they're camped at the lake."

"You have a long way to go," Hahami-na added.

"That is true, but the travel is through beautiful country and I enjoy it," Komus replied.

Manak-na's love of adventure was stirring. How he'd love to accompany the man to his home and back. He tried to cut out those thoughts, but they hung in the air before him. It hurt. He had already agreed that he would not adventure again. He had to throw those ideas away. It wasn't easy. Domur was acutely aware of how Manak-na would feel about hearing Aryna's curious comments. Aryna would have no idea the effects her comments would have on Manak-na.

Domur looked up. Ki'ti nodded. "Komus, how long would it take for a healthy woman with no children to make the same trip?"

"It might add a day or two, but nothing significant," Komus replied. "The way is not difficult. It depends on whether travelers are able to follow an austere regimen of walking with few stops and eating nothing but jerky."

Manak-na wondered what Domur was doing. Surely, she didn't want to make a trip that long! He was afraid to dream that they might make such a trek together. He tried to put his mind to other things and could not.

There was no time for stories. Slowly people went to their sleeping skins having feasted on new information.

When they had gotten comfortable in their sleeping skins, Domur whispered into Manak-na's ear, "I think we should find a few couples and accompany Komus on his way. We could see how his people would think of sometime in the future getting together for finding mates for our young ones, so we do not become too inbred. It's not like there are many people all over this part of the earth—and now the boatbuilders are gone."

Manak-na had his mind filled with adventure and this comment from Domur was something he was not prepared to entertain. "Are you serious?" he asked, not believing it.

"Of course," she replied. "I wouldn't ask something like that if I weren't very serious. I think it would do us good."

"Who would you choose to accompany us?" he asked.

"If I could choose, it would be Kai-na and Mitrak along with Tongip-na and Aryna. But they might not see this as something they'd like to do."

"Before we say anything, I'll find out tomorrow," Manak-na said. He cradled her in his arms and lay there listening to the hearth fires and the People breathing and participating in other activities. He wasn't ready for sleep at all.

In another part of the home cave, Ki'ti was devastated. Tiriku had not returned. She knew what to expect. She guessed that he'd never leave the grave of his special friend. She hoped he was eating, but somehow doubted it.

"Worried about Tiriku?" Untuk-na asked.

"Yes. I think we've lost Raven and Tiriku at the same time."

"I know it can happen with People like that sometimes, but with animals? Yet, I've never seen grief expressed more clearly than Tiriku expressed his after all the People left Raven's grave today."

"It makes me choke up every time I think of it," Ki'ti said quietly.

"What was all that about with Domur? Is she thinking about going with Manak-na on an adventure?"

"I would think there'd be more to it than that, my Love. If Domur wants to make that trip, it would have some benefit to the People, like planning a meeting for finding joining mates in the future."

"Now that would make sense sometime in the future."

"I agree. But no, Domur wouldn't plan an adventure for the sake of adventure or for Manak-na's sake. There would have to be a benefit to the People."

"Well, there are very few people anywhere around here. Those who were boatbuilders are now all gone. What will happen next, I wonder."

"Time will make all that clear. Now it's time for sleep."

"Sleep well," Untuk-na said to her. "Sleep well."

When Wisdom returned color to the land, it came with rain. Ki'ti was beside herself. Tiriku was still down by Raven's grave. He was getting soaked. She started outside and Untuk-na caught her.

"If you want to bring him up here, I'll go get him," he told her.

"Yomuk-na said he growled when he tried to pick him up."

"If he growls at me, I'll make it clear he has no choice."

"I would love it if you could bring him here," Ki'ti said almost choking. Her belly ripped apart each time she thought of Tiriku.

Untuk-na went down the path and found the little dog soaked, lying beside the grave of Raven. His muzzle still lay between his paws and his feet stuck out in the back. It was as if he hadn't moved. All that did move were his lovely brown eyes as he watched Untuk-na. Uneaten meat sticks lay near him.

"You have to come with me, Tiriku. It's time to come. Ki'ti needs you."

Tiriku sighed. He permitted Untuk-na to lift him to carry him back to the cave. It was clear that he was putting up with something he didn't want. When Ki'ti saw him, she was delighted. She wiped rain from his coat and wrapped him in a skin to warm his little body which was quite cold.

"Tiriku, I love you, my funny little special dog. I don't want to lose you. If you keep lying by Raven's grave you will lose your life. You must get back to living." She looked into Tiriku's eyes and tried to communicate her need for him. He just looked miserable. She handed him a piece of meat. He held it in his mouth. He let it fall to the ground. Ki'ti tried again. She scolded him, telling him he must eat the meat. He swallowed it. She gulped, knowing he was pleasing her, not eating. She just held him wrapped in the warm skin. He didn't fight. He just put up with her care. Ki'ti carried Tiriku over to Ahna where the two planned to work on the stories. She was afraid to put Tiriku down for fear that he'd just go back in the rain to die by Raven's grave.

When it was time for the evening meal, Ki'ti noticed that Tiriku was asleep. She put him down so she could eat. Then it was time for the men's council which would be very short that evening, or so she thought. As the meeting got underway, Ki'ti nodded towards Domur.

Domur said, "Last night I asked about accompanying Komus to his home. I had thought that with so few people around this part of the earth, it would be good to find people with whom to meet in the future so that young ones could find people with whom to join. I talked to Manak-na about it and he talked to Kai-na and Mitrak and to Tongip-na and Aryna. The six of us would like to accompany Komus to his home, if the People and Komus approve."

Ki'ti looked at Komus.

"I would welcome accompaniment on the trip. My people would find it interesting to consider future meeting."

Ki'ti looked up. No one was looking at her to speak. She asked whether any People felt the idea of the six going with Komus was not a good idea. All looked down. The six people would be accompanying Komus.

Elemaea looked at Ki'ti. Ki'ti was surprised but looked back and nodded.

"I would like to gather a few of my women's knives, pack them, and give them to Komus so that they can be taken as a gift of goodwill to his people."

"I would be grateful," Komus said, surprised at the offer.

"I have just finished a good supply of combs," Ekuktu-na said. "I would be glad to share some of them."

"I would be grateful," Komus said.

"I have some extra powdered ochre," Domur said, "I'd be glad to share that."

"I would be grateful. Please realize we can carry only so much extra," Komus said.

The People took his comment to mean that they needed to stop adding things for the People to send to his people. The meeting became quiet.

There was no story that night. When the meeting stopped, Ki'ti chatted briefly and then returned to her sleeping skins to find Tiriku. She was not surprised. While the meeting took place, Tiriku had left. She knew that his little body was on the cold rainy ground next to his Raven friend. It ripped her belly and caused her to weep. To be certain, Untuk-na went to the grave site and sure enough the dog was there. He touched Tiriku's head gently and told him he could stay. He also said farewell from Ki'ti and himself. Untuk-na would never forget the white face of the little dog with the sad eyes that looked at him the last time without moving any part of his body but his eyes.

When Wisdom returned color to the land, Untuk-na ran downhill to check on Tiriku. When he returned, he shook his head in a negative way when Ki'ti looked into his eyes. He called Tongip-na, and together they dug out the grave of Raven and made it larger. They laid Tiriku against the side of Raven, back to back, heads thrown back, beak to muzzle just as they'd done so many times in life. The graveside service was another eulogy said this time by Untuk-na. Ki'ti couldn't talk. All the People gathered—including Komus. Komus was fascinated. He had never known anyone to have a dog, let alone a raven. For them to have been so close made no sense to him, but he realized it was fact. Komus watched Domur sprinkle red ochre on the bird and dog. Children had found early flowers and covered the animals with them.

Each person who wanted to spoke about the animals. Then Untuk-na and Tongip-na covered the pair first with dirt and then with stones.

Ki'ti returned to her sleeping skins and covered herself and wept. She wept for Tiriku and Raven, for faithful love whether animal or person, for the temporary nature of life, for Raven's mate wherever she might be, for Untuk-na who was clearly the love of her life, for Wisdom's letting her know Tiriku and Raven. She wept until there was nothing left to weep. And then she slept. Untuk-na chose not to awaken her for the evening meal. Ahna presided over the men's council. Hahami-na glimpsed movement from the corner of his eyes. He elbowed Untuk-na who turned just in time to see an extremely tiny pup waddle over to Ki'ti and lift the sleeping skin with its muzzle and climb under. Where, he wondered, did such a tiny pup come from? He'd never seen it. It made Tiriku look big! He wondered when Ki'ti would realize she had another dog.

When Wisdom restored color to the land with a brilliant sunrise, Ki'ti awakened. As soon as she moved, a small dog moved beside her. She had grieved Tiriku. She wasn't dreaming. There was a small dog. She sat up. She looked under that sleeping skin and found the tiniest little pup she'd ever seen.

"Where did you come from?" Ki'ti asked. Then she laughed to herself. *Wisdom!* "You are so tiny, Little Girl," she said to the pup. "I will have to call you Ti'ti—tiniest of the tiny. Are you sure you're a dog?"

Ki'ti poked Untuk-na. He moved. She said, "I'm not ready for this, but here is the next dog. She is the tiniest dog I ever saw. Do you remember any dog this tiny being born around here?"

Untuk-na looked at the pup Ki'ti was holding. It looked smaller in her hand than when he'd seen it the previous night as it crawled into the sleeping skins with Ki'ti. "What did you name her?" he asked.

"Ti'ti. The tiniest of the tiny."

"That could get confused with Ki'ti if the People still called you that."

"I suppose so. She's adorable, isn't she? And she doesn't remind me of any dog I ever had. That's helpful. She is a dog, isn't she?"

Untuk-na laughed out loud. "Definitely. And she has to be related to the ones who were here before. When she knew you were in your sleeping skins, she just waddled over, stuck her muzzle under your skins, and climbed in. Just like she knew what to do."

"Speaking of knowing what to do, I suppose she knows to go out when she needs to go." Ki'ti put the pup down. Ti'ti scampered to the entryway and disappeared. Shortly afterwards, Ti'ti returned to Ki'ti. She knew what to do.

She'd lived with the other dogs all her short life. There was no dog privy scent in the home cave. She knew where to go.

In another part of the cave, Manak-na, Tongip-na, and Kai-na were meeting with Komus discussing what they'd need to take for the trip. The women were with their husbands listening and occasionally asking questions. All six of the People were excited to be taking a trip where they could make some speed and see different things. They were eager for the change. The men had already decided to carry more than their share of the weight. The women would have to be walking faster than they normally did, and until they got used to it, they'd need the lighter weights.

After all had been decided, Manak-na and Domur walked outside to the observation place. They climbed up on the platform built of stone, and they looked north.

"Domur, why did you choose to do this? I am excited to be doing this with you, but I feel that in some ways I'm not supposed to be adventuring."

"My husband," Domur said, "when you adventured on the sea, you left me and the People to do something for yourself alone. Of course, Wisdom made it so you had a tag along in Yomuk-na, but it was basically a thing you did for yourself. And you did bring back information for the People, not to mention bringing Ahna to be the next Wise One. But those were Wisdom's additions, not your plan. This is different because it's part of a group of People, and what you bring back in terms of information will benefit the People. It's not your doing it for yourself, but you're participating in a group effort to benefit the People."

"I see the difference you're pointing out. One is selfish. The other is not."

"To be brutally truthful, yes." Domur looked at him. She could see it still hurt him to know that he'd hurt her.

"Manak-na, I want you to stop carrying the fact that you once deserted me. You must get past that and live without continuing to put the past in front of your mind web. I am quite sure you'll remember that you made a commitment and that you'll keep it. Please, for both of us, turn loose of that memory that causes you to beat yourself. It's over and finished. Let's move from there to our future."

"How did I manage to have you for a wife?" he asked truly meaning his respect for Domur.

"I snared you before you were old enough to be wise, my Dear One. I knew how special you were and are."

"I love you." He lowered his head.

Domur took his chin in her hand and raised it. She said, "I know. I also love you." She kissed him.

The two looked north for a short while and then returned to the home cave to ready things for the trek that would begin with Wisdom's restoring color to the land.

That evening was quiet. The People had a very short men's council and spent time trying to help those who would be trekking to have everything they needed at the ready for morning.

Manak-na and Domur stopped to talk to Ki'ti. They sat on her sleeping skins beside her. "Is there anything special you'd like us to learn from this trip or share with the people of Komus from you?" Manak-na asked.

"I hope that by now you know what the People need, and you will do what you did when you went on your adventure—bring back everything new that you encounter to share. While you're gone, share carefully with those you do not know. Most of all take care of yourselves and the other four who go with you. Be certain that all six of you return as well as you leave. You must return before the season of cold days. This is very important, though for the life of me, I do not know why I'm saying that. I only know it's very important. Make your time count for something. Keep your eyes and ears alert for danger. Keep yourselves close to Wisdom and call out when you need help—without waiting. You have your garments for the season of cold days?"

"Yes, of course." Manak-na was surprised she'd ask that. It went without saying that hunters would be prepared.

"I know what you are thinking, my Brother. Check again for all six of you. There are three People going who do not hunt."

"I wonder whether I have forgotten something," Domur said absent-mindedly. Later they would find that Aryna had forgotten to pack her season-of-cold-days boots.

"Wise One, that tiny dog is adorable," Domur said watching Ti'ti play with a piece of Ki'ti's tunic.

"I think she is very special. How she came to be so tiny, I have no idea." Ti'ti stopped playing and looked deep into Ki'ti's eyes. The tiny dog curled up in the lap of her tunic and rested her head on Ki'ti's leg. Ki'ti began to cough. The cough had reduced but still lingered.

"Please be sure I am awake before you leave. I must say farewell for this trip," Ki'ti said with a gentle hand on Ti'ti's head.

"Of course, we will," Manak-na assured her. "Sleep well, my Sister." Manak-na extended a hand to Domur to help her stand. She took his hand eagerly.

Ki'ti smiled and nodded. She reached for Domur's other hand. Looking deep into Domur's eyes, she said, "My Sister, you have done so well. I approve of you so much more than you'd ever know. I must say this to you, so that you know." She squeezed Domur's hand.

Domur returned the squeeze to Ki'ti's hand. Use of the term Sister was very special and Domur's throat constricted at the word. She knew Ki'ti was talking about how she handled Manak-na's adventure. She probably knew the entire event, but Domur would never ask. She just knew Ki'ti was well pleased, which gave her a sense of gratification that would be achieved no other way than to hear it from the Wise One. Something was bothering Domur about this time with Ki'ti, but she couldn't reason out what it was. She was probably examining things with the long trek they were about to take in mind, she thought.

She and Manak-na went to check the backpacks that were ready at the entryway one more time, and then they would go to sleep. When they reached Aryna's backpack, Domur went to her friend and suggested she might need her season-of-cold-days boots. Aryna was horrified that she'd forgotten. She immediately got them and put them in the backpack.

Ahna went to Ki'ti and sat with her for a little while.

"Mother, you are not well," she said quietly.

"Shhh, Little Girl, I'm fine."

"Mother, don't pretend with me. *I know*. You have little air and your cough is not good. You keep pretending it's better, but it's worse."

"Ahna, you must remain silent about this. I do not want to trouble anyone. I will talk to Likichi about it. As long as I have no physical stress, I am fine. I promise."

"Do you also promise to talk to Likichi when Wisdom returns color to the land?"

"You have my word, Ahna." Ki'ti looked at the girl. There was no way to get past her scrutiny. Wisdom spoke to Ahna. Ahna would be a Wise One who would lead the People well, Ki'ti reasoned. She was so fit for the responsibility already. It was good. She was a person who asked so little, but then that was how she'd been raised. And Cam-na was good for her. He was to her what Untuk-na was to Ki'ti. It was a wonderful match.

Ahna left to return to Cam-na. She'd told him only that she was aware that Ki'ti was not well. She was worried. At least she'd gotten Ki'ti to agree to talk to Likichi when Wisdom returned color to the land.

The home cave bustled with activity as the seven readied themselves for the trek. Ki'ti met them at the entryway and put her hands on the shoulders of all seven, one by one. She said to each, "Go with Wisdom." Each was touched. It was special each time their Wise One did it.

They left for the trek before the morning meal. Wisdom had just returned color to the land. Fiery rays made lines on the morning sky. It was a lovely day as they entered the season of new leaves. Komus led, and the People paired from time to time with one and another to follow. The pace was vigorous, but each was able to take the speed. Manak-na, Tongip-na, and Kai-na had been generous in the extra weight they'd taken on. The women would be able to take on more weight gradually as they strengthened. Aryna was likely the least able to carry very heavy weights. She was slender and Minguat. But then, Tongip-na was her husband and he could more than make up for what she couldn't carry, since he was the largest of all the trekkers.

Back in the home cave, Ki'ti and Untuk-na ate while she told him that she'd talk to Likichi about the breathing problems. Untuk-na had been trying to get her to do that for quite a while. He wondered what caused her to do it this morning, but he didn't ask. He was just glad she would finally address the issue.

When they finished the meal, Ki'ti went to the back of the cave where Likichi was busy with the herbs.

"May I have some of your time?" Ki'ti asked.

"Of course, Wise One, what can I do?" Likichi carefully laid down a handful of herbs and seated herself on skins, gesturing to Ki'ti to be seated.

Ki'ti sat and Ti'ti crept into the lap of her tunic. "I have not been improving, Likichi. My breathing is tighter, that's all. Do you have some of the leaves Totamu used to help her breathe?"

"Oh, I missed that altogether. You should not pretend to be better when you're not, my Dear."

"I just don't want to worry anyone. I can do what I must as long as I don't have to walk up and down the hills. Trekking is impossible for me any longer." That was quite an admission for Ki'ti, and Likichi was well aware of the significance.

"Let me listen to your lungs," the old woman said crawling over to Ki'ti.

Likichi put her ear against Ki'ti's chest and back. She didn't like what she heard. Ki'ti could not see her alarmed frown.

"You're wheezing. I'll get the leaves and you can add them to the pouch you already have around your neck. I also want you to drink a lot of water.

Keep sipping it all day and evening. You've got to thin out what is in your chest so you can cough it up."

"How often do I use the leaves?"

"What I've added to your pouch, use whenever your breathing feels tight. I'll bring you gourds of hot water with the vasaka leaves steeped in it. When I bring that to you, I want you to drink it hot—and all of it. Off and on I'll bring some steeped chaga for you to drink. You need to drink it hot—and all of it. Promise me you will do as I ask."

"I promise, Likichi. What is this?" Ki'ti pointed to her chest.

"You probably acquired a problem from the ashfall when you were little. You were closer to the ground than most of us. You probably breathed a lot more of it than taller People, and it didn't get removed from your lungs. You know what lungs look like. You've probably got ash lodged in your lungs, where it has caused it to be hard for you to breathe. It's worse in the lower part of your lungs. So you have the upper parts that are still working. What you don't want is to let what's down there get so thick you can't cough it up. That's why I want you to drink lots of water. And you must not get overtired like you did. Having to lie on sleeping skins for days on end is not good. You need to be up and moving to get rid of what you can, but not moving to the extent that you get winded. Do you understand?"

"I understand well. Will this cause my death soon?" Ki'ti knew she needed to know what she could, but she wasn't at all sure she was ready for an answer. Ti'ti got up and headed towards the entryway.

Likichi gathered a handful of the leaves, and Ki'ti handed her the pouch from around her neck. Likichi put the leaves in the pouch and tightened the leather strap. She handed it back to Ki'ti, who put it back around her neck.

"As you are right now, you may be good for years. But if you don't take care of yourself, your time could be cut down quickly. Remember Enut? It's like that, I think. Even if you do take good care of yourself, I cannot truly say how long you have. I wish I could. Or, maybe not. I only know that you have a serious problem and must do what I told you. Think of it this way, you're immortal, until Wisdom calls for you."

"No one is immortal!" Ki'ti laughed a nervous laugh.

"I see it differently. I think we all are immortal until Wisdom calls us to come to the navel of the world."

"I love that, Likichi. I'll keep that in mind all day. It makes things more cheerful! It is a beautiful way to view Wisdom." Ki'ti ran the statement through her mind web savoring what it had to say about Wisdom.

"Good. Now, I'm going to make you some of that tea to help you breathe."

Ki'ti got up and Likichi stood, reaching back for a bundle of leaves. Likichi clenched her teeth. She was convinced Ki'ti had very little time.

Ki'ti walked back to the place where she and Ahna would go over the stories. Ki'ti noticed that Ti'ti was sitting by Ahna, waiting. "I kept my word," Ki'ti said to Ahna.

"I noticed, Mother. I am grateful. What did Likichi say?" Ahna smoothed out a place on soft skins for Ki'ti. Ki'ti sat, resting her back on the skins along the wall.

"She thinks that the lower part of my lungs is filled with ash from Baambas. The upper parts are doing well. She wants me to drink a lot of water and chew on these leaves. She wants me to be up and around daily but not to do anything physically stressful that would cause me to have trouble breathing. I'm not supposed to become overtired."

"Mother, if there is anything I can do to help you, will you promise to tell me?"

"I promise. One day you'll be Wise One. I'm sure you're ready now. Yes, I promise to let you know when you can help. In fact, you may find that I lean on you heavier and heavier far sooner than either of us knows. It is wonderful to know that when you are Wise One, I won't have a worry. You are a treasure."

"Mother, you must know that I love you with all my heart. You have shown me love and taught me to love. You have given me a life that I could never have dreamed I'd have. I will talk to Wisdom often and ask that Wisdom help your lungs work the best they can. I want you to live long."

Ki'ti looked at the young woman before her. "Ahna, my Dear, there is one thing I will ask of you now, so that I never forget. Right now I have Ti'ti. Whether I have another, time only will tell. When I go to Wisdom, will you take my dog and love it, as I do?"

"Of course, if that's what you want. I already love Ti'ti, and she cares for me too."

"That's why I asked you. I will make it clear to Untuk-na that I have made that request."

Likichi arrived with the gourd of steaming tea. "Now, drink this while it's hot," she said.

"Thank you, Likichi," Ki'ti said. She loved Likichi, the woman who'd been her mother before she was adopted by Emaea and Wamumur to be trained as Wise One. Ki'ti remembered that more and more often.

As Ki'ti drank the steaming liquid, she did actually feel freer to breathe. It was a definite help. She listened to Ahna review the stories for that evening. She began to wonder whether Ahna needed that supervision, and then realized that Ahna didn't, *she* needed something to do. Ki'ti told Ahna to continue to practice. She was going to walk around some, while she was able to breathe so well.

Ki'ti walked around the home cave until she found Untuk-na. She shared with him what she'd learned from Likichi. Untuk-na was alarmed, but he tried to hide it and did it well enough that Ki'ti didn't realize he was alarmed. He escorted them to a log where they sat together. Ki'ti remembered to tell him that when she died, she wanted Ahna to take care of her dog. That alarmed Untuk-na even more and required extraordinary effort on his part to appear to receive this news as simple fact, not an emotional punch in the belly. He realized that Ki'ti was preparing for death.

"Here's what I'm thinking," Ki'ti said, "I think that it's time for Ahna to take over. Remember that Wamumur and Emaea had me take over from them, so they had some time to live without the responsibility of Wise One, but they were available to me?"

"I remember that." Untuk-na was not in the least disappointed. He thought it wonderful that Ki'ti would consider taking time to live. Ahna certainly was ready to become Wise One.

"I need something to do. If I'm not Wise One, what will I do?" The anxiety in her face showed clearly to Untuk-na.

"Ki'ti, you are not defined by what you do but rather by who you are. You can still be Ki'ti, a loving wife, taking an interest in others, wanting the best for the People, doing whatever needs to be done that you can do—or just relaxing and enjoying what you see before you. When Wamumur and Emaea left the responsibility of Wise One to you, they were available to you only when you didn't have a clue what to do in certain situations. It didn't take you long to get past that need, but you did need it at first. They were like guides to you from more distance. You'd have that responsibility for a while. Then they just enjoyed life. Wamumur got busy with the home made from trees. Emaea helped with meat preparation, something she had longed to do. She also made parts of the home made from trees."

"You're right. They didn't have to have a list of daily duties. They just did what came naturally in life. I'm just not used to that. I think I could get used to it though." Ki'ti smiled at him as she savored the idea.

"You look like you're breathing better than you have in a long time," he observed.

"I am in Likichi's care now. She is bringing me steaming gourds of water made with a leaf to help breathing. She'll also bring some chaga. The treatment really is effective."

"Likichi is a wonder."

"She is. When Totamu died, I wondered how we'd get on without her. Everyone expected my Grandmother, Pechki to take the responsibility, but she didn't want it, and suggested Likichi would be better at it. From that time, Likichi has done great things."

"Well, I'm glad you're in her care. She won't forget when it's time for you to drink the steaming breathing liquid." The relief he felt was great.

"You're right!" Ki'ti laughed the laugh he loved. She knew that Likichi was devoted to fulfilling her responsibilities exceptionally well. Likichi'd stay right on her to be sure she got what she needed when she needed it.

"So when will you tell Ahna and the People?"

"I'll tell Ahna just before the men's council. I'll make the transition during the men's council."

"Why wait so long?" He was curious to know the answer.

"I would do just what was done with me. I didn't have time to get anxious about it."

"I see," Untuk-na replied.

From the entryway, Untuk-na could see that a couple of young hunters had returned with some deer. They weren't large, but they would contribute well to the supply. He put his hand on the entryway wall and looked out at the view. He loved the scene from the trees that blocked the view from below of the cave. What a great place this was! He was so relieved that Ki'ti had chosen this time to transition from Wise One. He knew that Ahna was well ready for the responsibility and he could see that already Ki'ti had relaxed a little. Perhaps, once the transition took place she could learn to relax and enjoy life. She would have to let go of Ahna to let Ahna make mistakes. That might be hard, but she'd find that Ahna would do well.

Children were gathered below the cave on the level ground. They were practicing with sling shots aimed at targets where Ekuktu-na had used blueberry liquid to paint various water fowl on leather. Leather stretchers were holding the targets. When the children reached a certain level of competency with the still stretchers, they moved down the flatland to where trees that overhung the land provided for a tethered large pouch filled with sand that could be set in motion. The children would practice with slingshots until they became proficient at moving targets. Then they'd practice with spears—first with still and then moving targets. Some of the children whose skills were great last summer had lost skill and had to work hard to regain it. Later adults would use the same practice ground for the same reasons, watched carefully by the youngsters.

Ki'ti walked around the home cave. She was chilled, so she put on her long pants and jacket and walked outside, enjoying the activity below. She felt a sense of joy at the decision she'd made. It was time, maybe, she thought, past time. She wondered how long Wisdom had planned for her to live. Would it be years, or less than a single year? There was no way to know. Life was precious. She wanted to get the most from every day she had left. Baambas, she thought, was still damaging all these years later. Who would have thought that something like ash could do to a person what it was doing to her. She felt a nudge at her ankle.

Ki'ti picked up Ti'ti and hugged the little dog. "You're just adorable, Little One," she said. Ti'ti licked her face and neck. "Ah, you bathe me?" Ti'ti looked at Ki'ti's face. The little dog was a happy pup. Ti'ti turned her head from side to side and looked into Ki'ti's eyes. Ki'ti hugged her and returned her to the ground. At least it didn't wind her to pick up the little dog.

Ki'ti felt in some inexplicable ways that suddenly each day was more sacred, more special—to be savored every moment. She felt she saw with different eyes, everything was in sharper focus. She didn't want to miss anything. She felt a certainty that she didn't have much time left. As time for the evening meal approached, she returned to Ahna.

"Are you ready for tonight?" Ki'ti asked her.

"Of course, Mother," Ahna replied from afar where her thoughts were in the story.

"I tell you, you are not." Ki'ti stood over her, holding Ti'ti on her arm against her rib cage where Ti'ti rested quietly.

Ahna looked up, clearly broken from her mind web practice. "What is it, Mother?"

"I want some time just to live without heavy responsibility, Ahna, my Dear One. Tonight I will lay down the responsibility of Wise One and turn it over to you."

Ahna began to protest, so Ki'ti raised her hand palm outward. She continued to stand over Ahna. "None of that. You've known all along that this would eventually happen. You're exceptionally well ready. I have no reservations whatever, knowing you're as suited as I—if not, better suited—to the task. The People will accept you without equivocation. It's time. I need to do this—now. From the time of the council tonight, I will lay down my responsibility. I will be available to you for guidance only, and I mean *only*, when you have tried with all you have to solve a problem yourself. I will not interfere with your carrying out your responsibility. Ask hunters for help. Ask other women. Use me only as a last resort. Do not fear making mistakes. You'll make some. Learn from them. Talk to Wisdom as often as you can." Ki'ti stood there reflecting on the spiral chipped in stone in the observation place where she'd told Untuk-na what it meant to her. Had she not gone from the point in the center and spiraled out? Had she not long ago begun her retreat in the spiral? She knew for a certainty that her retracing of the spiral was near the end point, what Ki'ti saw as the beginning and the end of life, but she had not received that information in a clear vision from Wisdom or a dream, instead it came from her own body signals, signals she'd never noticed until she slowed down this day. She was in strange pain. Pain she'd blocked. Now she was aware of its presence, if not its severity. She was glad the severity of the pain was blocked. It was deep in her bones. She silently sent a prayer to Wisdom to keep the pain blocked.

Ahna was sitting there with her head down. Ki'ti could see tears falling silently unchecked.

"Ahna, it is Wisdom's way. Look how far Wisdom went to find the right person to replace me. Look how hard it was to get you here. Wisdom knew this moment would come. Do not fret. Wisdom selected you from all those who live on earth at this time. When I die, my Dear, it is a temporary time before I see again you and all who are here. Death is an entry into another type of life. Separation is for a short time, really." She put her hand on Ahna's head. "Ahna, imagine my boundless joy to see Wisdom face to face. Just imagine!"

Those words cut through Ahna's grief. It transferred a sense of strength, if not the immediate reality of it. Ki'ti wasn't fighting death, but seemed to welcome the transition she'd make, even as Ahna was facing a transition. "Wise One," Ahna said, using the words while she still could and looking into the eyes of the only real mother she'd ever known, "I will toughen myself to make my transition as well as you are making the one you speak of making. I will seek to find the joy you speak of in the ultimate passage of this life."

Ki'ti stooped down and released Ti'ti. Ti'ti bounded to the entryway and went outside. Ki'ti did a firm palm strike. It was answered by one from Ahna.

Then Ki'ti hugged Ahna tight. Likichi arrived with a steaming cup of tea for Ki'ti's breathing. The evening meal was about to be served.

Untuk-na went to Ki'ti and asked how she was feeling. She said she was fine. Her eyes spoke more than her words. He looked at her blue eyes framed with the long brown lashes that he loved. She was tired, he could see. She appeared to be in discomfort, but he didn't press the issues with her. She would tell him when she was ready, or he'd ask when there were fewer People around.

They had smoked leg of large deer that night with many greens both cooked and fresh. Someone had taken the fat stored with blueberries in intestines and mixed it with some of the remaining nuts from storage they'd crushed that afternoon, and that added delicious rolled fruit and nut balls to the meal. Ki'ti smiled at Untuk-na while they ate. The meat and the greens were seasoned to perfection. Their People knew how to gather food, store it, prepare it for eating, and mix different seasonings to make their meals a feast. It was good, very good, Ki'ti thought.

After the cleanup from the evening meal the People gathered at the men's council. Ki'ti sat in her seat presiding. Ti'ti curled up in the lap of her tunic. Ki'ti began: "Tonight I have a change to make. All of you have known that for some time I have had difficulty breathing. Likichi attributes it to the ash following the explosion of Baambas. I am not well. I turn my responsibility as Wise One over to Ahna tonight. Ahna, you and I well know, is completely ready to serve as Wise One. From this moment forward, she is your Wise One. Ki'ti took Untuk-na's offered hand and stood up. She walked to the back of the group of People and seated herself with Untuk-na's assistance. There was dead silence in the home cave until slowly the palm strikes began. The People were accepting Ki'ti's transition and Ahna's becoming Wise One. It was a sign of sincere respect and acceptance. Nothing could have pleased Ki'ti more. The palm strikes lasted longer than anyone could have anticipated, but when they ceased, Ahna was seated at the place where the Wise One sat to preside over the council. She looked around and saw Ermol-na looking at her. She nodded.

"I wish to express the love we all have for Ki'ti." He carefully used her name. "She has served all of us so well. I will speak for the People. Ki'ti, if you have any need or desire that any of us can provide, ask. There is no one here who would not willingly stop what we're doing to help in any way at any time."

Ki'ti lowered her head as far as she could. She hadn't anticipated words like that.

Ahna looked up. Ki'ti was looking at her. She nodded to Ki'ti.

Ki'ti took the little pouch from around her neck. She emptied out the yellow owl. She pushed the leaves back into the pouch and put it around her neck. She handed the yellow owl to Untuk-na. Untuk-na took the yellow owl to Ahna. "That little yellow owl is for the next person who becomes Wise One after you. It will need a new pouch," Ki'ti said.

"Thank you, Mother," Ahna said forcibly keeping her voice from breaking.

Ahna looked up. All the heads of the People were looking down.

"That concludes the council this evening. There will be a story tonight." Ahna stopped speaking to give People a time to move around. All was utterly still. During that time, Untuk-na went with Ki'ti to their sleeping place. He unrolled the skins and helped her in. He covered her. Likichi brought her the vasaka and chaga teas. Once Ki'ti was well set, Untuk-na returned to the council.

Ahna began the story. She chose the story of Maknu-na and Rimlad, because in it Wisdom provided. It was a different story from what she had planned.

After the story People quietly turned to their sleeping skins. The evening had brought a great surprise. They were adjusting.

Chapter 9

The seven trekkers had been gone from the home cave for a moon. Komus led, followed by Tongip-na and Aryna, Mitrak and Domur, and Kai-na and Manak-na. They had arisen this day before Wisdom surprised them with a glorious burst of brilliant rosy glow to the whole sky. All were invigorated. They were nearing the big lake and there was a lot of excitement.

"I feel better than I've felt in a long time," Domur said to Mitrak. "Must be the exercise."

"I, too. It's as though I were young again," Mitrak replied fully in recognition that both she and Kai-na were the oldest of the People on this trek.

"Mitrak, I never think of you as older. We grew up together. Sometimes I forget. It's good to trek like this. It does make you feel vibrant. But it's impossible when there are young children and old people. And look at my belly. A lot of the fat I gathered around my middle has vanished." Both women laughed.

"Well, jerky has to be good for something," Mitrak laughed. "It certainly isn't creative cooking!"

Domur responded with a chuckle. Both women liked to eat good food. They had not grumbled, for they knew ahead of time there would be days and days of jerky, but they did like well-seasoned, freshly cooked meat. They also liked good, fresh vegetables available when the earth wasn't covered with white rain. They even would have been delighted to have what they normally just settled for—boiled plants they had cut into pieces and dehydrated to hard pieces in the season of warm nights and then boiled in the season of cold days to bring back tenderness. Rehydrated plants were not the same as fresh, but they were better than no plants at all. They missed their evening meals much more than they thought they would.

"Can you believe how much weight we're carrying now? At first I wondered how far I'd be able to travel with the light weight backpack. Now that we're carrying what is ours to carry, it seems lighter than those we carried at the beginning."

Domur laughed as she walked carefully through some scattered rocks. "We are becoming as well muscled as our husbands. Do you think we'd do well as hunters?"

"You might," Mitrak replied more seriously, "I can handle meat preparation when it comes to cooking. It still makes me retch when I smell a freshly slaughtered animal. I'd rather do many, many things than bleed and eviscerate a carcass." She almost retched just thinking about it.

"With as many People as we have, we've been spared a lot. Had we lived in very small groups, we'd have to do things we don't want to do. I love the size of our group now." Domur did a palm strike.

"I agree," Mitrak said echoing the palm strike. "Is that rain?"

Domur looked up. "Well, I think you're right and it looks like we'll be seeing a lot more. Look that way," Domur pointed off to the west.

"Hold up," Manak-na shouted from the rear. The rain was coming down heavier now.

Each of the People had a rolled gut sheet made of parallel split sections of animal gut sewed together to form the sheet. When rain fell, they unrolled the gut sheet and pulled it over their backpack and their heads. They had sticks that hooked to the gut skin above their heads and to the backpack, so that they walked with the backpack and their heads protected from rainfall. The sticks held it in place so their hands were free. They pulled the sheets up, hooked them to the sticks, and resumed trekking. Komus also had a rain protector. His was made of tightly woven grass. It was made so that his hands were free unless the wind was high.

The men and Aryna had been quiet during the trek. Domur and Mitrak chatted constantly. Sometimes the others would tire of the chatter, and at other times they'd find it interesting or humorous. It definitely added color to their trek. No one would have suggested they remain quiet. Komus found it fascinating. Women of the People were more open, more self assured, more outspoken than women of his people. Women of his people might have had the same thoughts as these women, but they would never have expressed them before hunters for fear of disapproval. These women, Komus realized, never questioned whether they were approved—they *knew* they were. It was insightful for him. He liked it. These women were strong. He wondered about the woman with the hair that once was yellow. There were white hairs among the yellow ones. Many white hairs. She was a quiet one. He wondered why. He'd never have guessed she was one of three survivors of a terrible war.

The rain came down harder and faster. It made pinging sounds on the gut sheets. They continued on. Rain would not stop the trek. Mixed with the rain were hard little white balls. The balls gathered on the ground. The trekkers wore coverings made for their feet for warm weather. It kept them from walking barefooted on the cold hard balls. The sky was dark and hail became larger. Lightning flashed and thunder roared.

"Glad I'm not an animal in the open all the time," Mitrak said loud so Domur could hear.

"Me, too. Imagine if we didn't have our gut sheets!"

"No, thank you, I'd rather not imagine that!" Mitrak laughed.

Komus stopped. On the hillside near where they were, there was a cave. Komus studied the landscape. Finally, he remembered. They walked towards the cave. He went inside and found the cave was free of animals and other people. Mitrak looked inside the container where she carried the ember for making fires. It had gone out. "We have to use a fire starter," she said. Komus produced one from his backpack. Aryna had already gathered some dry material that would ignite easily from the inside of the cave. She took it to Komus. Domur and Manak-na had gathered some twigs and were looking for dry wood. They found a few pieces of dry wood towards the back of the cave. They couldn't see well, so they would have to wait to explore the cave further when they could light a torch. They took what they had to Komus.

Komus noticed again that the People didn't need to talk a lot. They just knew what needed to be done and did it. He approved.

Kai-na stood in the entryway watching the storm. The air always smelled so fresh during a storm. Mitrak went to him and put her arm around his waist.

"What's it like when you go hunting, and a storm rises up like this?" Mitrak asked.

"We act like it's not happening, unless it is so bad that it frightens the animals, and then we look for shelter."

"You must've had some tough times."

"It's part of hunting. We have a responsibility to feed the People. That's foremost in our mind webs, but also foremost in our mind webs is that we have to be alive to do that. We try not to take risks that could be too great. We look out for each other carefully." Kai-na put his arm around Mitrak's shoulders and continued, "That is all the substance of being a -na hunter. We've had few accidents, because we train to be very careful. When I was injured, we were trying something very new. My injury showed us how to make the dropoff work better for us."

Mitrak was surrounded with a deep feeling of closeness to Kai-na but had no way to express it easily. She said, "I love you. I am so glad we live at this time and in this place. We are blessed of Wisdom."

He squeezed her shoulder. "I agree. Smell the wonderful fresh air. Have you ever smelled better?"

"It is so clean," she agreed.

A small hearth fire blazed behind them. They turned to see Komus making a torch from a piece of wood they'd overlooked. He seemed to have everything in his backpack. Even some tar for wrapping the end of the torch. He was warming it in his hands. They watched. Once he had it going, he headed to the back of the cave. He came forward with some dry wood to keep the fire going for a good while.

He looked at Domur and Mitrak. "Do you women think you can make a spit using some of this wood?" he asked.

The women looked at the wood he'd brought. "I think so," Domur said optimistically. Mitrak didn't say anything but wondered what the man had in mind. "We have nothing to put on a spit," Mitrak finally said, stating the obvious.

"I will strip off and ask Manak-na to do the same. We'll find something for the spit without soaking our clothing. After listening to you two this morning, I'm waiting for a great evening meal, well seasoned, and tasting good enough to last for another moon." He grinned from ear to ear as Manak-na began to strip off the leather clothing he didn't want to get wet in the rain. "This is a good place to stay overnight. We can start again when the sun shines in the morning," Komus added.

Aryna looked at Tongip-na. "Will you accompany me to search for greens?" she asked almost salivating.

"Of course," he agreed. Real food sounded wonderful. Both stripped off and were outside ready to find the other part of their evening meal.

Each of the seven trekkers was busy planning for the evening meal. Getting wet was a small price to pay for a belly full of good food on a trek like theirs.

It wasn't long before Komus and Manak-na returned with a medium sized boar. "Just the perfect size for us!" Manak-na announced from the entryway. "This will taste so good!" He stood by the fire shaking the water from his hair.

Domur brought him a skin and helped him dry his soaking wet skin by rubbing vigorously with the soft piece of leather. Mitrak looked at Komus. She took a similar skin and went to Komus. Excuse me, Komus, but I am going to help you. She began to rub his soaking wet skin with the soft leather. The man's cold skin warmed and began to glow a pinkish red color, just as Manak-na's skin, though the color of his skin was darker than Manak-na's. It was still easy to see the rosy glow. Mitrak did not give up until the man was dry and glowing. The same was true for Domur with Manak-na.

"You'll have to share this with the women of my people," Komus said with enthusiasm. "This is wonderful!"

Tongip-na and Aryna had already dried off before the men arrived with the pig. They took the pig and skinned it outside. The others had already bled and gutted it. They put the skin off to the side at some distance from the cave, since they had no plan to use it for anything, and prepared the pig for roasting. They put the pig on the spit and readied themselves to watch it, turning when needed.

Manak-na and Komus dressed and the cave was prepared for habitation near the entryway. Sleeping skins were rolled out for seating. It was a wonderful time for a break in the trekking while the rain fell and the storm thundered and lit up the sky. Life was good. Mitrak carried seasonings in little packages. She got a package and brought it to the hearth. Carefully she put the seasoning on the meat as Aryna turned the animal so she would cover all parts. It didn't take long before the scent filled the cave and turned the thoughts of all to food. It was not near time, however, so they had to do other things.

Komus checked his warm weather foot coverings and his clothing and backpack. Anything he had was scrutinized to see whether it needed fixing. If so, it got fixed during rest overs while they were not trekking. The others picked up the plan and soon all were checking everything. Aryna repaired a split in Tongip-na's season-of-warm-nights foot covering and Kai-na repaired a weakening strap on his backpack. The gut skins to protect from the rain were dried off and could be rolled and retied. Time was used well while they stopped for the rain. The torch Komus made warmed the cave and cast a cheery light. He had found a place in the rock wall where the torch fit, and put it there, where it was raised to eye level for the People.

"I like the raised torch light," Mitrak said with intensity. "We'll have to remember that when we return to our home cave. We could make holes to hold torches, if there aren't any usable wall spaces like this one already available. It's so much easier to see!"

"I agree," Aryna said. "With light like this, I could work longer on my sewing, because I'd be able to see so much better."

"You'd probably stay up all night, if you had light like this," Tongip-na teased her. "There'd never be time for us, and you'd be tired all the time from lack of sleep."

Anya looked at him horrified. "What an awful thing to say."

"Well, you tend to spend way too much time working. With light like this, you'd be able to extend the already long time." He grinned.

"I'm sorry."

"No need to be sorry. It's just how you are. I'm just not sure I'd want to have it so you could increase the time you spend working. I like to be with you, and there's so little time."

"You sound newly joined," Komus observed.

"Not at all!" Tongip-na laughed. "I love my wife and want every moment with her I can have."

Komus wondered whether the seeming initial disapproval was a reason for Aryna's quiet, but while he watched the interaction, he realized that Tongip-na wasn't really criticizing. There seemed to be some gentle teasing involved. It was a little confusing why the girl was quiet, but then, maybe it was just how she was.

The evening continued light hearted until Komus went to the torch and extinguished it in the dirt. They all laid aside what they were doing and rearranged their sleeping skins for sleep. All were more tired than they thought. With full bellies from a wonderful evening meal, quickly all slept.

When Wisdom returned color to the land, birds were singing and the rain clouds had disappeared, leaving a brilliant blue sky. The beginning promised a wonderful day and the trekkers were ready to leave. They prepared their backpacks and departed after carefully extinguishing the remains of the fire in the hearth.

They trekked hard, until they reached a hill. Before reaching the top of the hill, Komus said, "From there you can see the big lake."

All were terribly excited. It was the end of a quest for them that they had begun when they left the home made from trees. Instead of racing up the hill, they trekked as if nothing had happened. Upon reaching the top, they looked and it appeared that clouds were below them.

"What is this?" Manak-na asked Komus.

"Ah, I should have prepared you. Often the air is cloudy here and vision is blocked. But the lake really is there."

"If you say so," Tongip-na teased.

They continued trekking following Komus.

By nightfall they had reached the edge of the lake and a good place to camp that Komus knew about. They arrived at a propitious time while there was light left to see to start a fire and build some lean-tos. The foggy mist in the air had risen so they had some view of the lake and it was big! They were awed. Briefly they walked in the cold clear water soothing their aching feet.

"This trip may be shorter than I thought," Komus said. "My people may have moved to the place where we camp sometimes near the big lake. In this season we try to take seals."

"That would be interesting," Manak-na said with enthusiasm. Trekking two more moons did not sound like a good time any longer. His feet were very tired.

"How will you know?" Mitrak asked.

"If this foggy mist were not here, we'd know already. I hope that in the morning the fog has lifted. Then we'd see smoke from fires. My people camp right over that hill. You can see them from here along the lake's edge. Oh, I hope they're there. I have missed them so much."

"Komus," Mitrak asked, "Why did you go to sea?"

"I went because my father went and his father before him and his father before him on back in time to forever."

"Why did you go just because your father did?"

"It is our way. The first son does what the father does. The second and other sons do what they choose."

"I see," Mitrak said, and she did, but she did not understand at all. What if, she wondered, a son was an exceptional hunter, but because his father was a boatbuilder who sailed, he had to do that. What if he didn't want to follow what his father did? She thought she already understood that he'd have to do what his father did, regardless of whether he found it good. Maybe, first sons were not even permitted to find out where their special skills lay. Mitrak breathed a sigh of relief that she was People. The concept didn't seem to bother Komus, but it bothered her a lot.

When the trekkers awakened, they could see that there was a camp across the lake over the hill that Komus described. The mist was gone and the blue sky over the lake made it an exceptionally beautiful view. Komus opened his eyes and immediately looked to see if his people were camped nearby. He was delighted.

The trekkers got up and rolled up their sleeping skins. They pulled on their backpacks and began the trek over the hill while they ate jerky.

When they topped the hill, Komus's people recognized that there were strangers with Komus and they walked to meet them. Komus's son ran. He was a young man and had joined while Komus was gone. His wife was with him as he ran. She was a swift runner.

"Father, so good to see you," the young man said with a hug.

Komus held the young man at arm's length, looking him over. "You have matured, Ergi, my Son."

"Yes, Father."

A short, round faced, heavy woman waddled over to Komus. He embraced her warmly, turned to the trekkers and said, "This is Lugmi, my wife. This is Ergi, my son, and his wife, Nolsi. I'll introduce these people who travel with me when we reach our destination at the camp," he said smiling broadly.

Lugmi walked over to Aryna and took her by the arm and began to lead her to the camp. Aryna looked older than the others because her hair was grayer despite the fact that she was younger than Mitrak, but she couldn't understand why Lugmi singled her out. Komus asked her, "Why are you leading Aryna?"

Lugmi replied, "Is she not the Chief's wife?"

"They have no Chief, my Love," Komus replied.

Instead of letting go of Aryna's arm, Lugmi reached out and took Mitrak's arm, so she led two of the women. She began asking the women their names.

"If you'd have had a third arm, you'd have had all three," Komus boomed out in laughter.

The trekkers were startled by the change in Komus's behavior among his own people. Here was a man who was open and booming with joy. They had never seen anything from him but seriousness. This was a whole new world. The trekkers stole glances and raised eyebrows. They would all have admitted to enjoying it tremendously.

As they approached the camp many more people arrived to meet the newcomers. They gathered near a large hearth and all seated themselves in a circle with concentric circles around it, except where the concentric rings stopped for the place occupied by the chief. The newcomers were set into the circle. It was the way these people had of showing acceptance of them, Komus explained.

They talked and talked, communication being easy, since all knew the Mol language. Komus's people had a slightly different way of pronouncing some words, but it was clear what word they meant as they talked.

The People told that they originally headed towards the big lake, but they found it too cold to continue, so they settled in a place along the way. Komus interrupted to give their name of the place they settled and explain that they had rid the place of evil. His people were hushed, which startled the newcomers. The people of Komus looked suspiciously at the newcomers. They found it incomprehensible that anyone could rid a place of evil.

"How did you do that?" Lugmi asked timidly wondering whether these people had a form of spirit power.

"Our Wise One found a mummified man of the People. She realized he was evil. He was like us," Manak-na said, "People—not Mol or Minguat. He spoke mean spiritedly to our Wise One. She realized he should be buried so his spirit could go to Wisdom. He didn't want that to happen. She insisted, and our people buried him across the valley. Outside the room where the evil mummified man was, there was a painting that showed what the evil man had done. Our Wise One had that wall totally destroyed so it could not be reassembled. She did not want our People looking at the painting and learning evil from it. We hacked some large rocks out of there!" Manak-na mused.

"Good—that is good," Lugmi said, seemingly calmed. She still wondered about how their Wise One knew she needed to have the man buried and destroy the pictures to get rid of the evil.

Komus decided that confusion was in the air among the newcomers. He explained. "Many, many, many years ago, the man of whom you speak came to the Mol giants. They were dying out, and he managed to get them to follow him and his evil ways. The giants subjugated all of us. They would not let us continue to speak our language. We had to speak the language of the Mol. We tried so hard to keep our language, but all we could manage to keep was our way of doing things. They didn't seem to care about that. They would leave us alone as long as we spoke nothing but Mol and gave them gifts. They wanted special things: much food and things like a piece of jade or a purple bowl that had belonged to someone way back in our time. At least I think it did. They gave those things to the evil man. I suppose he ate the food we sent to feed them. There were more of us then. Many to the west moved further west to get away from the evil man. We didn't see that as an option, so we put up with things until the evil man died.

Some of our men went to take the special food and things, and they discovered that the evil man was dead. Oddly his spirit told our people to leave these things every time they were due. That was several times a year. The man said he wasn't dead; he had changed into a god. Our people were terrified and left the things for the dead man. When it was clear that nothing was happening to what we left, we stopped taking them. Passing the spot to go to the boatbuilders' place, I could still feel the evil from that place until now," Komus said obviously still awed. He looked at his people. "It's gone," he said with finality and conviction. "The evil is really gone."

Manak-na said, "If you have had things taken from you to give to the evil man, there are things laid on a table in the cave where his body was. You are free to come to our home and take back what was taken from you, if it's on that table. We have left those things alone. None of us wants what is not ours."

Komus's people were looking at each other in total disbelief. Later they would quietly question what kind of people could overcome such evil—wondering whether they had an even greater evil. After all, the evil man was one of the people like Manak-na. Maybe Manak-na and the others like him were evil. Only a couple of them were really Mol. Maybe Manak-na had cast a spell on them and on Komus to make them believe the evil had ended when it was about to get worse.

"This Wise One of yours," Monski, a hunter asked, "is a woman?"

"Yes," Tongip-na replied.

"How can a woman have the strength to fight a god?"

"First, the man in the cave was no god. He just wanted to see himself that way, and he seems to have convinced giants and others that he was. He was just an evil man. Second, the woman is our Wise One who communicates with the spirit of Wisdom. She is the storykeeper and storyteller of the People. She is tiny. She is not physically strong. She is very strong spiritually. Those things are different. She sees right to the heart of truth."

"But she is not among you?"

"No, she is not," Manak-na said. "She is considered a treasure among our People. She doesn't take risks such as this travel, for if we lose her, we lose our stories from the beginning of time."

There seemed to be some release of tension among Komus's people. Manak-na wondered whether they were frightened by the idea of their Wise One. It almost made him laugh, but he controlled himself quickly. He did not know these people. Maybe if they stood a little in awe of their Wise One, it would be a good thing. When he could, he whispered that among his People. Later, he smiled to himself. Why shouldn't they stand in awe of Ki'ti? He was her brother, and he did!

They spent time talking and getting acquainted until some of the women indicated it was time for their evening meal. All went to another area where they sat overlooking the beautiful lake. Each person took his or her bowl to the table where women filled it. Then they found a place on the hillside to eat. It was a restful time. Food always seemed to taste so good when it was eaten in the outside air. This time was no exception.

Mitrak asked Komus, "What is this meat? I think I have never eaten it."

He replied, "It is seal. Long, long ago, our people lived far to the south. That is why our skins are dark. For many reasons we migrated north. When we arrived, it seemed the thing to do to eat seals. They were plentiful and relatively easy to kill. They of all animals kept us healthy. We lived on the large land north of here where the boats turn toward the islands between the west and east. Our people left a warm land for one that is very cold. We have stories about the black and white seals they ate. They saved our lives. There are brown ones and grayish ones, but the black and white ones fascinated them. But that land is unstable. We had to move. How wonderful it was for our people of long ago to find this place with seals in a lake! When we don't come to the lake to eat seal, we are not as healthy. We have been eating seal ever since. A lot of our culture centers on seal, because we believe it gives us life."

"But you are inland. Seals don't live here." Manak-na was fascinated.

"They live in the big lake," Komus said, wondering whether he should share this privileged information.

"Seals in a lake?" Manak-na asked. "I thought they were only sea creatures."

"Well, what can I say? They live here." Komus wondered how they got to the lake, but didn't spend a lot of time thinking about it.

After the cleanup, people came to the newcomers, carrying tree limbs and branches, which they put in a sheltered area with a view to the lake. It was material for a lean-to, a very large lean-to; one that would accommodate more than the six newcomers. They helped the newcomers put it together, so they'd be prepared for sleep. Many evergreen branches were placed on the ground of the lean-to to make it soft and fragrant. Gourds of water were brought and placed under the sheltering roof, so the newcomers would not thirst. The People were grateful for the help and for the shelter. When they were in the lean-to alone, they spoke in the language of the People. They had not noticed any who could understand that language, but they took care what they said. There were none of Komus's people who spoke the language of the People.

When Wisdom restored color to the land, it was with great golden skies.

"When it looks like this," Mitrak said, "You'd expect to hear a shout from Wisdom." She combed her hair, picked her teeth, and tried to make herself tidy. "We've forgotten the gifts," she said to anyone who would listen.

"You're right," Aryna said. "Let's take them to the morning meal."

"Good idea," Kai-na added.

When Wisdom returned color to the land, they gathered the combs, tools, and red ochre and went to the place where the people of Komus planned to eat. His people had noticed that the newcomers had gifts, and they were eager to see what that meant. All gathered together to see what they could learn.

Manak-na spoke, "We brought gifts to you from our people." Tongip-na laid a small piece of leather on the ground. "These are combs for hair." He demonstrated how to use them, noticing that these people definitely had use for them. He laid them on the skin that was on the ground. "These are knives for your women to share. We have a young woman who has been making tools since she was a child. She made these for the smaller hands of women and for more intricate use. They can be used for preparing food or cutting items for sewing." He laid them on the skin beside the combs. "This is ground red ochre. Do you use it?" he asked.

The people looked at him uncomprehendingly.

"It comes from grinding red ochre rocks. You can see that I paint my face with it. It is something you can use for making marks on cave walls or putting on the skins of the live or dead. It is a preservative for skin." He laid the container on the skin on the ground with the combs and the knives.

"This comes from us as a gift with good wishes."

A very old man stood carefully, looking at Manak-na. "Your people have been very generous. I thank you for the gifts and for accompanying Komus home. I delight to know that the evil man is buried and can cause no more problems. We have also heard that the boatbuilders' place exists no longer. That cannot be. We will have to send more people there to rebuild. Those people will have to pass your place. Will you permit them to pass?"

"Of course," Manak-na said.

"Some of our people live on the other side of the sea. We cannot leave them without any communication available to this side of the sea."

Manak-na wondered who Komus's people on the other side were. All he recognized were Mol and People. He supposed that they were not really all that different. And some did have darker skins, but he thought it was the darkness of getting more than enough sun on the skin. Maybe not.

Newcomers watched as Komus's people came to look at the gifts. They tried combing their hair and discovered rats. Aryna was near a woman who tried to comb her own hair. Aryna showed her how to remove the rats before combing, so it wouldn't hurt so much. She did it so gently that the woman was grateful. When her hair was fully combed, she was smiling as she felt her silken hair.

The newcomers were ready to return home. They didn't want to seem too eager to leave, but they were anxious to return. They discussed it with Komus, and he understood. He assured them that his people would understand. At the evening meal there was discussion between the two people after Manak-na had made the admission that they had originally planned to trek as far as the lake to make that their home. The people of Komus made it clear that an adequate number of animals to take care of two sets of people could not be found at the lake. They asked the newcomers whether they hadn't noticed a lack of meat animals on the way up. They thought about it and agreed. They asked what happened.

"Years ago," a man said, "Before the people left for the west, we over-hunted. We had to feed ourselves and take food to the evil man. The animals began to die out, because they could not raise enough young to replace what we were taking. We have been very careful in the last few generations to come here to fish and eat more fish, and we always take as many seals as we are able. We need the seals for our health, and that way we can help land animals build up the herds again. But it will take a while. I'm glad you didn't come here to live. We might have fought over the few animal resources we have. That would not be good."

"I agree, that would not be good," Kai-na said.

"We have found our new home, and it is good," Manak-na added. "We like it a lot right where we are. The white rain is deep in the season of cold days, and that makes hunting difficult. To come further north would make things worse, we reasoned."

Komus added that he'd told them about having to wear double outside garments in the season of cold days just to go outside. He assured them he'd told them how difficult hunting would be in the cold times.

For the first time Manak-na wondered about his friend, Komus. He wondered whether the man was making things sound worse than they really were to prevent others from migrating to the area to eat seals. The idea consumed Manak-na's mind web. He could find no way to prove it, so he left it alone. He berated himself for being suspicious without foundation regarding a man he'd known for a while as a friend. After all, his people had no plans to move to the big lake anymore. It did, however, add an edge to the way he viewed Komus.

The newcomers assured them that they planned to leave in the morning. The people of Komus brought them a lot of jerky for their return.

Before the sun appeared in the sky, the People were gone. Manak-na and Tongip-na both had bad feelings. It was the way hunters felt when they sensed they were being stalked. The six of them discussed it. They made as little in the way of tracks as they could. They climbed over the hill and down the other side, keeping to the rocky ground. By the time they reached the woodland that edged the path, they had trekked far. Manak-na and Kai-na gathered branches that had leaves. They brushed out their foot tracks as they walked. When they came upon a forest with large width trees, they told the women to go uphill to guard their backpacks. The women were aware that there was a threat, and they were unwilling to hide while the men fought. They carefully retraced their way back down to the place near where the men waited. They had slingshots and a few women's spears. They could see quicker than the men the seven men who followed them. The men were trying to read the tracks that had been brushed.

Manak-na heard them before he saw them. He elbowed the other men. They were prepared. Each stood well hidden with spear raised. The men were almost on top of them when they each thrust their first spear into a man, killing three. They were on to their second set of kills when Tongip-na caught his foot in a root and fell. Manak-na and Kai-na speared two more of Komus's men. The remaining two were about to spear Tongip-na, when from the bushes three slingshots spun and the remaining two men were hit in the temple with rocks from the slingshots. One man, speared in the side, remained alive barely.

Domur went to that man and stood over him. "Coward!" she said with venom. "We brought you gifts and you tried to take our lives. What manner of men are you?"

The man had a spear sticking through his side. He was in much pain. He said, "We don't trust you. Your Wise One will come to demand food and gifts from us. You'll come to the big lake to eat our seals. We don't want you here. We thought if we could destroy you, we could sneak up on your people to destroy you all."

"Foolish man! We are the best friends you could have. We are People of our word." Manak-na breathed heavily and spoke in a measured way.

Domur stood there glaring at the man in anger. "Coward!" She spat out the word and roughly jerked the spear from the dying man making his blood flow more freely.

"We have to retrace our steps," Manak-na said, jerking his spear from the other dead man. Tongip-na and Kai-na pulled their spears free from the dead. Tongip-na noticed his spear point had broken. It was still useable but not quite as effective.

"What do you mean?" Tongip-na asked.

"I mean that we have to go back there to make it clear to all that their little plan didn't work, and that they had better stay away from us, or we'll return to destroy them utterly."

"What?" Domur was totally confused.

"If we fail to react they will judge us weak. They will come to destroy us. We have to stand up, *now*. When they see that three men and three women killed seven of their hunters, they'll think twice about taking advantage of us."

The People tied the dead men together and began to drag them to the top of the hill. They hoped going down would be easier. It was. They arrived at the camp to be met by Komus.

"What is this?" Komus asked in dismay, looking at the faces of the dead.

"These men followed us to murder us," Manak-na spat out the words.

"By all the gods," he turned to the old man, "are you all crazy? These people are my friends! You have done evil, when they have done nothing but good to you."

"We are trying to protect ourselves," the old man said quietly.

"That is a certain way to bring war upon us all," Komus said. He turned to his people. "I will no longer live where Punilok is leader. Replace him now, or I leave."

Punilok said in a quiet voice, "All those who will follow Komus walk to the far side of the creek."

All the people of Komus went to the far side of the creek except Punilok and his wife.

"How many of you knew what the hunters were doing?" Komus asked.

Two dead hunters' wives whose tear stained faces gave away their relationship to the dead bodies, stepped forward. "I knew," one said, and the other said, "I also knew."

"None of the rest of you knew?"

No one else indicated they knew.

"Why didn't either of you say anything?"

"Who would I tell?" one asked.

"I was frightened," the other added.

Komus said, glaring, "You are as responsible as these men for what has been done. The deaths of our own people are your responsibility as if you'd murdered them with your own hands. These People will never trust us again.

Before we lost seven hunters, they had three times as many hunters as we have. When I go back with some of you to the boatbuilders' place, we may all be killed, and it will serve us right. Such evil foolishness. Where did this evil arise? It must die!"

The People watched as Komus took on the leadership. They would never have guessed he had it in him.

"You two women and Punilok—over there," he ordered. They moved to the log where he pointed. "Who are the guards today?" he asked. Two men stepped forward.

"Where's the third?"

"We've only had two for a long time."

"Takuk," you are the third guard. "Guards get your spears—now!"

Punilok's wife ran to him and wrapped her arms around him.

The guards got their spears and returned to Komus. Komus looked them steadily in the eyes, "Kill them," he said. Komus's people were deadly silent. They were aching inside, but they were terrified to try to stop what was occurring. Without hesitating, the guards speared the four people.

Komus continued. "Eleven people died today. Eleven people! All for stupidity! We now have very few people to call our own. We will leave this place and trek to the boatbuilders' place. No longer will you live near the big lake. We will leave in the morning. I will ask you, Manak-na, my true friend, may we pass your cave on our way?"

"As long as you have no thoughts of murder," Manak-na said flatly.

"We will not, I assure you."

"Then, Komus and the people of Komus, you are free to pass by."

"I am so sorry, my friend. I hope that sometime, you will feel comfortable with me again. You have never done anything to deserve what happened to you today. I regret sincerely that it was my people who did it."

"Komus, I do not hold this against you, but it will be hard for me to trust your people."

"I don't blame you, Manak-na. They need strong leadership. I will try my utmost to provide it."

"Looks like you're off to a good start," Manak-na said.

Komus nodded. The newcomers left.

Komus headed to the place where his people gathered. They would be talking for a long time. He would not stop until he felt confident that he had authority clearly placed over every person in his group, starting with the guards.

By high sun the People had made it back to the place where the hunters tried to kill them. It was a sad place. "Try not to put this place into your minds," Tongip-na said. "It's best to forget some things." He pulled out his water bladder and took a drink.

"I agree," Manak-na said. "I'm not going to forget Komus's actions this day. I didn't know what we'd face there. He definitely wants to do what's right, and he wants to remain our friend."

"He does," Kai-na agreed. "When he ordered those three people killed, I couldn't believe what I was hearing. It's too bad about the old woman."

"What would you have done?" Manak-na asked, leaning against a tree trunk.

"I didn't think of it from that end," Kai-na replied. "Well, I'm not sure."

"I'd have done exactly what he did," Manak-na said.

"You would have?" Kai-na asked, shocked.

"I'd have done the same thing," Tongip-na said. "At times like that you have to do what's right even if it kills you, and you have to be decisive about it."

"Yes, Kai-na," I would have done what he did. "Remember hearing about the young man who abused Minagle—his name was Reemast?"

"I remember that. There's no real story about it. Reemast was never found again."

Manak-na looked up. He pushed off from the tree trunk. "Reemast was never found again, because two of the People with Wamumur's blessing killed Reemast and buried him."

"What?" Tongip-na shouted. "You're teasing." Tongip-na almost dropped his water bladder. As it was he soaked part of his tunic.

"I swear that I am not." Manak-na took a drink of water.

"You mean the People murder?" Kai-na asked.

"Of course, not! Murder means that there is ulterior desire for the person who commits the murder, some gain to be had from it—an example is a man who kills his friend because he wants his friend's wife. That's murder. Someone stands to benefit personally. Nobody wanted Reemast dead, but he would not give up his desire to harm Minagle. He burned hatred for her. It meant that the People would have to divide their time between whatever they were doing and guarding Reemast. Reemast would take no responsibility whatever, and he resented others guarding him. It was wrong, so Reemast was killed, not murdered, to protect Minagle and anyone else Reemast might want to hurt in the future. It was as Wamumur expressed it regarding Ghanya—the evil doer was like bad fruit that would cause the whole gathering of fruit to spoil. Better to eliminate the bad fruit than to destroy all the fruit. There is a huge difference between those two words, kill and murder. Wisdom tells us not to murder. Wisdom does not tell us not to kill. When those hunters sneaked up on us, was it in accordance with Wisdom for us to kill them?"

Everyone said, "Yes."

The women had listened carefully. Domur had heard Manak-na discuss this before, so she was not surprised.

Kai-na would spend much time thinking about the difference between killing and murdering. It expanded his mind web. He had thought the two words interchangeable. Clearly they were not.

They trekked and trekked possibly faster than normal, because they were happy to get as much distance from the people of Komus as possible. With the full moon, they could travel even later into the night, but they did not wish to encounter a bear on the trek. They would be very careful. Finally, when they were all fatigued, they stopped, put up a small lean-to, created a small fire, and slept. The bright rays of sun from the next day awakened them. They put out the embers of the fire and continued trekking.

For many, many days they continued to trek. They tired of jerky and decided to take the next animal they encountered so they could enjoy some real food before continuing on. It took three days to find a medium sized deer. Kai-na speared it and the group made a decent lean-to and a good fire and readied themselves to enjoy roasted deer. As they settled down to enjoy the scent of the seasoned deer, they heard noise of people. Tongip-na and Manak-na actually groaned.

"Are those the people of Komus?" Tongip-na asked, leaping to his feet.

"I don't know whether to say I hope so or not, but who else would they be?" Manak-na replied grabbing his spears.

Kai-na was on his feet and the women had pulled out their slings and some small rocks in readiness.

Komus and his people were trekking the path just as he said they would. While the People had been searching for an animal to fill their bellies, they had slowed. They knew Komus had a total now of five hunters and many women and children, some of the women were aged but not terribly old. These people were not a huge threat, but the three hunters and their wives were outnumbered.

The people of Komus came to a halt the moment they realized they had arrived at the camp of the People.

"I am sorry that we have overtaken you," Komus said while his people stood there wishing to be anywhere else.

"We must have slowed while hunting for deer," Manak-na said, noticing that Wisdom was about to suck color from the land.

"Camp here," Manak-na said. "We have enough to share. You might want to search for something to add to the meat."

Komus's hunters didn't need to be told twice. They began to set up the camp back down a good distance from the People. The women either tended children or began a search for vegetables while others set up a hearth. They worked very quickly as if they expected retribution when they did wrong. Komus had apparently been relentless in his taking authority. Manak-na approved in this case.

"We will have to post a guard tonight," Manak-na said to Tongip-na.

"I agree. This is definitely a time to be very careful."

They whispered among themselves preparing a guard for the night. Fortunately there were no clouds so their ability to tell time by the large and small snares would be easy. They planned to eat, sleep briefly, and then slip off to continue the trek long before the sun was up.

The meat was finally cooked and with the seasonings they had, it was causing not only the People but also Komus's people to salivate. Manak-na called to Komus. His people brought their bowls. The People generously filled the bowls of Komus's people. Those people thanked them and went to their camp to eat. Little was said between the two sets of people. The People brought their bowls with uncooked greens already placed in the bottom of the bowls. The meat was placed atop the greens. It was cooked to perfection, but then they had Mitrak with them.

They checked the sky. They found the tail of the small snare in the sky and the tip of the string where it would be tied. That was the star that never moved. They sought the tail of the big snare and found it. When the tail of the big snare pointed to the northeast, it would be time for Manak-na to awaken Tongip-na and Kai-na.

The two men went to sleep immediately. Manak-na guarded. At Komus's camp there was a little noise, but they were keeping the level of noise to a minimum. Mitrak, Domur, and Aryna lay on their sleeping skins, but they were not sleeping. They, too, felt that this could be a situation that could turn to attack.

Manak-na awakened the men when it was time. He asked if they'd like to start trekking, since he wasn't sleepy. They agreed and went to wake the women, who were not asleep. With great stealth, they rolled their sleeping skins, attached them to their backpacks, and stole off into the night, each with a large hunk of the deer meat in their hands. The remainder of the deer meat was left for Komus's people.

They walked rapidly, faster, they were certain, than people with children and older adults could walk. They continued the rapid rate for what felt like endless days with minimum sleep until they returned to their home cave.

It was high sun. People came to greet them, streaming down the hillside in great numbers. There was a festive air about their return, but it was as if a gray cloud hung off to the side. Manak-na figured it out as soon as he saw Untuk-na's face.

He walked to Untuk-na and placed his right hand on Untuk-na's left shoulder. He looked into his eyes. "What is it, my Brother?" he asked Untuk-na.

"Ki'ti is not doing well." His face was gaunt and serious.

Manak-na dropped his backpack and spears and ran up the hill, almost pushing People out of the way. He entered the cave at a run and then tried to slow. He found Ki'ti lying on skins near a small hearth towards the back of the cave. Ti'ti sat beside her arm.

"What is it, Ki'ti?" he asked with tremendous concern, kneeling at her side. Ti'ti moved toward Ki'ti's head. Ki'ti looked so lifeless and tired with dark circles under her eyes. She raised her head and he reached down and lifted her to hug her. She was too thin. He could feel her bones, as if she had no meat or fat at all but rather had a pouch of liquid that moved when he held her. He laid her back with extreme gentleness.

"Ah, Manak-na. I am so glad," she paused, "you made it back," she paused, "before I go to Wisdom." Her eyes closed and he feared she'd slipped off to sleep. In a few moments she opened her eyes again. "I've talked to," she paused, "Untuk-na." She shut her eyes, then, opened them moments later. "I want to talk to you." She closed her eyes as if struggling to breathe to get the words out. "So much has changed," she paused briefly, "too fast." She reached for his hand. Her hand was icy cold. "The changes," she paused, "are good. So far." Again she paused. "We have added," she paused and shut her eyes, "many different ones to become People." She lay still, barely breathing. "Eventually, they will add," she paused, "things that are not good." She lay still with her eyes shut, so that Manak-na was certain she slept. She opened her eyes, "Find a way," she paused, "to safeguard," she paused again, "our ways." She looked deep into his eyes. She could see how he hurt for her. "Brother," she paused, "do not weep," she paused, "for me." She shut her eyes and rested. "I go to see," she paused, "the face of Wisdom." She rested. "Imagine that!" The smile on her gaunt face made him forget for an instant how terrible she looked. "I need," she paused, "to rest." She shut her eyes and slept.

Manak-na was devastated. Although Ki'ti was younger than he, he had no memory of life before she was part of it. To see her like this ripped his belly apart. Ki'ti had always been there. He raced outside and up the hill. He topped the hill and slid and ran down the other side. He howled and shrieked and beat the ground with his fists. Finally emptied, he lay on the ground and looked into the trees. A raven perched above him.

"Don't say a single thing," he dared the raven. The raven was silent, as silent tears ran from the eyes of Manak-na. After much time had passed, Untuk-na came down the hill and touched the shoulder of Manak-na. Manak-na turned to look at him horrorstricken.

"No, she's not gone yet. I just came to see about you."

"I couldn't contain my grief so I came here to shout and wail it out. I'm back to myself, now," Manak-na said. "How long has she been like this?"

"A half-moon. One day she seemed to be adapting well and the next, she was like this." Untuk-na hurt with every word.

"She told me to safeguard the People against evil."

"She told me the same thing. She loves the People as if every one of us were one of her children," Untuk-na said. He was squatting on the ground. "She fears we'll change for the worse."

"I know," Manak-na added, getting to his feet. "How I love her."

"I, too. She doesn't eat. There is much liquid in her belly that pushes against her stomach. She has no hunger. It is very hard for her to breathe, probably for the same reason." Untuk-na leaned against a tree. He felt finally that he could share his grief with someone who would respond as he did.

Manak-na went to him and hugged him, something not forbidden or taboo, but done only on the rarest of occasions. Untuk-na returned the hug. "I love you, Brother. Ki'ti could not have had a better husband in the whole world. She adores you."

"Thank you, Manak-na. I, too, know the love she has for you. At first, I was envious of her love for you. I came to know how deep it was, but that it was sister for brother, different from our love."

"Had I been you, I might easily have felt the same way you did." Manak-na scratched his head. He hoped he hadn't picked up head lice.

"Will you tell me if you see any head lice. My head itches badly right here."

Untuk-na looked carefully. "No lice, you've got a patch of very dry skin there."

"What a relief!" Manak-na said.

"We are both charged with protecting the People against evil. That's an enormous responsibility. I hope you have some ideas." Untuk-na felt laden with responsibility. He had relief in being able to share it with someone else.

Manak-na shrugged. "We'll have to talk when things are not so emotional. We have another problem. Seven of Komus's people followed us when we left. They were planning to murder us. With the help of our women, we killed all of them. We dragged the bodies back to their camp and had it out. Komus had not known of the plot, until we dragged the bodies back, and he was horrified. He took over power and killed four other people, three of whom were complicit in the attempted murder. They are moving from near the lake to the boatbuilders' place. I think they will continue boatbuilding. But they will soon be passing by here. We need to be alert."

With a nod, Untuk-na agreed and the two of them climbed the hill and returned to the home cave in silence. Each thought about the need to safeguard their People from evil. Ki'ti was indeed Wise One, even if she had abandoned the title.

Domur met Manak-na at the entryway. "I am so saddened," she said.

"I, too. It rips my belly and my mind web." Manak-na wanted to hold in any more emotional outbursts. "I noticed that my backpack and spears are up here."

"Yes. Tongip-na brought the backpack and Kai-na brought the spears. You have thoughtful friends."

Manak-na nodded. He glanced back at Ki'ti. She was covered with her sleeping skins and appeared to sleep. Ti'ti was lying on the skins right beside her. He couldn't help smiling at the tiny dog. When anyone thought of Ki'ti, they thought of the dogs.

Likichi walked by and Manak-na stopped her.

She looked at him and hugged him. "I know it must have come as a shock to see her this way."

"Yes, Mother. How long does she have?"

"She could go at any time. She struggles to breathe. Sometimes it's as if it's just too much effort."

"I cannot imagine life without Ki'ti."

"Well, Son, you will soon have to. Just remember her at her best and think on that."

"How is Ahna taking it?" He asked with obvious concern.

"She grieves, but she stops by Ki'ti often and talks to her, asking her not to speak. She speaks of beautiful things she's seen or how someone was kind to another. She says things that give Ki'ti reason to hope all will be well. She loves Ki'ti. I think she's the only mother Ahna's ever had. Ahna will be a great Wise One. Already the People depend on her."

"That is good, Mother. Ki'ti must know."

"She knows. For that she thanks Wisdom for your adventure."

Manak-na laughed an open and genuine laugh. The release was helpful.

People gathered for the evening meal and the trekkers were delighted for it was exceptionally good. After cleanup the People gathered for the men's council. Ahna looked around and nodded to Manak-na.

"We had a good trip which I will share at a later time. We also had a bad time. Seven of Komus's people tracked us and tried to murder us after we left to head home. I do not know why they did that. We killed all seven of them. Our women are good warriors! They killed with slingshots!"

Domur, Aryna, and Mitrak looked down. The People murmured among themselves. That was something to approve. Suddenly, palm strikes began. Manak-na joined and then waited for them to stop.

He continued, "We dragged the bodies back to their camp. We saw Komus and told him what happened. He took control of power over his people right then. He discovered two women and one man were complicit in the attempt to murder us. He was horrified at what they'd done and had them slain before our eyes. The wife of one was slain with her husband. Komus is their leader now. He is leading them to the boatbuilders' place. I am not sure what he has in mind. He has few men now. Only five hunters. They are, however, following us."

People at the council looked around nervously.

"We need to be alert. I made them an offer. The evil man had giants working for him. They had subjugated the people of Komus in the area and insisted they give the evil man food and gifts from time to time. The items spread out in the storage cave are gifts given unwillingly to the evil man. I told the people of Komus that whatever was taken from them, they could take from there. I explained that we don't want what belongs to others. They may stop here to ask for their things."

Manak-na looked down.

Ahna looked at the People.

Yomuk-na looked at her.

"I will suggest that we take turns at the observation place. From there you can see part of the path far away. We will have warning when they come."

Ahna looked around.

Patah-na looked at Ahna. She nodded to him.

"I agree with Yomuk-na. That is a good place to observe whoever comes here. I'll be glad to participate in the observing. If you set up a plan to observe, Yomuk-na, just let me know when it's my turn. That is all I have to say."

Ahna looked up and noticed Hupu-na. She nodded to him.

"I, too, will participate. Let me know, Yomuk-na." He looked down.

Ahna looked up and nodded to Meta.

"I have good vision. Add me to your observers," she said enthusiastically.

Yomuk-na got Ahna's nod and assured the People he had enough observers. They would start after the morning meal.

Ki'ti from her bed could hear the meeting. She was so proud of the young People participating to protect all. And Yomuk-na's thinking of it. It was good. She drifted back to sleep.

Manak-na was proud of his nephew. For him to have foreseen the ability to have early warning and plan—it was good.

Ahna looked around and noticed Olintak. She nodded to her.

"We are running low on some of our medicinal herbs. If the weather is good tomorrow, any of you willing to join me to search for replacements please meet me at the entryway after the morning meal." She looked down.

Ahna looked around. She nodded to Sum-na.

"I want to go to the south tomorrow—two hills down. I saw some giant deer, females without young. I would like to take one. Anyone willing to come with me, let me know after the council. That is all I have to say."

Ahna looked up. No one looked at her. She said, "The council has ended for this evening." Because it was the season of warm nights, there was no story. The People headed towards their sleeping skins.

Untuk-na slid under the skins next to Ki'ti whose body was cold despite the covering of multiple skins. She moved, so he knew she still lived. His body ached for her to return to health. How awful it must be, he thought, to lie there and have so much to give, and struggle just to breathe. Ti'ti came over and looked right into Untuk's face. His eyes were shut but he felt someone looking at him. When he opened his eyes, he saw the face of the tiny dog looking at him, a thumb's length from his eyes. He reached out his hand and scratched gently behind the dog's ears. "It's okay, little Ti'ti," he whispered. For a long time Untuk-na listened to the labored breathing of the one above all he loved. Occasionally he'd let a tear fall from his eyes. When she saw one fall, Ti'ti licked the tear from his face. Finally, he slept.

When Wisdom returned color to the land the People had their morning meal. Yomuk-na and those who would take turns observing gathered to discuss who would take first watch, second, and so on. In the same area Sum-na and four other hunters gathered, ready for the hunt. The hunters left. Olintak, Lakop, Phelen, Yoah, and Luga met to go herb hunting.

Yomuk-na took the first turn at the observation place. His cousin Shud, Frakja-na's youngest son of fifteen years, joined him. "I'll help you look," he offered.

"As long as you keep your mind on what you're doing, that's good," Yomuk-na said.

Shud climbed up on the observation platform. The two watched carefully and during the time they spent there, no people were seen on the path.

Hupu-na came to relieve Yomuk-na. "Anything?" he asked.

"Not a thing."

"Can I stay with you?" Shud asked Hupu-na.

"As long as you keep your eyes on the path," Hupu-na said.

"I will," Shud said solemnly.

Again, while Hupu-na was watching, no people appeared on the path.

Meta arrived. "Anything?" she asked.

"No, nothing," Hupu-na replied.

Shud asked, "Can I stay with you?"

Hupu-na said, "He's been here with Yomuk-na and me. He keeps his mind on what he does."

"Very well, Shud." Meta couldn't understand why Shud wanted to stare at the path all day, but she was glad at the same time for company.

They watched and a giant doe with two fawns crossed the path.

"Now, that's something," Shud said.

"True," she replied.

Still no people were seen when it was Patah-na's turn to observe.

Shud asked, "Can I stay with you?"

Meta added, "He's been here with Yomuk-na, Hupu-na, and me. He is helpful and keeps his mind on what he's doing.

Patah-na looked at the young man carefully. "Very well," he said.

"I'll take one moment outside," Shud said.

He returned moments later after running to the privy.

Sum-na and the others returned with a giant deer. It was tough for them to carry it all. Two of the men each struggled to carry a quarter. Sum-na carried the skin rolled around the cleaned guts and carried over his shoulders.

They took it all to the meat preparation cave, where they'd return after the evening meal.

When it was time for the evening meal, Wisdom had already sucked color from the land. Patah-na and Shud went to the home cave to eat as soon as darkness came.

Untuk-na sat next to Ki'ti and watched her struggling to breathe. She had hardly wakened all day. She just slept, breathing somewhat irregularly with her chest moving as it had for days in an unnatural rhythm. He knew her body was shutting down. It hurt to watch, but he'd rather be nowhere else. He gently picked up her hand. It was so cold.

Ti'ti went to Untuk-na and sat beside him leaning against his side. She looked up at his face, and he reached down to pet her. She seemed, to him, not to understand. He thought she needed comforting.

Because there was nothing to report, there was no men's council. People went to their sleeping skins as if something were about to happen, but no one knew what. There was a sense of expectancy.

Two guards were at the entryway, out far enough that they were able to see in the dark without the hearth fires interfering. Low murmurs wafted on the breeze between them. There appeared to be no people out in the dark.

When Wisdom restored color to the land it was with a few white clouds and rays of golden light shining through. As soon as the guards saw the first glow of sunshine, they entered the home cave and their entrance stirred the People to awaken. Soon hearth fires glowed to flame and the morning meal was available. People rolled their sleeping skins up and put them against the walls of the cave, ready for places to sit for eating. Another day.

Yomuk-na took a handful of jerky and headed for the observation place, shadowed by Shud.

"Shud, what is it that interests you in the observation place?" Yomuk-na asked.

Shud thought how to put into words why he wanted to be there. "I am worried about these people of Komus who would have murdered our People. Imagine cowards who would murder women! I am outraged when I think of it. I want to do everything I can do to protect our People."

"Why didn't you volunteer, when I asked?"

"Yomuk-na, I am young yet. I haven't had a lot of experience. I can think, though, that if two people are here instead of one, there is a better chance that Komus's people won't slip by unobserved."

"You have thought well," Yomuk-na admitted. "That's why you've been so diligent?"

"Yes."

"I commend you Shud. Even Wisdom would approve."

"Thank you, Cousin." Shud glowed in Yomuk-na's praise. Yomuk-na remembered when Manak-na would praise him for some reason. He smiled to himself.

Yomuk-na looked at the place where the path was. "Look, Shud, what is that?"

"They have arrived. Should we not notify the People?"

"Yes. Let's go alert them and get the children up to the home cave."

The two went down the hill quickly and Manak-na whistled the signal for all to come immediately to the home cave. All arrived and the People went to the council place to hear what Manak-na was about to say. Through it all Ki'ti slept.

"We have observed Komus's people on the hill we can see from the observation place. They should be here before high sun. All people under the age of twelve must remain in the home cave. Are they all here now?"

Mothers looked around. Men did also. No child under twelve was missing.

"Very well, keep them supervised. I'd like to see seasoned hunters find trees for protection and go to the lower levels in case of trouble. Bring a supply of spears. I will meet the people of Komus on the level ground below. I will permit only two men to come to the cave where there are possessions that were given as gifts to the evil man. They may take what is theirs and be on their way. I will offer food for them to take with them for their evening meal, and enough to carry with them to see them through getting settled in their new home."

"Aren't you being too generous?" Arkan-na asked.

"I am being no more generous than I'd hope others would be if the situation were reversed. It will not affect our storage that much and could be the difference between their making it in the new place and starving. I do not want to have any part in the starvation of other people, even if there were evil ones among them."

"I see your point, Manak-na." Arkan-na still shivered when he thought of seven hunters attacking the six of his People, only three of which were male.

"I would like them to see that we are on alert, but that we are also thoughtful and generous. I want to give them absolutely no reason ever to consider attacking us again. I also want every man who has facial hair down there with spears ready. I want them to realize our strength is far superior to theirs. But be sure to keep a tree between you and them."

The men gathered their weapons. A few young women took their slingshots and some rocks and headed down also.

"Where are you going," Manak-na stopped Tiki, Luga, and Mona

Mona stood straight, making herself as tall as possible, looking up at Manak-na. "We are the most accurate with slingshots. We are going to climb the big trees and be ready to take aim from there. We have learned from your travel that women can kill if there is a need."

Manak-na stood there and laughed out loud. Hunters turned back to see what caused the mirth. That was definitely out of character with their present purpose.

When they discovered what the young women planned, they, too, laughed.

"What's even more amusing," Manak-na added, "is that I intend to take them up on their offer. Women killed some of these men with slingshots. We cannot trivialize them."

The young women stood stiff when they heard Manak-na's words. They wanted to jump and shout for joy, but they kept a solemn demeanor and went to look for suitable trees to climb. They needed trees with large openings so rocks from the slings would not be deflected.

By the time the men had positioned themselves, they could see Komus's people turning in their direction. When they were just about to the path to the cave, Manak-na stepped out alone to greet them. The people of Komus came to a quick stop.

"You have made good time," Manak-na observed.

The people of Komus were beginning to detect the men and young women all poised with spears and slingshots. They were startled but did not seem frightened.

"We have two things for you. First, you have your things that were given as gifts that weren't gifts but rather a type of extortion. You may send two men up to get what is yours. I will accompany them. Second, we have food for you to carry with you to keep you until you can make a store for yourself for the season of cold days."

"Manak-na, my people have already discussed this. We willingly forfeit the things that were taken as gifts because of how our people treated you. We do not feel that we have any right to accept your generous gift of food to help us."

"We don't want your things that were taken from you. You are quite free to get them. Just tell two of your men what they are and I will take them to the cave to get them. You err in not accepting the food we offer. You will need it to assure your passage through the season of cold days. I urge you to reconsider. It is a true gift, and gifts have no conditions regarding whether one has a right to receive—a gift is simply a transfer of something from one person or people to another without any condition of any kind."

Komus and the three hunters talked among themselves.

"We are willing to gather some of the gifts that were taken from us by the evil one, and we accept your very generous offer of food."

"Good. Tell the men what are the gifts you had to give the evil man."

The people of Komus talked briefly, and two men came slowly to present themselves to Manak-na.

"Good," Manak-na said, "Lay your spears down. Let's go." He began to lead the men up the hill.

At that precise moment, as if planned, quietly the dogs came down the hill from their assigned places. They reached the base of the hill, formed a line along the base of the hill, and sat there staring at the people of Komus. They did not offer to bite or snarl, only stared at the people with their golden eyes. Manak-na looked at the dogs and had to stifle the inappropriate urge to release his mirth in a booming laugh. How the dogs decided to do what they'd done escaped him, but he was grateful for the animals' action.

Komus's people were filled with terror. The dogs were wolves to them. They were in awe of the people from the beginning—they had rid a living place of evil; they were astonished when three men and three women returned with seven of their hunters dead; and to add to that, they had trained wolves to protect them—it was too much for the people of Komus to comprehend. As they grew back into a viable people the stories they would tell about these wolves magnified into legend, and from legend to myth.

The men went into the storage cave. There on the flat rock lay a number of gifts to the evil man. The men took three things, a piece of jade, a rock that appeared to have no meaning, and a small leather pouch.

"That is all?" Manak-na asked.

"I see none of the other things," one of the men replied.

"Look again," Manak-na suggested.

They did, but whatever they sought was not there.

"What are you looking for?" Manak-na asked. "I thought a purple bowl was taken from you."

"A string of bear teeth and another pouch made of caribou fur." The men were eager to go back down the hill. "That's all we came to get."

"Very well," Manak-na replied. "Let's go back down."

By the time they got down, men from the People had brought two stretchers piled high with food. They had skin coverings over them and were lashed onto the stretcher so that nothing would fall off. The people of Komus were amazed.

Manak-na walked over to Komus and put his hand on the man's shoulder. "Komus, how will you get seal?"

The man looked into his eyes. Manak-na noticed the fatigue in them—and sadness. Komus said, "I have thought of that. We can send smaller boats north to gather seals, maybe even some of the black and white ones, prepare them for us, and then return with them for storage. It won't be totally fresh, but it'll do. I'm surprised you thought about that, Manak-na."

"You had said your people need to eat seal for health and around it your culture is based. I am just concerned for you, my friend. We have offered meat, but we have no seal. Fare well, Komus."

"And you also, Manak-na." Komus turned and his people began the long trek to the boatbuilders' place. They tried to pick up the stretchers and found that they were very heavy. It took four men to carry one stretcher. Young men had to help because there were not enough older men to carry the stretchers.

Yomuk-na signaled to Shud. They returned to the observation place to assure themselves that the men did in fact leave. Untuk-na noticed and approved.

Girls climbed down from the trees and the men came uphill from their places near big trees. Dogs returned to their places. Their meeting had been successful, they all felt. It was clear that the people of Komus were slightly frightened by them. For the present that seemed a good idea.

"Untuk-na," Manak-na said, "please, add this to the collection on the ledge. It is the type of bowl from the Maknu-na and Rimlad story. It was from Komus's people, I think, but they didn't want it, or else they were unsure it was theirs. It will be good for us to see something from an old story."

Untuk-na took the purple shell and placed it on the shelf he'd made. He wished Ki'ti had known. Maybe deep in her sleep she did? He wondered.

They all went back to the cave to put away their weapons and chat among themselves. After the initial confusion they found places to sit and chat. Suddenly, from the relative quiet, tiny little Ti'ti threw her head back and began the most soulful howl anyone could imagine, and her size belied the volume she could put out.

Untuk-na ran to Ki'ti and found she no longer breathed. He rested his head on her chest and silently wept. Ti'ti continued the sad howl, her tiny mouth looking almost like a circle. Her eyes searched nervously while her head was thrown back and she continued to howl. She was inconsolable. Likichi came and put a band around Ki'ti's jaw, tying the band over her head, so her mouth would remain closed. She closed Ki'ti's eyes. No announcement was necessary.

The dog had done that. Oddly, the howl seemed utterly appropriate by the inhabitants of the cave, though it began to get on Likichi's nerves.

Ahna came over and picked up Ti'ti. "You're supposed to come with me little one," Ahna said. Ti'ti leaned her tiny body against Ahna and stopped howling. She looked up to Ahna's face with her too big eyes as if asking many questions in silence. Ahna stroked her little frame and tried to comfort her. "It'll be good in time, little Ti'ti. Give it time."

Some of the men went to the place where tools were kept in the storage cave now. They gathered tools for breaking up the grasses and for digging out soil. They would dig a grave for Ki'ti. As they began, honest tears flowed from their eyes and ran unchecked. They did not feel embarrassed or unmanly; they adored their former Wise One. She had played a part many times in the lives of each of them, making their lives infinitely better. How they would miss her! They dug deep.

Likichi, Ahna, and Elemaea cleaned Ki'ti and put her best tunic on her bony frame. They laid her on Ahna's chinchilla skin that was given her by Rokuk. It was Ahna's gift to cover Ki'ti in the grave. Men would carry her body down to the burial site in it. The women had done all they could do.

Domur carried a container of red ochre to where Ki'ti lay in the home cave. It was a large container. She began with Ki'ti's face and neck. She went to every part of her skin that was exposed and put the red ochre powder on her skin. She used a lot, but it didn't matter. She wanted Ki'ti to be preserved. Tears fell and she continued, rubbing the powder between Ki'ti's toes.

Some People were surprised when the chinchilla skin with Ki'ti's body was carried down to the grave and uncovered. The red ochre was covering Ki'ti completely. Somehow, though, to all it seemed right.

Ahna carried the little dog down to the grave site. Children had been scouring the hills for flowers and had amassed an extraordinary amount of them. She watched as they passed by Ki'ti's grave to toss in the flowers.

Ahna went to the place where she was supposed to stand by Ki'ti's grave. She held Ti'ti and thought back to her arrival among the People. She remembered how Ki'ti had treated her. She remembered when Ki'ti realized she had been given the memory for the stories.

Ahna wanted to weep, but she had responsibilities to carry out and could not take the time to weep. She felt she must honor Ki'ti by withholding her emotions and telling the story. Holding Ti'ti helped. The little dog snuggled as close to her as she could get.

The circle formed around the grave. To Ahna's left the People began to tell what Ki'ti had meant to them. This telling took a long time. Ahna had never seen a grave side honoring last this long. Manak-na later would tell her it was the longest he ever experienced. Stories of Ki'ti poured out of the People, things nobody had ever heard before. It would become legend. Ahna would need to make many stories for the People. She listened carefully. When the circle returned to her she shared her love for the woman who loved her and taught her to love. Then she began:

"In the beginning, Wisdom made the world. He made it by speaking. His words created. He spoke the water and the land into existence, the night and day, the plants that grow in the dirt, and the animals that live on the dirt, and those that live in the water and in the air. Then he went to the navel of the earth. There he found good red soil and started to form it into a shape with his hands. He made it to look a little like himself. Then he inhaled the good air and breathed it into the mouth of the man he created. The man came to life. Then he took some of the clay left from the man and he made woman. He inhaled and breathed life into her. Wisdom created a feast. He killed an aurochs, skinned it, made clothing for the man and woman from the aurochs, and then roasted the aurochs for the feast. The man and the woman watched carefully and quietly to see how he killed the aurochs, how he skinned it, how he made clothing from its skin, and how he roasted it. They paid good attention and they were able to survive by doing what they had seen done."

Ahna took a brief time to keep herself organized. She still held Ti'ti.

"The People were special and Wisdom pronounced that the man was to treat the land and the water and the animals and the woman the way he wanted to be treated—good. And the same was true of the woman. And it went well for a long time. But Wisdom hadn't made the People of stone. He had made them of dirt, knowing that they shouldn't have lives that would go on too long for they might get prideful and forget Wisdom. That is good because People should not be without Wisdom. They would die."

Ahna took another brief break to breathe deeply to keep from weeping.

"That is why the People return to Wisdom when they die. They are placed in the earth and Wisdom knows. When Wisdom hears of a death of the People, Wisdom waits until the grave is filled back. He waits until it is dark. Then he causes the earth to pull on the spirit of the dead to draw that person's spirit back through the dirt of the earth to the navel from which all People came, the navel of the earth where the red clay for making the first man was. The dead spirits depart for the navel of Wisdom. That is where they reside for all time. All People's bodies return to the dirt. But their spirit, that essence of the person made by the One Who Made Us, is pulled back to Wisdom in the place where first man was made, and Wisdom keeps all those he chooses with him there, safe and loved. There is a cycle Wisdom made: a cycle from the navel to the navel. He keeps the spirits of those whom he chooses and he destroys those whom he hates. Wisdom hates those who hate him, those who ignore him, those who would be hurtful to him or the land or water or to those living things Wisdom made including People."

Ahna looked up. What a tribute it was to Ki'ti to see all the faces in grief, having said such lovely things about her, faces tear streaked but reverently quiet. It was good. Ahna wanted to throw herself down and wrap her arms about Ki'ti's body, to weep, to be unreasonable. But she was Wise One and had severely restricted behavior expected of her. She had to be the mature one, the one who could be counted on to hold together. She would do it. She would hold together no matter what happened in her lifetime—out of respect to Ki'ti. She would be a good Wise One—for the sake of Ki'ti.

She put her free arm around Elemaea. "I loved her," she said.

"I know." Elemaea put her arm around Ahna. "Ahna, I will help you in any way I can."

"Thank you, Sister. I will always need you." The two walked up the hill hand in hand while Ahna carried Ti'ti.

Untuk-na stayed behind as others left. He knelt at the grave side and would not leave until Wisdom sucked color from the land. Then, he knew, Ki'ti was fully gone to Wisdom.

Manak-na went up the hill hand in hand with Domur. "Will you walk with me over the hill?" he asked.

"Of course," she replied.

They climbed to the top and Manak-na showed her the way he normally went to the bottom of the hill. They climbed the next hill to the place where the red ochre was. Domur had never seen the bald hill where the ochre was available and the strange stones were assembled.

"What is the purpose of these stones?" Domur asked, fascinated.

"I have no idea. I've never really examined them well."

The two began to look carefully at the stones. They had odd markings on them. They looked at the stones and realized that they were arranged in a circular manner and that the markings on the stones all faced the center of the circle. They tried diligently to make sense of the stones, but had to give up. Whatever the markings meant—they meant nothing to Manak-na and

Domur. Somehow it made them both sad. Some people at some time had meant to communicate something and now it was lost to time. Would it be that way with them? They wondered. They sat amidst the stones for a long while talking about just that. What wonders could the stones have revealed to them? How could a People capture what they knew and make it available to other peoples over a long time? They knew no way at all. All they had was their stories. Life was ephemeral, transient. If a storyteller died, all was lost, unless there was a replacement. Manak-na spoke of the tidal wave that wiped out the people at the boatbuilders' place and the one that took Tikarumusa's people. No one was saved. Komus would go to the boatbuilders' place, but did Komus know enough to restart the boatbuilding? How would they do with no seals living nearby? Who could know? Would he remain there or go to the other side of the sea? The People could have been wiped from the earth when Baambas blew. They weren't. Why? So many questions—so few answers. People would live, learn, make mistakes, discover brilliant things, then die or be destroyed, and lose it all. New people would start all over again, as if what was known before never existed. It seemed a terrible waste somehow. Or maybe it was a type of salvation—something in Wisdom's plan.

Manak-na stood. He reached for Domur's hand. She gave it readily, and he helped her up. They stood together, man and woman, and embraced in the center of the circle of stones. They had a long way to go before Wisdom called them. They would do their best to live well. Together.

Bibliography

Achilli, A., Perego, U.A., Bravi, C. M., Coble, M. D., Kong, Q.-P., Woodward, S. R., Salas, A., Terroni, A., Bandelt, H.-J., "The Phylogeny of the Four Pan-American MtDNA Haplogroups: Implications for Evolutionary and disease Studies," *PLoS ONE,* 3(3) e1764.

Adovasio, J.M., Page, J., *The First Americans: In Pursuit of Archaeology's Greatest Mystery,* Modern Library, Imprint of Random House, 2003.

Ao, H., Deng, C., Dekkers, M. J., Sun, Y., Liu, Q., Zhu, R., "Pleistocene environmental evolution in the Nihewan Basin and implications for early human colonization of North China," *Quaternary International,* 2010.

Bae, C., "The late Middle Pleistocene hominin fossil record of eastern Asia: Synthesis and review," *American Journal of Physical Anthropology,* supplement yearbook, 143(51), 2010.

Bae, K., "Origin and patterns of the Upper Paleolithic industries in the Korean Peninsula and movement of modern humans in East Asia," *Quaternary International,* 211(1-2), 2010.

Bailey, S., "A Closer Look at Neanderthal Postcanine Dental Morphology: The Mandibular Dentition," *The Anatomical Record,* 269, 2002.

Bailey, S. E., Wu, L., "A comparative dental metrical and morphological analysis of a Middle Pleistocene hominin maxilla from Chaoxian (Chaohu), China," *Quaternary International,* 211(1-2), 2010.

Bailliet, G., Rothhammer, F., Garnese, F. R., Bravi, C. M., and Bianchi, N. O., "Founder Mitochondrial Haplotypes in Amerindian Populations," *The Journal of Human Genetics,* 54, 1994.

Balter, M., "Child Burial Provides Rare Glimpse of Early Americans," *ScienceNOW,* Feb 2011.

Banks, W., D'Errico, F., Dibble, H., Krishtalka, L., West, D., Olszewski, D., Peterson, A., Anderson, D., Gillam, J., Montet-White, A., Crucifix, M., Marean, C., Sánchez-Goñi, M., Wohlfarth, B., Vanhaeran, M., "Eco-Cultural Niche Modeling: New Tools for Reconstructing the Geography and Ecology of Past Human Populations," *PaleoAnthropology,* 2006.

Bannai, M., Ohashi, J., Harihara, S., Takahashi, Y., Juji, T., Omoto, K., Tokunaga, K., "Analysis of HLA genes and haplotypes in Ainu (from Hokkaido, northern Japan) supports the premise that they descent from Upper Paleolithic populations of East Asia," *Tissue Antigens,* 55, 2000.

Bengston, John D., *In Hot Pursuit of Language in Prehistory,* John Benjamin Publishing Co., The Netherlands, 2008.

Benson, L., Lund, S., Smoot, J., Rhode, D., Spencer, R., Verosub, K., Louderback, L., Johnson, C., "The rise and fall of Lake Bonneville between 45 and 10.5 ka," *Quaternary International,* 235(1-2), 2009.

Boeskorov, G. G., "The North of Eastern Siberia: Refuge of Mammoth Fauna in the Holocene," *Gondwana Research,* 7(2) 2004, available in English in ScienceDirect, November 2005

Bogoras, W., *The Jesup North Pacific Expedition, Memoir of the American Museum of Natural History, Volume VII, The Chukchee,* Leiden, E. J. Brill, Ltd., Printers and Publishers, 1975 (reprint of the 1904-1909 edition). This publication is routinely referred to as *The Chukchee.*

Bolnick, D. A., Shook, B. A, Campbell, L, Goddard, I, "Problematic Use of Greenberg's Linguistic Classification of the Americas in Studies of Native American Genetic Variation," *American Journal of Human Genetics,* 75(3): 2004.

Bonnichsen, R. Lepper, B., Stanford, D., Waters, M., *Paleoamerican Origins: Beyond Clovis,* Center for the Study of the First Americans, Department of Anthropology, Texas A&M University, 2005.

Borrell, B., "Bon Voyage, Caveman," *Archaeology,* 63(3), May/June 2010. (possibility of seafaring by *Homo erectus* at 130,000 ya)

Bower, B., "Asian Trek," *Science News,* 171(14), 4/7/2007.

Bower, B., "Ancient hominids may have been seafarers," *Science News,* 177(3), 2010.

Brantingham, P., Gao, X., Madsen, D., Bettinger, R., Elston, R., " The initial Upper Paleolithic at Shuidonggou, Northwestern China," in *The Early Upper Paleolithic beyond Western Europe,* Ed. By Brantingham, P, Juhn, S., and Kerry, K., 2004.

Cannon, M. D., "Explaining variability in Early Paleoindian foraging," *Quaternary International,* 191(1), 2008.

Carmel, James H., "Homo sapiens and Neanderthals lived in peace, say researchers," The Times, United Kingdom, http://www.thetimes.co.uk/tto/news/world/middleeaste/article3552845.ece, 2013.

Catto, N., "Quaternary floral and faunal asssemblages: Ecological and taphonomical investigations," *Quaternary International,* 233(2), 2011.

Catto, N., "Quaternary landscape evolution: Interplay of climate, tectonics, geomorphology, and natural hazards," *Quaternary International,* 233(1), 2011.

Chauhan, P. R., "Large mammal fossil occurrences and associated archaeological evidence in Pleistocene contexts of peninsular India and Sri Lanka," *Quaternary International,* 192(1), 2008.

Chen, C., An, J, Chen, H., "Analysis of the Xionanhai lithic assemblage, excavated in 1978," *Quaternary International,* 211(1-2), 2010.

Chen, X-Y., Cui, G-H., Yang, J-X., "Threatened fishes of the world: *Pseudobagrus medianalis* (Regan) 1904 (Bagridae), *Environmental Biology of Fishes,* 81(3), 2008.

Chlachula, J., Drozdov, N., Ovodov, N., "Last Interglacial peopling of Siberia: the Middle Palaeolithic site Ust'-Izhul', the upper Yenisei area," *Boreas,* 32, 2003.

Ciochon, R., Bettis III, A., "Asian *Homo erectus* converges in time," *Nature,* 458, March 2009

Cione, A., Tonni, E., Soibelzon, L., "The Broken Zig-Zag: Late Cenozoic large mammal and tortoise extinction in South America," *Rev. Mus. Argentino Cienc. Nat.,* n.s., 5(1), 2003.

Coppens, Y., Tseveendorj, D., Demeter, F., Turbat, T., and Giscard, P., "Discovery of an archaic *Homo sapiens* skullcap in Northeast Mongolia," *Comptes Rendus Palevol,* 7(1), Feb 2008. Note: The findings are that the skullcap shows similarities with Neanderthals, Chinese Homo erectus, and West/Far East archaic Homo sapiens. Dating is possible late Pleistocene.

Corvinus, G., "*Homo erectus* in East and Southeast Asia, and the questions of the age of the species and its association with stone artifacts, with special attention to handaxe-like tools," *Quaternary International,* 117, 2004.

Coxe, W., *The Russian Discoveries Between Asia and America,* Readex Microprint Corp., 1966, copy of Coxe's document from 1780.

Cremo, M., Thompson, R., *Forbidden Archaeology: The Hidden History of the Human Race,* Unlimited Resources, 1996-2011.

Delluc, B., Delluc, G., "Art Paléolithique, saisons et climats," *Comtes Rendus Palevol,* 5, 2006.

Demske, D., Heumann, G., Granoszewski, W., Nita, M., Mamakowa, K., Tarasov, P., Oberhänsli, H., "Late glacial and Holocene vegetation and regional climate variability evidenced in high-resolution pollen records from Lake Baikal," *Global and Planetary Change,* 46, 2005.

Derbeneva, O. A., Sukernik, R. I., Volodko, N.V., Hosseini, S. H., Lott, M. T., and Wallace, D. C., "Analysis of Mitochondrial DNA Diversity in the Aleuts of the Commander Islands and Its Implications for the Genetic History of Beringia," *The American Journal of Human Genetics,* 71(2): 2002.

Derenko, M., Malyarchuk, B., Grzybowski, T., Denisove, G., Dambueva, I., Perkova, M., Dorzhu, C., Luzina, F., Lee, H. K., Vanecek, T., Villems, R., and Zakharov, I., "Phylogeographic analysis of Mitochondrial DNA in Northern Asian Populations," *The American Journal of Human Genetics,* 81, November 2007.

Dickinson, William R., "Geological perspectives on the Monte Verde archaeological site in Chile and pre-Clovis coastal migration in the Americas," *Quaternary Research,* 76, 201-210, 2011.

Dillehay, T. D., *The Settlement of the Americas: A New Prehistory,* Basic Books of the Perseus Books Group, 2000.

Dixon, E. J. and G. S. Smith, "Broken canines from Alaskan cave deposits: re-evaluating evidence for domesticated dog and early humans in Alaska." *American Antiquity,* 51(2): 1986.

Doelman, T., "Flexibility and Creativity in Microblade Core Manufacture in Southern Primorye, Far East Russia," *Asian Perspectives,* 47(2), 2009.

Elliott, D.K., *Dynamics of Extinction,* John Wiley & Sons, New York, 1986.

Elston, Robert G., Brantingham, P. Jeffrey, "Microlithic Technology in Northern Asia: A Risk-Minimizing Strategy of the Late Paleolithic and Early Holocene," *Archaeological Papers of the American Anghropological Association,* 12 (1) 103-116, 2002.

Erlandson, J., Moss, M., Des Lauriers, M., "Life on the edge: early maritime cultures of the Pacific coast of North America, *Quaternary Science Reviews,* 27, 2008.

Etler, D., "The Fossil Evidence for Human Evolution in Asia," *Annual Review of Anthropology,* 25, 1996.

Etler, D., "*Homo erectus* in East Asia: Human Ancestor or Evolutionary Dead-End?" *Athena Review,* 4(1) [Cannot locate year. The author is from Department of Anthropology, Cabrillio College, Aptos, California.]

Etler, D., Crummett, T., Wolpoff, M., "Longgupo: Early Homo Colonizer or Late Pliocene Lufengpithecus Survivor in South China?" *Human Evolution,* 16(1-12), 2001.

Fell, B., *America B.C.,* Artisan Publishers, 2010.

Fiedel, Stuart J., "Older Than We Thought: Implications of Corrected Dates for Paleoindians," *American Antiquity,* 64(1), 1999.

Finlayson, Clive, *The HUMANS WHO WENT EXTINCT, Why Neanderthals died out and we survived.* Oxford University Press, 2009.

Fitzhugh, W., "Stone Shamans and Flying Deer of Northern Mongolia: Deer Goddess of Siberia or Chimera of the Steppe?" *Arctic Anthropology,* 46(1-2) 2009.

Flam, F.: "Red hair a part of the Neanderthal genetic profile" *The Philadelphia Inquirer,* October 26, 2007.

Flannery, T., *The Eternal Frontier,* Atlantic Monthly Press, New York, 2001.

Forster, P., Harding, R., Torroni, A., and Bandelt, H. J., "Origin and Evolution of Native American mtDNA Variation: A Reappraisal," *The American Journal of Human Genetics,* 59(4): 1996.

Froehle, A., Churchill, S., "Energetic Competition Between Neandertals and Anatomically Modern Humans," *PaleoAnthropology,* 2009.

Gilbert, M. T. P., Jenkins, D. L., Götherstrom, A., Naveran, N. Sanchez, J. J., Hofreiter, M., Thomsen, P. F., Binladen, J., Higham, T. F. G., Yohe, R. M., II, Parr, R. Cummings, L. S. Willerslev, E., "DNA from Pre-Clovis Human Coprolites in Oregon, North America," *Science Express,* April 2008.

Gilligan, I., "The Prehistoric Development of clothing: Archaeological Implications of a thermal Model," *Journal of Archaeological Method Theory*, 17, 2010.

Gladyshev, S., Olsen, J., Tabarev, A., Kuzmin, Y., "Peleoenvironment. The Stone Age: Chronology and Periodization of Upper Paleolithic Sites in Mongolia." *Archaeology Ethnology & Anthropology of Eurasia*, 38(3), 2010.

Goebel, T., Waters, M., Dikova, M., "The Archaeology of Ushki Lake, Kamchatka, and the Pleistocene Peopling of the Americas," *Science*, 301(5632), 2003.

Goebel, T., et al, "The Late Pleistocene Dispersal of Modern Humans in the Americas, *Science*, 319, 1497, 2008.

Goldberg, E., Chebykin, E., Zhuchenko, N., Vorobyeva, S., Stepanova, O., Khlystov, O., Ivanov, E., Weinberg, E, Gvozdkov, A., "Uranium isotopes as proxies of the Lake Baikal watershed (East Siberia) during the past 150 ka," *Palaeogeography, Palaeoclimatology, Palaeoecology*, 294(1-2) August 2010.

Golubenko, M. V., Stepanov, V. A., Gubina, M. A., Zhadanov, S. I., Ossipova, L. Pl, Damba, L., Voevoda, M. I., Dipierri, J. E., Villems, R., Malhi, R. S., Beringian "Standstill and Spread of Native American Founders," *PLoS ONE* 2(9): eB29. doi;10.1371/journal.pone.0000829.

Goodyear, Albert C., "Evidence for Pre-Clovis Sites in the Eastern United States," unpublished and undated manuscript, [no longer has active link]

Grayson, D., Meltzer, D., "A requiem for North American overkill," *Journal of Archaeological Science*, 30(5), 2003.

Grove, C., "Ice-age child's remains discovered in Interior," *Anchorage Daily News*, 2/24/2011

Hall, R., "Cenozoic plate tectonic reconstruction of SE Asia," from Fraser, L., Matthews, S., Murphy, R., (Eds.), *Petroleum Geology of Southeast Asia*, Geological Society of London Special Publication 26, 1997.

Hapgood, C., *Maps of the Ancient Sea Kings,* Adventures Unlimited Press, 1966.

Hardaker, C., *The First American: the Suppressed Story of the People Who Discovered the New World,* New Page Books, 2007.

Haynes, C. V., Jr., "Younger Dryas 'Black mats' and the Rancholabrean termination in North America," *National Academy of Sciences of the USA,* 2008. (See also: for photographs http://www.georgehoward.net/Vance%20 Haynes'%20Black%20Mat.htm)

Henry, A., Brooks, A., Piperno, D., "Microfossils in calculus demonstrate consumption of plants and cooked foods in Neanderthal diets," *Proceedings of the National Academy of Sciences,* 108(2), 2010.

Hoffecker, J. F., *A Prehistory of the North: Human Settlement of the Higher Latitudes,* Rutgers University Press, New Brunswick, New Jersey, 2005.

Honeychurch, W., Amartuvshin, C., "Hinterlands, Urban Centers, and Mobile Settings: The 'New' Old World Archaeology from the Eurasian Steppe," *Asian Perspectives,* 46(1) 2007.

Hopkins, D. M., Matthews, J. V, Jr., Schweger, C. E., Young, S. B., *Paleoecology of Beringia,* Academic Press, New York, 1982.

Huyghe, P., *Columbus Was Last: From 200,000 B.C. To 1492 A Heretical History of Who Was First,* Anomalist Books, 1992.

Igarashi, Y., Zharov, A., "Climate and vegetation change during the late Pleistocene and early Holocene in Sakhalin and Hokkaido, northeast Asia," *Quaternary International,* xxx (in process), 2011.

Inman, M.: "Neanderthals Had Same 'Language Gene' as Modern Humans," *National Geographic News,* October 18, 2007, http://news.nationalgeographic.com/news/2007/10/071018-neandertal-gene.html

Irwin-Williams, Cynthia, "Dilemma Posed by Uranium-Series Dates on Archaeologically Significant Bones from Valsequillo, Puebla, Mexico," *Earth and Planetary Science Letters* 6 (1969) 237-244, North Holland Publishing Comp., Amsterdam.

Jackinsky, M., "Evidence of woolly mammoths on Peninsula grows," *Alaska Daily News,* 3/13/2011.

Jackson, Jr., L. E., Wilson, M. C., "The Ice-Free Corridor Revisited," *Geotimes,* Feb. 2004.

Jiang, Y-E., Chen, X-Y, Yang, J-X., "Threatened fishes of the world: Yunnanilus discoloris Zhou & He 1989 (Cobitidae)," *Environmental Biology of Fishes,* 86(1), 2009.

Jin, J. J. H., Shipman, P., "documenting natural wear on antlers: A first step in identifying use-wear on purported antler tools," *Quaternary International,* 211(1-2) 2010.

Johnson, John F. C., *Chugach Legends: Stories and Photographs of the Chugach Region,* Chugach Alaska Corporation, 1984.

Joling, D., "Warming brings unwelcome change to Alaska villages," *Anchorage Daily News,* 3/27/ 2011.

Joseph, F., *Discovering the Mysteries of Ancient America: Lost History and Legends, Unearthed and Explored,* New Page Books, 2006.

Khenzykhenova, F., "Paleoenvironments of Palaeolithic humans in the Baikal region," *Quaternary International,* 179(1), 2008.

Khenzykhenova, F., Sato, T., Lipnina, E., Medvedev, G., Kato, H., Kogai, S., Maximenko, K., Novosel'zeva, V., "Upper paleolithic mammal fauna of the Baikal region, east Siberia (new data)," *Quaternary International,* 231, 2011.

Kienast, F., Schirrmeister, L., Siegert, C., Tarasov, P., "Palaeobotanical evidence for warm summers in the East Siberian Arctic during the last cold stage," *Quaternary Research,* 63(3), 2005.

King, G., Bailey, G., "Tectonics and human evolution," *Antiquity,* 80, 2006.

Klein, H. S., Schiffner, D. C., "The Current Debate about the Origins of the Paleoindian of America," *Journal of Social History,* 37(2), Winter 2003.

Kolomiets, V. L., Gladyshev, S. A., Bezrukova, E. V., Rybin, E. P., Letunova, P. P., Abzaeva, A. A., "Paleoenvironment The Stone Age: Environment and human behavior in northern Mongolia during the Upper Pleistocene," *Archaeology, Ethnology, and Anthropology of Eurasia,* 37(1), 2009.

Komatsu, G., Olsen, J., Ormo, J., Di. Achille, G., Kring, D., Matsui T., "The Tsenkher structure in the Gobi-Altai, Mongolia: Geomorphological hints of an impact origin," *Geomorphology,* 74(1-4), March 2006.

Kornfeld, M., Larson, M. L., "Bonebeds and other myths: Paleoindian to Archaic transition on North American Great Plains and Rocky Mountains," *Quaternary International,* 191(1), 2008.

Krause, J., Orlando, L., Serre, D., Viola, B., Prüfer, K., Richards, M., Hublin, J., Hänni, C., Derevianko, A., Pääbo, S., "Neanderthals in central Asia and Siberia," *Nature LETTERS,* 449, 2007.

Kunz, Michael, M. Bever, C. Adkins, *The Mesa Site: Paleoindians above the Arctic Circle,* U. S. Department of the Interior, Bureau of Land Management, BLM-Alaska Open File Report 86, BLM/AK/ST-03/001+8100+020, April 2003.

Kurochkin, E., Kuzmin, Y., Antoshchenko-Olenev, I., Zabelin, V., Krivonogov, S., Nohrina, T., Lbova, L., Burr, G, and Cruz, R., "The timing of ostrich existence in Central Asia: AMS 14C age of eggshells from Mongolia and southern Siberia (a pilot study)," *Nuclear Instruments and Methods in Physics Research Section B: Beam Interactions with Materials and Atoms,* 268(7-8), April 2010.

Kuzmin, Y., Orlova, L., "Radiocarbon chronology and environment of woolly mammoth (*Mammuthus primigenius* Blum.) in northern Asia: results and perspectives," *Earth-Science Reviews,* 68, 2004.

Kuzmin, Y., Richards, M., Yoneda, M., "Paleodietary Patterning and Radiocarbon Dating of Neolithic Populations in the Primorye Province, Russian Far East," *Ancient Biomolecules,* 4(2), 2002.

Lam, Y. M., Brunson, K, Meadow, R., Yuan, J., "Integrating taphonomy into the practice of zooarchaeology in China," *Quaternary International,* 211(1-2), 2010.

Lee, H., "Paleoenvironment: The Stone Age. Projectile Points and Their Implications," *Archaeology Ethnology & Anthropology of Eurasia,* 38(3), 2010.

Lell, J. T., Sukernik, R. I., Starikovskaya, Y. B., Su, B., Jin, L., Schurr, T. G., Underhill, P. A., Wallace, D. C., "The Dual Origin and Siberian Affinities of Native American Y Chromosomes," *The American Journal of Human Genetics,* 70, 2002.

Lister, A., Bahn, P. G., *Mammoths: Giants of the Ice Age,* Richard Green Publisher, 1994.

Liu, W., Wu, X., Pei, S., Wu, Xiujie, Norton, C. J., "Huanglong Cave: A Late Pleistocene human fossil site in Hubei Province, China," *Quaternary International,* 211(1-2), 2010.

Lu, X., Xiong, D., Chen, C., "Threatened fishes of the world: *Sinocyclocheilus grahami* (Regan 1904) (Cyprinidae)," *Environmental Biology of Fishes,* 85(2), 2009.

Ma, S., Wang, Y., Xu, L., "Taxonomic and Phylogenetic Studies on the Genus Muntiacus," *Acta Theriologica Sinica* VI(3) 1986. (Translated by Will Downs, Dept of Geology, Bilby Research Center, Northern Arizona Univ., 1991)

Macé, F., "Human Rhythm and Divine Rhythm in Ainu Epics," *Diogenes,* 46(1), 1998.

Marwick, B., "Biogeography of Middle Pleistocene hominins in mainland Southeast Asia: A review of current evidence," *Quaternary International,* 202(1-2), 2009.

Mednikova, M., Dobrovolskaya, M., Buzhilova, A., Kandinov, M., "A Fossil Human Humerus from Khvalynsk: Morphology and Taxonomy," *Archaeology Ethnology & Anthropology of Eurasia,* 38(1), 2010.

Meltzer, D., *First Peoples in a New World: Colonizing Ice Age America,* University of California Press, 2009.

Merriwether, D. A., Hall, W. W., Vahine, A., and Ferrell, R. E., "mtDNA Variation Indicates Mongolia May Have Been the Source for the Founding Population for the New World," *The American Journal of Human Genetics*, 59, 1996.

Mol, D., de Vos, J., van der Plicht, J., "The presence and extinction of *Elephas antiquus* Falconer and Cautley, 1847, in Europe," *Quaternary International*, 169-170, 2007.

Moncel, M., "Oldest human expansions in Eurasia: Favouring and limiting factors," *Quaternary International*, 223-4, 2010.

Mueller, Tom, "Ice Baby: Secrets of a Frozen Mammoth," National Geographic, 215, 5, May 2009

Naske, C.-M., Slotnick, H. E., *Alaska A History of the 49th State*, 2nd Ed., University of Oklahoma Press, Norman, 1979.

Neel, J. V., Biggar, R. J., Sukernik, R. I., "Virologic and genetic studies relate Amerind origins to the indigenous people of the Mongolia/Manchuria/ southeastern Siberia region," *Proceedings of the National Academy of Sciences, USA*, 91, 1994.

Nikolskiy, P. A., Basilyan, A. E., Sulerzhitsky, L. D., and Pitulko, V. V., "Prelude to the extinction: Revision of the Achchagyl-Allaikha and Berelyokh mass accumulations of mammoth," *Quaternary International*, 219(1-2), 2010.

Norton, C. J., "The nature of megafaunal extinctions during the MIS 3-2 transition in Japan," *Quaternary International*, 211(1-2), 2010.

Norton, C. J., Jin, J. J. H., "Hominin morphological and behavioral variation in eastern Asia and Australasia: current perspectives," *Quaternary International*, 211(1-2), 2010.

O'Neill, D., *The Last Giant of Beringia: The Mystery of the Bering Land Bridge*, Westview Press, Perseus Books Group, New York, 2004.

Oppenheimer, S., "The great arc of dispersal of modern humans: Africa to Australia," *Quaternary International,* 202(1-2), 2009.

Orlova, L. A., Kuzmin, Y. V., Stuart, A. J., Tikhonov, A. N., "Chronology and environment of woolly mammoth (Mammuthus primigenius Blumenbach) extinction in northern Asia," *The World of Elephants – International Congress,* Rome 2001.

Osipov, E., Khlystov, O., "Glaciers and meltwater flux to Lake Baikal during the Last Glacial Maximum," *Palaeogeography, Palaeoclimatology, Palaeoecology,* 294(1-2) 2010.

Palombo, M. R., "Quaternary mammal communities at a glance," *Quaternary International,* 212(2), 2010.

Park, S., "L'hominidé du Pléistocène supérieur en Corée, *L'anthropologie,* 110, 2006.

Pei, S., Gao, X., Feng, X., Chen, F., Dennell, R., "Lithic assemblage from the Jingshuiwan Paleolithic site of the early Late Pleistocene in the Three Gorges, China," *Quaternary International,* 211(1-2), January 2010.

Pietrusewsky, M., "A multivariate analysis of measurements recorded in early and more modern crania from East Asia and Southeast Asia," *Quaternary International,* 211(1-2), 2010.

Pimenoff, V., Comas, D., Palo, J., Vershubsky, G., Kozlov, A, Sajantila, A., "Northwest Siberian Khanty and Mansi in the junction of West and East Eurasian gene pools as revealed by uniparental markers," *European Journal of Human Genetics,* 16, 2008.

Pitulko, V., "The Berelekh Quest: A Review of Forty Years of Research in the Mammoth Graveyard in Northeast Siberia," *Geoarchaeology,* 26(1), 2011.

Ponce de León, M., Golovanova, L., Doronichev, V., Romanova, G., Akazaqa, T., Kondo, O., Ishida, H., Zollikofer, C., "Neanderthal brain size at birth provides insights into the evolution of human life history," *Proceedings of the National Academy of Sciences,* 105(37), Sept 2008.

Potter, B. A., Reuther, J. D., Bowers, P. M., and Relvin-Reymiller, C., "Little Delta Dune Site: A Late-Pleistocene Multicomponent Site in Central Alaska," *Archaeology: North America,* CRP 25, 2008.

Powell, E., "Mongolia," *Archaeology,* 59(1) Jan/Feb 2006.

Prokopenko, A., Kuzmin, M., Li, H., Woo, K., Catto, N., "Lake Hovsgol basin as a new study site for long continental paleoclimate records in continental interior Asia: General contest and current status," *Quaternary International,* 205, 2009.

Quade, J., Forester, R. M., Pratt, W. L., Carter, C., "Black Mats, Spring-Fed Streams, and Late-Glacial-Age Recharge in the Southern Great Basin," *Quaternary Research,* 49(2) 1998.

Ransom, J. E., "Derivation of the Word Alaska," *American Anthropologist,* 42, 1942.

Razjigaeva, N., Korotky, A., Grebennikova, T., Ganzey, L., Mokhova, L., Bazarova, V. Sulerzhitsky, L., Lutaenko, K., "Holocene climatic changes and environmental history of Iturup Island, Kurile Islands, northwestern Pacific," *The Holocene,* 12, 2002.

Reich, D., et al., "Genetic history of an archaic hominin group from Denisova Cave in Siberia," *Nature,* 468, 7327, 2010.

Rose, W. I., Chesner, C. A., "Dispersal of ash in the great Toba Eruption, 74 ka," *Geology,* 15, 1987.

Rudaya, N., Tarasov, P., Dorofeyuk, N., Solovieva, N., Kalugin, I., Andreev, Daryin, A., Diekmann, B., Riedel, F., Tserendash, N., Wagner, M., "Holocene environments and climate in the Mongolian Altai reconstructed from the Hoton-Nur pollen and diatom records: a step towards better understanding climate dynamics in Central Asia," *Quaternary Science Reviews,* 28(5-6) 2009.

Ruvinsky, J., "The Great American Extinction," *Discover,* 28(8) 2007.

Saillard, J., Forster, P., Lynnerup, N., Bandelt, H.-J., Nørby, S., "mtDNA Variation among Greenland Eskimos: The Edge of the Beringian Expansion," *The Journal of Human Genetics,* 2000 September; 67(3): 718-726.

Saleeby, B. M., "Out of Place Bones: beyond the study of prehistoric subsistence," Arctic Research of the United States, *U. S. National Science Foundation,* 2002.

Sattler, H. R., *The Earliest Americans,* Clarion Books, New York, 1993.

Schepartz, L. A., Miller-Antonio, S., "Taphonomy, Life History, and Human Exploitation of Rhinoceros sinensis at the Middle Pleistocene site of Panxian Dadong, Guizhou, China," *International Journal of Osteoarchaeology,* 2008.

Schrenk, F., Muller, S. *The Neanderthals,* Routledge, 2005.

Seong, C., "Tanged points, microblades and Late Palaeolithic hunting in Korea," *Antiquity,* 82, 2008.

Shen, G., Fang, Y., Bischoff, J. L., Feng, Y., and Zhao, J., "Mass spectrometric U-series dating of the Chaoxian hominin site at Yinshan, eastern China," *Quaternary International,* 211(1-2), 2010.

Sher, A., Weinstock, J., Baryshnikov, G., Davydov, S., Boeskorov, G., Zazhigin, V., Nikolskiy, P., "The first record of 'spelaeoid' bears in Arctic Siberia, *Quaternary Science Reviews,* 30, 2010.

Shichi, K., Takahara, H., Krivonogov, S., Bezrukova, E., Kashiwaya, K., Takehara, A., Nakamura, T., "Late Pleistocene and Holocene vegetation and climate records from Lake Kotokel, central Baikal region," *Quaternary International,* 205, 2009.

Smith, T., Toussaint, M., Reid, D., Olejniczak, A., Hublin, J., "Rapid dental development in a Middle Paleolithic Belgian Neanderthal," *Proceedings of the National Academy of Sciences,* 104(51), Dec. 2007.

Snodgrass, J., Leonard, W., "Neandertal Energetics Revisited: Insight Into Population Dynamics and Life History Evolution," *PaleoAnthropology,* 2009.

Starikovskaya, Y. B., Sukernik, R. I., Schurr, T. G., Kogelnik, A. M., and Wallace, D. C. "mtDNA diversity in Chukchi and Siberian Eskimos: Implications for the Genetic History of Ancient Beringia and the Peopling of the New World," *The American Journal of Human Genetics*, 63, 1998.

Stephan, A. E., *The First Athabascans of Alaska: Strawberries*, Dorrance Publishing Co, Inc., Pittsburg, 1996.

Stone, R., "A Surprising Survival Story in the Siberian Arctic," *Science*, 303(5642): 2004.

Stringer, C., Finlayson, J., Barton, R., Fernández-Jalvo, Y., Cáceres, I., Sabin, R., Rhodes, E., Currant, A., Rodriguez-Vidal, J., Giles-Pacheco, F., Riquelme-Cantal, J., "Neanderthal exploitation of marine mammals in Gibraltar," *Proceedings of the National Academy of Sciences*, 105(38) Sept. 2008.

Stringer, C., *Lone Survivors: How We Came To Be the Only Humans on Earth*. Times Books, Henry Holt & Co., LLC, New York, 2012.

Strong, S., "The Most Revered of Foxes: Knowledge of Animals and Animal Power in an Ainu *Kamui Yukar*," *Asian Ethnology*, 68(1), 2009.

Sykes, B., *The Seven Daughters of Eve*, W.W. Norton & Company, New York, 2001.

Szathmary, E. J. E., "mtDNA and the Peopling of the Americas," *The Journal of Human Genetics*, 53, 1993.

Tamm, E., Kivisild, T., Reidla, M., Metspalu, M., Smith, D. G., Mulligan, C. J., Bravi, C. M., Rickards, O., Martinez-Labarga, C., Khusnutdinova, E. K., Fedorova, S. A., Torroni, A., Neel, J. V., Barrantes, R., Schurr, T. G., "Mitochondrial DNA 'clock' for the Amerinds and its implications for timing their entry into North America," *Proceedings of the National Academy of Sciences, USA*, 91, 1994.

Tarasov, P., Williams, J., Andreev, A., Nakagawa, T., Bezrukova, E., Herzschuh, U., Igarashi, Y., Müller, S., Werner, K., Zheng, Z., "Satellite- and pollen-based quantitative woody cover reconstructions for northern

Asia: Verification and application to late-Quaternary pollen data," *Earth and Planetary Science Letters,* 264(1-2), 2007.

Tattersall, I., *Masters of the Planet, The Search for Our Human Origins,* Palgrace Macmillan, 2012

Than, K., "Neanderthals, Humans Interbred—First Solid DNA Evidence: Most of us have some Neanderthal genes, study finds," May 6, 2010 for *National Geographic News,* http://news.nationalgeographic.com/news/2010/05/100506-science-neanderthals-humans-mated-interbred-dna-gene/

Tianyuan, L., Etler, D., "New Middle Pleistocene hominid crania from Yunxian in China," *Nature,* 357, June 1992.

Tong, H., Moigne, A.-M., "Quaternary Rhinoceros of China," in English, *Acta Anthropologica Sinica,* Supplement to Volume 19, 2000.

Torroni, A., Sukernik, R. I., Schurr, Ti G., Starikovskaya, Y. B., Cabell, M. F., Crawford, M. H., Comuzzie, A. G., Wallace, D. C., "mtDNA Variations of Aboriginal Siberians Reveals distinct Genetic Affinities with Native Americans," *The American Journal of Human Genetics,* 53, 1993.

Vasil'ev, S. A., Kuzmin, Y. V., Orlova, L. A., Dementiev, V. N., "Radiocarbon-Based Chronology of the Paleolithic in Siberia and Its Relevance to the Peopling of the New World," *Radiocarbon,* 44(2), 2002.

Vialet, A., Guipert, G., Jianing, H., Xiaobo, F., Zune, L., Youping, W., de Lumley, M.-A., de Lumley, H., "Homo erectus from the Yunxian and Nankin Chinese sites: Anthropological insights using 3D virtual imaging techniques," *Comptes Rendus Palevol* 9(6-7), 2010.

Volodko, N. V., Starikovskaya, E. B., Mazunin, I. O., Eltsov, N. P., Naidenko, P. V., Wallace, D. C., and Sukernik, R. I., "Mitochondrial Genome Diversity in Arctic Siberians, with Particular Reference to the Evolutionary History of Beringia and Pleistocenic Peopling of the Americas," *American Journal of Human Genetics,* 82(5), 2008.

Wagner, D. P., McAvoy, J. M., "Pedoarchaeology of Cactus Hill, a sandy Paleoindian site in southeastern Virginia, U. S. A." *Geoarchaeology,* 19(4), 2004.

Waguespack, N. M., Surovell, T. A., "Clovis Hunting Strategies, or How to Make Out on Plentiful Resources," *American Antiquity,* 68(2), 2003.

Wang, J., "Late Paleozoic macrofloral assemblages from Weibel coalfield, with reference to vegetational change through the Late Paleozoic Ice-age in the North China Block," *International Journal of Coal Geology,* 83(2-3), 2010.

Waters, Michael R. et al., "Redefining the Age of Clovis: Implications for the Peopling of the Americas," *Science,* 315, 1122, 2007.

Waters-Rist, A., Bazaliiskii, V. I., Weber, A, Goriunova, O. I., Katzenberg, A., "Activity-induced dental modification in holocene Siberian hunter-fisher-gatherers," *American Journal of Physical Anthropology,* 143(2), 2010.

West, F. H., Ed., *AMERICAN BEGINNINGS: the Prehistory and Palaeoecology of Beringia,* The University of Chicago Press, Chicago, 1996.

Wiedmer, M., Montgomery, D., Gillespie, A., Greenberg, H., "Late Quaternary megafloods from Glaial Lake Atna, Southcentral Alaska, U.S.A., *Quaternary Research,* 73, 2010.

Woodman, N., Athfield, N., "Post-Clovis survival of American Mastodon in the southern Great Lakes Region of North America," *Quaternary Research,* 72(3), 20009.

Wu, X., "Fossil Humankind and Other Anthropoid Primates of China," *International Journal of Primatology,* 25(5) 2004.

Wu, X., "On the origins of modern humans in China," *Quaternary International,* 117(1), 2004.

Wu, X., Schepartz, L. A., Norton, C. J., "Morphological and morphometric analysis of variation in the Zhoukoudian Homo erectus brain endocasts," *Quaternary International,* 211(1-2) 2010.

Wu, Y-S., Chen, Y-S., Xiao, J-Y., "A preliminary study on vegetation and climate changes in Dianchi Lake area in the last 40,000 years," partial in English, *Acta Botanica Sinica,* 33(5), 1991.

Wynn, T., Coolidge, F. L., *How to Think like a Neanderthal,* Oxford University Press, 2012.

Xiao, J., Jin, C., Zhu, Y., "Age of the fossil Dali Man in north-central China deduced from chronostratigraphy of the loess-paleosol sequence," *Quaternary Science Reviews,* 21, 2002.

Xiangcan, J., "Lake Dianchi," *Experience and Lessons Learned Brief,* final version 2004.

Xu, J-X., Ferguson, D. K., Li, C-S., Wang, Y-F., "Late Miocene vegetation and the climate of the Lühe region in Yunnan, southwestern China," *Review of Palaeobotany and Palynology,* 148(1), 2008.

Yahner, R. H., "Barking in a primitive ungulate, *Muntiacus reevesi:* function and adaptiveness," *The American Naturalist,* 116(2), 1980.

Zang, W., Wang, Y., Zheng, S., Yang, X., Li, Y., Fu, X., Li, N., "Taxonomic investigations on permineralized conifer woods from the Late Paleozoic Angaran deposits of northeastern Inner Mongolia, China, and their palaeoclimatic significance," *Review of Palaeobotany and Palynology,* 144(3-4), May 2007.

Zhang, Y., Stiner, M, Dennell, R., Wang, C., Zhang, Sh, Gao, X., "Zooarchaeological perspectives on the Chinese Early and Late Paleolithic from the Ma'anshan site (Guizhou, South China)," *Journal of Archaeological Science,* 37(8), 2010.

Zhu, R., An, Z., Potts, R., Hoffman, K., "Magnetostratigraphic dating of early humans in China," *Earth-Science Reviews,* 61(3-4) June 2003.

Zorich, Z., "Did *Homo erectus* Coddle His Grandparents?" *Discover,* 27(1) Jan. 2006.

No author designated. "Bone fossil points to a mystery human species," *USA Today*, Mar 25, 2010. [Three types of humans lived within 60 miles of each other in southern Siberia.]

FROM THE INTERNET:

America's Stone Age Explorers http://www.pbs.org/wgbh/nova/transcripts/3116_stoneage.html (8/23/2010)

Ancestral Human Skull Found in China (80,000 to 100,000 ya) http://news.nationalgeographic.com/news/2008/02/080220-china-fossil.html

Ancient bison bones supports theory about Ice Age seafarers being first in Americas http://www.thaindian.com/newsportal/world-news/ancient-bison-bones-supports-theory-abo... (9/5/2010)

Archaeology of the Altai Republic http://eng.altai-republic.ru/modules.php?op=modload&name=Sections&file=index&req=viewarticle&artid=20... (1/30/2011)

Archaic Human Culture http://anthro.palomar.edu/homo2/mod_homo_3.htm (9/9/2010)

Bamboo http://earthnotes.tripod.com/bamboo.htm (9/13/2010)

Berelekh Map http://www.maplandia.com/russia/magadanskaya-oblast/susumanskiy-rayon/berelekh/ (8/31/2010)

China map http://en.wikipedia.org/wiki/File:China_100.78713E_35.63718N.jpg (8/20/2010)

Chukchee Society http://lucy.ukc.ac.uk/ethnoatlas/hmar/cult_dir/culture.7837 (4/5/2011)

Chukchi Directions of time and space http://www.cosmicelk.net/Chukchidirections.htm (4/5/2011)

Chukchi Language http://en.wikipedia.org/wiki/Chukchi_language (4/5/2011)

Cro-Magnon http://en.wikipedia.org/wiki/Cro-Magnon (8/12/2010)

Denisova Cave (Siberia) http://archaeology.about.com/od/dathroughde-terms/qt/denisova_cave.htm (8?31/2010)

Dover Bronze Age Boat http://indigenousboats.blogspot.com/2008/01/dover-bronze-age-boat.html

Earliest Humanlike Footprints Found in Kenya http://donsmaps.com/erectus.html (9/11/2010)

Face of a Neanderthal woman http://www.femininebeauty.info/neanderthal-woman (8/23/2010)

First Americans http://www.nmhcpl.org/First_American.html (8/23/2010)

Four-horned Antelope http://en.wikipedia.org/wiki/Four-horned_Antelope (9/15/2010)

Geography of China http://en.wikipedia.org/wiki/Geography_of_China (9/3/2010)

Historical earthquakes in China http://drgeorgepc.com/EarthquakesChina.html (9/24/2010)

Historical SuperVolcanoes and Archeology Indicate Nuclear Winter Climate Models Exaggerate Effects http://nextbigfuture.com/2010/04/historical-supervolcanoes-and.html (8/20/2010)

Hominid Tools http://www.handprint.com/LS/ANC/stones.html (8/23/2010)

Homo erectus http://humanorigins.si.edu/evidence/human-fossils/species/homo-erectus (8/12/2010)

Homo erectus http://en.wikipedia.org/wiki/Homo_erectus (8/12/2010)

Homo erectus http://www.archaeologyinfo.com/homoerectus.htm (9/5/2010)

Homo erectus Survival http://www.archaeology.org/9703/newsbriefs/h.erectus.html (9/5/2010)

Homo neanderthalensis http://humanorigins.si.edu/evidence/human-fossils/species/homo-neanderthalensis (8/12/2010)

Humans wore shoes 40,000 years ago, fossil suggests http://www.stonepages.com/news/archives/002825.html (8/27/2010)

Hydropotes inermis (Chinese water deer) http://www.ultimateungulate.com/Artiodactyla/Hydropotes_inermis.html (9/8/2010)

Ice Age Climate Cycles http://earthguide.ucsd.edu/virtualmuseum/climatechange2/03_1.shtml (1/29/2011)

Images of Neanderthals http://www.talkorigins.org/faqs/homs/savage.html (8/23/2010)

La Ferrassie Neanderthal Reconstruction http://s1.zetaboards.com/anthroscape/topic/2448167/1/ (8/23/2010)

Late Pleistocene, now-extinct fauna of the southwest http://www.saguaro-juniper.com/i_and_i/history/megafauna.html (8/22/2010)

Meet the Neanderthals http://news.bbc.co.uk/2/hi/science/nature/1469607.stm (8/23/2010)

Mousterian http://en.wikipedia.org/wiki/Mousterian

Muntjac (barking deer) http://www.itsnature.org/ground/mammals-land/muntjac/ (9/8/2010)

Neanderthal http://www.crystalinks.com/neanderthal.html

Neanderthals more intelligent than thought http://www.msnbc.msn.com/id/39324819/ns/technology_and_science-science (9/24/2010)

Neanderthal reconstructions http://www.daynes.com/en/reconstructions/neanderthal-4.php (8/23/2010)

Origins of Paleoindians http://en.wikipedia.org/wiki/Origins_of_Paleoindians (8/22/2010)

Pedra Furada, Brazil: Paleoindian, Paintings, and Paradoxes, http://www.athenapub.com/10pfurad.htm (2012)

Pompeii-Like Excavations Tell Us More About Toba Super-Eruption http://www.sciencedaily.com/releases/2010/02/100227170841.htm

Quaternary Period http://www3.hi.is/~oi/quaternary_geology.htm (8/31/2010)

Red hair a part of Neanderthal genetic profile http://seattletimes.nwsource.com/html/nationworld/2003975496_neanderthal26.html (8/26/2010)

Rethinking Neanderthals, Joe Alper, Smithsonian.com, Science and Nature, June 2003 http://www.smithsonianmag.com/science-nature/neanderthals.html?c=y&page=1

Sacred Bones, Fields of Stones, Dr. Francis Allard Earthwatch Journal, October 2002, www.earthwatch.org

Savoonga artist to explore traditional native tattoos, Anchorage Daily News http://www.adn.com/2011/04/02/1788951/savoonga-artist-to-explore-traditional.html (4/5/2011)

Shamanism in Siberia http://www.sacred-texts.com/sha/sis/sis04.htm (4/5/2011)

Shiraoi Ainu Village http://members.virtualtourist.com/m/tt/52254/

Signs of Neanderthals Mating With Humans http://www.nytimes.com/2010/05/07/science/07neanderthal.html?_r=1 (8/26/2010)

Simple techniques for production of dried meat http://www.fao.org/docrep/003/x6932e/X6932E02.htm (9/27/2010)

"Skin Deep," a program on the Smithsonian Channel with Penn State anthropologist, Nina Jablonski http://www.smithsonianchannel.com/site/sn/video/player/latest-videos/skin-deep-full-episode/2180530922001/

Solutrean http://en.wikipedia.org/wiki/Solutrean (8/23/2010)

Stone Age Columbus http://www.bbc.co.uk/science/horizon/2002/columbusqa.shtml (8/23/2010)

Stone Age Site Yields Evidence of Advanced Culture http://history.cultural-china.com/en/51History9459.html (9/5/2010)

Stone-tipped spear invented earlier than thought, researchers say, http://www.latimes.com/news/science/la-sci-hafting-spears-201221116,0,6983702.story (11/17/2012)

Straight-tusked elephant http://en.wikipedia.org/wiki/Straight-tusked_Elephant (10/3/2010)

Synoptic table of the principal old world prehistoric cultures http://en.wikipedia.org/wiki/Synoptic_table_of_the_principal_old_world_prehistoric_cultures (9/8/2010)

Transmitting the Ainu wisdom http://www.town.shiraoi.hokkaido.jp/ainu-tradition/yamamaru/index.html

Umiaq skin boat http://en.wikipedia.org/wiki/File:Umiaq_skin_boat.jpg

Volcanic Ash http://geology.com/articles/volcanic-ash.shtml (8/20/2010)

Zhirendong puts the chin in china http://johnhawks.net/weblog/fossils/china/zhirendong-2010-liu-chin.html

Zhoukoudian Relics Museum http: www.china.org.cn/english/features/museums/129075.htm (9/5/2010)